THE GAMBLER'S GAME

THE GAMBLER'S GAME

BASED ON A TRUE STORY

JAMES DARNBOROUGH

PINEWOOD MEDIA

First published in the United States 2024

Pinewood Media Inc.
5419 Hollywood Boulevard Ste C-102
Los Angeles, CA 90027

Print ISBN 978-0-9971340-4-9
E-book ISBN 978–0-9971340-2-5
Audiobook ISBN 978-0-9971340-3-2

Library of Congress control number: 2023950939
Cover design by Valentina Pino

www.thegamblersgame.com

For Priya

PROLOGUE

Two commissionaires, clad in their impeccably tailored red coats, stand guard at the entrance to the Casino de Monte Carlo. As he climbs the steps toward them, they greet him by name out of acknowledgment and respect.

All the waiters, croupiers, and dealers at the Salle de Jeux know Mr. William Darnborough well, as he has taken this walk many times over the last four years. Their eyes are filled with secrets and whispered rumors, and they follow his every move. He strides through the great labyrinthine room, exuding an unsettling combination of serenity and unwavering determination, a predator navigating his hunting ground with considered purpose.

He is dressed impeccably in a hand-stitched black dinner suit with a rose-gold cravat, and his Italian leather brogue shoes click on the marble floor as he crosses the atrium.

He enters the Salle Garnier, with its high, glass-domed ceilings and ornate chandeliers, and he nods an acknowledgment to Joseph Agid, and Viscount Kilmorey. In the Salle Touzet, he sees four croupiers at the roulette table, two on either side of the wheel and two at either end of the double-sided table. The man in charge, the Chef de Partie, sits on a tall chair behind the wheel and respectfully acknowledges Mr. Darnborough. He has heard acquaintances call him Bill, but he does not greet him by name, as this is not permitted.

Bill stands at the middle of the table. Always the middle, as this gives him the best opportunity to place his chips exactly where he wants them in as short a time as possible.

The dealer spins the wheel and fires the ivory ball in the opposite direction, announcing, "*Faites vos jeux, messieurs.* Place your bets, gentlemen."

One of the other players hurriedly piles more chips onto the section of the table dedicated to the first dozen numbers, a desperate attempt to defy the mounting pressure. Another fellow gambler casts furtive gazes in Bill's direction, his eyes darting back and forth as if searching for a sign, a hint of the impending move. Even though his mind is racing, Bill remains stony-faced and taps his fingers rhythmically on the table.

As the ball slows, the croupier looks up and around the table. "*Les jeux sant faits.* The bets have been placed." Bill springs into action as if a jolt of electricity has surged through his body. With an astonishing display of agility, he employs both hands to unleash a torrent of chips from his reserve. Each chip finds its place with calculated precision, meticulously distributed across the third dozen. The towers of chips resemble a model of the Manhattan skyline and represent ten thousand glittering dollars that will be won or lost in this moment.

As the ball hurtles toward its destination, time slows to a crawl. The dealer prevents any last-minute additional bets as he waves his white-gloved hand over the table and insists, "*Rien ne va plus.* No more bets."

"Now it is in God's hands," says one of the other players, his voice carrying a sense of resignation mingled with reverence. Whispers of suspense ripple through the crowd that have gathered to watch the ball complete its cruel dance, their voices charged with a mixture of hope and trepidation.

Bill, at thirty-five, exudes an air of quiet refinement. His chiseled features, accentuated by a clean-shaven face and impeccably combed-back, dark hair, lend an aura of sophistication. Behind this suave façade, lies a story etched in the lines around his eyes, a tale of clandestine affairs, shadowy encounters, and hidden secrets. Once innocent and hopeful, his eyes now bear the scars of a life lived on the edge as he watches the ball drop.

PART I
THE BALLPLAYER

1888 – 1891

CHAPTER 1

"*B*atter up!" The words echo through the spring air, signaling the first day of tryouts for the Bloomington Reds. Bill stands confidently within the pitcher's box, ready to showcase his talent. His stepfather, Charles Parke, the hotshot lawyer, thinks being a ballplayer makes you lower than a dog, "and you don't make much money, besides." Still, from what Bill has seen, these baseball players are heroes who represent all his dreams and aspirations. They get to go on trains to exciting places he has only read about in the newspapers. This could be his big break, his ticket out of the dire circumstances that loom over his life in Bloomington, Illinois.

He doesn't put much stock in what his stepfather says, nor his mother, Alice, who says even worse things about ballplayers. She wants him to go to college and get a proper job with prospects. But what gives her the right after the things she's done? Or at least been accused of. Bill has never been sure if she was guilty, and she denies everything, of course, but he isn't so sure he can believe her.

The inaugural season for the Central Interstate League is 1888, and ten teams from Illinois, Iowa, and Indiana will fiercely compete for the title. The Reds already have a star pitcher in Clark Griffith, but they need more hurlers to get them through the season. Bill aims to be one of the chosen ones—though it seems as if half the male population of Bloomington have turned up hoping for a spot on the team, and manager Will Conners is only looking for a handful of contenders to fill gaps in the roster.

A burly figure, a wad of tobacco nestled in his cheek, takes his position in the batter's box, spits on the ground, and glares at Bill with contempt.

"Let's see what you've got, kid," sneers Conners.

Bill is determined not to be intimidated. If he's to have an exciting life at all, he can't be. His entire future depends on it.

At the tender age of eighteen, Bill possesses a physique that belies his youth. His well-built frame, sculpted by rigorous boxing training as a member of the school team, boasts broad shoulders that radiate strength and determination. In his hand, he cradles a nine-inch circumference, five-ounce ball—a compact sphere that holds within it the potential for triumph or defeat.

He tries to remember everything he has ever learned about balance and breathing, but his mind is in overdrive. He has been practicing this since he was a small boy, but never has so much been at stake.

He looks at the catcher, then at the batter, then glances away as he winds up and takes a deep breath. He pivots his left leg, and all the tension leaves his body as he feels like a flexed bow on the point of releasing an arrow. Fastball. The batt whiffs—a miss! The catcher grins at Bill and fires the baseball back to him.

Bill doesn't show his thrill, just reaches up his hand for the ball, which lands with a satisfying thwack and sting in his bare hand. Some players have started wearing leather gloves to protect their hands, but Bill thinks they're unmanly, as most players do. Anyway, he doesn't have money to buy one.

"Again," says Conners, who has now moved directly behind Bill to get a better angle. And Bill hears his long-dead father's voice: "It's all in the fingers and wrist."

Bill thinks, *That's right, Dad,* and this time, he throws a curveball, and he has kept his elbow in tight so that the batter has no idea what's coming. Another miss.

"Again," repeats Conners. Bill nods at the catcher, stares at the batter, and a moment later, the ball explodes out of his hand.

The air sizzles, and in an instant comes the sound of the pop as the ball lands in the catcher's mitt. The catcher stands and flicks his wrist as he grimaces from the sting of the ball. Another swing and miss! The batter's scowl deepens as he rests his bat on his shoulder and spits in Bill's direction. Bill again holds back his smile, though it is clear that Conners is impressed.

Throughout his life, Bill has seldom seen his name in print, save for the occasional appearance on the team sheets adorning the school notice board. Yet now, in a moment that brims with significance, he yearns to impress Emily Irvine, bearing a tangible testament to his identity in his hands—the team roster printed in *The Bloomington Courier*. Even though the role of starting pitcher is reserved for Griffith, there is his name emblazoned in bold print: *WILLIAM NELSON DARNBROUGH—pitcher*.

Recollections of his father's words resurface as he recalls the tale of his grandfather altering the spelling of the name to ease pronunciation. A desire, inexplicably etched in Bill's mind, takes root—an aspiration to change the name back to its original spelling of Darnborough.

He had hoped Emily would be dazzled, but she looks up from the newspaper at him with big, sad eyes as if he's betrayed her somehow.

Bill had met Emily in English Literature class when they were both sixteen and plucked up the courage to flatter her about her insights and the eloquent way she expressed herself. For a while, he thought they would be inseparable as they explored Bloomington together, laughed at each other's jokes, and even stole kisses under the old oak tree behind her parents' house in Franklin Park.

"I know I always wanted you to do well," she says, "but what happens if you do really well and get traded to St. Louis or somewhere?"

He folds the paper and angrily shoves it under his arm.

"Come on, Em, can't you see? This is something big. You ought to be happy for me. Imagine if I'd got a place at a college far away, but this, this is even better. This is better than college as it's an adventure. I'm going to travel and meet people." She just shakes her head, and her eyes fill with tears.

"But you could come with me."

"Of course, I could not come with you, Bill," she whispers. "You know my parents would never allow it. My place is here. Anyway, what about college? You're still going to Illinois State, aren't you?"

Even though he has been studying college-level mathematics at high school, and his place is guaranteed, where would that lead? Everyday life, from all he has seen, only makes people miserable. Ever since he was thirteen, when he first read Jules Verne's *Around the World in Eighty Days*, Bill has harbored a yearning to explore, and this could be the very beginning of his journey. His joy becomes tinged with sadness at the prospect of leaving Emily. He likes Emily but is not about to let her tie him down.

The home of the Bloomington Reds is Wilder Field on Franklin Avenue, conveniently situated near the brewery, and three thousand avid fans turn up on the season's first game. Emily is not one of them. Nor are Bill's mother and stepfather there. Charles has made it clear that he has more important things to do, and Alice is simply scandalized that her son is becoming "one of those no-good, ne'er do-well ballplayers." And, anyway, to keep in line with Bloomington's most upstanding ladies, she would not dream of attending a game unescorted by her husband—even if she didn't think baseball was the most un-Christian pursuit in the world. Alice and Charles say that they want their best for him, but Bill has no trust in his mother and right now just wants to hear a crowd cheering for him and see his name in the newspapers.

The first game is against the Danville Browns, and Bill's hands and throat grow sore from clapping, hooting, and cheering his teammates from the bench. By the next day, he's a bit disheartened at not getting a chance to face even one batter, as Conners keeps Griffith in the pitcher's box throughout the first two days of play.

On the third day, the players on the bench stand up to watch a menacing bank of thunderclouds roll in across the long horizon, and soon everyone is running for cover from a torrential downpour and loud cracks of thunder as lightning streaks across the heavy sky.

It's his third day, and Bill still hasn't thrown a pitch. Still, he tries to stay optimistic as he and his teammates joke and laugh together, waiting out the storm. He has had his first taste of being in front of so many fans and is walking a little taller. And tomorrow, they are heading out south on the train to Springfield.

On the long train rides through the countryside, Griffith likes to tell the new players stories, and most of them are quickly bored and head to the back of the car, where there's always a card game in progress. Bill, though, sits and soaks up Griffith's stories like a sponge. He stays quiet, but there is intensity while he listens to Griffith, and the gears are turning in his mind. Griffith leans closer to show him the millimeter variance in the way he grips the baseball that will make all the difference if Bill can master it. Bill nods and closes his eyes for a second like he's seeing himself throwing a quick strike straight down the middle of the plate.

The telegraph poles keep time as they pass by the window, and Griffith takes to telling Bill everything. How his family had come over from the old country—"mine, too," volunteers Bill, then is quiet again—and made it possible for Clark to have a far better life than he would've back there. He talks about his father, who was killed in a hunting accident in Missouri after the family had attempted the Oklahoma Territory journey, leaving Clark's poor, widowed mother to return to Bloomington with all five of her children.

"I'm sorry. I know how that feels," Bill volunteers, "My father died when I was nine," then says nothing more about it. When Clark asks about Bill's mother, Bill says only, "She still lives in Bloomington, but we don't talk much."

Bill has the impression that Clark feels slightly anxious about him as he starts to offer advice on more than pitching. As the train rattles past the Illinois prairie, Bill wonders if this is what it's like to have a big brother.

"Listen, kid," Clark says gruffly. "This is how I learned about the importance of doing things yourself. I was only thirteen, and me and some other kids saved $1.25 to buy a baseball. We sent this kid twelve miles on horseback to buy the ball. The damn thing burst on the second time I slugged it. You see, the kid only spent a quarter on a cheap ball and kept the change for himself."

Bill glances out of the window and smiles.

"What?" asks Clarke.

"Well, you've got to hand it to the kid. It was quite a smart move."

Clark leans back and sighs as he pops the knuckles on his calloused hand. He will probably have to start using a glove soon, though every player decries them, Clark loudest of all. But even Bill can see his hands look beat up. "I know, kid," he says, "I guess the moral of this story is: don't trust anybody."

Bill feels like time is accelerating. He is thrilled to travel across state lines for the first time with the Reds—once even as far as Rockford, Indiana, over 250 miles away. He gets plenty of time in the box and has mastered his fastball, which he can hurl high or low in the strike zone, in on the batter, or away from him. He can now also throw a fadeaway curveball that breaks away in the opposite direction than the batter expects. In a game against the Crawfordsville Hoosiers, Bill smashes out a triple, showing that he is more than useful with the bat. His confidence builds, and he gets his fair share of the newspaper coverage as the team wins more games. He tries not to pay too much attention, just to stay focused on doing what he needs each game, but Emily, even though she wants him to quit baseball, adores him and keeps a scrapbook with newspaper articles.

A short time ago, the papers made mention of the remarkable fact that Pitcher Keefe of the New Yorks had won eighteen straight games. Our own Darnbrough has won the last ten games in which he has pitched.
—The Pantagraph, Bloomington, Illinois. August 23, 1888.

"And you still won't come out and see me play?" Bill teases, but she blushes and shakes her head.

It's the last game of the 1888 season, and Conners has summoned Bill to his "office"—a corner table in the bar inside the main building of the nearby Meyer and Wochner Brewery. Bill sips his beer and wonders if his place on next year's team is as secure as he'd thought as Conners talks gruffly for a few minutes, dissecting every slight mistake on each pitch Bill has just made in the game.

Then, Conners clears his throat. "Well, kid," he says. "I won't beat around the bush anymore. An offer has come from the Denver Grizzlies. It may as well have been a telegram, considering it's only a few lines." He continues, quoting from the letter this time. *We think Mr. Darnbrough needs a lot of work, but he did fine this year, and we feel this offer is more than generous.*

Bill looks at Conners with a fixed stare, trying hard to conceal his excitement. *Denver!* He knows nothing about the place except that it must be a thousand miles away.

"Well, Bill, there's no reserve clause on your contract for next year and probably nothing I can do to convince you to stay, as I know it's what you've been aiming for. It's high altitude in Denver, so you can expect more home runs off your pitching, but otherwise, what d'ya think?"

Bill is completely lost for words. His heart is beating double-time, his throat has closed, and words just won't come out. This is his ticket out of Bloomington, the very thing he's been dreaming of, but right now, he feels frozen in fright at the thought of accepting it. Maybe deep down, he had always thought things would improve with his mother. Despite everything she's done, if he leaves town to play ball, he can kiss the idea of any reconciliation with her good-bye. And Emily, too. Maybe he'd been hoping she'd come around to being a ballplayer's girl, but her parents, both teachers and prominent in the town, insist that she concentrate on her studies.

Bill is already far away from college. *Denver*, he thinks, and he clears his throat, stands up straight, and thrusts out his hand. "Mr. Conners, it's been an honor, and I won't ever forget you."

Conners shakes Bill's hand and smiles. "Just remember to keep your head down out there, kid. They don't call it the Wild West for nothing. Take care you don't get shot in the street by some outlaw, all right?"

Bill swallows. Is it really that bad out there? Well, he's going to find out. "All right, sir. Thanks."

Conners leaves, and Bill goes to join his teammates at the bar. "So," says Clark Griffith, "I guess you're leaving us."

"Denver!" says Bill. He still can't believe it.

Clark grins. "I'll see you in the Western League, then, because I'll be with the Milwaukee Brewers."

Bill hopes he'll see his former teammate over the winter around Bloomington, but, just in case, he suggests that he and Clark sign baseballs to each other as keepsakes of the season. Clark signs his simply: *To Bill, with best wishes, Clark Griffith.* As Bill and Clark join their former teammates in a rousing toast, Bill vows to himself to keep the ball. Not only has Clark been his best friend this season, but he has a feeling Clark will become a big star in the baseball world.

Bill thinks maybe he will, too.

"To the Reds!" Clark shouts, holding his beer aloft.

"To the Reds!" echoes Bill and the rest of the boys, and then they drink and cheer some more. It is a bittersweet moment for Bill to know this team is now a thing of the past as they have become like a family to him—at least the closest to one he can imagine.

Bill is unsure of exactly how the circumstances of his transfer have occurred, but he has been promised $1,200 a season and an attractive signing bonus. He decides to wait until spring, when it's time to go, to tell his mother about his new job. In the meantime, he keeps his head down and dutifully attends classes at Illinois State University.

"YOU CANNOT THROW AWAY your education for a hobby," shouts Alice, looking for support from Charles, who sits in his armchair, trying to hide behind the newspaper. "We have worked hard to make sure you get the best start in life, Bill."

Bill has managed to stay quiet for months, but now is not the time to quarrel, as he knows this is an argument he cannot win. His mind is made up, and he must stand before his mother and take it.

"And you're leaving in two days?" Alice exclaims, her tone incredulous. "You didn't give us any warning? How long have you known about this? Bill, you're no son of mine any longer." She gets up and storms out of the room. Bill is unsurprised, yet the words still sting. They listen as she stomps upstairs.

Charles sighs. "She doesn't mean that entirely, you know. You're her only son, and she wants to be proud of you. We'd like to see you follow me into the law, you know."

Bill sighs, too. "I know." He holds back from saying that there's not a snowball's chance in hell of that.

Charles folds his newspaper, appearing to be deep in contemplation. Bill had expected shouting and threats—this quiet thoughtfulness makes him uneasy. Finally, Charles swallows and says, "Bill, do you know the best way to win a fight?"

Despite everything, Bill smiles. "Don't bring a knife to a gunfight?"

"No," says Charles, keeping a straight face and fixing his stare. "The best way to win a fight is to not be in the fight in the first place. Where you're going will not be like boxing in the schoolyard. There is no shame in living to fight another day. Remember that."

"Thank you, sir. I'll be careful," says Bill, and Charles gives him a man-to-man nod. Bill guesses, all in all, this is about the best he could've hoped for.

It's March 21, 1889, and Emily comes to see him off at Old Shakopee Road, where the stagecoach will take him on the long haul to Peoria on the first leg of his journey. He could have taken the train south to Springfield, but this way is cheaper. Bill gives her a reassuring smile as she once again blinks up at him with those pretty eyes.

"Don't worry. I'll be back," he says, though they both know that it won't be any time soon.

The driver helps him hoist his bag onto the roof rack, and before he steps up to the stage, Emily grabs his sleeve. "Until the end of the season, Bill. That's all I'll wait. You know I want to get married."

Bill's heart feels crushed in a fist, but he smiles. "Thank you, Em. I don't deserve it." She does not appear satisfied by this, but he squeezes her hand, kisses her cheek, and finally succeeds in making her smile, though perhaps she senses it, too—part of him is already long gone. He climbs aboard the coach as she waves goodbye, and he grins and waves back.

After the bone-rattling ride to Peoria, Bill will be boarding a series of trains changing at Galesburg, Quincy, and Kingston across the northern border of Kansas until finally arriving in Denver, nearly one thousand miles later. He has one bag containing two baseballs, a personal grooming kit including a sharp switchblade for shaving, a change of clothes, and an old pair of size nine baseball shoes with built-in steel cleats.

Bill holds the distinction of being the youngest pitcher ever signed by Denver. Despite this, he is optimistic that the Grizzlies will quickly embrace him, paving the way for a future brimming with fame and fortune.

CHAPTER 2

"*J*ust arrived?" says the stranger.

Bill has rolled into Denver's Union Station, still optimistic despite being wholly exhausted and unsure where he will stay. He does not want to appear lost and confused, although his small-town demeanor is a dead giveaway, and it's not long before a well-groomed gentleman, exuding an air of respectability, offers his assistance.

"Yes! Do you know a good place for a room, just for tonight, until I get something more permanent?"

"Sure thing," he says, and Bill is relieved as the man seems sincere enough.

"See this road here," the man continues, "that's Wynkoop Street. Follow it down to 16th and turn right. There's a boarding house halfway up there called The Meadows Hotel. It's no palace, but they should be able to help you."

"Thank you so much," says Bill, and his confidence returns. If everyone in Denver is as helpful as this, he should have no trouble at all. He hitches his bag over his shoulder and heads off to 16th Street.

To the west, Bill's gaze captures the majestic snow-capped mountains of the front range. However, as he shifts his attention toward the center of town, he notices the bustling activity that contrasts with the serene grandeur of the Rockies. There are signs everywhere for hardware, laundry, dress, and hat makers, and sure enough, he sees the sign for The Meadows next to a notice that reads "Rooms for rent by the day, week, and month." As he enters the building, he feels the heat from the log fire and realizes how cold he is. On the left is a bar that also serves as the hotel reception.

"Good day, sir," says Bill to the mustachioed man who stands behind it, polishing a glass. Bill is trying his hardest to be as polite as possible. His stomach rumbles, anticipating the food he can smell, maybe meat fried with onions. "I need a room for tonight, please. In fact, maybe for two nights."

The barman looks Bill up and down with an expression that says he's not impressed. "One dollar a day or six dollars for the week. Shared bathroom."

"Fine," says Bill, reaching in his coat pocket for his wallet. "I'll take...wait..." Bill is now searching in his other pockets and getting increasingly flustered. The barman has seen this many times before and walks away to serve a waiting customer.

Panic sets in. Bill's money is gone. No matter how many times he checks all his pockets, his wallet with the little cash that is the sum total of his wealth is nowhere to be found. He puts his travel bag down, empties the contents on the ground, and has to scramble to collect one of the baseballs which has rolled away toward the door. The barman sees the rolling ball and returns to look curiously at his gear.

"Are you here to play baseball?" he asks.

"Yes! I'm playing with the Grizzlies," says Bill, gathering his belongings and his composure. "I'm starting this season. I'm a pitcher."

The barman laughs like that's funny. "Well, we need all the help we can get after last year."

"Look," says Bill, "I've got a problem. I've lost my wallet. Would you mind if I stayed the night and got you the money tomorrow? I'll pay for a whole week."

"Sorry, mister, you have my sympathy," says the barman as he walks around the bar, "but we have house rules here, and the number one rule is cash in advance for the rooms, no exceptions."

He won't budge, even when Bill tells him his name and promises to get the money first thing in the morning. "I don't know anyone in Denver," Bill says, almost pleading now.

"So, how are you going to get the rent tomorrow if you don't know anyone here?"

Bill's face heats up as he realizes the barman has made a valid point. He is absolutely going to have to figure out a way to get his signing bonus partly paid in cash in the morning. He'll have to locate Dave Rowe, the Grizzlies' manager.

But where did he lose his wallet? He tries to retrace his steps. He remembers using it to buy a sandwich and a beer when the train stopped in Kingston. Since then, it had been safely tucked away in his left inside coat pocket, where it always lived. Aside from the ticket inspector, he hadn't talked with anyone since arriving in Denver. Except for the well-dressed gentleman who *kindly* recommended the Meadow Hotel.

Like a cold, hard slap in the face, Bill realizes that he has been the victim of a pickpocket. How could he be so naïve? He takes pride in his situational awareness on the field and in public places. But he knows his one weakness is that he is too trusting—especially when he needs help.

There is nothing to do for it now unless he wants to head back to the train station and try to find the man and fight him for his wallet, a plan he quickly realizes is not apt to go in his favor. Anyway, he can hear his stepfather's voice in his head, saying the best way to win a fight is not to get into the fight.

"Which way to River Front Park?" Bill asks the barman.

"Not far," he says with genuine empathy. "Go back up 16th to the station, cross the tracks, and turn right at Bassett."

"Thanks. I'll be back."

Bill tosses his bag over his shoulder once more and heads for the door. The walk back up to the station seems much longer now, and it's getting dark and considerably colder. The air is indeed much thinner than Bloomington up here at over five thousand feet, and

Bill turns up his coat collar as he nears the baseball field. He keeps his eyes peeled for the pickpocket, but there is no sign of him. There are no gas lamps on the streets up here, and the light is fading fast as he nears the park.

Ensuring no one is in sight, he tosses his bag over the padlocked gate and climbs into the grounds. Heading to his right, he discovers a spot beneath the bleachers and, using his bag as a makeshift pillow, lies down and does his best to keep warm. As he peers up between the slats, it looks like even the stars are shivering in the cold. He is exhausted, physically and emotionally, and despite the chill and lack of food, sleep comes easily, at least for a few hours.

Waking with a start, he hears jangling keys and the creak of the main gate. A man enters and starts walking with a sense of purpose across the field toward the main sheds. Relief is followed instantly by apprehension as Bill stands up, raising his hand to the back of his neck as he fights the soreness. He walks around to the side of the bleachers and tries not to startle the man.

"Good morning!"

The man whirls. "Who the devil are you? How did you get in here?"

"It's a short story," says Bill cheerfully. "My name is Bill Darn-brough from Bloomington, Illinois, and I'm the new pitcher. My wallet was stolen, and I didn't know where else to go."

The man swallows, removes his hat to scratch his bald head, and calms down. "Right. Get your bag and follow me. We've got a stove here, and we'll get some coffee down you before we decide what to do." Bill follows eagerly. Coffee!

Over a steaming cup, Bill learns that John Backman is the player-caretaker of the Denver Grizzlies, and, as far as Bill is concerned, he is a saint. Curiously, John behaves as if this sort of thing happens at the start of every season, and he lends Bill five dollars without any hesitation, promising to ensure Dave Rowe takes it out of his signing money in a few days. He tells him to get some food, secure a room at the Meadows, and be back at the field at eight o'clock sharp the following morning.

There is a different manager on shift at the Meadows this time, and Bill decides not to trouble him with his story and pays for two nights. He plans to keep extremely close track of the three dollars he has left.

Dave Rowe displays minimal interest in Bill's less-than-ideal arrival in Denver and promptly steers the conversation toward business. The Grizzlies, currently holding the sixth position in the Western Association baseball rankings, are the focus of Rowe's attention, and he looks eager to assess Bill's pitching abilities. Following a dazzling demonstration of fastballs, Bill swiftly delivers a formidable curveball, only to hear the familiar words again: "You'll be starting as our second pitcher."

"Great!" Bill says, still over the moon at the prospect of playing at this level with some of the best players around.

Wanting to put the events of his first evening in Denver behind him, Bill decides that, as long as he stays on his guard, he ought to explore the town some more.

Someone at the bar at the Meadows has told him about Madden's. The owner, Eugene Madden, is a second generation Irishman and a councilman, and his brother is the police captain, so he is probably a valuable person to know.

Bill walks in to find a no-nonsense drinking establishment. Groups of railroad workers known as tarriers and returning prospectors gather around tables, but they do not seem to mix with each other much. Bill overhears what sounds like an exaggerated tale being told by one of the prospectors. There don't appear to be any games or gambling, but a man in a derby cap plays the fiddle, and some men sing with raised glasses. Bill catches the words to the chorus as he makes his way to the bar: *You'll never find a coward where the shamrock grows*.

As Bill takes a first sip of his beer, a young man of about twenty-one arrives at his side and orders a beer for himself. He is a bear of a man, easily six foot and broad-shouldered with a perfectly trimmed handlebar mustache. Bill catches his sideways glances—is he spoiling for a fight? He pretends to ignore him until, after some time, the man breaks his silence and speaks up.

"I know who you are," he says in a mildly threatening voice.

"You do?" says Bill, feigning absent-mindedness and planning his escape.

The stranger grins to see that he's unnerved Bill. "Sure! Bill Darnbrough! Don't you remember me?"

"Holy smokes!" Bill nearly splutters. "Art Twineham! I didn't recognize you and didn't expect to see anyone I knew here!"

Art laughs. "Well, here we are," he says, raising his glass. "Who would have guessed that, just two years ago, we thought we'd never make it out of the backwoods?"

Bill raises his glass. "It's great to see you, Art." He pauses. "But what are you doing here?"

"I'm catching for the Grizzlies now. I signed months ago, and I've been here since February. Means we're gonna be teammates again."

"That's great. Congratulations." Bill sips his beer, feeling relief at having someone familiar with him in this new town.

"What do you think of Denver so far?" Art blurts, and without waiting for an answer, he leans in. "I've been here before. My first piece of advice is to keep eyes in the back of your head. Heard of Soapy Smith?"

Bill sips his beer. *Cool as a cucumber*, he thinks, without having ever understood exactly what the old cliché means. "Can't say I have," he says, realizing that Art is trying to throw him off balance.

"He's the guy you don't mess with," says Art. "And I am dead serious about that. Started out as a plain, old-fashioned conman with the shell game and three-card monte." Art demonstrates moving his hands over each other to make sure Bill gets the idea. "Before you know it, his gang members are swindling any poor sucker in rigged poker games. Last year, he opened the Tivoli Club down on Market Street. He's got his fingers in all the pies and basically runs this town."

Bill has a tiny smile on his face. He looks unconcerned. Arts gulps his beer and goes on. "Listen, Bill, there are a few things you need to know in this town if you want to keep your shirt. Many savvy travelers have been taken for a ride on the streets of Denver.

22

And the police are in on it, too. And the Irish. And the Italians. You've really got to watch yourself."

"All right, Art, sure, I understand," says Bill, then gives Art a friendly slap on the back and orders two more beers.

"That's Michael," Art says, pointing to the barman. "He's here direct from Kilkenny, Ireland."

"I wonder if I'll see Ireland one day," Bill ponders aloud as Michael delivers the fresh beers and Art and Bill clink glasses.

"Stick with me, pal, and you'll at least see the back side of Denver," Art promises. "By the way, have the folks from Old Judge been in touch with you yet?"

"The cigarettes? No, why?"

"You know, the new baseball cards you can get in the packets?"

"I don't smoke."

"You never saw them in Bloomington?" says Art. "They're everywhere now. They take our photograph and put it on a baseball card, and it says your name, the team, and your position. William Darnbrough, Denver, pitcher. That's how everyone knows what we look like."

"I've never had my picture taken," says Bill.

Someone starts singing the opening lines of "My Wild Irish Rose," and a group of tarriers quickly join in. After a moment, the entire saloon bellows the chorus, and Art joins in, his chest swelling with the sound of it: *My wild Irish Rose, the sweetest flow'r that grows. You may search ev'rywhere, but none can compare with my wild Irish Rose.*

"You'd better learn the words, pal," Art says with a laugh to Bill when it's over. "I'll teach you!" Bill smiles slightly to the cheers of the railroad men, and Art and Bill both drain their glasses.

"All right," Art tells Bill. "Much as I'd like another, we'd better not make a late night of it. Got to make a strong start on the first day, and practice starts early tomorrow." Bill shrugs, smiles that slight smile, and slides off his barstool. Art hurries to follow him out. "Listen, I'm going to put in a good word for you with Dave Rowe, all right? He trusts me."

Outside, the night air is cool. "I think things are going to go all right for me here, Art," Bill says, shoving his hands into his pockets and looking up at the night sky.

On the walk back to his hotel, Bill reflects that the Irish have a much easier go of it out here compared to back east, where even in Bloomington, the "No Irish Wanted" signs are everywhere. The Burlington and Union Pacific Railway expansion is proving to be a lifesaver for many of them, and work is plentiful in Denver. Probably better odds at a decent wage than prospecting, he decides.

Bill opens the door to his room and flops onto the bed. Still fully clothed, he looks up at a large, brown water stain on the ceiling and vows to give himself every opportunity at a better life. Tonight was fun, and he's glad he happened into Art and equally thankful to have him as a teammate. Nevertheless, Bill has a lingering feeling that this isn't the life he's destined for. Not precisely. He does think that coming to Denver has got him closer to wherever he's meant to end up—and he hopes it won't take long. There are many hotels and rooms above saloons to choose from, but where he is now is convenient and cheap, and that's all that matters right now.

As he drifts off, Bill's last thought is that he should write to Emily. He feels a pang of guilt, considering he practically abandoned her.

Then again, now he has chartered a new course, one that appears to be propelling him upwards.

CHAPTER 3

*B*ill joins the Grizzlies for warm-up drills and practice at River Front Park the following morning. Moving at speed between bases is crucial, and split-second decisions are made using instinctive reflexes.

There are at least six balls in play as the outfielders throw fast and accurately to each other and the bases. Two players wield their bats and hit practice balls all over the park, which are scooped up and returned with lightning speed. Bill is impressed and surprised with their professionalism and commitment, as there were not even limbering up sessions in Bloomington. The players on Bill's old team were focused on outfoxing their opponents by treading on the catcher's feet with sharpened cleats, tripping up runners, and generally being as abusive as possible.

Denver looks to Bill like a team that wants to win by being in better shape and playing to its strengths rather than the other team's weaknesses. Dave Rowe is demanding on the sprints, and Bill is keen to make the best impression, so he pushes himself harder than the senior members of the team. He feels like he is on trial today, and while his past pitching record at the Bloomington Reds will be considered, he also needs to be seen to be pulling his weight. He is the youngest player to be signed to Denver in the team's history, but somehow, he needs to become the opening pitcher.

Most of the team chew and spit tobacco, and many pitchers use the spit from a chaw to make their gloves more supple. Bill is no exception and uses a spitball regularly after John Backman insisted he start wearing a glove. Unsurprisingly, he is nervous as he throws practice pitches at the left-handed Jim Curtiss, one of the Grizzlies' formidable hitters. Left-handers are in high demand, and Curtiss is no exception. Fortunately, Bill's swerving pitch breaks away from the straight line to the catcher's right, and the deception leaves all of them, especially Tom Dolan, the stand-in catcher, suitably impressed.

Shortly after, he is called to the manager's office once more. As he enters, he sees Dave Rowe seated behind a desk, and also present in the room are John Backman, Jack Keelan, and Hank Steely. These three individuals are senior team members and therefore afforded management status. The door opens behind Bill, and in walks Art. The others look serious, but Art cannot conceal his smile as the conversation unfolds. Everything is happening so fast as Backman hands Bill his two uniforms—white for home games and blue for the road. Both have a D for Denver embroidered on the front.

"So, are you all set, Bill?" he hears someone say.

"Let me get this straight," says Bill. "Sayer left, and now I'm the new starting pitcher?"

"Right," says Hank Steely, "you and McNabb will rotate."

"Just like that?" says Bill, trying hard to stifle his elation.

"Yup, just like that," says Art as he swings his arm in a ghost pitch arc. "Pack a bag. We're off to Sioux City on Tuesday!"

In the early spring of 1889, Denver is fast becoming a destination rather than just a way station for prospectors, and new neighborhoods are cropping up outside of town. To celebrate his success, Bill decides to take the northbound streetcar to the end of the line and explore.

The foul-smelling vapors of the stockyards and tanneries hit Bill right to the back of his throat as the open-sided streetcar nears its destination. It is evident at once that life here is hard as, aside from the terrible stench, there doesn't appear to be any attempt at street cleaning, and the people walk without any display of pride or contentment.

The imminent collapse of the Austro-Hungarian Empire has seen new arrivals from all over Eastern Europe, as Czechs, Croats, Poles, Slovaks, Slovenians, Serbs, and Russians seek better opportunities in America.

The Slavs have settled right here, in the north of the town, along the banks of the South Platte River where the smelter factory is located. The Union Pacific and Burlington railway yards and the stockyards are here, and the settlement is named Globeville after the Globe Smelting and Refining Company.

Bill decides against venturing into any of the run-down saloons. He has heard that they are often held up as the laborers use them to cash their paychecks.

Globeville might as well be another country, and it seems to Bill like all eyes are on him. He may be a stranger to Denver, but he feels like an utter intruder here. His palms are sweating by the time the southbound streetcar rings its bell to depart—not nearly soon enough, as far as Bill is concerned.

Three days pass by quickly, and the team loads up all their combined gear onto the train at Union Station headed for northwest Iowa. When Bill was born, this trip would have taken at least a week on a stage or in covered wagons, but by now, the entire U.S. is crisscrossed with a spider's web of railroads. The team has the use of the Pullman sleeping car, although the dining car is too expensive, so they have to dash for food, water, and coffee at each stop.

"Hey, Bill, have a seat!"

Tom Dolan, Ed McNabb, and the shortstop, Bill White, are playing cards, and Tom beckons Bill to an open spot. Bill looks at Tom as he shuffles the deck with great dexterity and hesitates for a moment.

"Thanks, fellas, but I'm not much of a card player," he says.

"Come on kid," says Ed, "we're only playing poker for pennies."

"Right now," says Bill, "I need every penny I've got!"

"Suit yourself," says Ed.

Bill is trying to determine how many hands he would have to win to buy a new pair of cleats. Hundreds probably. Train poker seems like a decent way to pass the time, but what's the point unless you could win some serious cash? On the flip side, what if he lost what little he had? What if the ante increases after a few whiskies, and they are no longer playing for pennies? Aside from this, he doesn't know how to play poker. He decides that if he ever plays cards, he'd better learn the rules first.

They travel along the Platte River for two days, stopping at Julesburg, North Platte, Kearney in Nebraska, then change trains at Columbus to continue north to Sioux City. The first-class passengers enjoy the scenery seated on rich upholstery, surrounded by luxurious velvet hangings, and carved mahogany. They drink fine wines and enjoy sumptuous meals, but Bill can only dream of joining the esteemed ranks of the Transcontinental elite.

On the first game day, the cable cars run the fans down to Evans Driving Range, Sioux City's combined racetrack and baseball field. The Cornhuskers have a strong record in the Western Association, having come third in the last season, and Bill has studied their form from newspaper articles. Although anxious about the left-hander, Monk Cline from Kentucky, he is his usual, confident self.

Three groundsmen are out on the field putting down chalk lines around the batter's and pitcher's boxes, and a further two are watering down the dirt with a hosepipe. One holds the hose over his shoulder while the other directs the water. The two managers meet in the middle, and Dave Rowe shakes hands with Jim Powel, the Huskers' manager and first baseman, but it looks like there is no love lost between these two, and this tense encounter sets the tone for the game.

Baseball is a team game, although, out on the field, as far as the pitcher and batter are concerned, it is one man against another man. When it is the Grizzlies turn to field, Bill soon makes a fine mess of the ball using pine tar, which makes the ball behave less predictably. The stickiness of the tar gives Bill a better grip, but its brownish-black color makes it hard to detect that the ball was white at the start of the game. He uses his wrist to good effect, never giving a hint of the type of delivery, and most of his victims fall into the swing-and-miss category as the ball becomes harder to see at high speed.

When Monk Cline steps up to the plate, Bill's confidence wavers. He looks around the perimeter to confirm that his outfielders are completely focused as if anticipating a resounding crack of ball on bat.

Bill winds up. Throws. The ball sails up…up…

And hits Cline right under the chin! Cline drops like a sack of potatoes. The crowd gasps as one and rises with everyone craning to see. Cline is flat on the ground, and players from both teams are running toward him. Bill gets there first and looks down at his rival, prone in front of Bill's dusty cleats. Cline lets out a moan. The umpire and Dave Rowe are shouting at each other. Someone runs up with a bucket of water and drenches Cline, who sputters and opens his eyes. Bill lets out a sigh of relief, glad to see that Cline's windpipe has remained intact. The last thing he wanted to do today was kill someone. All he wanted was to let Cline know he wasn't going to be intimidated, wasn't going to let any guy crowd the plate.

Both managers are called to the batter's box, and a severe warning is dished out to Bill. If the umpire had been certain that Bill intentionally hit Cline with an illegal pitch, he could have ejected him from the game, and if it persisted, he could have disqualified the team entirely. Thankfully, Cline recovers sufficiently to walk to first base, and the game continues.

Despite their best efforts, the Grizzlies are down 5-6 to the Huskers, and the mood after the first day is somber. A small wooden shed behind the outfield fence serves as the visitor's changing room. The paint peeling off the walls reflects their mood as the players mainly stare at their shoes.

Dave Rowe probably didn't know what to expect from this kid out of Bloomington, but it sure wasn't to knock down one of the biggest hitters in the league the first time he faced him.

"Have you heard the term, chin music?" says Dave to Bill, not intending it as a question and loud enough for everyone to hear.

"That's not me, Mr. Rowe," says Bill. "I didn't mean to hurt him."

"You love lefties, don't you," says Dave, showing off his full set of tobacco-stained teeth. Similar to John Backman, the caretaker, Dave Rowe is reminiscent of a non-commissioned officer from an army regiment who knows when a lesson has been taught. He is not in the business of unnecessarily disciplining his troops, and on this occasion, there is no need to belabor the point. Bill thinks Dave is impressed and decides it's time to toughen up. Throwing in on batters is part of the game, right?

After two more losses to Sioux City, the Grizzlies' season has started on a sour note. On the trip back to Denver, Bill does his best to keep his mind on the bigger picture. Someone has left a copy of the *Omaha World-Herald* newspaper on the train, and Bill reads an extensive editorial about the upcoming World's Fair to be held in Paris from May to October. The coverage is wildly enthusiastic regarding the American contingent, which promises to be prestigious and varied. Thomas Edison will be demonstrating his new phonograph and the entertainment will be sure to thrill with Buffalo Bill Cody and Annie Oakley performing their Wild West shows daily.

Reading about the largest pavilion, The Gallery of Machines, Bill imagines a mechanical device that can deliver baseballs at a batter to practice without the pitcher. He conjures up an image of himself manning the stall, wearing his American baseball uniform, while visitors marvel at his new invention.

The article has many illustrations, including one of Gustave Eiffel's newly completed tower, which people can climb for five francs. There is also a reference to the fact that Eiffel also built the iron frame of the Statue of Liberty. Another illustration shows the grand pavilions on the Esplanade des Invalides with trams at the entrance. The paper says the organizers expect up to a staggering thirty million visitors over six months.

Bill neatly folds up the paper and leans back to reflect, staring out the window at Nebraska's gently rolling hills, peppered with occasional homesteads. Despite the world's major events, he finds himself ensnared within his own small one, preoccupied about his pitching performance over the last three days.

Art falls into the seat beside him, breaking into his thoughts. "The world certainly looks heavy today, Bill," he says and laughs.

Bill laughs a little in return, grateful for his friend's good humor. He doesn't know quite how to explain where his mind has been. "Sometimes I guess I think if I squint hard enough, I can see my way clear into the future and the whole world," he says. "But then it turns out I just keep seeing the past, my own little thoughts, and the things I was running away from back home."

"Boy oh boy," says Art, "think of all you'd be missing if you hadn't! If I wasn't playing ball, I guess I'd be working in a brewery, then getting fired for drinking all the merchandise."

Bill smiles. The telegraph poles appear to pass slower now, and time seems to stand still at that moment for Bill. For the first time, he is questioning his decision to leave Bloomington. What if he gets let go from the team, with insufficient money to return home?

"Look, Bill; you win some, you lose some. You can't go getting all downcast every time things don't go your way. And life's too short to be contemplating which forks in the road we should have taken. All I know is, win or lose, you're the number one pitcher around here. Pretty soon, the whole town of Denver will know your name, and all the girls will follow you home, so you'd better be sure you've got a quality lock on your door."

Bill manages another smile at that, and he turns to see all his teammates in various states of travel. Tom, Ed, and Bill White are playing cards again while others are reading books and newspapers, and some are staring out the windows. Bill knows they have all taken similar risks to be here.

Anyway, what does he really stand to lose, other than some ball games? After all, his reasons for getting out of Bloomington had been good, and he still clings to the conviction that his dreams and aspirations lie far beyond the confines of his hometown.

CHAPTER 4

*T*he *Streets of Doom* is the nickname given to the area between Larimer Street and Union Station in Denver. It is said that if you can make it through this part of downtown without encountering any of Soapy Smith's gang members and succumbing to their wizard-like financial cons, you are either a local or even a wizard yourself.

After two wins in a row against the Minneapolis Millers and Kansas City Blues, Bill and Art have agreed to go out tonight to celebrate, especially since Art made a spectacular barehanded catch at the fence to cement today's victory. They make their way toward the Tivoli Club at the southeast corner of 17th and Market. The streets are full of people laughing and shouting like the whole town is celebrating, and Art and Bill walk with their chests puffed out, knowing they're at least part of the reason.

They've agreed to dress modestly so as not to attract unwarranted attention, and certainly not to carry any weapons or large amounts of cash. Bill has taken to keeping the little money he does have in three different places: A little in his wallet, some folded into his sock, and a few bills in the breast pocket of his shirt. He learned his lesson quickly after that first day here in Denver.

Art spends the rest of their walk explaining the rules of faro, a card game played at the Tivoli in addition to poker and roulette. It seems to Bill that all Art is really doing is showing off, throwing around phrases such as *burning off the soda, gaffed dealing boxes* and *cat hops*. Bill thinks it will be much simpler to learn the game by seeing it first-hand. He reminds himself not to drink too much tonight despite the strong temptation. When he returned to his room this evening, he found a letter from his mother—the first she'd written him since he'd been away. *Give up this sinful game and come home. All can be forgiven.* Bill had crumpled the letter and thrown it into the trash, then fished it out again and dropped it into the fire in the lobby on his way out. She was the one person in the world who could really make him see red. What right did she have to sit in judgment of him? To talk about *sin* and *forgiveness?* Just because *she* got off scot-free and took up going to church?

He takes a deep breath to calm himself. He's already decided—he just won't write back. He wants to focus on the business at hand. He's a grown man on his own in the city, and who cares what his mother thinks?

"By the way, Art," he says, to distract himself from his thoughts, "why do they call this guy Soapy Smith?"

"His real name's Jefferson Smith," responds Art, being careful to keep his voice low. "He used to sell bars of soap, and he had this scam he ran. He'd stand in front of a crowd with a pile of soap bars wrapped in plain paper, then unwrap some and re-wrap them in bank notes. Ones, fives, even tens. Then, he'd cover them up again with plain paper and put them back in the pile while spinning some spiel about how this is the best soap anybody's ever seen, and he's willing to stake all this money, so you'll try it, right? Then, he'd offer the soap for sale at, say, twenty-five cents per bar, with the chance you pay your quarter and get ten dollars in return. The first buyers were always his own cronies, and they'd get the soaps wrapped in notes and start shouting out about their winnings, so, before you know it, everyone in the crowd's clamoring to buy a bar of soap, which in reality is only worth about five cents. And guess what?

Nobody else would get a bar wrapped in anything but plain paper. Of course!"

Bill is starting to see that there are many ways to get ahead in the world and that he will have to watch out for men with questionable morals and values.

"By the way," says Art. "You know the barber's shop at Union Station?"

"Sure."

"Don't ever go in there. I hear they shave a "V" into your neck if they think you're a good mark for Soapy's gang. The "V" is for "victim," and they can see you're a good target.

As they enter the saloon on the ground floor at the Tivoli, Bill touches Art's shoulder as they reach the bottom of the main staircase that leads upstairs. There is a sign mounted above them.

"What does *Caveat Emptor* mean?" Bill asks.

"It's Latin," says Art. "It means *let the buyer beware.*"

"Want some company, sweetie?" slurs an over-made-up working girl to Bill, who does not answer but manages a slightly embarrassed smile. Her oily black hair is straight, and her breath is 100% proof. Bill thinks she must be about the same age as Emily, maybe eighteen. Art doesn't appear to have even noticed her, and Bill wonders how often he must come to joints like this.

At the top of the stairs, they turn to the right and enter the main gambling room. It has a bar at one end with red, white, and blue Union flags draped around the mirrors. Curiously, a Cuban flag is also hanging beside one of the shelves packed with different varieties of whisky. Bill has to swallow back his nerves when he notices a couple of toughs seated at a table by the bar staring at them as they edge forward.

"Come on," says Art, gesturing to Bill.

Fortunately, people generally concentrate on their chosen games and pay the two young ballplayers no heed. Bill knows he looks even younger than he is and is glad for Art's size, which should keep any men from wanting to tangle with them.

Bill carefully takes in his surroundings. He can see at least five poker tables, each with players focused on their cards, only occasionally pausing to sip a drink or glance up at the dealer or other players. On the right side of the room are three tables with a small crowd gathered around playing what must be faro. Further back, on a raised wooden platform is a roulette table with two players standing on the near side. Apart from some occasional bustling at the faro tables, the room has an unnerving hush compared to the saloon downstairs.

Art towers over the other men jostling for drinks and has no difficulty getting the barman's attention. Soon, armed with a bottle of whisky and two shot glasses, they choose a small table off to the side of the room to observe.

When they see the amount of money on the nearest poker table, they exchange looks with raised eyebrows. Their paltry baseball salaries would probably not even stretch to a seat at that table, and Bill begins to think that this visit is premature, that he should come back when he has more ready cash.

He tries to analyze the type of people in the room. They are already risk-takers, as anyone who has made it as far as Denver is a speculator of some description. If some have been prospectors, then this is the place for them—they are used to danger and fear. However, most of them look like they ran out of luck long before they walked through the door of the Tivoli.

Bill finds he is calculating the odds of getting shot in this place. The gun laws in Denver are strict, but no one searched them when they arrived or even asked if they were carrying weapons. He imagines the chances of getting stabbed here at the Tivoli, or just plain punched in the face, would be increased when men cheated or drank too much. He consoles himself with a reminder that life-threatening perils are considerably less here than ten miles west out of town, and that's just due to the rattlesnakes. Anyway, he can't help being curious. "Let's go look at the faro," he says.

"Sure, why not?" Art picks up the bottle of whiskey and follows Bill over to the closest table. Six men are gathered near the side of the oval table, opposite the dealer, and Art explains the basics to Bill.

The images of thirteen playing cards are stenciled onto a board that rests on the table, and varying piles of chips are piled on top of them as the dealer pulls cards from a mechanical box known as a shoe. Each player lays their stake on one of the card images, and the dealer draws two cards. The first card is placed on the right side of the shoe, the second next to it. Players with bets on the same card as the first drawn card automatically lose, and any that match the same number win double their original stake. Any remaining bets that had neither won nor lost stay on the table until the next two cards are drawn.

"It gets more complicated," says Art. "At the end, you can predict the order of the last three cards and win big."

"How the heck could you do that?" asks Bill, a little too loudly, and the players all look up, though they show only a fleeting interest in these two tourists and return to the game.

"You see that thing over there," whispers Art, "that looks like an abacus? That shows all the cards played so far, so we can see which cards are left."

Bill laughs slightly. "There's not going to be a *we* at this tonight, pal. You have a go. I'd like to see you hit a home run at this."

Art smirks, hands Bill the whisky, and pays the dealer five dollars in exchange for chips and a penny which can be used to reverse the bet. He places one chip on the six and another on the two. The dealer draws an eight and then a ten. One of the other players has a chip on the ten, and the dealer places another chip of the same color on top of his bet. The dealer scoops up all the other chips as another player lets out an audible groan.

Art twirls the side of his mustache as he places another two chips on the jack and the ace. This time, the dealer draws an eight and an ace. Art looks like he has just been served a slice of his favorite hot blueberry pie as the dealer multiplies his bet by a factor of one. The other chip disappears, although he doesn't seem to mind. Within a relatively short time, Art has lost all his chips and completely forgotten about the penny.

He comes around the table to Bill and retrieves the whisky bottle. Bill is unsure what to say and is relieved when Art speaks first. "I think the deck is rigged, Bill," he whispers. Bill considers Art's diagnosis and decides this must be the refrain of many gamblers, as no matter if the odds are stacked against them, an unrealistic optimism dwells within them.

"Hey, that's nothing." Art says as he downs another shot of whiskey. "Five bucks? Ben Thompson lost $3000 in Leadville not long ago and shot out all the lights." Art pauses a moment and tilts his head. "Although come to think of it, Doc Holiday did shoot a guy over a disputed five-dollar bet."

The casino room is now so thick with smoke that it is hard to see from one end to the other. Bill watches Art pour another shot with a peculiar gleam in his eye and decides he'd better keep his friend distracted before he gets big ideas about avenging his five-dollar loss.

"Let's go and see the roulette."

There are charismatic and fun croupiers, and then there are croupiers who look like they would rather watch the paint dry on the casino's walls. This dealer falls into the latter camp. "No more bets," he mumbles. Even the felt on this table is worn out, with fading numbers, although the wheel turns just fine as the ball starts its inevitable descent. Bill decides to follow the lead of another onlooker and just watch and learn for a few minutes.

The dealer always spins the ball in a clockwise direction, and the wheel rotates counterclockwise. The numbers are spread in a particular way to separate the red and black, odd and even, and high and low numbers in a balanced pattern.

This is Bill's first visit to a roulette table, and he is fascinated as he watches the two players place their bets on the numbered grid. There is silence around the table as everyone eagerly anticipates the spin of the ball before it lands in a slot. If that number corresponds with the number that the player has placed his chip on, he wins. The players have different colored chips so the dealer can easily see who has won. Bill is transfixed, and an excitement stirs within him as he watches the ball tumbling from the wheel and jumping from fret to fret.

"How much are chips worth?" Bill whispers to Art.

"One quarter a chip, young fella," says the dealer who has overheard the question.

"Go ahead, get two bucks' worth, Bill, and have a go," says Art.

Art stands, looking at Bill, who is deep in thought, until finally he says, "Not tonight, Art, I've seen what I need to see," and he turns away from the table.

"But you can place an outside bet and double your money," says Art. "See, here," he points to the black and red diamonds and then to the odd and even zones.

"Got it, thanks Art," says Bill, "but I don't think I trust myself to walk away like you did." As he walks toward the door, Bill stops momentarily and turns to look at the roulette table one last time.

The gas streetlamps on 17th Street light the way toward home, although Bill and Art do not part company until they are well clear of the Streets of Doom.

Bill has trouble drifting off to sleep despite the whiskey. "The house always wins" is a term he has heard somewhere before, and it occurs to Bill that the devious Mr. Smith has come a long way since the soap bar con. Subconsciously, his eyes are circling from left to right as he pictures the roulette wheel spinning around and around. He can hear the clutter of the ball and starts imagining which numbers he would pick.

The questions keep coming, making sleep impossible. Surely, the house doesn't always win? Otherwise, nobody would play? There must be a way to beat the system? What would Emily and his mother think of him gambling? Is there a trick to roulette? Does he have the sense to know when to walk away?

You see, there are gamblers and gamblers. Now, these crap-game men only make tinhorn gamblers, for this reason: When a man runs up against one of them, he loses his money slowly, but surely. He wins a little occasionally and becomes fascinated with the game. Then he winds up by becoming a gambler himself. But when they run up against me it's off with them. They're just paralyzed. I take everything they've got in short order, and they just throw up their hands and swear they'll never gamble again—and they don't. I tell you, I'm a reformer.

—Soapy Smith, as quoted in the Denver Evening Post, March 18, 1898

CHAPTER 5

*D*owntown Denver is alive with cosmopolitan progress, and the streetcars are packed with smartly dressed folks who all seem remarkably healthy looking to Bill, who goes out to explore every chance he gets. One morning, he's standing on a streetcar gripping a leather handhold and working to keep his footing against all the bumps, rattles, and shakes. He looks out at the busy retail district of 16th Street streaming by, when a gentleman whose attire would be befitting of a banker or a lawyer addresses him directly.

"Young man," he says, "I hope you beat St. Joseph this weekend, as I've got a wager." This is quite a shock to Bill. He can't believe that, first, he's been recognized in public, and second, that a gentleman of this man's standing should be a baseball fan.

"It's a team effort, sir," he responds with a smile. "We'll do our best."

"You'll do a damn sight better than that, son," says the man. "We're all rooting for you. Do you have any idea how much respect you carry around here? Has anyone told you that, even though they don't all show up to the games, all the men in the foundries, the stockyards, the tanneries, and the mills all root for you? When you're out there, young lads are running from the park to give updates on the scores."

Bill wishes that Dave Rowe would take some lessons from this man on inspirational speaking when, spontaneously, cries of "hear, hear!" and applause ring out through the car from the other passengers. Bill looks around, astonished, then thrilled, and he does a little bow to acknowledge the crowd.

Before he even has a chance to tamp down his surprise, the man tugs his sleeve. "By the way, I was at the press room gathering last week. That's how I recognized you. Listen, son, I know you've got your hands full now, but what about the off-season? You're going to need a job, aren't you? To stay in Denver? Why don't you come see me, and let's talk about it."

The man hands Bill a card. *JOHN ARKINS*, it reads. *Editor, Rocky Mountain News*.

Bill has sudden visions of himself as a sportswriter, attending boxing matches all winter long. What could be better than that? Also, he likes how this man calls him "son"—it plucks a string in his heart that he didn't even know was there. "Thank you, Mr. Arkins! I will!"

The Denvers won from St. Joseph this morning. The cause of this change was timely hitting in the seventh inning and the admirable work of Darnbrough in the box. McNabb started in to pitch the game, but in the third inning a hot liner from Curtis's bat hit him on the arm and injured him so badly, he had to retire. Darnbrough pitched for seven innings and held the visitors down to two single hits, and he led the team in batting, having two hits for a total of five bases in three times at bat. His support in the field was faultless and the entire nine worked hard to win and showed what kind of ball they are capable of playing when they take proper care of themselves and act like they had some elixir on hand.

—St. Joseph (Missouri) Herald, August 29, 1889

Madden's is Bill's preferred watering hole, a place he considers top-notch. There, he takes pleasure in setting his shoe upon the brass rail at the base of the bar. However, Art Twineham, determined as ever, refuses to concede defeat so easily.

"Don't you want to try it? You didn't even play one hand before," Art pleads as they head once again for Madden's.

Bill smiles the little smile that he knows Art hates. Even after all these months playing all these games and the long miles traveled on the train together time and time again—well, he might be able to tell from a slight twitch of Bill's lip what pitch he's going to throw, but other than that, he guesses Art cannot tell for one damn second what he's thinking.

"Come on, Bill," Art says. "I know you wanted to try that roulette wheel."

Bill laughs. "I'm not sure why, but I see that thing in my dreams, and the last thing I need is to try it."

"I see the faro table in my dreams! Plus, girls, leaning over it." Art sighs, then leans closer to Bill and lowers his voice. "You know, there's girls in these places who'll—you know—and it doesn't cost much, either."

Bill says, "You want to catch something?"

Art straightens up, draws back, and laughs but looks frustrated. "You mean to tell me you don't believe in chasing your dreams? Having a good time? God knows, nobody lives forever, Bill."

A cloud passes over Bill's face for a second, and then he grins. "That's why I'm going to climb the ladder quick, Art." He slaps Art's shoulder. "And I'm not going to let any soap-man grease the rungs, if you know what I mean."

Art shakes his head slowly. He couldn't know that Bill is—in his mind at least—already someplace miles ahead of where Art stands, someplace Art will probably never even get to in his life. "No, Bill. No, I really don't know what you mean."

Bill just gives that little smile again, shoves his hands into his coat pockets, and starts to whistle a tune as he pushes the door to Madden's.

IN LATE SEPTEMBER, back from a road trip to Omaha, Bill visits Arkins at the offices of the *Rocky Mountain News.* His dreams of being a sportswriter are short-lived as Arkins wants him to work in the advertising department once the baseball season ends. He offers to pay Bill a handsome commission for all the advertising he secures for the paper and, when the baseball season starts again in the spring, give him time off for games and practice.

Though slightly disappointed that his job won't involve attending sporting events, Bill recognizes immediately that this is a far better deal than he could've hoped for. Many players have to look for new jobs at the end of each summer.

"Considering you're our ace pitcher," Arkins says, "business owners will be thrilled to meet with you, son. I have a feeling you'll be our most successful ad man yet." He stands, shakes Bill's hand, and claps him on the shoulder. Bill leaves feeling like he's moving up in the world.

He writes to Emily about his new job, thinking she'll be proud, but her reply is sour. *I guess this means you're not planning to come home to Bloomington this winter, and I guess I ought to tell you that Tom Edmondson has been calling on me.*

Bill thinks of writing to his mother but doesn't. She hasn't written to him, either, except once, months ago.

THE DENVER GRIZZLIES end the season with a win-loss record of 51-70, finishing sixth in the league, and Bill with a pitching record of 12-14 compared to Ed McNabb, who recorded 3-18. Bill's earned run average of 4.37 secures his spot on the team for the next season, and Dave Rowe confirms he will be the starting pitcher. After a celebration with Art and the others, most of whom are heading back to their old hometowns for the offseason, Bill moves into his own rented rooms with a shared bathroom down the hallway.

He reports to work at the *Rocky Mountain News* office every morning, and the clacking of the typewriters increases in volume and haste as the daily stories unfold and deadlines beckon. The paper has a wide circulation with competitive advertising rates, and within a few weeks, Bill has a healthy client base of new advertisers. While the work isn't his true passion and is far from what he had envisioned, he realizes he has a natural talent for it.

He suggests grouping similar businesses together on the ad pages in the same way that retailers like to group themselves together on a street. Arkins agrees, and soon, the new layout is implemented. There are soap makers next to toothpaste tubes with clever little keys to squeeze out every last millimeter of the paste, bespoke tailors near the hat and dressmakers, flour and sugar brands in a clump, plus a large half-page illustration showing the dry goods center on California Street.

As winter sets in, Bill is amazed at how clear and crisp the air has become, but it is dry on his throat. The snow drifts on the streets make navigating between meetings hard, and he has to circumnavigate the enormous piles of snow that the rotary plow deposits on the sidewalks. It's his first Christmas away from Bloomington, and he finds he doesn't mind one bit. If he's longing for anything, it's for spring—for baseball.

One evening, Bill has stopped for a beer after work and casually walks down Blake Street when he passes one of the working girls leaning on the railings. She winks and smiles at him, then, without any warning, seizes his hat and playfully chuckles as she tosses it down the stairwell to the outdoor basement.

"What the hell do you think you're doing?" cries Bill, his voice echoing as he descends the stairs in pursuit of his hat. As he reaches the bottom, he is taken aback by the stairwell's unexpectedly large area, and suddenly, emerging from the shadows, two men materialize and launch a barrage of blows upon his head and stomach. He attempts to defend himself as best he can, but their surprise assault overwhelms him, and before he knows it, he's sprawled on the floor. Swiftly, one of the men delves into Bill's jacket and removes his wallet, but by now, Bill's consciousness has faded as his world turns to darkness. In mere moments, the attackers ascend the stairs and vanish onto the street without exchanging a single word.

The next thing Bill is aware of is pain. His head is pounding, and his ribs are on fire as his surroundings come into focus. He raises his hand to shield his eyes from the bright light of a sparkling chandelier looming over him and begins to register voices.

"Rest easy, my dear. We'll take care of you. Don't worry." It is a woman's voice, and although severely disorientated, he can see her more clearly now. She is middle-aged but still quite beautiful, and her smile is accentuated with full red lipstick.

"Where am I? How did I get here?" Bill manages.

"One of my girls saw you getting a thumping." She turns to indicate a serious-looking man in a suit. "John here, recognized you, and he brought you over the road."

John's suit is tight on his large frame, and he looks like he escaped from a previous profession of wrestling gorillas at the circus.

"I am grateful," says Bill. "But who are you?"

"My name's Mattie Silks," says the woman. "I run this street."

Bill takes in his surroundings. He is lying on a red velvet couch, and there is a small table next to him with a crystal decanter and glasses. Behind Mrs. Silks, in addition to John, are two younger girls in bright cotton dresses.

"The one on the right," says Mrs. Silks, following Bill's gaze, "That's Kitty. She's the one that saw what happened and called Big John to help you." Kitty flashes a wide smile as she gracefully executes a mock curtsy.

"Oh, wait," says Bill, "is this—?"

"Yes, my dear," says Mrs. Silks, "welcome to Denver's little slice of paradise. John tells me you're a famous baseball player, and that's why I agreed to take you in. Honestly, I'm quite surprised you haven't been here before. Most of the team have, you know." She turns to smile at the others. "And the team before that, and the team before that."

Bill tries to sit up, a grimace crossing his face as his hand instinctively moves to his side. The sensation suggests bruised ribs, yet he feels a sense of relief knowing that his ordeal could have culminated in a far worse outcome.

"Just rest for a while, my dear," says Mrs. Silks. "You see, I have a reputation at this end of town, and I don't like my girls or my customers getting knocked around."

"Well, I'm very grateful," says Bill, looking over Mrs. Silk's shoulder, "Thank you too, John."

"Right," says Mrs. Silk with conviction as she claps her hands. "Just remember, it wasn't one of my girls that set you up tonight. We don't tolerate any of that nonsense around here."

"Got it," says Bill, trying his hardest to smile. He never imagined his first visit to a brothel would be as a patient.

On a chilly morning in late December, Bill enters the newsroom, removing his winter coat and hat and hanging them on the stand tucked into the corner. He stamps his boots on the ground, attempting to stave off the cold, and catches sight of John Arkins gazing at him through the glass window of his office. He knows the editor had taken a big chance hiring him, but he feels it's paying off. Bill is hardly ever at his desk as he's always on the go from one meeting to another, as if he is moving fast between bases. He refers to his advertising deals as "home runs" and hopes Arkins admires his spirit. Bill thinks he might be able to run the whole advertising department in the not-too-distant future—and probably double its revenue.

He is formulating a plan. He needs to meet the "right" people in town. Baseball is everything, but right now, in the winter, he could become the advertising manager of Arkin's dreams if he were better connected to the affluent folks.

Maybe wait until that bruise around his eye has faded, though.

CHAPTER 6

*A*s 1890 arrives, Bill makes a case to John Arkins about needing some help meeting people outside his baseball circle. Arkins agrees and speaks to his wife, Margaret, who comes up with the idea to invite Bill to the new Broadway Theatre.

The Broadway near 16th Street has become the premier uptown opera venue. The two-week inaugural season is to be given by The Emma Juch Grand English Opera Company, who are performing six operas beginning and ending with *Tannhauser*. Seeing an opera has never been high on Bill's wish list, but this is where the well-heeled people of Denver society are headed, so he's naturally curious.

He feels like an imposter as he rents a white tie and dress suit with a crimson waistcoat for the evening. The tailor must not be a baseball fan, as he doesn't recognize Bill and treats him with mild disdain, perhaps thinking that he is yet another "gold digger," although not of the mining variety.

The opulence of the theater astounds Bill as it is unlike anything he has seen before. From their box, he has a perfect view of the orchestra pit and can hear the ensembled musicians tuning their instruments. As he gazes across to the people on the other side, he gets an idea of how his position must look. The boxes have heavy crimson and gold drapes hanging down from domes that look to him like golden onions. The stage has a painted scrim with a street scene titled: *A Glimpse of India,* and the enormous ceiling reminds him of an ornate ribbed scallop shell.

Bill is elated to be surrounded by such grandeur and joins in the spontaneous applause from the entire auditorium as the conductor enters and turns to the audience to bow. Silence descends as he taps his baton on the lectern and the music bursts from the orchestra as the vast curtains are raised. Bill looks anxiously at his new acquaintances as if seeking their approval. Is he sitting in the right place? Are they sure he should even be here? Arkins smiles and hands him a little set of binoculars.

Within moments, Bill's apprehension is dissolved, and he is captivated. He looks at the program to see who plays each role and becomes entirely transfixed by Emma Juch, who plays the role of Elisabeth. Even though she sings in German, Bill can recognize that she is an exquisite soprano. Every time she takes a breath to sing, Bill feels himself become tense and goosebumps rise on his arms. From their vantage point, he can easily see right into the orchestra pit and is fascinated that so many talented people are contributing to such a lavish production. The multi-colored sets are vivid works of art, and he is transferred to another realm for three hours without a thought of the outside world.

After the final curtain has fallen, Bill remains in his seat longer than the others, as if anticipating another act.

"How did you enjoy your first taste of the opera, Mr. Darnbrough?" Mrs. Arkins enquires.

"Well, thank you so much for inviting me, Mrs. Arkins. She was fabulous, wasn't she?" says Bill. Mr. and Mrs. Arkins exchange a glance and a smile, and all three are well aware that Bill has little idea what *Tannhauser* is about.

Almost immediately, Bill decides to investigate Miss Emma Juch further. He convinces himself that this is simply a case of harmless admiration, although he becomes more and more determined to meet her somehow. It turns out that, in addition to having a heavenly voice and being bewitchingly attractive to behold, she is from Vienna, Austria, and can sing perfectly in German, Italian, French, and English. The program from the Broadway Theater further informs him that she has toured all over the United States from New York to Los Angeles and appeared in a leading role at Her Majesty's Grand Italian Opera in London.

Emily Irvine of Bloomington seems like a lifetime ago as Bill sets his sights on a gem so rare it is seemingly unobtainable. He decides to consult with Art first, and they meet at Madden's the following day. Bill blows in his hands to warm them, stomps the snow off his feet, and fills in his friend about last night's opera, particularly Miss Emma Juch.

"She's major league, Bill," concludes Art after no more than three seconds of deliberation following Bill's enthusiastic pitch. "I understand you love a challenge, but this woman is probably related to European royalty!"

"But, Art, I knew from the moment she started to sing on that stage that she was someone I had to know. Almost as if I'd known her already—"

"You sound like a deranged infantryman, Bill," interrupts Art, "back from the war with half his mind lost on the battlefield! Mark my words, this is a battle you cannot win."

Bill shakes his head. "My mind is set, Art. Everyone doubted me when I said I would play pro ball someday but look at me now."

Art takes a drink. "As to baseball," he says, "you had a plan. At the moment, concerning Miss Juch, you may be up a ladder, but you'll need the entire Denver Fire Department to hoist you up into the clouds, because that's where she lives."

Returning to his room, Bill is once again lying on his bed, looking up at the ceiling and now preoccupied with a plan to arrange a chance encounter with the delightful Miss Emma Juch.

He had not realized until seeing her that, far from being aloof about women, as his friends have often accused him, or being hesitant to involve himself because of what happened between his own parents, he has simply been waiting for a *remarkable* woman. One who, as Art puts it, resides in the clouds, the upper echelons of experience.

Bill guesses it's vain to think he could make his way up there, too, but there's just no denying what he knows in his heart—Miss Emma Juch is the girl for him. All he has to do is meet her.

He knows absolutely no one in the entertainment business, let alone those connected to opera. And Miss Juch is only in town for two weeks, so he must work quickly.

He decides that it's high time he got to know the Italians. If most operas are sung in Italian, surely the Italians must be well connected in those circles.

CHAPTER 7

*B*ill wastes no time as he is now on a mission. The next day, he visits Siro Mangini at his tavern known as Christopher Columbus Hall on Larimer Street to talk about advertising in the *Rocky Mountain News*. Mangini is one of the most prominent Italians in town, so Bill figures that if anybody knew about opera, it would be him.

Bill imparts a convincing argument for the Christopher Columbus Hall to advertise in the newspaper by explaining that so many Denver residents would love Italian food—they just don't know enough about it.

"Many folks think Italian food is just for Italians, but it's not, is it?" Bill says. "Perhaps you could put more Italian paintings on the wall, and people would feel like they're going to Europe for dinner?"

As their business is concluded, Bill casually asks, "Do you go to the opera, by the way?"

Siro laughs. "Not me. Look around. If my customers knew I drove around in a nice carriage and went to the opera, they would realize that I am not one of them and would go to Luigi's place on 14th Street. Now, try some of my ravioli."

Augustine Roncaglia of Columbia House and Peter Albi, who

owns a tavern on 15th Street, respond similarly. "The only singing we see is at church on Sundays," laments Albi.

Bill has had one of his best days selling advertising, but his new acquaintances, while aware of the new opera house, have not actually visited.

Bill thinks that Signore Siro Mangini's magnificent ravioli is something that Miss Juch would enjoy, but perhaps he needs to plan somewhere more upscale to take her to dinner. He knows that to ask her out in his initial approach would be overreaching, but nevertheless, he practices how he'll greet her in front of the mirror on the cupboard door.

"Good evening, Miss Juch. It is indeed a pleasure to meet you. I'm planning a trip to London next year, and I understand you know the city well. Is there anything, in particular, you would recommend?"

Miss Juch invades his every thought, and sleep becomes an inconvenience.

He decides that his next move should be to meet the Germans who run the main brewery and many of the taverns. Bavarian House, Saxon Hall, and Mozart Hall are just some of the more upstanding establishments. Moreover, Bill has read in the *Rocky Mountain News* about the new Turn Hall, which has opened on Arapahoe Street. In addition to being a drinking hall, it has an exercise club and is a center for the arts, hosting concerts, plays, lectures, and even opera. Many prominent Germans, particularly those in the liquor business, have become members of the Denver aristocracy. Looking back, he really should've thought to start here in his quest for an introduction to the beautiful Austrian singer.

The gas lamps cast circular shadows on the sidewalk as Bill approaches Turn Hall. Built of brick with a brown sandstone façade and occupying four city lots, the formidable building has two huge imposing turrets, and a usually confident Bill feels pangs of anxiety as he crosses the threshold of the vast entrance hall. He is anxious that the people he meets may all speak in German, and "Guten Abend mein Herr," "Good evening, Sir," is all he knows.

A man adorned with a glorious mustache, unlike any Bill has

ever laid eyes upon, extends a warm and cordial welcome. Misinterpreting Bill's position at the newspaper, he embarks on an elaborate tour of the building. From the fencing room to the gymnasium, the bowling alley to the ballroom, every nook and cranny is unveiled with meticulous detail.

Finally, his mustachioed companion ends the tour and gives Bill a printed flyer advertising the upcoming performance to be given by the famous pianist Ignacy Paderewski.

"Is he coming far for his concert?" enquires Bill.

"Mr. Paderewski is a world-renowned virtuoso from Poland," replies his guide in a hushed voice to express the gravity of this event. "He will arrive in his own private railway car with his Steinway grand piano and play four nights at the Broadway. We have an exclusive evening for our guests here at Turn Hall before his public concert, and he has promised to play Robert Schumann's *Traumerei* for us."

Cold air whips into the entrance hall as the front door opens, and a man wearing an elegant-looking winter coat walks in. He removes his hat as he takes in the scene.

"Darnbrough? Bill Darnbrough of the Grizzlies?" he exclaims. "What are you doing here? Oh, never mind, why don't you just come in and meet everybody! What a thrill it is to see you. And in the middle of the off-season. I didn't know any of the players stayed in Denver all winter." Bill is unsure who this stranger is or how he recognized him, but nevertheless, he dutifully follows him up the main staircase as he is happy to have an introduction.

The room is heavily veiled in a haze of cigar smoke with leather couches, plush armchairs, and polished low tables. Bill notices ornate bookshelves with leather-bound works of German and English literature, and the paintings on the walls immortalize wild boar hunting scenes, picturesque European landscapes, and military figures on horseback.

"This is my brother-in-law, John Millheim, and this here is Philip Zang," says the man enthusiastically. Bill shakes each man's hand in turn, making sure to look them straight in the eyes as his stepfather had taught him. He has noticed that they all have well-tailored suits with expensive looking cravats, and, most strikingly, they all have first-class mustaches. He puts his hand up to his upper lip for a brief moment as he considers whether it may be time for him to follow the trend.

The conversation starts off inevitably around the exceedingly cold weather they are experiencing. Another man joins the group and is introduced to Bill as Adolph Coors, who wastes no time engaging in conversation once he has discovered Bill's background.

"Tell me, Bill," says Coors, "do you think baseball and beer are a good match?"

Bill lets out a small chuckle. "I thought you fine gentleman would be discussing finance and philosophy, and it's a relief you'd like to talk about beer. Anyway, yes, Mr. Coors, baseball fans drink all manner of things, but I suppose they do drink beer. Honestly, I have to concentrate on my job out there, so I don't give it much thought."

"I see," says Coors.

"It appears our friend in the brewing game has hit on an idea," observes Millheim.

"It seems to me," says Zang, changing the conversation, "that the west will develop at a great pace thanks to Vanderbilt and Morgan and the others for getting the railroad tracks laid out at an incredible speed."

There is a moment of silence around the table as the others look at Bill. He feels this is a test to see if he has anything interesting to contribute beyond baseball.

"I agree," says Bill, "but it's more than that. Look at all the towns that have sprung up thanks to the gold and silver prospectors. Many survive and thrive thanks to clubs like yours promoting education and the arts and culture. I think the arts and culture play the most important role in any city, aside from good, decent employment." Bill tries his hardest to steer the conversation toward music and entertainment and finally gets his break when Adolph Coors raises his voice again.

"Who would have believed that this little town would have built so many theaters and music halls in such a short time?"

"The opera!" Bill exclaims, surprising everyone with his enthusiasm. "I had the good fortune to attend a showing of *Tannhauser* recently at the Broadway, and what a fantastic performance. Have any of you gentlemen seen it?"

The German businessmen look at each other with knowing smiles.

"We Germans are most proud of Wagner," says Millheim, "particularly if you are from Leipzig, but, as I am sure you know, he composed *Tannhauser* while living in Dresden."

"Ah-ha!" says Bill, "But isn't Miss Juch from Austria?"

The Germans are gracious enough not to laugh at Bill's naivete.

"It sounds like you have done your research well, young sir," Millheim responds as he tips the end of his cigar into the ashtray.

Bill swallows back his nerves, then says, "Do any of you know Miss Juch, by any chance?"

"We make a point of inviting many famous individuals who represent the best in the arts to the Turn Hall," says Zang, who clearly has some standing at the club. "Did you know that we have a private audience with the great pianist Ignace Paderewski in two weeks, right here, next door in the music hall?"

"Yes, the man who gave me a tour earlier told me," says Bill. "Going back to Miss Juch, though, if I may, is there any way I could meet her while she's in town?"

The Germans exchange looks again, this time with furrowed brows. Clearly, they all know that an introduction out of the blue would be entirely inappropriate. He is only a ballplayer, after all. Bill detects their obvious concern and goes ahead with his prepared pitch.

"You see," he says, "my family is from England originally, and I'm planning a trip there next year to try and trace my roots. Miss Juch has recently been in London, and I'm hoping she could advise me on places of interest that I should include during my travels."

There is a long silence around the table as Bill's far from plausible story is considered by all present.

"Of course, Miss Juch will attend the piano recital," says Zang. Bill barely hears the mocking in his tone. "That is her last night in Denver, and she has no performance scheduled herself. Perhaps you may become acquainted with her there?"

"Excellent!" says Bill. "How do I buy a ticket?

CHAPTER 8

"My advice is to try your luck at Soapy's place," says Art.

"I don't think you heard me," responds Bill. "The problem with that is that I hardly have enough left to cover my rent. I don't get paid for another two weeks and must find a way to meet Emma Juch at Paderewski's concert." Art looks pensively at Bill, unable to come up with an alternative suggestion.

"You see, the night of the concert is her last day in town," says Bill, looking out the window. "I'm going back to the Broadway, and maybe I could see her on her way out after the performance." Bill can see that Art is growing impatient with him now and would prefer if he would stop chasing dreams and become his full-time drinking and gambling partner.

After one week, they meet again, and Bill reports back that his pursuits have been unsuccessful, as the doormen are under strict instructions not to let anyone near Miss Juch.

Bill is keenly aware that the gulf that separates him from the higher echelons of society is wealth. After much consideration, he finally agrees to return to Soapy Smith's, as he reasons that life would be so much easier if he could win a little money. He has managed to find a book that describes basic roulette strategies and has started making notes with a pencil. Flipping back a few pages at one point, he realizes that his notes look like insects have crawled all over the page, leaving imprints. Bill smiles at the idea that only he could decipher the meanings in the same way that only a pharmacist can read a doctor's prescription.

The roulette table is busier this evening and Bill finds himself once more transfixed by the spinning wheel. There is a bare light-bulb over the table and the ball gives off a sparkle each time it passes the left-hand side as if sending a signal. The noise of the ball jumping from fret to fret as it decides where to land reminds him of the clacking of the telegraph ticker tape machine in the newsroom. Bill watches the other players and tries to make sense of their betting strategies, but with only a rudimentary knowledge of the odds, he cannot seem to pluck up the courage to place any bets of his own. One thing he does learn, though, is that he will need a lot more money in reserve if he is to have any chance of winning.

"Well?" asks Art, who has come over from the faro tables.

"Well," says Bill. "How's about this? I get paid in a week, and we can come back?"

"You mean you still haven't had a go?"

"Not yet, my friend. I need a strategy."

"Nuts to your strategy," says Art. "Place your bets."

Bill stands for a moment with the same apprehension he feels standing in the pitcher's box facing a left-handed batter. His eyes lock with Art's, and a chill runs down his spine as he sees a glint of admiration in Art's expression. Bill can sense that he's being tested, and the weight of the moment hangs heavily on his shoulders. With a deep breath, he musters the courage to reach into his wallet and pull out a crisp five dollar note, which he slides nervously across the table to the dealer.

The man taps a finger on the numbers grid, indicating that he cannot physically give him the note but must place it on the table. He receives his twenty-five cent chips, which are white with green flecks. Unlike poker, where players are known to throw all manner of personal objects of value onto the table, in roulette, only chips issued by the casino are considered bona fide currency.

Then he waits. He watches the other players who rush to place their chips around the grid and on the outside betting zones. This is the first time he has been so close to the roulette wheel, and he observes and listens as the ball jumps from fret to fret before finally coming to rest in a pocket of its choice.

Bill has picked one chip off his pile and is moving it from finger to finger in his right hand. Art taps him on the shoulder and waves his hand in the direction of the table to encourage him to take the plunge. One of the players leaves the table, goes to the bar, and is replaced by a tall, astute-looking man with round glasses who looks like a bank teller rather than one of the Tivoli's typical customers. All the players seem to have an air of confidence and a sense of purpose as far as Bill is concerned, and he is aware that the dealer is glancing at him regularly now during the ball spin as if wondering what he is waiting for. They both know that the odds will not improve as time passes, so Bill eventually makes his move.

He takes a deep breath and, with a handful of chips in his left hand, uses his right hand to place individual chips on the 5, 11, 17, 23, 29 and 35. He has laid bets straight down the center column, missing every second number. In addition, he places two chips on black and two on even, and now nearly half his chips are gone, so he sits down.

"No more bets," calls the dealer.

The wheel spins for around twenty seconds, which feels like an eternity. During this time, when all eyes are fixed on the ball, Bill imagines the various methods that *Caveat Emptor* is living up to its warning. Could the dealer have a pedal beneath the wheel or a magnet setup that could influence the outcome?

The ball does its customary merry little dance with irritating deception until finally coming to rest in the number five pocket. The dealer places his wooden marker on red five, and at 35-1 odds, Bill has just won $8.75. He lets out a great sigh of relief at his victory and the dealer counts out his chips, which he then pushes to Bill, who turns to look at Art and mimics holding a drink to his lips. The big man obliges and heads to fetch a celebratory beer from the bar. Once he has settled down, Bill remembers his total stake was $2.50, so in fact, he thinks he has only won $6.25. Still, that's the alternative of an additional week at the hotel paid for on his first go, so now comes the tricky decision. He waits out the next spin and decides to stay at the table, as surely his prediction skill has resulted in this great triumph.

Bill's strategy is to place precisely the same series of bets as before, no more, no less. His game plan pays off as this time, the ball lands on red 23. Incredibly, he has just won another $9.25, including his original stake. He takes a break during the next two spins and watches the other players place bets similar to his. Clearly, they are impressed with his strategy, which makes Bill smile, considering he barely knows what he is doing. He feels like an imposter and remains totally calm without overtly celebrating. His face and demeanor are impassive as, once again, he places the identical bets, and this time it comes up 22. Although he does not have a bet on 22, this is an even, black number at 1:1 odds, so he has still won another two dollars.

Cautiously removing the winning chips off the even zone and the black diamond, he replaces the same bets for the fourth round. This time, the winner is the house as no bets have been placed on red nine.

"Cash me in." Bill can hardly believe the words have come out of his mouth the moment he speaks as he pushes his pile of chips toward the dealer. He has not suddenly looked at his watch as if realizing he is late for a pressing engagement and has not conferred with Art on strategy. It just happened.

Bill is elated at winning and feels an unexpected sense of superiority over the other players, who will no doubt continue playing until they have exhausted all their funds. He receives "value chips" to the tune of $12. The other players barely acknowledge him and carry on as if he had never been there. This is not the kind of establishment where the customers exchange pleasant conversations to pass the time. He stands up and walks to the cashier, who is in a small, metal-bar-fronted office at the end of the room.

"I'm telling you, Bill, you were on a roll," says Art, holding two beers. "I saw you from over there. That was not beginner's luck, but a higher power was speaking to you. It's your destiny to—" Bill cuts him off mid-sentence.

"Look, Art," he says. "I have no other income besides my base-ball salary right now, and I'm still learning this game. If I had carried on, eventually I would have lost and then would probably never want to come back to a roulette table in my life. I like this game, but I need to be patient. Isn't the secret of being a good gambler mainly knowing when to stop? All I needed was enough money to buy a ticket to the concert so I can meet Miss Juch. It's just a matter of keeping your eye on the ball, old pal." He doesn't want to admit that his heart has never been pounding quite like this, even in the middle of a ballgame.

Bill arrives at the Turn Hall with only minutes to spare before the great Ignacy Paderewski takes to the stage. They were right, he had brought his own piano, and it is a magnificent white Steinway. As the handsome maestro strides across the stage, he runs a hand through his large mop of untidy dark hair.

The applause goes on for minutes, and Bill realizes that this man is undoubtedly as popular as the reputation that precedes him. The program lists the various pieces he is to perform, and none seem familiar to Bill, so he redirects his attention and scans the audito-rium looking for Emma Juch. As much as he strains without standing up, it is impossible to locate her as he is almost in the back row.

Paderewski plays Chopin's *Polonaise* with great gusto and vigor-ously hammers the keys. His performance is as eccentric as his hair, and the audience enthusiastically responds at the end of each piece. As the break for the intermission is announced, Bill finally spots Miss Juch as she stands and walks toward a side exit door accompanied by John Millheim, who he recognizes from his meeting at the club. Heading out the back door and skirting around the hall down a corridor, Bill finds himself in a lounge bar area and sees Miss Juch, who is by now surrounded by a small group of admirers. He inserts himself into the melee by pretending to be making haste to the bar and feigning surprise to see Millheim.

"Herr Millheim," Bill exclaims, "how good to see you again." Fortunately, Millheim recognizes Bill and returns the greeting.

"Mr. Darnbrough, welcome back to the Turnverein." No doubt recalling their conversation, Millheim smiles as he turns to Miss Juch.

"Miss Emma Juch, please allow me to introduce one of Denver's brightest young sportsmen, Mr. William Darnbrough."

Bill can't believe it. He is actually meeting the woman he's been dreaming of nonstop for weeks. He notices her gray eyes and then looks down at her sheer elbow-length cream-colored gloves as he gently takes her hand.

"What a great pleasure it was to see you at the opera, Miss Juch," he says and is pleased that his voice comes out smoother and stronger than he feels.

"You are a sportsman?" she says in a distinct Germanic accent. She speaks very softly for someone with such a powerful singing voice.

"Yes, I'm lucky enough to be on the Denver baseball team." She smiles automatically, although it is clear from her expression that she has little or no interest in baseball. Bill, quick as a flash, follows up.

"I'm so pleased to meet you as I was hoping you could tell me about London. I understand you have visited many times, and I plan to go there soon." Millheim and the other gentlemen in attendance seem momentarily stunned by this young upstart's impertinence but show even more surprised by her response.

"London is full of wonderful people, and I adore the English. They are so polite." She looks from side to side, seemingly aware that the men hang on her every word. "My advice is to also travel around Europe. You should see the south of France these days. It is quite magnificent. I would highly recommend a visit to the fabulous opera of Monte Carlo."

"Monte Carlo," repeats Bill.

"Yes," she says, "the Garnier Opera is my favorite place in the whole world, and the sea and the mountains are so beautiful." She gives him a little wink, which nearly causes his heart to stop. "There is also the chance, Mr. Darnbrough, of winning a bit of money at the grand casino. Or, perhaps, a lot."

Bill has calmed himself enough to smile. "Will I see you there, Miss Juch?"

She smiles back, more deeply this time, and—is it his imagination?—bats her eyes. "Perhaps."

At this point, Millheim has decided that Bill has monopolized Miss Juch quite enough and interjects. She smiles at Bill as the others gather around her again like bees around their Queen.

"Tell us, Miss Juch, where are you performing next?" quips one excited supporter, and in an instant, Bill is relegated to the sidelines.

He is quickly plotting his next move when Philip Zang comes up and grabs his sleeve. "Here, come shake Paderewski's hand, Mr. Darnbrough."

Zang maneuvers the two of them directly into the path of the great maestro and says, "Mr. Paderewski, great performance tonight, Sir. I would like to introduce you to one of Denver's most famous sports stars, Mr. William Darnbrough."

Paderewski nods at Bill without smiling or offering his hand. *Perhaps he doesn't shake hands*, thinks Bill, *for fear of damaging his livelihood. Maybe his hands are insured?* In the instant that their eyes lock, Bill considers all the exotic places this man has visited—Rome and Madrid this year alone according to Millheim.

"I really enjoyed your performance," says Bill, to which Paderewski simply manages a slight smile and another nod before he walks on, seemingly in a hurry. Bill turns to look for Miss Juch, although she has also disappeared, and he is left standing next to Zang.

"One day," he says, "I'm going to see all the places he's seen."

CHAPTER 9

*B*ill sits at a table in Madden's, drinking coffee with Art.

He realizes maybe it's foolish to dream that someday he really will find Miss Juch at the opera in Monte Carlo, but, right now, he doesn't care how thickheaded it is, and, in his off-hours away from the newspaper, it's all he can think about, even as weeks have gone by.

His one other distraction is his roulette bible. Bill reads the fundamentals of roulette, which are not as straightforward as he had initially imagined. He is seeking an answer to an age-old question. Is there a strategy for placing your bets? How can you employ skill as opposed to simple luck to increase your chances of a big win?

"Hey, Bill." Art is tugging his sleeve, and Bill is brought back to reality. "It's starting."

There is a loud commotion coming from the street. Other people in the saloon get up and go outside to investigate. Bill and Art follow, Bill tucking his little book into his inside coat pocket.

It is the morning of March 17, 1890, and Denver's second St. Patrick's Day parade is about to start. Bill, Art, Bill Fagan, and Danny Flanagan run up to Blake Street to see the sight. The sound of drums and flutes becomes louder as the marchers get closer, and

Bill can see what looks like the entire police department leading the way.

"Good time to rob a bank," Bill whispers to Art.

Some of the policemen are on foot, some are riding on horseback, and they are followed by marching drummers and flute players. A large crowd is on either side of the street, many wearing green hats and coats. They cheer as the proud-looking police move by in front of them and then even louder as some creative folks throw green paper streamers out of the office windows on either side of the street. Next in the procession are the saloon owners with horses towing wagons packed with beer barrels and their taverns' names on banners draped over the sides. The most prestigious-looking wagon is from the Denver Brewing Company, which is drawn by two majestic white horses.

Next in line are the councilmen who appeared to have placed themselves strategically behind the police just in case of any trouble. James Doyle, Andrew Horan, William Gahan, and John Conlon are all dressed up in their Sunday Best with their own variations of green scarves, cravats, and green ribbons around their hats. The politicians are followed by a procession of not so well-regaled railway workers, men from the smelting foundry, and the mill workers. Their banners show them to be from the Irish Progressive Society, Irish Fellowship Association, St. Patrick's Benevolent Society, the Order of Hibernians, and Eugen Madden proudly leads his Irish Land League.

The valiant men of the Denver Fire Department bring up the rear with three carriages for water hoses, an extendable ladder, and a giant brass bell that has its own wagon drawn by a pair of sturdy draft horses. The publisher of the Irish American newspaper, *The Rocky Mountain Celt* is taking good advantage of the parade by having a kid run around handing out free copies of the paper to onlookers.

"Free *Celt*! Free *Celt*!" he cries with great gusto as if it's a statement to gain the release of a political prisoner. The newspaper's owner is sure to attract more advertisers as this is only the second time Denverites have realized how many Irish live in the city.

More drummers and flute players have been joined by men

playing fiddles, and the street is packed with onlookers cheering and clapping.

"It appears the fine ladies of the abstinence society were not invited today," says Art, raising his voice almost to a shout.

Indeed, they were not, and the taverns and saloons do a roaring trade well into the night. Around midnight, Bill realizes that somehow, he has slipped into an Irish accent, as have many other revelers. The parade has had the extraordinary effect of making everyone question their heritage and decide that they must have at least a little Irish in them. This is perfectly feasible, Bill decides, and until he gets to England to check parish records, he may as well be Irish. At least for one night.

The following morning, Bill looks into the mirror, feeling he has aged five years overnight. Taking advantage of some samples his newest advertising client sent him, he cleans his teeth with Dr. Sheffield's toothpaste in a tube. After forty push-ups, he feels a little healthier and goes downstairs to pick up the newspaper.

As he often does, Bill takes the tram up to Castle Marne on 16th and Race for breakfast. It is an imposing building made with rusticated lava stone and contains a Victorian parlor that serves an excellent full breakfast—a necessity after the St. Patrick's Day shenanigans. He selects an armchair next to the fireplace as the courtyard is still too cold in the mornings at this time of year.

Mrs. Peiker brings a steaming coffee urn to refill Bill's cup. Since her husband's passing, Mrs. Peiker has run Castle Marne on her own and always manages to appear at precisely the right moment. Usually, only overnight guests are allowed in for breakfast, although she has a soft spot for Bill as he is always on his own and makes little fuss.

"What's the good news, Mr. Darnbrough?" she asks. Always the same question.

"If I were a rich man, Mrs. Peiker, I'd be off to Europe for the next World's Fair," says Bill, putting down his newspaper.

"You are rich, Mr. Darnbrough," she says, "you have youth, good health, and your whole life ahead of you to see the world."

The morning sun glints through Castle Marne's magnificent six-foot stained-glass window, and Bill marvels at the light, then wonders what the light is like in Paris, London, and Monte Carlo. He is determined to see for himself, one day, as unlikely as that may seem.

He realizes that what he knows for sure right now is that if he is to have any hope of this kind of success in life, he has to start from where he sits. Which means he must become a great pitcher. Not a good pitcher, as he has been to this point, but a world-class pitcher, like Cy Young or Kid Carsey.

World-class, he thinks again, liking the way it sounds.

IN THE NET at River Front Park, Bill pitches to Bill Fagan, the left-hander from New York. He practices as much as possible with left-handers as he always needs to be prepared for the unexpected. In between games, he trains with any and every available catcher, and he has also set up a padded dummy with the help of John Backman. The dummy has a black box painted in the middle to replicate the strike zone, and he gathers a large bag of balls and practices for hours until his arm is numb.

"So, what ya been up to over the winter, Bill?" asks Fagan.

"Well, I went out west and found gold, and now I own the team, so you can call me Sir from now on."

Fagan stops in his tracks and looks around to see the smile on Bill's face. "You know Bill," he says, "one day, your sense of humor is going to get you punched right in the face, and you won't get up for two days."

Bill laughs.

As they sit on opposite benches in the shed that has come to serve as their changing room, Bill looks up at his teammate.

"Do you know why there are so many Bills around, Bill?"

"No idea," replies Fagan.

"Well, it's because of the French invading England," says Bill.

"Wait, when did the French invade England?" asks Fagan.

"Quite a while ago. 1066, in fact. The French King was known as William the Conqueror, and the English eventually started calling their sons William. That's why there are so many Williams around."

"You are quite strange, Bill," says Fagan after a moment of thought. "Full of surprises. You grew up in a different neighborhood than me."

"I read a lot about the old country," says Bill. "I'm going to go there someday."

The winter snow has left the grass at River Front Park a rust-colored brown, and after re-seeding, the groundskeeper wheels his water hose up and down the diamond and all the way to the outfield fences. There is a lot of dirt, but he takes pride in his work, which will look well-cared-for—at least for the first game. Hammer blows can be heard from the carpenters on the east side, who are laboring on the extra bleachers, so named as they have been bleached by the sun. Many of the simple planks are being replaced with more elaborate ones with backrests, thanks to a private donation from a local sports enthusiast. More groundskeepers underneath the stands clear up bottles left by vagrants over the closed months.

THE FIRST HOME game of the 1889 season is against Minneapolis Millers, who seem to find the thin air to their advantage as they have not hit so many home runs in one inning since '86. Bill's frustration is evident as the batters seem to connect with his pitches just when it is needed.

He tries to remember his breathing and the importance of staying calm. As he stands in the pitcher's box, he looks around at the crowd, and his confidence returns. I belong here, he says to himself. He winds up, keeping his feet square to his shoulders and bringing his hands up to his chest. The release of the ball is like a cattle whip. Tom Dolan feels the sting of the ball in his glove from Bill's fastball many times that day.

It was a scramble, but after a fair amount of kicking and fault-finding, the Grizzlies kept up their momentum in the final game and beat the Minnies 12-11.

After the customary shaking of hands with the opposing team, the Grizzlies head to the shed. There is a new coat of white paint, but already, there is an overwhelming stench of sweat and old socks.

"Why do the pitchers always stink so bad?" says Jack Conner.

"Hey, that's not true. I raise the tone of this place when I come in," is Bill's retort.

"Who's up for a celebration at Hanover's?" asks Art.

"The German place?" asks Frank Hoffman.

"What's the matter, Frank, worried we might meet your sister?" jokes Brickyard Kennedy. Frank stands up and steps toward Brickyard with a menacing glare.

"My sister is dead."

"I'm so sorry, Frank," stutters Brickyard, taken aback. "I had no idea. I was only joking." Fortunately, the uncomfortable silence that follows only lasts a few fleeting moments.

"I vote we go to Madden's. What d'ya say, Billy?" Billy O'Brian, like Brickyard Kennedy, prefers the Irish taverns, and together they have quite a reputation for drinking and fighting. It's never too severe, and, of course, they would never actually get arrested for their behavior on account of the local police having mainly Irish roots and the fact that they are both well-known baseball players.

Bill looks at the others and weighs up his options as Danny Flannagan stands up.

"We're off to Madden's, and that's final," says Danny, mustering some authority.

Danny is good friends with Michael Flaherty, the barman at Madden's, and he orders the first round as the others languish around one of the larger tables. The game had gone on until almost dusk, so the music has already started, and it's not long before people are stamping their feet in time to the fiddles. Glasses are clinked together, although Bill's mind wanders again as he thinks the violin cases must be easier to carry around than a Polish piano. He thinks of the spinning roulette wheel and feels for the little instruction book tucked inside his coat pocket. He decides to revisit the Tivoli Club sometime over the next few days—just to observe, of course.

THE NEWS OFFICE is alive with chatter as Bill arrives and immediately realizes something big has happened. He worries war has been declared or someone has been assassinated.

"Bill," says Ned Shaffer, the sports columnist, "have you heard?"

"Heard what?"

"Soapy Smith attacked Colonel Arkins last night. Beat him over the head with his cane!"

"I don't believe it," says Bill, stepping back. "Is he all right?"

"Not exactly," says Shaffer, "He's alive, and he's been taken home—the doctor is with him. They arrested Soapy Smith and one of his henchmen, Banjo Parker. It's retribution, they say, for all the stories against crime and corruption we've been printing."

"I need to get to his house and see him," says Bill, anxiously looking around for his hat in blind panic before realizing it is still in his hand.

"Don't go there. He's got all the care he needs." Shaffer looks at Bill, and it is obvious the news has profoundly impacted him. "Come and get a coffee," he says.

Bill is feeling anger boiling up inside him and is already plotting revenge. Arkins has shown him great kindness since he arrived in Denver. He wants to hit Soapy Smith where it really hurts—his money.

If only he was the greatest roulette player in the world, he could completely clean out the Tivoli Club.

CHAPTER 10

The rule which says pitchers are always the poorest batters on the team is quite reversed in ours, as Darnbrough is one of the best batters on the club, while Healey and Hoffman hold their own.

It is predicted on all sides that our boys will wrap themselves in the silk pennant and glory this season. The grounds on Broadway are within easy reach of the city and are excellent in every respect, the capacity being about six thousand. Last Sunday the grandstand and bleachers were actually jammed. There were at least two hundred vehicles on the lower end of the ground, and while it is conceded that the elite of the gentle sex never turns out on Sunday, last Sunday was somewhat an exception of the rule, as several of the well-fed darlings of Capitol hill were out in all their glory and pug dogs.

The Denver, Omaha, and St. Paul clubs are now a tie, at the head of the Western Association with a percentage of .750."

—Aspen (Colorado) Chronicle, August 15th, 1890

oward the tail end of the baseball season, the entire city of Denver is in a frenzy over the success of their Grizzlies. Unfortunately, the final games are away at Kansas City, putting the Grizzlies at a disadvantage, and a long train ride away. Tom and the boys have their regular game of poker going on and a bottle of whiskey to help pass the time. Bill is sitting by himself, reading his roulette instruction manual. Recent visits to Tivoli have not been successful—he always manages to stop himself before he loses too much, but he hasn't been winning, either—and he is trying to figure out why.

So far, he hasn't worked out much of anything, but he has gleaned one key piece of information: in European and French roulette, there is only one zero pocket on the wheel, while the American wheels have 00 and 0 pockets. This influences the way the numbers on the two types of wheels are distributed and tips the odds further in favor of the house. Probably invented by Soapy Smith, Bill thinks with a grimace as he imagines him swinging from the gallows. John Arkins has recovered well, but the rumor is that Smith has escaped trial by heading west.

In need of a distraction from a throbbing headache, Bill decides to take a walk and explore the train. He should see what life is like in the dining car, if only for something else to put on his wish list. Five carriages later, he opens the connecting door only to realize that he must have come the wrong way as he sees the entire car packed with railway workers. Nearly all are sleeping haphazardly, using whatever space they can find. Those who are awake have a vacant look in their eyes as if they are looking for something but only see as far as the middle distance.

These are the men who built the railway I am traveling on, thinks Bill, and they have so little. Most of them look Chinese, and Bill guesses they have a meager future at the end of the line. He turns to go back the way he came, grateful for all the freedom he has. The dining car can wait.

The Transcontinental Railway, which has its easterly point in Omaha, Nebraska, and goes to Sacramento, California, was built in just six years, almost entirely by the hands of Chinese immigrants. It is truly one of the most outstanding engineering achievements the world has seen and is largely responsible for the 1890 census declaring that the American Frontier has disappeared. Bill and his teammates can easily crisscross the midwest compared to twenty years previously when they would have had to use stagecoaches at great expense and time. The overland trip from Nebraska to California would have taken five or six months through the arid desert and rugged mountain terrain and cost between one hundred and two hundred dollars. The Transcontinental Railroad made the same trip possible in just five days from fifty to seventy-five dollars.

As the train pulls in at Kansas City's Union Station in the West Bottoms, Bill is still thinking about how the railroads have completely changed America as he grabs his hat and kit bag. A collective sigh of relief comes from the carriage as they finally reach their destination.

Their first stop is a gloomy boarding house, which they will have to endure for the next four days.

"Well, it's not the Midland," says Dave Rowe in response to the grumbles from the players, "but consider yourselves lucky—it's not a boxcar either!" Not impressed, they agree to head straight to a tavern after the long journey.

The State of Kansas enacted prohibition in 1881, yet the resilient residents of the western side of the area circumnavigated this restriction by simply traversing the state line to Kansas City, Missouri. O'Malley's on 16th Street is like a beacon to those who have visited before, and Tom, Brickyard, Jack, and the others lead the way.

Art moves almost as fast as he does between bases as they approach the saloon. After a few beers and much complaining about the train and the state of the rooms most of them have to share, the conversation turns to the business at hand.

The Kansas City Blues had won the league title the year before, and nobody present believes this will be a fun vacation.

"Jim Manning," announces Jack, "he can slug right or left-handed, you know." Manning is the Kansas second batsman, outfielder, shortstop, and assistant manager to Charlie Hackett.

"Right," says Tom, "but he can only throw with his right arm."

"You Irish zounderkite," snorts Jack, "How does that help us?"

"Well, if you're going to resort to name calling, gibface, then I suggest we take this outside," says Tom, whose Irish temperament ensured he never missed an opportunity for a good punch-up.

"Gentlemen," interrupts Bill, "we have only one common enemy here, and we need to muster all of our team spirit for this one."

"Wise words for one so young," says Art with a sideways smirk.

"Seriously," says Bill. "We all know each other well, but out on the field, we need to be able to talk to each other with just a look. We all need to know how many outs there are, and that comes from General Shortstop over here," he continues, pointing to Bill McClennan, "and we need —"

"Hold it, Bill," interrupts Brickyard, "may I remind you that we have been over all of this a thousand times this season and that right now, we have arrived at Missouri's finest Irish drinking establishment, and we should be celebrating that fact."

Bill looks around at his teammates' faces, feeling unexpectedly philosophical. He realizes that even though they can be irritating, many of them will be gone at the end of the season, and he will miss them. He can't believe that he was the pitcher on the school team in what seems like a moment ago. Now he has friends from all over, from places he'd never heard of. They even have a Canadian, Milt Whitehead, from Toronto, on the team. The others always make fun of him for his pronunciation of "out" and it is unfortunate that "out" is used so often in baseball.

"Anyway," says Frank, "who's got a limerick?"

"Another beer?" says Art, draining the last of his glass. "Bill, you want one?"

"Sure, thanks, Art, and I've got one," says Bill. "A limerick, I mean." The music and singing is getting louder, so the gang leans in to hear.

"There was a young pitcher from Denver, who threw with incredible splendor. The fans would cry out, boy, that man has some clout, we should call him the Denver Avenger."

"Not bad for a sassenach," cries Danny.

"What's a sassenach?" asks Art.

"Same as a bodach," says Danny with a smile, "it means I like him." Danny gives Bill a hearty slap on the back as Brickyard joins in the chorus of "Where the River Shannon Flows."

Danny and Billy O'Brian also join in, although they mumble most of the next verse as they only know the chorus. When it comes around again, all three of them sing like they are on the stage at the Broadway.

Where dear old Shannon's flowing, where the three-leaved shamrock grows. Where my heart is, I am going to my little Irish rose. And the moment that I meet her, with a hug and kiss, I'll greet her, for there's not a colleen sweeter where the River Shannon flows.

The manager and two barmen usher them outside at closing time, and they carry on singing entirely out of tune down the road toward the hotel.

There were no supreme revelations that evening, although it was generally agreed that if they were not prepared by now, then it was too late. For Bill, it was just another night before a game, and he is not much of a drinker, so once back at the hotel, he falls asleep with the roulette book tented over his chest.

Over the following three days, the games against the Blues descend into near chaos as umpire Henderson loses his cool on many occasions. During one play, Bill tries to steal home from third base but is caught by Pears, who raps him twice on the back with the ball. Henderson dismisses Pears for a violation, and the crowd cries for him to "carry the rule book." Only twenty minutes later, the Grizzlies storm the field to protest a bad call, and a mass brawl nearly erupts. Continuous wranglings and disputes result in many spectators leaving the ground in disgust, although, eventually, Kansas prevails 11-9.

The cold beers in the saloon do nothing to lift the mood of the defeated Grizzlies. Art swears at himself, or everyone, or no one. It's hard to tell. Bill displays no trace of emotion as usual, although his eyebrows arch as a young boy, out of breath from running, approaches him with a small white folded piece of paper. The writing on the front clearly says *Darnbrough*, and as he unfolds it, he sees a handwritten note that simply reads, *Come and find me outside.* It is signed by Charlie Hackett, the Kansas City Blues manager.

He tells the others he has arranged to meet an old friend, and they think nothing of it.

"Well, well, young Mr. Darnbrough, that was quite a show you put on for us this week."

"Thank you, Mr. Hackett," replies Bill, admiring Hackett's three-button gray suit and his polished shoes. He looks more like an owner than a manager.

"Look, kid," says Hackett, "I'm not going to mince words. We want you to come and play for us next season." And with that, Hackett turns and walks away, leaving Bill standing alone, speechless. Has he just been traded?

The train ride back to Denver gives Bill plenty of time to wrestle with the pros and cons of moving to Kansas. To play for the team that currently leads the league is an enticing prospect for Bill. However, it has taken him two years to get to know his way around Denver, and he has a job with the newspaper, albeit not one with great prospects and even though he feels an allegiance to John Arkins, it is, after all, just to pay the bills. Perhaps he could find something similar in Kansas City? If he left the Grizzlies, could he ever go back to Denver? Would his teammates see him as a turncoat, or would they encourage him to pursue his career?

Many of the other players are simply traded without any say in the matter, and if Bill is to have any chance at getting to the majors, he must roll with the punches. He has recorded a 12-14 record with a 4.37 earned run average (ERA) in 32 games with the Grizzlies and batted in 41 games with a .232 average. All very good, but a move would mean a healthy signing bonus, which would be very useful right now.

Finally, he decides that he must seek advice. Art is his closest ally, so he goes around to his rooms and offers to take them both out for a drink. This time, Bill chooses a place less boisterous than Madden's, and they settle down on hardback chairs in a corner of Schumann's, one of the finer German taverns.

"So, what gives, ace?" asks Art. Bill glances around for the sixth time since they sat down and lowers his voice as if to impart national secrets.

"I've been traded to the Kansas City Blues team."

"I know," says Art; "everyone knows."

"What? How? What do you mean, everyone?" says Bill.

"You really should understand this little world we live in, Bill," says Art. "There are no secrets, and it's a dog-eat-dog world out there, so we do what we can to get ahead."

"Fine. But I'm not having an easy time with this, Art. I don't want to walk out on you guys."

"Think about it," says Art. "What do you have to lose? Let's weigh up the pros and cons."

"Good idea," says Bill.

"Right," says Art. "On the one hand, you have a position here as the starting pitcher for as long as your arm holds out and a town that loves you even when we're losing. You have adequate funds thanks to your charm with the advertisers around here, and if you really set your mind to it, you could easily find yourself a female companion."

"You are making it sound pretty damn ideal, Art," says Bill.

"Maybe so, but consider this," counters Art, "Is this as good as it gets? You won't make it to the majors with the Denver Grizzlies, and you'll never own the newspaper. You'll be the advertising director at best, I imagine. If you don't take this chance to play with the top team in the league, you may live to regret it, as you will never know where it may have taken you. Don't make the mistake of putting loyalty above opportunity."

"You're a good friend, Art, and I appreciate your counsel," says Bill. "Looks like I'm off to Kansas then. Are you sure you don't want to try out for the Blues, and you could come with me?"

"Nice try, Bill," says Art, "and I appreciate the sentiment, but they want you right now and that's just fine. Anyway, I've been traded to a new team, so consider yourself lucky."

"You've been traded as well?" says Bill. "Where to?"

"Ottumwa. It's in Iowa, near the Illinois state line. Manager by the name of Stancliffe told me I would be the catcher all season, which is better than hanging around here hoping that Dolan would spike a finger or something."

"When are you going? What are you going to do this winter?"

"I'm going home for the winter," says Art. "Back to Galesburg. Who knows, I might meet a pretty young girl and start a family."

"I'd better warn them you're coming," says Bill with a wry smile.

"Damn right! Lock up your daughters, folks! Not to worry, Bill, our paths will cross again soon enough, trust me. By the way, seeing as I'm not going to be around pretending to be your guardian angel anymore, you should get yourself some protection. I think a Colt .45 would do nicely."

The Tivoli Club is less tempting without Art's encouragement, but Bill still finds himself standing at the edge of the roulette table, taking notes in his little roulette bible. Occasionally, after payday, he will throw a couple of chips on red or even but dares not risk losing his rent money. He recognizes that the only method he can use to become successful at roulette is to arrive with a large cash reserve, so, for the moment, he needs to concentrate on making some money.

After five months of selling advertising, Bill's last meeting in Denver is with John Arkins at the *Rocky Mountain News*. It's a tough meeting as Bill has come to look at Arkins as something of a father figure. Nevertheless, he has his last paycheck to collect and needs a reference.

"The advertisers will be saddened to hear of your departure, Bill," says Arkins as they sit casually in his office for the last time. "But I am a man of my word, and I did promise to let you go when the season started again. I suppose I should have guessed another team'd snap you up." Arkins sits back in his chair, no doubt quite proud of himself having aided in Bill's education by taking him to the opera.

"You're not our archetypal advertising rep," he continues, "and from now on, they will have to deal with a boring salesman that discusses circulation numbers and returns on investment instead of last week's game. I'm joking of course." Bill thinks this is what it must be like for so many people when they leave their place of employment. For the first time, the boss imparts meaningful sentiments and almost treats him like an equal instead of hammering on about targets and deadlines.

"Right," says Arkins. "Well, Bill, you're welcome back anytime. We need more people like you on the staff. From what I hear, even as a salesman, you ask all the right questions. In fact, I wish some of our reporters would ask all the right questions once in a while."

"Thank you, Mr. Arkins," says Bill. He wants to say something about Soapy Smith but thinks better of it. "Just one more thing. In the event that I don't make it all the way to the majors, could you please write me a reference?"

As Bill walks down the stairs, he whispers to himself, "The adventure continues." Perhaps this is how his life will work out, constantly on the move with no attachments. It has only been two years since he left his mother and Emily behind, and it feels like there are many unresolved issues in Bloomington, but he must fight on if he is to get to the big leagues. In the meantime, he takes Art's advice and buys himself a Colt .45 pistol from the hardware store on 8th Avenue, although he vows to keep it at home unless he is traveling.

CHAPTER 11

$\mathcal{T}$he train ride from Denver back to Kansas City is 640 miles, takes thirty-two hours, costs around the same as a week's lodging, and there is no dining car. The majority of the land they cross is completely flat, and Bill can see fields in all directions as far as the horizon. During the journey, a traveling companion has regaled with great enthusiasm about how fertile the soil is in Kansas for wheat growing.

"And the broom corn!" exclaims his fellow passenger. "The broom corn grows as high as a house! It's so high it sweeps the clouds out of the sky!" Another passenger tells a tale of a gigantic potato, "so huge that the farmer used the cavity it left as a cellar." If the passion of these men is anything to go by, then Kansas is the hot ticket, and Bill hopes the locals can show an equal amount of zeal for baseball.

This time, Bill is no longer a tourist, and his attitude toward this new place has changed. It is hard to believe that the city he encounters was a tiny fur-trading outpost only ten years earlier. The Board of Trade building on 5th and Delaware now dominates the downtown skyline, and the population has doubled in the last eight years to 135,000. Signs for hotels line the streets as if the "Heart of the

Union" is expecting a continuous stream of visitors. Walking down Minnesota Avenue, Bill sees carpenters, bricklayers, painters, and plasterers hard at work building new office and residential buildings. Next to the streetcar track, he has to jump out of the way of workers hastily laying asphalt on a recently graded road. One aspect of the street that strikes Bill is the network of dozens of telegraph lines. *These must be for businesses to connect with their suppliers*, wonders Bill.

He tries three hotels before settling on the Hotel Victoria on 9th and McGee. Although the rates are bordering on extortion at three dollars per day, Bill feels he deserves a treat, at least for a short while.

The Hotel Victoria has boasted of being the first of its kind in America to have a bath in each suite. Bill takes full advantage of this fact, and the hot water is a welcome relief for the journeyman's bones. After drying off, he goes to the window to draw the curtains for the night and realizes the whole street is lit up with electric lights. Bill might not be immediately thrilled about the move to Kansas City, but the golden twinkle of the lights fills him with optimism.

Over one million head of cattle pass through the Kansas City stockyards every year. Judging from the crowd of cattlemen gathered for breakfast at the Hotel Victoria, Bill has arrived at the epicenter of the cattle trade. It is clear that many visitors take this opportunity to catch up with old acquaintances, and they talk in hushed tones about the trials and tribulations of their business. He overhears one rancher describing his encounter with rustlers: "It gets worse every year. I've hired four extra hands this season, and I have to house and feed them and pay them bonuses for keeping the herd safe when we move pastures."

From what Bill can ascertain, these men take their business very seriously, although they do not brag to each other about their latest achievements. Instead, they use this time to collaborate on the latest two and four-point barbed wire fencing and which abattoirs offer the best deals. This world is utterly alien to Bill, and he would not volunteer to get up before the sun every day to check fences and be on a constant lookout for cattle thieves.

Bill currently grapples with two primary concerns. The first is the imperative to increase his earnings, given that accommodations with baths and exploring Kansas City necessitate more financial resources than his modest pitcher-in-waiting salary provides. The second concern is the crowd reaction when playing against Denver at River Front Park. He realizes there is little he can do about the second issue, so he has to set about making a plan to acquire more funds.

Charlie Hackett is single-minded in his mission to keep the Kansas City Blues at the top of the league. He has little interaction with Bill but gathers the team for a pre-season speech.

"They're trying out two umpires this season," says Hackett, "which means we have to ease up on the abuse. No spiking or spitting at the umpires, boys—the owners don't appreciate the fines. Anyways, the crowd will give them all the abuse they deserve, so let's just get out there and play our game. This is our season, boys."

It is obvious to Bill that this is a no-nonsense team with purpose and focus. He meets the whole crew, and they welcome him into the fold, although he knows he has started at the bottom of the pile again and has a long way to go to prove his mettle.

By the time the crowd has filled Association Park, Bill feels a great sense of relief at being on the home team as thousands of fans have turned up at the Kansas ballpark. Many wear bowler and Marlow hats, and some have stove pipe hats, making it hard for people directly behind them to see the action. There is a high hill behind and to the left of him where more fans arrive in carriages to watch from the loftier position. They really should increase our wages, thinks Bill, seeing the long queues at the concession stands. Today's opener is against the Lincoln Rustlers, and Bill gets quite a shock when the familiar frame of Tom O'Leary steps up to the plate. He knows O'Leary from Bloomington and guesses that it's not just he who has been moving around lately. Bill is frustrated, as he should be the one in the pitcher's box. He saw the move to Kansas as a step up, but he seems to have moved backward. He desperately wants to drive a few fastballs straight past O'Leary into the catcher's mitt, but can only bide his time in the outfield. He watches on as the Kansas City Blues lose their first game of 1891.

As with Denver, Bill is keen to explore his new hometown, and the spring sunshine feels good on his skin as he investigates the local area. One afternoon, he finds himself completely lost. He has walked down an alleyway and come across a small square where a group of young boys are playing baseball. They have assorted sweaters to mark the bases, although the bat and ball seem grown up enough.

"Hold up," says one of the lads upon seeing Bill, "you're Bill Darnbra from Denver. Came in this season."

"Yes, that's me. How did you recognize me?"

"My Dad collects all the cigarette cards with the pictures on and gives them to me. I know all the players."

"I see," says Bill. "Who's winning?"

"Not you, that's for sure!" says another boy with cuts on his shins. "Why aren't you the starting pitcher anyway, Mr. Darnbra?"

"Good question," says Bill, not knowing how to follow up on that one. There is little point explaining the politics or managerial strategy to these youngsters who worship their team and all its players.

"What's your name?" he asks the kid with the bat, who seems to be the spokesman for the gang.

"I'm Willy," beams the boy. "Home Run Willy, they call me," he says as he takes a swing through the air.

"Well, it is a pleasure to make your acquaintance, Home Run Willy," says Bill. "Keep practicing, and I'll look out for you in a few years." Bill turns and walks away, leaving the future stars of Kansas City to their game. He resumes his wandering, returning to contemplation of his own predicament. His quest to become a world-class pitcher has stalled, as has his study of roulette, and, as for his old dream of Emma Juch? He's read recently in the newspaper that she's heading for a months-long tour back East, which means he has absolutely zero chance of crossing paths with her anytime soon. And, sure, it was a crazy kid's dream to think he had any chance with her in the first place, but giving up the dream still stings.

He realizes that the act of letting her go is a clear indication that he is no longer a kid. He decides he won't even bother to write to his mother to tell her he's moved to Kansas City. He's a grown man now.

He feels slightly consoled by the thought and begins to whistle as he makes his way down the dusty street, imagining himself throwing a blazing strike down the middle of the plate the very next chance he has.

That opportunity doesn't come soon enough. Jack Devon is another pitcher recently acquired by the Blues, and Bill decides to confide in him over a beer.

"The thing is," says Jack, "we are all at the mercy of A.G. Spalding, and there's nothing we can do about it unless we start another league."

"I don't get it," says Bill, "why can't we just get paid fair and square? It's us players who bring in the crowds;—just look at all of them last week."

"Too right," continues Jack, sipping his beer and wiping some froth off his mustache. "Let me explain. Unless you are a top base stealer like King Kelly, our pay is capped by the National League, which at this time is run by the iron hand of our fearless leader, Albert Goodwill Spalding. He's crushing the Player's League with lawsuits, and they won't survive the season. It's all about the money these days, and his sporting goods empire will make sure he has complete control over everything."

"Yes, I heard Kelly was signed to Boston for $10,000," says Bill, "I wouldn't mind a slice of that."

"Of course, you would," says Jack, taking another sip of his beer. "You know, the way the game is going, there will only be a dozen or so teams with enough clout to carry on next year anyway. The likes of you and me will be coaching high school kids and saving up to see the Phillies."

That night, Bill reads more of his roulette bible, but he knows he should be contacting the local newspapers for a real job in the advertising department. He gets off his bed, goes to the writing desk, and putting an ink pen to the Queen Victoria Hotel stationery, he composes a letter to Eugene Field, the editor of the *Kansas Times*. He repeats the same note to John Hardcourt of the *Star* and Jock Campbell of the *Kansas City Journal-Post*. *"I have some ideas regarding increased advertising revenue which I would like to share with you and a letter of recommendation from John Arkins of the Rocky Mountain News..."* An idea is forming in his mind whereby a joint venture exists between the baseball fraternity and one of the newspapers. He could offer simultaneous advertising space in the printed paper and on the boards around Association Park.

The Kansas City Blues lose the next two series against St. Paul Apostles of Minnesota and the Minneapolis Millers. Bill is frustrated at not being picked to pitch. Each time the umpire calls, "Play Ball," it feels as if he is talking to everyone else except him. To make matters worse, the team is now being charged to rent their own uniforms. One week before they are due to board the train for Denver, Bill confronts Charlie Hackett.

"The owners had to pay to get me here, Mr. Hackett, so don't you think this game of all games would be a good time to use me? After all, I know these players well, and in case you think they know my style too, I have some new tricks up my sleeve."

"Fair enough, Bill," says Hackett, meeting his eyes. "Right now, what have we got to lose? You can start against the Grizzlies."

With only hours to spare before leaving for Denver, Bill has been summoned to the offices of the *Kansas City Star* on Wyandotte Street. William Rockhill Nelson had started the *Star* five years earlier and created a healthy advanced subscription circulation, but he was behind the *Kansas Times* in terms of advertising revenue. Bill has done his research well and knows that some fresh ideas are needed. Unfortunately, despite being a famous pitcher in Denver, only diehard baseball fans in Kansas City know who Bill is, and this meeting is not attended by Nelson or his partner Sam Morss. Instead, Bill is greeted by Wayne Powell, the assistant editor, and George Wainwright, the sports columnist, who no doubt had heard of Bill and was curious to listen to what he had to say.

"Sorry about your run of bad luck this season," is Wainwright's opener as they sit at a long table in the conference room. It's an uphill battle for Bill from that moment on as he shares his plan for simultaneous advertising on large signs around the ballpark at the same time as print ads run within the newspaper.

"This all sounds very complicated," weighs in Powell with a shake of his head. "We're doing well with our current accounts." He casts a smile at Wainwright, and Bill realizes his proposal was dead in the water before he even walked into the room.

As he leaves the building, Bill feels that this is their loss and that the *Times* will love his idea as soon as he gets a chance to propose it to them. Baseball has taught him to keep calm and optimistic, even when things aren't going your way. He's whistling another tune as he walks north on Main Street, heading for the hotel to pack his bag for the journey to Denver.

CHAPTER 12

*A*s they settle down on the train, the conversation turns to baseball folklore. Bill talks with Frank Pears about the early days when the Knickerbockers played at the Elysian Fields and how Joseph Smith played in Missouri before founding the Mormons. Charlie Hackett relates a tale of how the famous explorers Lewis and Clark played ball with the Nez Perce Indians on their way back from the Pacific.

"Because the Nez Perce could not understand English," declares Hackett enthusiastically, "they mainly explained everything by hand and drawing lines in the dirt, but every word had to be translated. The captain spoke in English to the corpsman François Labiche, who spoke in French to Charbonneau, who spoke in Hidatsa to his wife, Sacagawea. She then spoke in Shoshoni to a Nez Perce captive from her tribe, who repeated the words in the Sahaptian dialect!"

Time passes quickly when there is good conversation to be had on a long train ride, and as they come toward the outskirts of Denver, Bill is in familiar territory. He can't wait to see all his old teammates, even though he anticipates a degree of awkwardness, considering they are now on opposing sides.

On game day, the Blues ride in carriages painted with team

colors down 16th Street to River Front Park. People line the sidewalks on both sides as they make their way toward the ground, some cheering, some booing. The atmosphere is electric with anticipation. Kansas City may not be having their best season, but they were top of the league last year, and the Grizzlies are on the warpath.

The wood and iron grandstands overflow with fans known as bugs and cranks with a splattering of crankettes in their midst. Bill spots the men of the volunteer fire company on standby should a wayward cigar start a fire, and for the first time he has seen, a band marches out onto the field. Any minute now, he is expecting a speech from the mayor, but luckily, everyone is spared that torture, and the two umpires proceed to their designated spots. As is customary, the visiting team bats at the top of the first inning, so Bill takes his place on the bench in the visitor's dugout.

Tom, Brickyard, Edgar, and the other Grizzlies have all seen Bill, although they barely acknowledge him as this is serious business and there is no joking around in the outfield as everyone is entirely focused on the game. The plate umpire points at the pitcher, and his cry of "play ball" echoes around the ground.

In their first outing, the Blues score one run, and things are looking up for them. At the bottom of the first, Bill walks across to the pitcher's box. He hopes there will be very little pitcher rotation this time, and his confidence and determination move into high gear. He must ignore the crowd and even his own teammates in the moment it takes to wind up his delivery. The first pitch is the most important for him. There is a moment of stillness, and a hush descends upon the crowd. Bill is thinking of Cy Young, the pitcher for the Cleveland Spiders, who is the fastest hurler the game has ever seen as he throws his own cyclone at the right hander, Parke Wilson.

Bill's fastball takes approximately half a second or 500 milliseconds to travel from his hand to the home plate, and it takes Parke Wilson about 300-400 milliseconds to blink. Swing and miss, strike one. Swing and miss, strike two. On his third pitch, Bill decides on a change-up that is deliberately slower than his usual fastball and designed to sneak past the batter. Wilson is no fool and has anticipated this as the crack of his bat reverberates around the field. Frank Pears runs for the catch, and Bill cringes to see the sun is definitely in Frank's eyes. As he reaches up high, the ball hits his glove, then jumps up again, but he manages the catch. Finally, things are going well for the Blues, and they stay on top and record an 8-2 win.

They agree to meet in the hotel lobby in one hour to go out and celebrate. They don't know where yet, although Bill suspects it won't be Madden's as the Grizzlies will likely be there. There has been enough entertainment on the field and no need to start any trouble. Even though opposing teams normally get on well together, the last thing they need is for the Denver sports pages to run with *Grizzlies and Blues take the fight to the streets.*

Bill goes upstairs to change and sees a note has been passed underneath his door.

It reads:

Bill, these are interesting times in our business, and I have a plan that I would like to share with you. Please meet me at Jones's at 7 p.m. today. Yours faithfully, Dave Rowe.

Jones's is a run-down dive along the streets of doom—ideal for a rendezvous when you don't want anyone to overhear confidential discussions. Bill walks in to see only four other patrons in the whole place, one snoring loudly with his head resting sideways on a table. Two others are playing fifteen ball pool on an old billiards table in a corner, and the only other guest looks like he is relating his life story to the barman, who is cleaning glasses and pretending to be interested. Bill buys himself a bottle of beer and sits at a small table with his back to the door.

"You know he drowned," Dave booms.

Bill turns, smiling to see the familiar face. "Who did?"

"Schlitz," says Rowe, pointing to Bill's bottle. "Just off the coast of England; I believe they're called the Scilly Islands. On his way to Hamburg, Germany. Ship ran aground—everyone drowned."

"Ah," says Bill, his grin widening. "This is why you're the manager. You're full of insightful information, and you also have the ability to sneak up on people even when they're expecting you." Dave grins and goes to the bar to fetch a beer for himself.

"To your good health," Dave announces as he clinks bottles with Bill.

Bill nods at him but says nothing. It seems to him that Dave has an agenda, and it's probably top secret, so he needs to show he knows when to keep quiet.

Dave leans in. "Listen, kid. What we're about to discuss is strictly confidential and goes no further than these four walls." He looks around and corrects himself. "This table, in fact."

Bill blinks. Gives nothing away. "That's fine, sir," says Bill.

Dave nods. "Listen, Bill, I'm a player first and a manager second, so we're on the same side, if you know what I mean. And I'm sure you know that the owners are gunning for more control. Here's the bottom line, Bill. People are reading about the magic twelve in the National League, and they come out expecting greatness from us every week as if we're the Phillies or Boston." Dave swigs his beer. Bill realizes his palms are sweating but does his best to maintain an aura of confidence. "What they don't understand, Bill, is that all these outfits are loaded, and those teams can afford huge signing bonuses to attract the best players in the land. Teams in our league cannot."

"Sure," says Bill, "but the bleachers were jammed this week, and they were every game the last two seasons. It isn't like the fans aren't interested."

"Maybe," Dave's voice carries a weight of skepticism. "But don't kid yourself; that's not a lasting reality. Remember my words. Here's the cold truth—you know I can be direct—it's a lost cause. Unless you can somehow claw your way into the big leagues, our world of professional baseball is a sinking ship."

Bill's body tenses, a reflexive response to Dave's blunt words. He scans the surroundings, his eyes searching for something, anything, to ground himself. With a mixture of disbelief and confusion, he swallows hard and lifts his beer to his lips, taking a measured sip. Setting the bottle down on the table with a distinct clink, Bill leans back in his chair as if the conversation itself has pushed him away.

The grand aspirations he's harbored, the visions of making it to the majors, suddenly seem to disintegrate before his eyes.

"Why did you want to meet me, then, Dave?"

Dave can't help but smirk. He pulls out four *Old Judge* cigarette baseball player cards from his inside coat pocket and lays them out on the table one by one. The images are of himself, Bill, Monk Cline, and Dave's brother Jack Rowe.

"You may know that my brother Jack owned the Buffalo Bisons in New York?" he ventures.

"Sure," says Bill, "I also know he was the star of the '87 World Series with the Wolverines. But didn't the Bisons disband when the Player's League collapsed?"

"Yes, exactly right," says Dave, "and that's why it was a clever move to sell up to some New York capitalists right before the league went under."

Bill's eyes narrow. "Why am I here, Dave?"

Dave loses the smile and looks serious now. "Kid, the other three of us offered ourselves as a package to the highest bidder, which happened to be the Lincoln Rustlers. I want you to come with us. I want us to be unbeatable."

"Thank you, Mr. Rowe," says Bill. "I'm very grateful that you picked me to come with you. I just have one question."

"Your reserve clause?"

"Yes, Sir," replies Bill, knowing full well that Kansas has the option to renew his yearly contract. They could even decide to sell or trade him unless he is released.

"You let me worry about Charlie Hackett," says Dave. "It will all be taken care of."

Bill takes a deep breath. He feels honored to be included in the company of some of his heroes, but this is a big decision. Can he trust Dave to "take care of Charlie Hackett?" What does that even mean? Will Lincoln be his only path to the major leagues?

"Dave," says Bill. "Thank you for this. I mean it. Thank you for trusting me, and you have my word that this will go no further than these walls. But—"

"But?"

"Well, sir. I need to think about it for a night, that's all. Lincoln, Nebraska is so far away from everything." Bill knows this is not the answer Dave wants and hopes he can respect his integrity regardless of the outcome.

"Good," says Dave, clinking his bottle with Bill's once more. "Don't take more than tonight to decide, mind you. There's many moving parts in this game, but we need you, Bill. We need our ace pitcher."

CHAPTER 13

*B*ack in Kansas City, guilt gnaws at Bill's conscience as he sits alone in the dimly lit bar downstairs at the hotel. He retreated into silence during the train ride back, unable to engage in meaningful conversations with his teammates, fearful that any slip of the tongue would reveal his involvement in Dave Rowe's scheme. He feels like a conspirator, a turncoat, and a fraud, even though he hasn't done anything wrong—yet. He prides himself on honesty and trustworthiness, and this situation is making him uncomfortable. He is restless and decides to go for a walk to clear his mind.

There is no rational explanation for how he manages to be standing outside J.D. Kelly's tavern by the railroad bridge. It wasn't planned. He steps through the door to find the saloon is set up like any other, with glass bottles lined up on mirrored-backed shelves behind a long bar. There is an old piano whose ivory keys turned yellow many years ago, and it remains untroubled by human hands this evening. There are no bar stools, leaving men to stand, drink, and murmur among themselves. To the right of the bar are three small tables with men playing cards, and beyond them are two faro tables and a roulette wheel. He stops at the bar, orders a small whiskey, and makes his way over to the tables.

The setup at Kelly's is even less sophisticated than the Tivoli Club in Denver, but Bill gets a perfect vantage point from which to observe and learn. The roulette table has well-worn faded numbers on the green felt grid, and the dealer is nonchalant in his delivery of the ball to the wheel. There are three players at the table and the croupier acknowledges Bill with a simple nod as he stacks up chips. This is how Bill wants it—no attention to him, but his complete attentiveness to the game.

The players use variously colored chips to distinguish their bets, placing them in what appears to be a random manner before and during each spin of the wheel. Bill looks for patterns in their betting style rather than patterns of the winning numbers. He has a fair understanding of the dynamics of the wheel from his book, but theory is no substitute for watching other, more experienced gamblers at work.

After about twenty minutes, one player has emerged, favoring the bets outside the numbers grid. He tends to go for evens, reds, and occasionally places a chip or two on the dozens. The dozens are the "1st 12" including the numbers 1 to 12, the "2nd 12" featuring the numbers 13 to 24, and the "3rd 12", which are the numbers 25 to 36. Bill notices that this player does not appear to have any significant system to his betting, although he wins small amounts quite often, which means he can stay in the game longer. He rarely places his chips on the actual numbers and remains perfectly calm throughout—never punching the air when he wins or banging the table when he loses.

The other two players place bets of varying denominations all over the table, and Bill tries to determine whether they have good or bad strategies. Sometimes, one of their numbers comes up, and the winner lets out a whoop or a sigh of relief, depending on the size of the win. He sees how the chips are received when one of the players places a five dollar note on the table, and the dealer exchanges it for fifty white chips. Unlike the piano keys, the chips are shiny.

He plans to start making notes of the odds and payouts on his next visit, but for now, he is gathering intelligence, which is a good enough place to start. The main thing to remember, Bill decides, is the house edge. For example, if he bets on red, his odds are not 50/50 as there are eighteen black numbers and eighteen red numbers, but also two green numbers, zero and double-zero. Using his notebook, he works out that his odds of winning on red are, in fact, about 47.3%. It turns out that studying mathematics may be useful after all.

As he leaves Kelly's, he is glad to be a little bit wiser and, aside from two small whiskeys, no poorer. He hears a tugboat sounding its horn and wonders if it has traveled down the Missouri River from Nebraska. He realizes that the moment has come to stop drifting with the current.

Before giving his final answer to Dave, he has one more thing to do in Kansas which will determine his immediate future. The next Kansas City Blues game is tomorrow at home to the Sioux City Corn Huskers, but somehow, he has to make time to meet with the *Kansas City Times*. He has hand delivered his letter of introduction and feels confident that they will respond with a request for a meeting. The Queen Victoria letterhead and his past record with the *Rocky Mountain News* will surely have an impact. He goes downstairs to the hotel lobby to check for any correspondence, and the duty manager hands him a letter as expected. Only it's not from the newspaper but from Dave Rowe in Denver.

As a tongue-in-cheek reference to Bill's English heritage, Dave opens with a Shakespeare quote, "The game's afoot." The letter details a healthy signing bonus and an immediate starting pitcher spot for Bill next April with the Lincoln Rustlers. There is no indication of how long the contract will run or even if there is any contract. Furthermore, his departure from Kansas will have severe repercussions unless Dave has somehow convinced them to release him from his current contract.

A move to Lincoln is a bold plan, but at least it is a plan, and right now, any kind of plan seems better than none.

Bill walks down Broadway until he reaches the tranquil bank of the river. Taking a seat on a vacant bench in the park, he fixes his gaze on the tugboats, skillfully maneuvering colossal barges, their movements cloaked in an air of mystery and menace. Bill ponders his choices once again, grappling with the daunting task of assessing his options.

His immediate thought is that he can't stay at the Queen Victoria any longer, as he has forsaken decent meals for a private bathroom, which seems illogical. He has not heard back from the *Kansas City Times*, and there are no immediate alternatives for a supplementary income. He has no overwhelming allegiance to the Blues despite being given the opportunity to start the most recent game. In general, he reflects, Kansas City has not been that hospitable compared to Denver. In his mind, his pros and cons list seems to weigh decidedly on the negative, and it feels like he is convincing himself to follow one of the river barges north.

Trust is a scarce commodity in Bill's circle, yet Dave Rowe has seen fit to share a promising opportunity. As the decision settles within him, like a coin falling into a slot, the time has come to decide what to do between October and next April when he'll start playing with the Lincoln Rustlers. The easiest option is to stay in Kansas over the winter, so, back in his hotel room, Bill writes again to Eugene Field at the *Times* and Jock Campbell at the *Journal-Post*.

On his last day at the Queen Victoria, the highly-anticipated reply arrives from the *Journal-Post*, and Bill has been summoned to their offices for an interview with Frank Garner, the features editor. It turns out Frank has a healthy respect for Bill's abilities and agrees to take him on, although not in the advertising department. It is not exactly what he had hoped for, and Bill spends a lengthy winter working on production and research in various departments at the *Journal-Post*. However, it covers the rent for his significantly less lavish room, and he remains focused on his work.

One thing he knows for sure: spring always comes around again.

CHAPTER 14

he train pulls into Nebraska City for a brief stop, and Bill
picks up a copy of the *Nebraska State Journal*. It seems that
Lincoln, Nebraska, in 1891, is in turmoil. The economic downturn
that affected most of the country has finally caught up with them.
Bill reads that last year's drought ensured a terrible crop harvest for
the third year in succession. Could he possibly be going to Lincoln
at a worse time? Perhaps spring will usher in some good tidings after
such a brutally cold winter.

Inside the carriage, the troubles of the outside world seem far
away, and a tranquil ambiance pervades as the train glides across
the vast Nebraska prairie. The steady chugging of the steam engine
combines with the train tracks' rhythmic clatter, creating a soothing
melody that resonates within the compartment. Warm sunlight
filters through the windows, giving a gentle glow to the scene. There
are three pretty young women sitting by the opposite window, and
Bill is certain the one with the piercing amber eyes keeps stealing
stares at him. The man opposite is smiling at the girls, showing off a
prominent gold tooth. Brave man, thinks Bill, walking around with a
gold tooth.

In a sudden, heart-stopping twist, the peaceful atmosphere is shattered as the carriage door violently crashes open, and three men wearing bandanas over their faces enter with pistols drawn.

"This is a robbery!" cries the lead man.

Bill feels a surge of adrenaline and fights the temptation to glance up at his case, which rests on the rack above his head, concealing his Colt .45. He is not the only passenger with a pistol, though, as two rows in front of him, a man shouts.

"Railroad police! Hands up!"

The gang leader points his weapon directly at the lawman as the second man fires a shot through the carriage ceiling. No words are necessary as this puts an end to the policeman's brief but courageous stand as he lowers his gun to the floor, realizing that he is outnumbered. Better to live to fight another day.

"No more heroics, or they'll be killins today," says the first man, who, it is clear now, is in charge. He moves to pick up the railroad man's gun and says, "Whoever fires the first shot will be responsible for what happens next. Put your valuables in the bag and stay calm." Curiously, all the passengers except the policeman have stayed calm. Bill would have expected screams, especially from the young ladies sitting to his left, although they appear perfectly serene and seem to be using secret gestures to communicate with each other. The man with the gold tooth has stopped smiling.

Bill reaches for his wallet inside his coat pocket as the third robber with the bag approaches. He is careful to keep his free hand in the air as he notices a wave of blonde hair pocking out from underneath the hat of the bag handler. Their eyes meet, and he realizes that the third man is actually a woman, and judging by the eyes, a very pretty one at that. He instantly checks himself as a liaison with a train robber is surely an even worse idea than one with a traveling opera singer. He adds his wallet to the growing pile of acquisitions as the woman points her gun to his pocket watch. Reluctantly, he unties the watch from his waistcoat and places it in the bag as a lady cries out from further up the carriage. Bill tries to stand up to see what is happening. The woman's male companion has been pistol-whipped by robber number two in the side of the head. In any hold-up, one of the gang is often a hothead, prone to overreaction, and this was no exception. As Bill contemplates his options, he feels cold metal against his neck.

"Sit down," comes the whisper as Bill realizes he has a gun pointed right at the back of his head.

The leader and hothead exchange a momentary stare, and then, as quickly as they had arrived, all three head for the far carriage door. The leader turns just as they are nearly out of sight.

"Don't nobody be followin' us as we got plenty o' bullets."

The assailants disappear through the connecting door to the next carriage, and almost instantly, all the passengers become intimate friends. The mainly silent carriage turns into a flurry of urgent conversation.

"How will they get off the train? Where's the guard? Maybe they killed him?" One man silences the passengers quickly with, "Let's go after them."

Clearly, that is not at the top of the list for most of the others. A young woman is using a scarf to bandage the head wound of the pistol-whipped man as his wife is crying beside him. Bill remains outwardly calm as he feels in his sock for his money and silently thanks the Denver pickpocket for his lesson. The pocket watch was not expensive, and he had no sentimental attachment to it, so as far as hold-ups go, this one could have been much worse for him.

The man seated opposite Bill leans in toward him.

"That was Bert Curtis and Peg-Leg Watson, mark my words."

"Really?" says Bill.

"Yes sir, saw his limp. Not sure about the little one, but that was them for sure. The Pinkertons have been after them for a while now. They'll get them in the end. Always do."

By now, the conductor has arrived from the next carriage, but he has no answers for the passengers, many of whom are still in distress.

"Ladies and gentlemen," he begins before being bombarded with a hail of shouting questions and accusations of negligence.

"I'll sue the railroad for this," says one man with newly discovered courage.

The conductor explains they will stop at the next station to investigate and give medical attention if required. This does little to calm the situation, as shock and fear quickly and inevitably turn to anger.

Bill has surprised himself with his ability to stay calm, which may be connected to his baseball experience. Even when he does not have complete control of a situation, he has realized that he does have control over how he reacts. He leans up and opens the window a fraction to let in some cool air. This is what I need, he thinks, to be able to keep a cool head when all around me are losing theirs.

The piercing tone of the sharp whistle and the clanging of the bell signal their arrival at the next station. Steam billows and swirls, enveloping the locomotive in a ghostly shroud. A flurry of urgency consumes the station master and other railroad officials as they try to work out how the robbers got off the train. They search all the carriages in case they are still on board, but there is no sign of them, and the general consensus is that they must have jumped at one of the slower bends. Train hold-ups are becoming more regular now, but the railroad owners are eager not to make too much of a fuss about it as they don't need the bad publicity. After only twenty minutes, the locomotive clangs its commanding bell and they continue their journey.

Everything is very well organized as a sketch artist has material-ized who will be going through the carriages taking descriptions. His presence brings reassurance, a symbol of justice in motion, but the bandanas and hats make it difficult to substantiate the many different accounts. Amid the organized chaos, a sense of order returns, but it transpires that Bill is not the only passenger who spotted that robber number three was a blonde woman.

As the journey resumes, Bill returns to his roulette bible to continue his education. The man opposite Bill has been replaced at the last stop by another gentleman in an expensive-looking suit and coat with a bright cravat. He has a perfectly trimmed mustache, a reassuring smile, and a relaxed demeanor. He waits until Bill turns a page to speak.

"They say there are no true systems, and you cannot beat the house in the long run. Do you believe that?"

"From what I gather, the likelihood of getting shot over a game of roulette is quite slim, so the odds seem to be in my favor," remarks Bill, a wry smile creasing his lips. He looks at the stranger, a sense of amusement dancing in his eyes, fully embracing the façade of a roulette player. Even though something about the stranger has him on his guard, he welcomes the opportunity to talk with someone not obsessed with catching train robbers like everyone else in the carriage.

"My name is Gerent, Gerent Duvalier," says the man offering his hand to Bill. He shakes his hand.

"Bill Darnbrough; a pleasure to meet you, Mr. Duvalier."

"Please call me Gerent," he responds. "Forgive me—I am so rude, but roulette and all games of chance interest me greatly, and I couldn't help seeing your book cover."

"Not at all," says Bill, trying to place Duvalier's accent. Perhaps French, he thinks, as he carefully lays his book and pencil on the table separating them.

"I'm just trying to learn the principles," Bill continues, "and to decide for myself if it really is a game of chance or if it is possible to create a system. Do you play?"

"Ah ha," says Duvalier. "Be careful. Did you know that if you add up all the numbers on the wheel, the total is 666, the devil's number?"

"I did not know that," says Bill, trying not to sound sarcastic. "Fascinating."

"But that is not important," says Duvalier. "You are correct to ask the question. The biggest question of all, of course—is there a system? Yes, I have played on occasion, but I'm more of a card man. Roulette is slightly different over here than in Europe, you know?"

"How so?" asks Bill. Of course, he knows the answer to this question, but he is intrigued and wants to test the stranger.

"The American version has a double zero, whereas the European one has only a single zero. This changes the odds for the player and the house. It may not seem like much, but it adds up."

"So, what is the advantage for us in America?"

"No real advantage unless you own the wheel, of course," says Duvalier with a chuckle. "In Europe, the house edge is 2.7 percent, whereas here it is 5.26."

Bill notices that Duvalier has avoided his question regarding the system and decides to let their conversation play out. After all, it's a long train journey, so why not gain as much information as possible?

"Do you know about biased wheels?" Duvalier asks. "This is about as close to having a system as you'll get. Listen carefully." Duvalier leans in closer to Bill. "You would think that each spin of the wheel would be completely random, but certain irregularities can be seen from the wear and tear of the wheel. Sometimes, the frets become loose, which means the odds of the ball landing in the same numbers increase. Noticing these slight abnormalities requires a great deal of patience and confidence."

At this point, Bill is starting to wonder if Duvalier has a hidden agenda. Why would he share these trade secrets with someone he had just met on a train? Perhaps he wants to use Bill to place bets in a saloon from which he has been banned? Maybe he needs money and wants to split any winnings, claiming his advice resulted in the wins.

"Have you heard of Joseph Jagger?" he asks Bill in a hushed tone that suggests he has inside information.

"No, I don't think so," Bill replies.

"About eight years ago, an Englishman named Joseph Jagger won big at the casino in Monte Carlo. I know how he did it. You see, he was an engineer, and for more than a week, he used six clerks to record the results from all six roulette wheels at the casino and discovered that one of them showed a clear bias toward a group of nine numbers. So, he bet large amounts on those numbers only. Nobody knows for certain how much he won, probably around $120,000." Bill's heart has sped up at the mention of Monte Carlo. "How do you know he used clerks, and if so, why didn't the casino stop him?"

Duvalier dismisses the question with a brush of his hand. "It's not illegal, but I would not advise such trickery in a place like Soapy

Smith's in Denver or Tiger Alley in Leadville, but in Monte Carlo, they expect a certain amount of gentlemanly conduct."

"You know Soapy Smith's?" says Bill.

"Certainly, I have been there several times, but I would avoid it if I were you, as it is very unusual for anyone to get out of there with a profit. They will always find a way to get their money back if you win."

"You know, he left Denver," says Bill.

"In Monte Carlo," says Duvalier, completely ignoring Bill's comment, "The casino introduced spirit levels, and they change the metal dividers each night so that even if the wheel were biased, it would be to a different set of numbers the next day. Fortunately for Jagger, he knew when to quit and got back to England."

"Next station, Lincoln," calls out the conductor as he passes through the aisle. "Next station, Lincoln."

"That's me," says Bill, standing up to hoist down his bag from the overhead shelf.

"Me too," says Duvalier, doing the same. "How long are you staying in Lincoln?"

"Quite some time, I hope," says Bill. "I'm joining the baseball team, the Rustlers, as starting pitcher."

"You don't say," says Duvalier, revealing an Americanism demonstrating that he has been this side of the Atlantic for some time. "I'm good friends with Jimmy Macullar, the manager. We go way back to Baltimore days."

"What a small world. Maybe I'll see you at the next game, then?"

"For sure, I'll be there," responds Duvalier, who now seems to be trying even harder to use American terms as a means of acceptance. Bill grins, then realizes he has no idea if Jimmy Macullar will still be on the team by the weekend, but he certainly won't be the manager, assuming Dave Rowe's plan has worked out as expected.

Bill bids Duvalier goodbye on the station platform and approaches a porter who is loading bags onto a buggy. "Pardon me, do you know the way to the St. Charles Hotel?"

"Sure," the porter replies, "It's not far. Down there," he points, "in between 7th and 8th on the far side of O Street."

"Right," says Bill, turning with a thank you nod and thinking he may have been better off walking around in circles. Perhaps he'll ask another stranger on the way for clarification. He looks around for Duvalier, but he is nowhere to be seen.

Fortunately, there is no need for further instructions, as he soon finds 7th Street and then the south side of O Street, where the imposing façades of the brick buildings loom large, casting long shadows across the whole area. The St. Charles Hotel reception has a framed photograph on the wall, showing the outside of the hotel and the adjacent Hargreaves Brothers' hardware and grocery store draped in Stars and Stripes flags. The rates on display show $1.00 or $1.25 per day, although, before booking his room, Bill checks that the Rowe brothers have arrived.

"Yes, sir," says the young man behind the desk, "Is your name Mr. William Darnbrough, by any chance?"

"Yes, that's me."

"Excellent, your room is already paid four weeks in advance. Please sign here," he says, turning the guest ledger around and handing Bill a fountain pen. He snaps his fingers, and an elderly man, remarkably swift on his feet, appears and offers to carry Bill's one bag.

"Thank you, I'll manage," says Bill, hoisting his bag over his shoulder and holding out his other hand for his key.

"You will find Mr. Rowe in room thirty-one on the third floor, Sir," says the clerk. The room key has a round leather tag attached with the number 32 stitched into it. Bill takes the stairs two at a time up to the third floor. His room is sparse but clean and bright, with a good view over most of the rooftops of downtown Lincoln. There are few tall buildings here, so it feels good to be in a lofty position. Bill is hoping everything works out, as it would be nice to stay right here for the remainder of the season, at least. He takes off his shoes, lies down on the bed to test the mattress, and, staring up at a perfectly white ceiling, tries to work out why Dave Rowe would pay for a whole month's lodgings.

CHAPTER 15

*J*olted by a sudden, thunderous pounding on the door,
Bill awakens, momentarily disorientated. He takes in the
surroundings and the high ceiling and realizes someone
is talking to him from behind the door.

"Bill, it's Dave Rowe. Are you alive in there?"

"Hold on, I'm coming," says Bill as he runs a hand through his
hair and makes his way over to the door.

"Glad you made it," says Dave as he puts both hands on Bill's
shoulders and grins from ear to ear. "Get your shoes on. We're
going downstairs, and the others are waiting."

Next door to the hotel is the much smaller, single-story Occi-
dental Saloon with a prominent sign advertising *Cool Fresh Beer.* Dave
holds open the door for Bill, and they go through a second entrance
which is designed to keep the heat or cold out depending on the
season. As it is only late Spring, the temperature still drops by over
20 degrees as the sun goes down, and Bill is glad they spent only
fifteen seconds outdoors as he left his coat in his room. The bar is
not busy this evening, and Bill soon spots Monk Cline and Jack
Rowe talking at a table in the far corner. They stop at the bar to get
two beers and walk over.

"Monk, you know Bill," Dave says, and Bill shakes Monk's hand. "Good to see you again, Monk."

"Likewise, Bill," says Monk, "as long as you don't throw a fastball at my head." He laughs.

"This is my brother, Jack," announces Dave. "Jack, meet Bill Darnbrough, the fastest fastball this side of the Mississippi."

"Good to know you, Bill," says Jack, standing and shaking his hand.

"Good to meet you, Jack," says Bill, "I recognized you from your pictures, of course."

Bill is in awe of the great Jack Rowe and decides the best play is to sit and listen. He is simultaneously excited and anxious as his future is now entirely in the hands of the men seated around this table in a saloon in Lincoln, Nebraska. It's not exactly a predictable set of circumstances, although this is the thrill of it. He likes the unpredictability as it feels like a real-life game of roulette.

"Now," says Dave. "We all know why we're here." Dave looks at his brother and continues. "The Player's League was a great idea with the most honorable intentions, but we are coming to the 20th Century, and nothing will be the same, especially for the hard-working man. Sorry, I know you didn't come all this way for a lecture, but it's been a long road for all of us, and now is the time for us to make the most of our talents before it's too late. Agreed?"

"Agreed," the other three reply in unison.

"So, here's the deal," continues Dave. "Monk here has played all over the known baseball world since '82 and knows all the tricks, and you, Bill, naturally, are the star attraction with the meanest, most feared fastball Lincoln will have ever seen. I'm the new manager, and Jack has so much money now that he just wanted a nice vacation." The laughter comes at just the right moment and a relaxed atmosphere replaces the tension everyone around the table feels.

"How does it feel, Bill?" asks Jack.

"How does it feel?" says Bill, repeating the question to give himself a moment to compose an answer. "Good. Great, I mean good. I'm not sure." He must be more nervous about the whole thing than he realized. "I guess I need to stop worrying about every-thing and just get on with the game. When I'm out there, in front of the crowd, I'm perfectly focused and in charge, but here, right now, I'm not sure. I don't want any part of the politics, that much I do know."

"Good answer, Bill," says Jack, reaching over the table with an outstretched hand, which Bill takes as a sign of "Welcome to the club."

Monk goes over to the bar and returns with four more beers.

"The good news, Bill," says Dave, "is that we're at home for the next game, the first game you're in. We meet the Apostles next week, and you're the man in the box."

"Great!" says Bill, who turns to Jack, "Jack, I hope you don't mind me asking, but why are you really here?" There is a long pause as Jack leans back slightly in his chair but maintains his fix on Bill.

"Like my brother said, I'm on vacation." There is silence around the table as the other three are now staring at Jack, waiting for a further explanation. He crosses his arms, smiles and says, "I'm biding my time, gentlemen. Spalding has ensured that the corpora-tions and politicians are taking over the game, and it's an unpre-dictable time for baseball back east. Being with my brother and playing ball is just about as good a vacation as I could hope for. I wouldn't want to be anywhere else but right here with you, having a beer and planning our fates."

"I was in my last year of high school when you played in the World's Series," says Bill, not looking up from his beer as if embar-rassed to be on the verge of sharing his admiration for Jack. He wants to make it clear how much he respects him and how his career has influenced his own path. After waiting for the right moment, he has decided that now is as good a time as any.

"I know you know this, but you may not know that we all know this as well. You were the starting shortstop for the Detroit Wolver-ines in '87, and you won the National League pennant with a 79-45 record and then beat the St. Louis Browns in the World Series. You hit for a .318 average and were ranked as tenth highest in the league's position players. 130 runs scored, 30 doubles, and 239 total bases." The other three are staring at Bill in complete silence. "Well, numbers have always been a strong suit of mine," he offers, punctuating his statement with a modest shrug and a small, understated smile.

Dave Rowe grins and raises his glass, and soon everyone is toasting to Bill and the Rustlers' success this season.

Association Park is dry and dusty as the team assembles on the field. Somehow, it feels to Bill as if this is the calm before the storm. Dave Rowe has been confirmed as the new manager, and he gives a rousing speech about the importance of giving the good people of Lincoln something to be proud of. The drought has left much misery, and times are hard, so baseball is the one thing that can bring everyone together.

The St. Paul Apostles have George Bausewine as first batter, who is the same age as Bill, although six foot two and 207 pounds. One of his tricks is what has become known as the "chop," where he hits the ball down to give the runners more time. The Rustlers fall behind 7-0 in the first inning, and Dave gives another rousing speech.

"All right, boys, don't go out there and try to hit seven home runs. Take it one base, one run, and one pitch at a time—that's the only way to do this."

Unfortunately for the Rustlers, this is easier said than done, and they get slaughtered 15-4. The Lincoln cranks are not impressed, and it looks like they are headed for a thumping defeat until the Sunday game.

The date is Sunday, April 26th, 1891, and at the bottom of the fifth inning, Bill is poised and focused, winding up for a pitch. The moment of anticipation is abruptly shattered as the county sheriff, accompanied by a pose of deputies, descends upon the field, intending to disband the game. Chaos ensues as the crowd of more than 3,500 spectators becomes engulfed in a frenzy. Like a tidal wave crashing onto the field, a multitude of spectators storm the park, their emotions running high. Players and cranks intermingle, a sea of fans overwhelm the sheriff, and Bill worries that these confrontations will soon turn into all-out aggression.

The deputies are outnumbered and as one daring individual takes the opportunity to relieve the sheriff of his pistol, the atmosphere becomes charged with a mixture of adrenaline, anger, and defiance. Dave Rowe and the players try to restore calm, and eventually, order is re-established, and the sheriff has a chance to explain what is going on.

The deputies issue tickets to the players for violating the state's "blue law" which prohibits, among other things, "any person fourteen years or older from sporting, rioting, quarreling, hunting, fishing, or shooting" on a Sunday.

ON THE FOLLOWING THURSDAY, Bill stands in a crowded courtroom with thirteen of his teammates, his sweating hands shoved into his suit coat pockets. He can't believe that after all the shenanigans with his teammates and the dubious saloons he has frequented, he faces possible jail time just for playing baseball on a Sunday.

Beams of sunlight filter through the old sash windows, and a hazy veil of smoke has settled over the packed room. The proceedings are continuously interrupted by boisterous baseball fans, determined to make their presence known.

"I will have order in my court, or the room will be cleared!" cries Judge John Hall for the third time. Reporters have come to the Lincoln County courthouse from as far away as Des Moines and Denver as this is a landmark case.

Frank Lewis and J.R. Webster are prosecuting the trial, and they do not question the observance of the Sabbath as a day of rest, but rather the term "sporting." The question they put before the court centers around if baseball is included under the definition of "sporting" and therefore subject to Nebraska's "blue laws."

"There were no wagers placed by players or spectators," argues Charles Magoon for the defense. "The game did not disturb any churchgoers and was in a closed setting, only open to spectators who had purchased tickets. Furthermore, none of the players profited from Sunday's game as they are all on weekly salaries."

There is a possibility that the Judge is a baseball fan as, after only a moment of deliberation, he determines that the defendants were not liable and dismisses the action. A huge cheer goes up from the crowd.

Bill is equally fascinated by the proceedings and experiencing renewed relief that he didn't try to follow in his stepfather's footsteps and become a lawyer. He wonders if the case will be written up nationally, if his mother will see his name in the Bloomington paper and take it as proof that he has become just as notorious as she'd feared he would when he set out to play baseball. Just as they prepare to leave, Gerent Duvalier appears at Bill's side.

"What are you doing here?" says Bill.

"I was curious," replies Duvalier, "just like everyone else in this town. Now that you are a free man, why don't we get together to test out your roulette theories one evening?"

"Sure," says Bill, deciding that even though he is still uncertain if he trusts Duvalier, perhaps he could learn something from him.

BILL and the team celebrate their victory at O'Leary's Tavern on P Street. It is an unusually warm evening, and the ice-chilled glasses are a welcome respite after the stress of their courtroom appearance. There is something about surviving a legal prosecution that bonds people, and that experience will forever tie Bill's teammates. The conversations are easier now, and they all speak freely about their pasts.

Bill is not the only player to have moved around a lot over the past years, and the hometowns of the team members are a testament to the railroads, as with each passing year, travel becomes more accessible. Stories of growing up in Brooklyn, New York, or Boston are exchanged for tales of life in rural Ohio and Mississippi. Half of the team are new to Lincoln, and they exchange tips on places to go and new discoveries.

Until recently, the majority of people passed through Nebraska on their way to somewhere else, and the wagon rivets across the landscape grew deeper with each passing decade. From its humble beginnings as a good place to extract salt from the flats of Salt Creek, the city has acquired a worthy reputation as a place to start a family and earn a good living. In 1891, Lincoln has several schools, a functioning, full-time fire department, new hotels, diverse entertainment, and various newspapers. There is also a new hospital, a telephone exchange, a state capitol building, and an asylum that houses 400 of Lincoln's 37,000 citizens.

GERENT DUVALIER APPEARS to have no interest in putting down roots in Lincoln and has no family that Bill is aware of. His only interest seems to be making off with as much loot as possible from the poker tables. It is not exactly clear what his long-term intentions are, but he appears to enjoy playing the role of mentor to Bill. He introduces him to a tavern called Goodfellows in the North Bottoms neighborhood, which has the outward appearance of a quiet drinking establishment, although inside is a haven for the lowest of Lincoln's society.

Each time the front door swings open, all heads swivel in its direction, and Bill's entrance with Gerent is no exception. Many of the patrons are recent Volga-German immigrants from Russia, and there is no hero's welcome for the ace pitcher here as they have absolutely no interest in baseball. Nearly all the occupants are concentrating on one of two challenges. Either to get as drunk as possible, in the shortest amount of time, for the least amount of money, or to win enough money gambling not to care how much the drinks cost.

The roulette table is a single-sided, short table with two buffalo-sized men acting as overseers on either end in addition to the croupier operating the wheel. They must have arrived at the busiest time as six players with additional onlookers are at the table. Bill is fascinated by the frenzied activity during the betting phase, followed by the complete silence and concentration as the players await the ball's descent.

Bill quickly realizes that he and Gerent have two distinctly different psychological approaches to the game. Gerent seems intent on employing a master magician's strategy by deceiving the house. He regularly whispers, mainly criticizing the other players' tactics, and irritatingly, he tries to predict the outcome of the next play with "this time it will be even red" or "watch it land on black this time." Invariably, he gets it wrong, although when it comes time for him to play, he falls uncharacteristically silent.

Bill is still new to the game, but his limited experience has shown him that an astute player would succeed with patience and at least some form of systematic method. He notices one of the players does have a system that he repeats. He places a single chip on 1, 16, 28, and 30, with three square bets in the first, second, and third dozen. This means his payouts on the single bets are 35-1, and the square bets, which are split between four numbers, have odds of 8-1. This player sits in the middle of the table opposite the dealer, which means he can stretch easily to place his bets at each turn.

To see his winnings substantially accumulate would take Bill much longer than he intends to stay at Goodfellows. However, he can see that this strategy ensures that the player can remain at the table for as long as he can hold out, unless he gets greedy. He usually gets a hit on one of his numbers every four or five spins, and there is no doubt that overall, he wins slightly more than he loses, but it is a thin margin. Clearly, this man has no immediate prior engagements and is content to outstay all the other punters at the table.

Gerent's patience dwindles rapidly, and after only about six spins with minimal bold betting, he turns to Bill.

"Come on, Bill, take my spot here and have a go."

"Right," says Bill, as he very calmly takes out one crisp five-dollar note and three dollar coins. "Dollar chips," he says to the dealer.

Goodfellow's chips are made from clay and shellac with a curious inlay stamp. Bill can't decide if the inlay represents a pitch-fork, a cactus, or the Greek letter Psi, and now is probably not the ideal time to enquire. He waits for the dealer to collect the chips on the table and spin the wheel again.

"Place your bets," growls the croupier from under his bowler hat as he shoots the ball around the wheel.

Remaining completely calm, Bill places three chips in a pile on the second dozen, covering 13-24, and a further three chips on the third dozen, covering 25-36. The other players are busy in their own worlds with last minute indecisions as Bill places his last two chips on the corners of 2/6 and 7/11.

"No more bets," calls the dealer, and the ball leaps from fret to fret before coming to rest in the 34 pocket. Bill has just won $9, which gives him a profit of $1, which the dealer pushes to his spot at the table. Without any reaction, Bill places the winning chip off the grid and repeats the exact same bet with his remaining eight chips, and this time, the ball lands on red three, and he wins another dollar. He repeats the bet three more times, winning one dollar each time.

"This is incredible," whispers Gerent.

"Cash me in, please," says Bill, ignoring Gerent as he knows the Frenchman will insist that he up the stakes.

"I understand your logic," says Gerent, "but did you accurately assess the odds?"

"Eighty-six percent," answers Bill, "which is why I stopped. I wanted to prove a point. That system covers thirty-two numbers, so you can only lose on six numbers, including the zeros. I made five bucks, which is exactly what I wanted. Plus, I was watching the other guys, you know, how they placed their bets and how they reacted when they won or lost. There was a lot going on."

Gerent is unsure how to respond as Bill turns to leave.

"You staying?" says Bill.

"Yes. Wait," says Gerent. "How did you know how to do that?"

"Igor Romanoski. He's in the book," Bill pats his coat. "Russian roulette player."

CHAPTER 16

*T*he Rustlers are playing for their very survival, and they need the support of the whole town and beyond. The allure of roulette and evenings out with Gerent is enticing, but Bill wants to stay focused on winning games that can be won.

The next home game is against Denver on June 1. Bill is anxious that this may be his last shot at moving out of the minor leagues as another pitcher, Hank O'Day, has recovered from injury after coming over from the New York Giants. If Bill can put in an outstanding performance against his old team, he might still have a chance to get to Baltimore or even Boston. Players all over the country are breaking their contracts as the teams struggle to survive, and Bill must concentrate on each game as his entire future is at stake. It is a dry and dusty day, and the crowd is restless for a good victory, with all eyes on Bill to help secure a memorable win.

The visitors' team roster includes the formidable pitcher Henry Fournier, who can hurl the ball over the plate with alarming speed. His curveballs claim their first victim as Lincoln's left-hander, Jesse Burkett, is sat down in the first inning. The eight-thousand-strong crowd grows restless until the second inning when the Rustlers start to get some runs.

Owen Patton slams one to Denver's Joe Werrick, but Werrick overthrows wildly to first base, and Patton makes it to third. Bill steps up to the plate and swings as hard as a lumberjack on his first pitch, sending a grounder straight to Werrick, who dashes toward the plate to cut off Patton. During the confusion, with a gritty haze of dust swirling all around, Bill uses his speed and makes it all the way to third. His breath comes in labored gasps—he can feel the dust in his lungs and tries to spit out as much of it as possible.

The game is tied 2-2 until the fifth inning when Dave Rowe hits a giant home run, and the crowd goes wild as the new manager makes his mark. Bill stays alive on the base paths and makes it to second after a grounder from Wilson which Fournier picks up and unwittingly tosses to Bill White, who is nowhere near the bag. Monk Cline's sacrifice advances everybody, and then Harry Raymond smashes out a two-bagger, giving the Rustlers two more runs.

Once again, Dave Rowe steps up and, this time, manages a hit to left-center, giving Raymond a run. At the end of the inning, Lincoln is ahead, 6-3. In the eighth inning, Fournier steps up to the plate and Bill stares him down from fifty feet away in his position in the pitcher's box. Once again, he has to force the dusty air deep into his lungs. He decides that a fastball is the only option, and Fournier has no chance to swing as the ball drills him on the elbow. The physicians run onto the field as Fournier collapses onto the ground, wincing in pain. He will live, but he is out of the game, and Keefe is bought in as his replacement.

Brickyard Kennedy gets on and scores on Joe Lohbech's triple, and then White scores two runs, giving Denver the lead 7-6. The crowd now settles into a quiet intensity, which turns into groans of disappointment as Lincoln fails to score a run in the ninth inning, and Denver wins the game.

"Rats," says Monk as he sits down opposite Bill on the bench in the visitor's shed. "You reckon Fournier'll be back tomorrow?"

Bill shrugs. "He looked all right, and it was his left elbow, so he'll probably be fine to pitch." Monk spits on the ground. "Next time, aim for the other elbow."

Fournier does not return to pitch the following day, and despite his best efforts, his replacement, Keefe, is no match for the Rustler's bats, and Lincoln wins the game 7-1.

In the final game of the series, however, Keefe seems to have regained his composure and Lincoln are at his mercy as he continues to confuse batters with changeups and unexpected deliveries. Denver gets a man across the plate in the first inning for one run, and then it is Bill's turn in the pitcher's box.

"You all squared away?" asks Dave Rowe as Bill warms up his arm.

"Sure, boss, I've got this."

Bill then proceeds to get three of Denver's biggest sluggers out in quick succession, and Denver is shut out until the sixth inning. There are short, sharp plays from both sides, and Denver gets another man across the plate at the bottom of the sixth. Lincoln are now down by two, and Dave takes this moment to call his team out of the dugout onto the field.

"We're in a hole, boys," he says. "You see all these hard-working folks," he says, pointing around the grandstand and bleachers. "Sure, they came to see a ball game, but you know what they need? They need to see their home team win. If we win this one, we're on top of the league, so let's give 'em something to remember."

They return to the dugout for the seventh inning, and Jack Rowe steps up to the plate. Keefe acknowledges a signal from the catcher and lets loose a ripper, which Jack manages to drive straight toward White. The ball must have hit something on the turf as it takes a bad hop past White, and Jack makes it to first base, which gets a huge roar from the crowd.

Next, Burkett drives one to McGarr, who fields it well as Jack sprints to second. Umpire John Gaffney calls Burkett out at first, which is greeted with a great howl from the cranks, but protests are in vain as Gaffney, whose nickname is "Honest John," is not known for reversing his decisions.

Dave Rowe now steps up and misses Keefe's first two pitches as they whizz by like cannon shots. On the third, he lifts one away to center, and his brother makes it to third.

A hush descends as Bill walks to the plate, twirling his bat from hand to hand. He looks incredulously at the umpire as the first pitch he sees is called a strike, but regains his composure quickly. In the split second after the next pitch leaves Keefe's hand, a magnificent crack echoes around the field as Bill thumps the ball deep into right-field down the first baseline.

Dust is everywhere as Jack Rowe powers over the plate, followed by the sprightly Phil Tomney, which puts the Rustlers in the lead by two runs.

The crowd throws up hats, cushions, and anything else not attached to something, and the cheers can be heard all over Lincoln. Some of the cranks throw silver dollars onto the field at Bill in recognition of his saving the game with his timely hit, and Lincoln goes on to win the game 3-2.

As the other players leave the field, Bill remains in the diamond. Usually, the crowd is quick to head for the exits to avoid the crush, but today, everyone has stayed in their place to applaud their team. Bill soaks in the atmosphere and claps towards the main stand as a gesture of appreciation for their support. Surely, he thinks, with this level of enthusiasm, the league must survive. Most importantly, if he can maintain this level of personal success, one of the Eastern teams is certain to offer him a contract.

Darnbrough displayed his usual good nerve and superb judgement and caused three of the most accomplished sluggers in the Denver aggregation to lay down before his prowess . . .
—Lincoln Journal Star, June 1, 1891

CHAPTER 17

*G*erent is playing poker at O'Rourke's tavern on L Street. Bill waits at the bar, watching the game from a distance, and decides right then never to play this game. There seems to be little entertainment compared to roulette, and the players are perpetually grave looking. There is a break in the game, or has it ended? Bill is unsure as Gerent comes to the bar and shakes his hand. Bill orders them both a beer.

"Did you see the news from Monte Carlo?"

"Yes, I did," says Gerent. "Lucky Englishman."

"What exactly does it mean—he broke the bank?"

Gerent slugs his beer. "It means this Mr. Charles Wells won so much money that they could not afford to pay him his winnings and had to borrow money to pay him."

"But it's the casino at Monte Carlo," Bill says, and his toes tingle as if with a minor electric shock. "How could they possibly run out of money? It's the most famous casino in the world, and they're backed by a Royal family."

"That is what I intend to find out," says Gerent, smiling.

"What do you mean?"

"I'm going to France to find out for myself. Now, please excuse me, Bill. I see that my adversaries have returned to the table, so I must join them." Bill watches him return to his poker game, feeling no closer to an answer on anything.

Initially, he suspected Gerent had ulterior motives—perhaps driven by money or some sort of scheme. He was captivated by how this man could embrace the existence of a wandering gambler. Gerent's financial sources seem undefined, and with no dependents, he leads a life skirting the fringes of society. Except for baseball players, he has yet to cross paths with someone so well-traveled.

If Gerent goes to Monaco, he will miss him as he has few people he can call friends, given his own somewhat nomadic lifestyle. Lost in his contemplations, he wonders what Art Twineham, John Arkins, and even Miss Emma Juch are doing right now.

A TOKEN *of our appreciation* is all the note says. It is signed by Dave Rowe, and the envelope also contains four folded five-dollar notes. Bill is sitting on the bed in his room, admiring the artwork on the bills, wondering if there is some hidden agenda from the manager or if this is simply a pitcher's bonus. One thing he knows for sure, a gambler should only play with money that he can afford to lose. This is cold, hard cash that was unexpected, so why not double it at the roulette table? Just for one night, he has a chance to behave like one of the major leaguers back east and stand shoulder to shoulder with the high rollers.

Goodfellows is not exactly where the high rollers hang out, but it has become familiar territory and is close enough. As he walks to the bar, a man in a stove pipe hat stops him by the door.

"You're the Frenchman's friend, aren't you?"

"Yes, I suppose so," answers Bill.

"They found him about an hour ago back there," he points down toward the ally.

"Is he all right?"

"Stone dead. Stabbed, they say."

The newspapers are quick to insinuate that Duvalier inhabited the darker underworld of Lincoln's seedy gambling fraternity and frequently racked up debts. This is the first time Bill has witnessed the repercussions of not squaring your bets. Part of him wants to get to Monte Carlo as fast as possible to honor his friend, but does he want to spend his whole life running the gauntlet? Selling advertising and playing in the minor leagues will not give him the opportunity to find out—there has to be another way.

To compound matters, as if losing his only acquaintance outside of baseball is not bad enough, the league announces that it will be closing down until "suitable financial arrangements are made."

Nobody hangs around to mourn the team's demise, and all the players scatter like frightened crows in a field. Bill feels like he has lost an elderly relative who had been slowly edging off life's mortal coil, as even though the inevitable has happened, it is still a shock.

He has no savings and no prospects. Maybe next spring, he can probably find some semi-pro team somewhere. But what about the winter? He has so little money that he can't afford to travel far and still hope to pay for living expenses afterward. He is contemplating an approach to the *Lincoln Journal Star*—surely their advertising department could use his fresh ideas—when he receives a letter, forwarded from Denver, from his stepfather. His mother is ill. They think it might be cancer.

CHAPTER 18

*H*is mother doesn't look very sick. Maybe a little pale, a little older. As he sits at the breakfast table listening to her lecture him, Bill wonders if his stepfather made up a story just to get him home. Charles has long since left to go to the office, and the remnants of the fried eggs Bill's mother had cooked for him are cold and congealed on his plate.

"I just don't want you to get discouraged," his mother says. "The important thing now is that this silly *baseball* pursuit is in your past. Because, obviously"—she throws an expansive gesture to the room, "a person can reinvent themselves, Bill. You just have to be very careful in how you go about it."

Bill grits his teeth. Years of rage have built up within him and right now, with everything that has happened, he's had enough of his mother's preaching and can't hold it in any longer. "I don't know how you kept Charles from finding out." His voice is so cold and hard it surprises him.

His mother's eyes dart as if she's afraid a neighbor may have overheard him, but all the windows are closed. She brushes off his words with a gesture, composing her face to look calm. "The things people will say," she says, "when they get an idea in their heads that's just plain wrong."

"I doubt they would've kept you in jail for two months if there'd been nothing to it."

Her gaze is like glass. "The point is, Bill, I left all that behind me. I'm respectable now. I'm the secretary of the Ladies Aid at church and the wife of a lawyer—not of a dirt-poor farmer like your father. You can make yourself into anything you want to be. Whose son you are doesn't matter. Your no-good father doesn't matter."

"Don't say that about him!"

"Oh, I know you always liked him, Bill. Who could blame a boy for admiring his father? But did you never see things from my point of view?" She stands and begins clearing the plates.

"Your point of view? You took the one person I looked up to away from me, and I've been running ever since. You left me with creepy Aunt May and her drunk husband, and then you took me away from everything I knew. To what? A new town where I had no friends because you had your sights set on another man—one to take care of you."

"Us, Bill, us. Take care of us."

"Mother, why don't you tell me the truth? You've never told me the truth about what happened! I was nine years old, my father died suddenly, and my mother was accused of poisoning him and sent to jail. They called you the *She-Devil Poisoner of Lebanon* in the papers. You thought I didn't see it, but I overheard Uncle John bad-mouthing you to the neighbors. Can you imagine what it was like for me when they dug up his body to look for evidence? You don't have any idea what that was like for me. The things people said about you."

"Your father ate something that didn't agree with him," she says coolly, wiping a plate with a circular motion. "The rest was just idle talk. They found no evidence, remember?" Then, she turns abruptly to glare at Bill over her shoulder. "And remember our agreement, Bill. You will never breathe a word of this to Charles. Or it's the both of us who will lose everything."

Bill glares back. He realizes he's starting to lose control, but he breaths deep and it feels good to let it all out. His mother has finally shown a slight weakness, a chink in her armor. He has tried to respect her for so long because that is what she demanded, but now, he is seething with anger. She wants him to erase his real father and say he's a lawyer's son. She wants him to go back to college and set up a law practice of his own. Chicago is as big as her dreams get. She wants to visit him and go shopping at Marshall Field's with enough money to buy anything she wants. It's different now, though, as he has tasted freedom. Three years away, and yet here he is, back in his mother's house, about to be caught up in her web once again.

She's still looking at him, but her eyes have softened. This a well-practiced move that Bill has seen many times before. She wants to bring him back to a time long ago, when he needed her, and went out of his way to love and support her. When he did what she wanted. They had some good times together but now he vows he will never tell her of his own, bigger dreams.

"We're a team, aren't we, Bill?" she says. "Haven't we always been a team?" *Good God, no*, he wants to say, but what comes out of his mouth is, "Yes, Mother. Of course."

He's good at staying quiet, he reasons, and that's all she's really asking him to do. Bill tells himself that his current situation is just a bad spin of the wheel. He knows the most intelligent, practical course of action would be to get a job selling advertising in one of the local newspapers. He's determined not to stay under his stepfather and mother's roof for more than a week, tops.

But he can't believe how stuck he feels. His mother complains that she is in terrible pain, and has a strange mass in her midsection, and she's seeing the doctor again tomorrow. When she says what a comfort it is to her to have Bill home, she might as well have handcuffed him to her wrist.

It's his fourth night back in Bloomington when he walks into the Bouquet Casino.

PART II
THE AMERICAN GAMBLER

1891-1903

CHAPTER 19

"*P*restidigitation," says Mr. Lewin, fixing his stare at Bill.

"Right," says Bill. "What does that mean?"

"That, my boy, is why we have eagle eyes. Palming, switching, ditching, and stealing cards from the table. It means sleight of hand, and some of the folks who come in here could probably make a good living as magicians."

Hiram T. Lewin runs the Bouquet Cafe, a restaurant and bar at 206 N. Center Street on the west side of Courthouse Square in Bloomington. Under a separate license, he also runs a modest casino in the backroom behind a connecting double door. Lewin recognized Bill from his baseball days and saw how intently he watched the roulette wheel last week. After Bill explained the situation with the league, Mr. Lewin realized he could be an asset to the place and immediately offered him a job.

"It also happens in roulette," continues Lewin. "Would you be able to spot someone past posting bets?" An inquisitive look comes across Bill's face.

"You mean folks placing bets after "no more bets" has been called? For sure. I'll keep an eye on the totals and will always be on the lookout for distractions."

"Watch this," says Lewin, leaning his broad shoulders over the roulette table. He holds a fistful of dollar bills and passes them to an imaginary dealer. At the same time, he slides a chip one square over from where it was initially placed. "Like everyone else around the table, you will be distracted by the paper money. That's called misdirection, which happens more often than you'd think."

"Everything else is easy," continues Lewin. "You know why my daughter is so good at piano?"

"No, I don't," answers Bill, "please tell me."

"Practice. She plays for hours and has been since she was about seven. You'll get good at adding up the totals in no time, but a really great dealer needs to have awareness to such a degree that you can see something suspicious before it's even happened. One thing to look out for is players pretending not to know each other, who are, in fact, playing together. Technically, it's not illegal for folks to play together, but in my experience, the best strategy is to assume that everyone is a crook and they are out to swindle us."

"So, besides folks coming to eat, how many people come in here just to play roulette?" asks Bill.

"It varies. A good many work around here, clerks and such. It depends on the weather, payday, and sometimes, if the poker tables are busy, some folks just can't resist making a bet. If two people are at the roulette table, more are likely to join than if nobody's playing. Some nights, it gets real busy, and I'll have Jim as dealer and you act as his second pair of eyes so you can concentrate on the chips and the cash. One thing we can never get wrong is the payouts. Always take as long as you need counting up the winnings as it's better to be slow and get it right than make a mistake, and things can get nasty real quick."

"Right, Mr. Lewin," says Bill. "Who's Jim?"

"Jim and Larry take turns behind the bar, and Jim's handy around the casino. By the way, please call me Hiram."

Bill and Hiram spend another forty-five minutes at the table, with Bill showing off his counting abilities. He has a good handle on the payouts after months of studying odds using his notebook and roulette bible and watching hours of roulette in Lincoln. Hiram is a tall, well-built man with short black hair and is clean-shaven, but it seems to Bill that middle age may be catching up with him as he has a bad cough. The most important lesson learned as he watches and listens to his new mentor is that the croupier must never take his eye off the layout. He will hear when the ball slows down and need only glance to see the winning number. Otherwise, his concentration is always on the table itself, not the wheel.

After explaining some basic rules of the house, such as not becoming friendly with any of the players, Hiram tells Bill to start at lunchtime on Wednesday to ease him into his new life as a croupier.

The news that he will be working at a steakhouse that is also a casino does not go down well with his mother and stepfather.

"You should believe in something with a passion and have a desire to help your fellow man," says Charles. "To think you would do this to your poor mother when she's already ill and we're facing a very uncertain future. Until you can come back here with a plan to contribute to society in a meaningful way, you are not welcome under my roof."

Bill shrugs, kisses his mother's cheek, grabs his hat from the hook by the kitchen door, and heads downtown to rent a room.

HIRAM HAS EXPLAINED to his wife, Ruth, and daughter, Libby, that the new croupier has recently been out West and knows everything there is to know about roulette and will surely be a big asset to the casino.

The Lewin family sits down for lunch the following day, which is always served at two in the afternoon, just before Hiram goes downstairs to work.

"Father," says Libby, "I don't see what harm it would do if I played piano for your patrons between three and five in the afternoons. It would make the place festive. It would probably even bring more people in."

Her mother looks scandalized, and it takes Libby the entire meal to wear the two of them down. They finally agree to three to four on Mondays and Tuesdays only, the casino's slowest days, and she will have to make the most of her time.

Bill does not notice Libby standing framed in the doorway as he is at the roulette table trying to decipher his own handwriting in his notebook. She fixes her eyes on the piano, tips up her chin, and crosses the room as if making an entrance on the stage of a grand concert hall, her thick skirts brushing the dusty plank floor. She slides onto the piano stool, arranging herself so that her bustle hangs over the back edge and her skirts sweep elegantly around. She poises her hands above the keyboard and gently begins to play *Fur Elise*, which sounds tinny on the out-of-tune piano, but she plays on regardless.

Bill is immediately transfixed. The double doors are open, but the gambling area is empty, so he sits on one of the chairs behind the roulette table, watching and listening to Libby play. She is wearing a day dress made of green and black brocade, with ringlets in her hair. Hiram must have heard the piano from the office as he comes out to check on her. Bill jumps up and starts stacking and re-stacking chips before placing random piles of bets around the grid, pretending to practice the payouts. There is hardly anyone else in the place at this hour on a Monday, but Bill has visions of Libby's father sitting on a rocking chair with a shotgun over his lap and decides that any approach will have to wait.

EACH NIGHT, when he returns to his room, Bill writes down at least two new roulette systems. This evening, a regular player has placed twelve chips down the middle column on alternate rows in a criss-cross pattern. Each bet is split across two numbers, and the man plays the same bet for at least eight spins and comes out ahead when he stops playing. Bill can't know the exact winnings over such a large number of spins as he has to concentrate on the other players simultaneously, but he is optimistic that this system has worked well, so he gives it a name. "The Zigzag Split." Most players continue to play until their funds have been completely depleted, but this man knew when to walk away. He will look out for him and watch more carefully next time.

The following evening, he notices a safe bet, which would typically enable a player to prolong his visit to the table. He plays just under the maximum outside limits on the first and third dozen, with varying middle numbers covered. His coverage of numbers 13 to 24 is generous and would have been well rewarded had not the ball chosen to land on double zero. Bill instantly confiscates his entire stake, which will go toward the next delivery of steaks and whiskey. As the man is about to get up from his chair, a drink magically appears by his side. The man does not speak—he just sits, takes out his wallet, and passes Bill another ten-dollar note to change for chips. As Jim walks away, he turns and nods to Bill, who gives him a tiny half-smile in return.

In the late afternoon, just before the casino's bustling hours, Libby, who has been playing the piano a couple of afternoons a week for reasons unbeknownst to Bill—considering the piano's terrible tuning and the absence of an audience—glides past Bill's table. She pivots, a subtle smile gracing one corner of her full lips.

"You know, I don't really know anything about baseball," she says, "but I hear things."

This is the first time she has spoken to Bill, and he is taken aback. He notices the elegant curve of her neck and the intriguing slope of her nose.

"I've heard, for example," she says, "that you, sir, can throw a baseball as fast as a bullet in a straight line right where you're aiming it." She bats her eyes. "I don't believe it, though."

Bill laughs at that. "I'm retired," he says.

"Good," she says. "I've also heard baseball players have terrible manners." Another bat of her eyelashes. "But—as fast as a bullet? Maybe you could show me sometime."

"There used to be a practice net at Miller Park. Why don't we go and see if it's still there? Would you like to go for a walk down by the lake?"

"I'd like that, Bill," smiles Libby, "How about Thursday morning on your day off?"

———

SURE ENOUGH, as they round the path from the Summit Street end of the park, they can see a small group of young boys taking turns throwing balls at the net.

"We used to call this "the pocket," says Bill as he walks up to the net and fondly touches the sturdy scaffold frame. "Which one of you youngsters can lend me a ball to see if the old man can still hit the net?" The boys stare at Bill, unsure what to make of him. Grown-ups don't normally come here. This is their territory. The tallest of the group looks up at the stranger, perhaps with a glimmer of recognition, but says nothing as he grudgingly hands him his baseball.

"Why thank you, young sir," says Bill.

When the ball whacks the wire, Libby cheers him and squeals, and he notices the way the sun gleams on her pinned-up hair.

"Hey, mister!" shouts one of the younger boys, but the taller one holds him back, and they form a little line to get back to business.

"Keep practicing, boys," Bill calls over his shoulder.

They walk on together, stopping by the stone bridge at Mirror Lake. It's early November, and the boat houses are all locked up for the winter. A brisk wind is sweeping dead leaves past as Libby twirls her parasol. "I don't think I've ever met a man as strong as you," she says, then looks up from under her eyelashes and leans in. "What's that?" she says, touching his coat pocket.

Bill reaches inside the pocket and pulls out a baseball.

"You had your own one all the time?"

"Sure," says Bill, "but I wanted to show them that it's possible to throw it that fast, even with one of their balls. Just in case they thought my one was special, you know."

She is very close now, but he backs away and keeps walking. He must be careful, he thinks. A companion is a tempting option, but a relationship with Libby would also mean a relationship with Hiram and the café. There is still so much of the world Bill wants to explore, and he can't afford to get stuck in this town. He passed Emily Irvine on Oakland Avenue two weeks ago, but she didn't see him. He's heard she is married now and has a son who's one year old.

Even in the past, he knew he had to get out of town, and in the present, he must uphold resolute determination to avoid being lured back into a mundane existence.

CHAPTER 20

*H*iram is watching Bill. He is sure of it. There is no action at the roulette table, and across the room, Hiram is talking with a customer at the bar, although he keeps looking over in Bill's direction. Eventually, he comes over.

"You know, Bill, the best thing you can do in your life is marry the right woman. The second-best thing to do is read. I read a lot. Did you know that Roman soldiers used a chariot wheel to play roulette?" He doesn't wait for Bill to answer. "An arrow was placed under the wheel and pointed to the winning marked space. The Greeks also played with a shield revolving on a metal point, and they used ten numbers."

There is a pause. He removes his glasses, wipes them with his handkerchief, and puts them back on. "Bill, I need to know your intentions with my daughter."

"My intentions?" says Bill, completely taken aback.

Hiram's bushy eyebrows draw together in a frown. "I've seen the way you look at each other."

Bill has been unaware of looking at Libby much at all. In fact, he's tried his best not to.

"I know you took her to the park," Hiram says in an accusing tone.

There is a long silence between them as Bill chooses his words carefully. Hiram has been a valuable mentor, and Bill certainly doesn't want to lose his job.

"Your daughter is a beautiful girl—" he begins.

Hiram claps his hands and grins. "Oh, this is thrilling!"

Bill feels the blood draining from his face.

"I knew it!" Hiram went on. "I just knew there was something there. I couldn't hope for a better fellow for my daughter, Bill, honest."

"Mr. Lewin, I—" says Bill, but he stops himself. He doesn't want to disappoint Hiram, but he'll have to extricate himself somehow. Very carefully.

LIBBY TAKES to stopping by Bill's table on her way back upstairs after her hour at the piano on Mondays and Tuesdays and then always leaves just when he's starting to get interested in the conversation.

He can't refuse when Hiram invites him to join his family for Sunday dinner one week, and then the next. Despite harboring a desire to escape, the idea of belonging to a loving family is starting to grow on him.

He spends the Christmas holiday with the Lewins, although for them, the Jewish festival of Hannukah falls between December 25 and January 2 in 1891. Despite turning down their kind invitation to attend the new temple on Monroe and Prairie Street, Bill tries his best to understand their traditions. He spends New Year's Eve working at the saloon, and a week after that, he and Libby head to the park to go ice skating.

Miller Park is transformed in the winter with a blanket of snow, ensuring the only sounds are the gentle crunch of their footsteps and intermittent melodies of chirping birds. He almost doesn't know how it has happened, whether he has asked her, or she suggested it to him, but no matter, they are walking toward the rink, skates slung over their arms, laughing at some joke he's made about how he'd better not fall and break his pitching elbow if he ever hopes to play ball again.

She links her arm through his. "Oh, Bill," she says, "you don't want to play baseball again, do you?" She looks up at him, smiling, and, despite the cold, his cheeks burn from her closeness.

He reminds himself that his mother is scheduled for surgery next week, and then he will get out of Bloomington. But skating with Libby is fun, and at the end of the day, with the sun setting against the frozen horizon and children scattering toward home, she pulls him into the dark corner of the warming shed. She looks up at him with wide eyes, her pretty face rosy from the cold, he finds her impossible to resist, and leans down to kiss her.

From that moment onward, she becomes an intoxicating presence in his life. Whether seated at her parents' dining table or watching her from across the saloon as she plays the piano, the promise of warmth and affection and another tender kiss lingers like a captivating drug. He has never been afflicted like this before, and it's a weakness; he knows that for sure, which he cannot abide by, but neither can he seem to deny it.

His mother has her surgery—something feminine she won't discuss. He brings her flowers, but Charles has hired a nurse and makes it clear they need little, if anything, from Bill.

BILL HAS the feeling that Libby is in love with him now, which only makes him more restless. He sees her anxiety whenever he mentions baseball—"Next season, I could be anywhere," is met with her singing a cheerful tune as if she knows something that he doesn't.

It's a Thursday in late February when she finds another opportunity, once more in the dark corner of the deserted warming shed. The night descends outside, and no one is going to come in, especially not after she bars the door from inside. He smiles and kisses her eagerly. They're both wrought up—it's not pretend, and his heart is going wild. "Bill," she whispers. "I've never—"

She whispers closer in his ear. "I want you to—"

He leans back, eyes wide. He knows he should stop, it's clear. He's an honorable man.

She whispers warmly in his ear again. She guides his hand. He follows.

Some fumbling later, and then a groan from him, and he thinks, "Now she has me. What have I done?" Even as he holds her tight, he wants to let go.

"Oh, Bill," she whispers, gently touching his face.

CHAPTER 21

"*Not* so fast, my boy," says Hiram defiantly. "There are some things you should know." Bill stares intently as he continues. He had no clear vision of how this conversation would unfold, but it is certainly deviating from his expectations.

"Libby is my most precious possession, and should you ever hurt her, we will duel in the street. But there is something else. In our faith, it is traditional for our own children to take over our businesses, but with you as my son-in-law, Bill, I am confident you will do a good job running things around here when I'm gone."

"Thank you for trusting me, Sir, but I didn't mean—that is, I'm not sure—perhaps we should talk about this—" Bill stutters before Hiram cuts him off.

"I've built this place from nothing. I know it's not much, but I'm proud of what I've achieved, and I need to know that I can trust you. Ruth and I didn't raise our daughter to be a saloon keeper, and I don't expect her to have to worry about the day-to-day business of the casino."

"I understand." Bill murmurs, his gaze unwaveringly locked onto Hiram. A shiver runs down his spine, the hairs on the back of his neck standing on end. He can't decide if it's exhilaration or fear causing this reaction.

Bill finds himself thrust into marriage before he can even wrap his mind around the situation. Married! It's the very fate he had vehemently strived to avoid, now a stark reality he's forced to confront.

THE WEDDING IS a modest civil ceremony, and, after extended deliberation from every angle, Charles and Alice do decide to grace the occasion with their presence but depart even before the reception at the café commences.

Bill is indeed smitten by Libby, and he enjoys her company and loves coming home to their new apartment late at night and crawling into the warm little bed beside her—yet he cannot shake the doomed feeling of a man aboard a sinking ship.

Hiram and Bill start spending much more time together as the mentor teaches his student everything there is to know about simultaneously running a restaurant that is also a casino.

"It's a balance," says Hiram. "Give the people a sense that they are entering a high-end joint without excluding the masses. Keep it nice, but don't spend too much doing the place up, or folks will think you are making too much money off them."

One early May evening, Bill is focused on the roulette table and doesn't immediately recognize Frank Pears until he hands over a five-dollar note and asks for five stacks.

"Howdie, Bill," says Frank, "I heard you were here." After all this time, Bill is surprised to see his old teammate from Kansas, but the shock is immediately replaced with relief as he needs someone to talk to.

"Frank, great to see you," says Bill, "but we'll have to wait until I get a break to catch up properly." He quickly returns his attention to the three other players at the table and announces, "Place your bets, please."

As Frank and Bill walk down the road, Bill explains.

"It's a policy, you know, not to be too friendly with the players. The other players get jittery, thinking that I'm friendly with you and will somehow let you win. There's no way I could do that, of course."

"Of course not," says Frank, smiling as they enter O'Leary's.

"No, really, there isn't," says Bill, "I can't predict anything about roulette, and that little ball completely defies the natural laws of gravity."

"Good to know," says Frank as they order two beers.

"I'll cut right to the chase, Bill," he continues as they sit with their drinks. "I'm here as a representative of Tun Berger—you know he's the catcher at the Pittsburg Pirates?"

"I've heard of him," says Bill as he sips his beer.

"Well, he's doing a spell as manager of Rochester in New York, and he asked me if I could find a good pitcher for this season. So here I am."

Bill can't believe his luck. As long as his arm holds out and Hiram and Libby are on board. "I appreciate the offer," he says, "but I have to speak to my wife and father-in-law as it is their place, after all, and I'm lucky to be running it now."

"I understand, Bill," says Frank. "But remember, it's just for the summer."

"Just for the summer," repeats Bill.

A fire has been reignited within him, and he decides the best course of action is to speak with Hiram before Libby. "This may be my last shot at the majors," he says.

"I get that, Bill," says Hiram. "But you need to understand that you have commitments and responsibilities now. Hopefully, you'll have a family of your own soon, and this place needs constant supervision," he adds, waving his arm around the saloon. Bill stares at his father-in-law, unsure how to follow up, but it seems Hiram has conceded that he can't stop him.

"I won't pretend that I'm not disappointed, Bill. Of course, it would be great publicity for the place if you did make it to the majors. So, I wish you luck."

"Are you joking? I'm not leaving my mother!" Libby has not reacted well to Bill's suggestion that she go with him.

"You're supposed to be here to help my father!" she yells. "To help me!"

"I'll only be gone for the summer."

"It's a boy's game! You're leaving me to go off and play when you're supposed to be a husband and, one day, a father."

Bill is relieved when it's time to climb aboard the train. He can already imagine the texture of a baseball in his hands, the feel of the summer sunshine on his face. He sent word to his mother and Charles that he would be gone for the summer. Bill didn't waste time going to see them as not even Alice could dissuade him from this decision. Libby, Ruth, and Hiram have come to the station to bid him goodbye. Libby stands on the platform, scowling, her arms folded across her chest. Only Hiram waves back to Bill as the train whistle blows and the steam cranks the pistons into motion.

Rochester Flour Cities baseball team is so named due to the twenty or so flour mills along the Genesee River. At one point, Rochester's High Falls was the largest flour producer in the world, although most of the players on the team now work at local firms Bausch & Lomb, Eastman Kodak, and Western Union, which have their headquarters here.

Highly accomplished and experienced players like Spud Johnson, Bill Watkins, and Sleeper Sullivan have all heard of Bill, although, as with all new players, they treat him with suspicion. Third baseman Chippy McGarr knows Bill from Lincoln, but that does not mean they are friends, and McGarr does not do much to aid Bill's integration.

Libby's letters from Bloomington are full of complaints: her father is getting sicker, the apartment is too hot, she's lonely, and this isn't what married life should be like—not one bit. Bill has to concede that there is no point in getting defensive, as she does have a point.

The team plays three home games against the Buffalo Bisons, the Troy Trojans, and the Binghamton Bingos and two away games against the Albany Senators and the Philadelphia Athletics. During the Syracuse Stars game, Bill's pitching is abysmal throughout as he has no focus, and his pitching arm is beginning to really ache. The afternoon sun stings and he turns his collar up to protect his neck. As each minute passes, he can only think that everything he ever dreamed of will never come true. Syracuse has signed the familiar face of Henry "Frenchy" Fournier, who had done a spell at Omaha after Denver. Even though he is a few years older than Bill, it looks like his throwing arm has endured better than Bill's as Fournier continues to pitch with near-perfect accuracy.

> *You could hear Rochester blood curdle at Culver Park yesterday afternoon at about 5:55 o'clock, while at the same hour what little Syracuse blood there was on the spot was coursing through the veins of its prospectors as merrily as the salt would allow.*
>
> *Darnbrough was thumped all over the lot in the second inning and in the third and sixth innings, the home team did some terrible slugging. But the Stars won."*
>
> —*Rochester Democrat and Chronicle, June 24, 1892*

IN LATE JUNE, a letter arrives from Libby that begins, *Sweetheart, bad news.*

Her father coughs nonstop and stays in bed whenever he's not working. She's afraid of what will happen to the casino, which he can barely manage now. *You need to come home, Bill,* she writes. *Now. I need you. Your future is here. Anyway, with your pitching as bad as you describe, it is time for you to admit that your dream of being a major leaguer will never come true.*

She's right. But that doesn't mean he doesn't resent her a little bit for saying it.

The next day, a letter arrives from Hiram. *I sure would appreciate it, Bill. Knowing the place was securely in your hands would mean so much to me.*

Bill doesn't want to let Hiram down, and Libby's right that it's his only future now, especially given that he's heard rumblings he may be cut from the team anyhow.

Tun Berger is not entirely surprised when Bill resigns. He has started only six games this season, and it has become obvious that his arm cannot take the strain of so many games in the pitcher's box.

Darnbrough has decided to keep out of baseball the remainder of the season and last night he left Rochester for Bloomington, IL., his home where he will engage in business with his father-in-law. The young pitcher has played in very hard luck this season. At the outset, he hurt his arm severely and although he has gone into the box several times, he's not been in good shape since he signed with the Rochester team. He has shown though that he is an excellent pitcher. In the game that he pitched at the beach, he held the Buffalos down to a double and a scratch single and there were only two putouts in the outfield at that. Few pitchers have made a better showing than that this summer. If his arm was in better shape, he would be a valuable man for any team in the association. Darnbrough is one of the most gentlemanly players who ever wore a Rochester uniform. When his arm comes round, he will be welcomed back to Rochester.
—Rochester Democrat and Chronicle July 1, 1892.

As HE BOARDS the train this time, he shudders at the prospect of caring for an ailing father-in-law and a demanding wife. He feels like a man marching into an intense and unrelenting ordeal. Yet, in the midst of the journey home, a thought emerges: "Don't make the most of it; make the best of it." Bill's inherent optimism rekindles. This is his path now, his future, and he is determined to extract the best from it. If he can stay committed, he could even make himself a rich man.

On July 1, 1892, Hiram Lewin signs over the title of the Bouquet Café to William Darnbrough.

CHAPTER 22

Mr. Will N. Darnbrough, the proprietor of the Bouquet chop house, has scored a tremendous hit with his new 15-cent dinner. He has certainly surprised the people with his departure, for he gives you Delmonico fare at soup house prices. If you have not already tried this dinner, you should do so. Businessmen will find it cheaper than eating at home.

—Bloomington (Illinois) Daily Pantagraph, July 14, 1892

*L*ibby asks her mother to teach her about keeping the books now that her husband owns the restaurant and casino, but Bill insists that he do the accounts himself. She talks about the children they will have together, and Bill is enthusiastic about the pursuit of creating their own family in certain predictable ways. Still, for some reason, Libby does not get pregnant despite their efforts.

While Bill continues to dedicate himself to the success of the Bouquet, a sense of personal emptiness plagues him. His unfulfilled dream of playing in the majors weighs heavily, and the constant trouble with his shoulder adds to his despair. Occasionally, he reminisces about the opera singer and his dreams of going to Monte

Carlo, but these desires now feel distant, like the dreams of a different man.

Hiram's absence from the casino becomes increasingly frequent, and he opts to have his meals in his room. Whenever Bill does catch a glimpse of him, he seizes the opportunity to gather as much information as he can about the restaurant side of the business—how to treat the customers and select the most suitable menu offerings. At the age of just twenty-three, Bill finds himself burdened with numerous newfound responsibilities, but his enthusiasm to exchange ideas with Hiram remains unwavering. He suggests extending the opening hours and eagerly shares his thoughts. Bolstered by Hiram's guidance, Bill's confidence steadily grows.

Marketing and promotion are high on his list of priorities, and working the newspaper angles comes naturally after his experience with the *Rocky Mountain News*. He deftly secures editorial coverage in the *Daily Pantagraph* in addition to running ads.

He takes the time to tour the competition, including—over Libby's objections—going as far as Springfield to visit Harry Lane's place on East Washington Street. Lane's upstairs casino features poker, dice, and roulette, with horse racing bets taken in the basement. This place has twenty-five employees and is open day and night. Lane is known around town as the "boss gambler," with most law enforcement and local council members either on the payroll or wise enough to turn a blind eye. Bill decides that there is no need to try and scale his business to such a degree but he is determined to spruce things up and entice more high rollers into the Bouquet.

He meets with Horace Richardson, who owns Tryner & Richardson cigar manufacturers in Bloomington, and starts selling his cigars in the bar. The homemade cigars on offer are priced at ten cents and Bill buys them directly from Richardson at four cents apiece. The cigars are called "Bouquet."

When Bill announces he intends to buy another roulette table, Libby takes some convincing as it means they will have to take on another full-time croupier. Finally, when he shows her the potential profit margins, briefly explaining the house "edge," she capitulates, and they take delivery of a new H.C. Evans wheel from Chicago.

Everything will be merry at the Bouquet tomorrow. The genial young propri-etor, Mr. William Darnbrough, will treat his friends to a delightful turkey lunch and serve all of the regular hot drinks, including Tom and Jerry, egg nog, etc. This is in addition to the immense variety of choice old liquors which have just been imported from the old Pompeiian vintages, which for strength and purity are not equaled by any stock in the state. Call upon Mr. Darnbrough.
—*Bloomington (Illinois) Daily Pantagraph, December 20, 1892*

JUST AS BILL, Libby, and her mother sit down for supper at home, they hear a gunshot from inside the building. The sound is a muffled crack, although there is no doubt in Bill's mind what it is, and he runs up to the apartment, taking three stairs at a time. He assumes Hiram has had an accident while cleaning his pistol.

Hiram Lewin is lying dead in his bed with a .38 caliber Colt revolver beside him. Bill's heart races as he tries to absorb the scene, the impact of the gunshot still reverberating through his mind. He has shot himself in the chest and appears to Bill to have died instantly, as it is less than a minute since the shot rang out. Libby and Mrs. Lewin rush into the room, and Libby stifles a scream with a trembling hand over her mouth. In a state of shock and despair, Ruth Lewin drops to her knees and starts crawling toward the bed. Bill acts swiftly to block her path to shield her from the blood-soaked sheets and Hiram's lifeless body. The housekeeper appears at the door momentarily, turns, and runs down the stairs and out into the street and it is not long before the surrounding residents hear of the tragedy.

Sometime later, Bill sits alone in Hiram's room, looking at his motionless body, thinking how peaceful he looks. His shock slowly turns to resentment that Hiram could be so selfish and leave him alone to deal with his wife, daughter, and the business. He holds his head in his hands as he remembers his father and the countless questions he wishes he could have asked him. He owes much to Hiram, a proud man who went to great lengths to disguise his suffering. Resentment transforms to sorrow as Bill yearns for just one more week with his mentor.

Bill had no idea that his mental state had deteriorated to such an extent that he would take his own life. He must have been planning this for some time. Perhaps that's why he signed over the casino so abruptly?

The coroner arrives to inspect the body, the pistol, and a letter Hiram wrote to his wife. The text is rambling and mostly incoherent, and it is clear that his physical and mental state had severely worsened over the last several weeks. Hiram Lewin was forty-six years old, and the coroner returns a verdict of death by suicide.

After the funeral, Ruth Lewin is still in shock. She agrees that Bill and Libby should divide the business activities, with Libby taking care of the properties and Bill running the café and casino operation. Hiram owned two additional buildings on South Center and East Jefferson Streets, which Libby oversees, and the building on Main Street and two lots in Mason City.

Determined to honor Hiram's legacy, Bill pledges to go to extraordinary lengths to ensure the saloon thrives under his command. Among his initial endeavors is a much-needed upgrade to the bar, where he sets in motion a plan to acquire a selection of high-quality wines, beers, and spirits, adding an air of sophistication and refinement to the establishment.

Seeking solace and a glimmer of joy amidst the somber atmosphere, Bill ventures to Peoria and purchases three spirited Irish Setters from a reputable dog breeder. As the train carriages whisk them back home, the sight of these youthful canines, with their floppy ears and vibrant red coats, prompts many passengers to comment and ask to pet them. At home, the mere presence of these magnificent creatures breathes new life into the air, instilling a renewed sense of optimism within the confines of both the house and the saloon.

Will Darnbrough was in trouble, but a step ladder saved him. A traveling man stepped into Darnbrough's Casino the other day and called for a drink of old Kentucky whisky. Mr. Darnbrough called his attention to the labels on the barrels giving the age and brands of the goods he sells. The drummer was one of those shrewd fellows who are up to snuff and said he did not believe there was a barrel of '86 whisky in the town. Mr. Darnbrough was at sea for a minute only, but quickly recovering himself, grabbed a step ladder and invited the drummer to mount it and examine the government stamps on the heads of the barrels, which prove conclusively the age and brand of the goods. The salesman was satisfied and quickly begged to be excused, and squared himself by saying, "Come on boys; it's on me!"

—Bloomington (Illinois) Daily Pantagraph, April 1893

THE FOLLOWING YEAR, Bill retains the revered J.W. Evans & Sons of Bloomington to refurbish the restaurant and bar, which includes two new double doors to the casino area, making it more appealing. He has a large chandelier installed, a varnished mahogany bar, and new liquor dispensers in front of a long wall mirror, which has the dual effect of brightening the bar area and making it look twice the size.

As with baseball, when Bill puts his mind to something, he becomes entirely focused. Driven by this visionary spirit, he decides the Bouquet needs a rebranding to propel it to new heights. He convinces Libby and Ruth of the transformative power of his latest endeavor, and in September 1894, "Darnbrough's Café and Casino" is officially launched with as much publicity as possible.

The next two months unfold with a flurry of activity, each evening teaming with customers and the sweet sound of roulette chips being swept into the coffers. It seems that nothing can dampen the mood until one evening, Bill receives a distressing message from his mother. His stepfather, Charles, has been taken ill with bilious fever, leaving him weak with jaundice skin. The local doctor's efforts to provide a remedy prove futile, and Charles's condition rapidly deteriorates. Days pass with somber anticipation until on November 16, 1894, Charles Parke dies at his home on East Mulberry Street.

Bill's concerns for his now twice-widowed mother prove to be short-lived. He is anxious that she is unlikely to find a third husband at fifty-two, but she seems content enough as the old man has left her a good pension to survive on. Within a mere two weeks, she announces that she is moving east to Massachusetts.

Like many other states, Illinois has quickly become a litigious society, and Bill has his fair share of court cases. One such case involves a suit brought against him by Strickle Bros., who contend Bill owes them nearly $50 for framing a picture to be hung in the casino. *The Pantagraph* reports that the *attending circumstances surrounding this case are somewhat peculiar.* It is a painting of considerable size and depicts a three-chimney stack White Star liner crossing the Atlantic. Bill had chosen this painting as it suggests wealth and travel, two things that he and most gamblers desire above all else. The framers had decided to place the artwork face down on the floor in order to attach the hanging wires. Bill had arrived at the door, which was open just enough for one of his dogs to nose it open and bound in, causing considerable damage to the canvas. In his defense, Bill claims that the damage to the painting is in excess of the value of the frame and was caused by the negligence of Strickle Bros. The judge's summation turns into a lecture about the importance of dog leashes and door latches, ultimately ruling that Bill is not liable for the cost of the frame and Strickle Bros. are not responsible for the cost of the painting.

"We'll call it a draw," says Bill across the aisle as they leave the courtroom.

Bill drafts in new employees, including Dan Fitzgerald and George Schmidt, both expert bartenders from Chicago, with John Mittler running the kitchen in the café. In addition to whiskeys and wine, they serve Anheuser-Busch, Faust, and Pilsner beer, and *The Pantagraph* reports that *Schmidt makes the best cocktails in Bloomington.* Jim continues to do an excellent job of ensuring the regular roulette players are well-lubricated. By November 1895, the papers report that Darnbrough's Casino offers a "champagne lunch" with oysters.

"Are you sure that oysters are right for us?" says Libby, whose words strike Bill as more of a statement than a question.

"For sure!" replies Bill. "Any month with an "r" in it is good for oysters!"

"What do you mean?"

"The oyster season. September to April."

"But don't you think that's a bit extravagant?"

"Not at all," replies Bill confidently. "You see, eighty percent of our profits come from twenty percent of our customers, so let's make sure we get the big spenders in here."

Libby does her best to reign him in, but Bill seems determined to create his own little Monte Carlo in Bloomington. In December, he purchases a brand new mahogany upright Briggs piano, telling Libby it's for her. However, he hires a kid from the Wesleyan College of Music to play in the evenings.

IN THE SUMMER OF 1896, newspapers report that gold has been discovered in the Yukon Territory, Canada. As "Klondike Fever" spreads, some of Bill's regular customers announce that their odds of finding gold are better than winning at Bill's tables. Dan and George are always quick to remind them that they have a better chance of getting home alive on the streets of Bloomington than in the lawless frontier towns.

One evening, Jim and Dan have to throw out one of their regulars, Mike McHugh, who has been drinking for far too long and has become quarrelsome with some of the other customers at the bar. As Bill is closing up the casino at around midnight, he sees McHugh belligerently shouting at passers-by on the west side of the square. He recognizes Thomas Middleton, a local policeman arriving to speak with McHugh, although the cop does not anticipate the reaction. McHugh pushes Middleton to the ground, grabs his baton, then starts kicking him in the head. Bill rushes over and, remembering some boxing moves from school, lands enough punches to make McHugh drop the baton and run off down Washington Street.

Sergeant Dunn comes over to see Bill the following day.

"We do not recommend folks take the law into their own hands, of course, Bill, but I thought you should know that we caught McHugh last night thanks to your description."

"Glad to be of service," says Bill. "How's Middleton?"

"He had a few teeth loosened, but he'll survive. I heard the papers have picked up the story already. You wouldn't know anything about that, would you? Thomas Middleton is one of the oldest and best men on the force, and I need my officers to be seen as professional at all times, you see."

"Someone did come round to see me earlier, but I stuck to the facts, Sergeant."

The Pantagraph did run the story on page nine of Friday's edition and credited Bill with saving the policeman's life. This is priceless publicity for Bill, as the casino owners are often seen as the bad guys, so this will go a long way to uplifting his standing in the community.

A few months later, four students from Indiana University arrive intent on playing a roulette system they must have worked out for themselves in their dorm rooms at college. Bill is on his guard whenever strangers arrive as he recalls Hiram's words, "Assume everyone is a crook." There seems to be a leader as he is issuing instructions to his friends before the play commences. They wait until enough space is free at one of the tables and place their stakes seemingly randomly, covering most of the numbers. The croupier that evening is John Thackery, although Bill keeps an eye on proceedings from behind the wheel as he suspects the boys have a plan. None of the three players place bets on the same numbers, an immediate giveaway that they are working together.

There are many reasons that working as a team can increase the outcome in the player's favor, the most obvious being that whoever wins, the takings will be split amongst the group. These students are not wheel watchers as they seem intent on setting to work with great haste. Bill has seen people watching the wheels for hours, looking for biases, although he habitually dismantles and rebuilds both his wheels to prevent this. Bill thinks that perhaps the students are mathematical geniuses who have methodically devised a probability strategy, although their ruse soon becomes evident.

On one spin, John has called for the bets to be placed, and three players cover numbers in each section nearest to where they are standing. The fourth player is closest to John, and at the exact moment the ball drops, he asks him to change a ten-dollar bill.

Momentarily distracted from the layout, John fails to notice one of the other boys moving a small stack of chips onto the number that came up. Bill spots it immediately and calls Dan and Jim, who join him beside the table.

"There is no argument to be had here," Bill says, addressing the group. "We do not tolerate cheats in this place, and my word is final." The boys are looking around like startled deer as more of the customers from the bar arrive to see what's happening. "I saw you moving your chips after the dealer called no more bets, and the ball had dropped," continues Bill defiantly. "You have no defense, but I will not press charges. However, you are not welcome in this establishment ever again, and if you attempt to come back, we will have no hesitation in calling the police." The boys do not put up any argument as they shuffle toward the door as spontaneous applause breaks out.

"Good for you, Bill!" shouts one of the regulars.

Bill had decided long ago that acting swiftly and confidently was the best way to deal with cheats. Arguments often follow disputes, which only cause play to be delayed, which costs the casino money, so in many cases, the house will return the player's original stake and ask them to leave. Any serious trouble could cost him his license.

Bill is only 26, but he has learned a vast amount about the psychology of the gambling community in a few short years. He notices regular players who once had gold pocket watches are now replaced with less ornate cases, and many coats are long overdue for a steam cleaning. The customers do not usually speak with the croupiers, but occasionally, they confide in Bill their innermost secrets as if the casino is a place to confess one's sins.

One such regular visitor, whom Bill has known for at least two years, explains that a large tax bill has arrived, and he is in danger of losing his house. Rather than telling his wife, he wants to win enough playing roulette to pay the bill and be done with it. This is the conundrum faced by all casino owners. Bill has a business to run and should not let personal circumstances interfere with the profit margins, but his heart gets the better of him, and he sends the man on his way, instructing him to talk things through with his wife.

TOWARD THE END OF 1896, a large number of advertisements start to appear in the local press aimed at struggling farm owners—six percent loans with land as collateral. In late November, The Big Four Railway and others start offering round trip "home seekers excursions" to Arizona, Indian Territory, North Carolina, Okla-homa, Texas, and Virginia. Bill also notices an advertisement in *The Pantagraph* for the "True Southern Route," a train with a Pullman sleeper suite that can take you all the way to Los Angeles direct from Bloomington. He cuts out the ad using a letter opener and places it in a file inside his desk drawer.

Hiram's suicide has affected Bill more than he initially realized, and he has become fearful that his own life will become as perpetual as the roulette ball. He has a recurring thought of going around and around, slowly losing momentum until he stops with only a grave-stone in the place of a fret. He worries about speaking with Libby about his restlessness for fear of upsetting her, but this only makes matters worse.

Life has become unfulfilling, and his thoughts drift off to Paris and maybe even Monte Carlo one day. The routine of the café and casino has left him feeling unchallenged after the exhilaration of baseball. While Libby seems content with leisurely strolls in the park with the dogs, Bill's patience wears thin. What has happened to the grandeur of the opera, the pristine white Steinway pianos, and dreams of the enchanting French Riviera? He starts to loathe the customers complaining about their trivial lives. While Bill is well aware that the casino ensures his financial stability, as his enthusiasm diminishes, so do the casino's finances.

In December 1896, J.W. Evans & Sons issue a writ to foreclose a lien against the café as the latest fixtures used for additional remod-eling have only partially been paid. Libby insists on seeing the account ledger and is horrified to discover Bill has spent a fortune on salaries, furniture, and alcohol—including champagne imported from France. Even the casino is losing money as most of the regular customers have disappeared.

Bill has no defense. "I'm sorry, Libby," his voice barely a whisper like a child who has been caught stealing, "I thought—"

"That's the problem," she cuts him off. "You didn't think. To you, this was all just one big gamble. My father built this place up from nothing, but to you, it was all a game."

"I know. I did exactly what he told me *not* to do. The regular guys were the bread and butter of this place as I thought if I did the place up like a palace, then royalty would come."

"William Darnbrough," Libby spits, "in what world would royalty come to Bloomington? You are a fool and a disgrace."

The end of Darnbrough's Café and Casino comes quickly. The wholesalers, Oberkoetter & Co., join J.W. Evans & Sons in a rush to make it to the top of the list of creditors. Ike Hirsch, who owns the liquor store at 109 South Center Street, petitions the court stating that he will pay the creditors and purchase Darnbrough's property at a fair market value.

William N. Darnbrough's chop house and buffet on the west side of the square was closed this afternoon. Trade has been slack this past few weeks and this is given as the cause of the trouble. Mr. Darnbrough expects to embark on other business. He is the well-known baseball pitcher of former years.
—The Daily Leader, Bloomington, Illinois, Jan 29, 1897.

Despite this enormous setback, Bill is starting to think bigger than Bloomington again. He can't stop himself and begins to formulate a plan. There is no doubt that he is feeling like a gambler now—full of unrealistic optimism. When he tells Libby he is thinking of going to New Orleans or St. Louis to look for a new location for the casino, she asks him to leave, and it appears the casino is not the only thing coming to an end. Bill can see that Libby's newfound stature as a woman of property renders the allure of the casino irrelevant in her eyes, and she wastes no time asserting her independence.

A suit in replevin has been instituted by Mrs. William N. Darnbrough to gain possession of those fine-bred dogs. A few weeks ago when Mr. Darnbrough's chop house was shut up by a constable on an attachment writ, among the property seized were the three dogs. Mrs. Darnbrough claimed them as her own property and began suit to gain possession of them. The case has been set for trial in a justice court today, but it has been postponed for a week. These dogs are among the finest in Bloomington.

—The Daily Leader, Bloomington, Illinois, Feb 9, 1897.

CHAPTER 23

*B*ill lies in his bed and stares up at yet another ceiling marred by stains. The clattering of the hot water pipes in the little room above The Gem Saloon serves as a perpetual reminder of this chronic state of affairs. Bill feels sorry for Libby and Ruth, although with their properties, at least they will have financial security. He grapples with a sense of shame but takes solace in the fact that he has a small amount of money saved from his time at the casino and his stint in Rochester, along with two respectable suits.

Finding resolve, he repeats to himself, "The adventure must continue," and this phrase becomes his new mantra, a reminder that life is a constantly unfolding journey, and he must embrace it with courage. There is no time for self-pity and dwelling on the mistakes of the casino, as that will only hinder his progress.

One thing is certain: if his new venture is to have any chance at success, he will need a business partner. Bill's idea could be dangerous, but his optimism eclipses the risks.

He has sent telegrams and called acquaintances old and new, including his friend, Art Twineham, in St. Louis, where he has been playing for the Browns. He receives no reply from Art but hears from someone else that he has immigrated to China, undoubtedly experiencing something similar to the wanderlust they talked about all those years ago in Denver.

Finally, Bill receives a return telephone message from Walt Adams, one of his regulars from the café.

"This is an adventure with two objectives," Bill begins as they sit on either side of a small table at the Gem saloon. "First, we have an opportunity to become very rich, and secondly, we can have a great deal of fun along the way."

"What do you mean?"

Protection will be a prerequisite, and Walt is over six feet tall, with a dark, full mustache that reminds Bill of the lawmen from out west. His suit has seen better days, but, on the upside, Walt was a useful boxer a few years back, and above all, Bill has never seen him lose his temper.

"I'll explain. If we play it right, Walt, this could be the highlight of a lifetime."

Walt takes a large gulp of his beer.

"The plan is to go to St. Louis and buy a roulette wheel. Then, we offer our services to saloons on the edge of town that run card games already. Set up our wheel and split the proceeds with the house. We then take our profits and play our own game on the roulette tables in the center of town, at the legitimate casinos."

Walt has both hands on the table in front of him and does not reach for his beer this time. He has the look of a child looking at an arithmetic problem on the teacher's board without any idea what it means.

Bill leans closer to Walt across the table.

"Imagine you own a bar somewhere in a run-down part of town, and you have some regulars but no passing trade. Business is just ticking over, and you're always worried about how you can afford to pay for the next delivery." Walt stares at Bill, not touching his glass. "This is the life of a saloon owner," Bill continues. "Mundane is an understatement. One day, two smartly dressed gentlemen present you with an opportunity with no strings attached. They suggest spicing up the place with a little roulette action and cutting you in on the proceeds. You are not required to invest in this venture and have nothing to lose."

"Sure," says Walt, "but don't you need a special license or something to run a back-room casino?"

"Yes, replies Bill. "That's why we target saloons that already have cards or dice, or both. If anyone questions us, we can claim that we assumed that the proprietor had the required license."

"And then?" asks Walt.

"Then we take the winnings and hit the high-roller casinos. We don't need to try and double our money or anything because that's how you lose. What we can do is make ourselves a tidy sum at each place as long as we keep moving." Bill smiles and sips his beer while he lets the idea sink in.

"Why do we keep moving?"

"Good question, Walt," says Bill, looking around the saloon and lowering his voice. "We don't want to attract any attention you see, and also, we may be carrying large amounts of cash."

Once again, Bill finds himself traveling with one single bag. He has his trusty switchblade for shaving and other personal items, but there are no baseballs or boots this time, only a spare suit. He is a gentleman traveler, looking like any other businessman on the train, and uses the time to explain some basic roulette principles to Walt, who has agreed to a fifteen percent stake, and to the wisdom of beginning in St. Louis, which is a home rule city with strict gun control laws.

"Many people are fooled by probability," he tells Walt as he pulls a coin out of his pocket. "Heads or tails?"

"Heads," says Walt. Bill spins the coin in the air, catches it in his right palm, and flips it over onto the top of his left hand. A robed Lady Liberty, wielding her shield and holding an olive branch, sits on his hand facing them.

"Tails. Again, heads or tails?"

"Heads." Once more, the quarter lies liberty side up.

"Again," says Bill.

"Heads," says Walt.

"Tails." Bill places the coin on the table and says, "You're probably thinking that if this coin lands on tails every time, then there must be a trick, say a hidden piece of thread or a magnet, or perhaps it's a double-sided coin, right?" Walt nods impatiently, no doubt hoping that Bill will carry on flipping until he wins.

"If I flipped this coin 21 times, the probability of it coming up tails every single time is something over two million to one. I'm not going to get all philosophical about this, but the reality is that there are no tricks, and this is a perfectly normal coin. But here's the important part. Whatever happened a second ago counts for nothing every time I spin it over. The chances of it landing on heads or tails are back to 50/50. People make this mistake with roulette every single day. For example, if they see the ball land on black on several successive turns, they assume that this must be the moment that it switches to the other color. I've seen folks with notepads writing down every single number for hours, and it makes no difference. Are you following this?"

"Yep," says Walt, "It's different in cards, of course, as the cards get used up, but on the wheel, the numbers are always there."

"Exactly!" says Bill. "This is important to know because I don't want you putting everything on red just because black has come up in the last nine spins." They get up and go to the dining car, and Bill is relieved that Walt seems to be smart as well as tough. This should be a good partnership if Bill can segment his life and emotions.

The Southern Hotel is located at the corner of 4th and Walnut Street in downtown St. Louis, and Bill and Walt check into their separate rooms. This is Bill's first time seeing such a dynamic and exciting city, and his impatience to explore gets the better of him. He knocks on Walt's door.

"I'm thinking we should stretch our legs after the journey. You coming?"

St. Louis in 1897 is the fourth largest city in the USA behind New York, Philadelphia, and Chicago. The roads are busy with people dodging street trollies and carriages, and they stop at the corner of Chestnut Street as the Wainwright Building comes into view. It is the tallest building either of them has ever seen, built out of terracotta bricks and ten stories high.

The springtime fashion in this city is how Bill had imagined Paris as the women wear brightly colored dresses with large floral hats, and many younger men now wear straw boaters. The streets are loud with trolly bells sounding off their right of way, although it is quieter down by the banks of the Mississippi, which they reach in less than ten minutes.

"See that," says Bill, pointing at a vast side-wheeler riverboat, "We are never, ever, going on one of those."

"Why not?" asks Walt.

Bill needs to preempt Walt's desire to see the riverboats because he cannot afford to lose what little money he has in reserve. The roulette wheel will be expensive, and he needs to cover their table bankroll.

"Plenty of gambling on those beauties, but there's no chance I would mix with poodles and circus clowns. These riverboats have become an embarrassment to any self-respecting gambler, more like a series of fairground attractions."

Walt looks longingly at the riverboat. "Are you sure we shouldn't get on board? You know, for research purposes?"

"Not a chance, my friend. We have work to do. Speaking of which, let's head back to the hotel and aim for an early start. Busy morning tomorrow, shopping."

"Shopping?"

"Yes, Sir. We're buying our props."

CHAPTER 24

"*I* thought this was a game of chance," says Walt to Bill as they inspect the wheel.

"That it is," says Bill as he spins a ball around the rim, "but the odds favor the house." They are looking at a George Mason roulette wheel for sale at Sullivan's Sports Emporium on Locust Street. It supplies the riverboats and saloons with a wide variety of goods ranging from decks of playing cards to faro tables.

"Aside from our wits, the wheel is our most important asset, Walt," says Bill as he looks over the merchandise. "If there are any imperfections whatsoever, somebody will exploit them, and we cannot afford to take any chances." Bill takes out his pocket tape measure and notes a height of eleven inches and twenty-five inches in diameter. There is ornamental foliage on the outside, accentuated with gold leaf, and the inscription on the turret reads, "The Geo. Mason Co. Makers, Denver, Colo." There are eight diamond canoes on the ball track, and it is a magnificent looking wheel.

"Wait a moment," says Bill, looking up at the store owner who has joined them. He points at the wheel. "There is only one zero."

"Ah yes," says Sullivan, "This is probably going to be shipped to Europe." Bill eyes him with suspicion as he moves to the next table.

Sullivan follows. "This is a free-spinning B.C. Willis. Satinwood and rosewood, hand-painted with gilt detailing over a maroon background. See this," he points, "that's a nickeled stand with a nickeled rim, guaranteed to last for decades."

"How much?"

"For $225, I'll throw in a felt numbers layout."

"All right, we'll come back to that in a moment," says Bill, pulling out his notepad from his jacket pocket. "I have a list here of supplies, and if you can procure these additional items, I think you will find you'll get a healthy profit." Sullivan smiles as Bill starts reading off his notes.

"I need chips," begins Bill. "About two thousand should do it, something with a unique motif, also, a table limits sign, four ivory balls, a rake, a table cover, and a stopwatch." Sullivan does not hesitate for a moment.

"Come and take a look at this, gentlemen." He unlocks a cabinet and places a wooden case on the countertop. He carefully opens the lid with a tiny key and says, "This is an oak chip case with brass handles and three drawers containing eighteen hundred chips in white, pink, yellow, and green. The denominations are fifty cents, $1, $5, $10, $20, $50, $100, and twenty-six $500 chips. They are mother of pearl, and the motif you see here on the backside is a trident."

"A trident?" says Walt.

"Yes, that'll do nicely," says Bill.

"I don't have any stopwatches at the moment," says Sullivan, "but I can get you a rake and a table-limits-sign frame with a stand by tomorrow."

"Excellent," says Bill, "don't worry about the rake; we'll use our hands, but we'll be back for the sign. How much for everything?"

Some haggling ensues, but Bill has noticed that the shop also sells "te-to-tum" loaded dice, so it is clear that some friendly bartering is allowed. Walt's imposing frame comes in useful before they have even started, as Sullivan backs down when he takes one step closer at the point of a dispute. They have just acquired the only necessary inventory to start his new business for less than a Kansas cattleman pays for two miles of new heavy wire fencing.

Bill has arranged to meet with Bill Gleason, the St. Louis Browns' shortstop, at Compton's saloon in the Gate District.

"I'm guessing this has nothing to do with baseball," Gleason says, "so it must be important."

Bill explains the purpose of their visit to his town and asks for advice on the most suitable gambling joints to look out for. Gleason, born and bred in St. Louis, has no problems explaining and highlighting the lesser-known activities in his town that the riverboat visitors rarely get to see. It becomes clear that St. Louis, like many other cities, has passed laws against gambling that have been repealed, circumnavigated, ignored, or the presiding bodies have been bribed. Gleason says that many of the saloons in St. Louis are German owned, partly because the Germans had stayed loyal to the Union during the Civil War, and there is also a definite French influence. "The city is named after a French King, after all," Gleason points out.

Bill makes notes of the recommended saloons. The plan is becoming a reality. They return to the Southern Hotel, and Bill sets up the new wheel on the breakfast table in his room. They push the writing desk in front of it and roll out the green felt numbers grid. Bill explains to Walt the disadvantages of betting with only a small amount of chips.

"Volume is the only way to beat this," says Bill. "You will need to memorize the odds, but otherwise, it's common sense."

"Easy for you to say. You've been at this for years," says Walt.

"Maybe," says Bill, "but you've been playing cards against people for years, and with this, you are not playing against other people, and you are the bank. Don't worry, I'll always be there with you, looking out for cheats." Bill rotates the zero pocket to the top of the wheel and shows Walt how all the even numbers from two to 18 and all the odd numbers from 19 to 35 are located to the left of the zero pocket.

"If you place bets on all even numbers from two to 18 and on all odd numbers from 19 to 30, you will have covered the left side of the wheel."

"Ah. So, all the even numbers from 20 to 36 and the odd numbers from one to 17 are on the right of the zero?"

"Exactly! You've just covered the other side. Also, use numbers 2, 19, 8, 15, 34, and 28 as reference points for the dozens."

This is a critical moment, as Bill has just explained why so many roulette players fail. Many people play the layout instead of playing the wheel. The ball doesn't drop on the layout.

Walt has a natural ability with numbers and, as they role play, taking turns as croupier and player, he soon has a good grasp of counting winnings. However, Bill reminds him to always check before handing over substantial amounts.

"Anything over $20," says Bill, "and you turn to me and say the amount out loud." He's feeling jittery, and he doesn't know if it's from nerves or the excitement that all of his plans are actually taking shape.

That evening, Bill and Walt visit three saloons Gleason recommended along Chouteau Avenue near the railway tracks. Bill's experiences traveling with baseball teams have shown him that the bars near the railway tracks are usually unlikely to be visited by the more affluent citizens of the town, and these are no exception. One place has poker and faro games running every night, "just fine, thank you," and has no interest in roulette. The second has no enthusiasm to run any gambling at all.

"Third time, lucky," says Walt as they arrive at the corner of Jefferson Avenue. Harry's saloon is located on the same block as O.K. Harry's Steel Company, making it a convenient stop for shift workers. Harry himself is actually called Hans, and he resists the idea at first, although Bill finally convinces him that he has nothing to lose and much to gain. Hans will not need to buy a roulette table, will not have to train or pay any croupiers, and will receive twenty-five percent of the profits every night at precisely eleven o'clock. Bill tells Hans he doesn't have to worry about using his safe, and they will take care of the payouts with enough cash in reserve to cover the value of chips in circulation. They agree to run the game for six days starting next Monday and then re-visit the arrangement.

"This is it," says Bill, turning to Walt with a broad smile. "We're nearly there."

Walt wants to visit the Turkish baths at the Lindell Hotel on 6th and Washington the following afternoon to celebrate but shows his disappointment when Bill reminds him that they haven't got anything to celebrate just yet. Despite this, he does treat them both to a well-deserved haircut at William Roberson's barbershop in the hotel's basement. The uncertainty of the outside world temporarily fades away in the tranquility of the barbershop and seems to provide a respite from Walt's frustrations.

"Ready for the big time?" says Bill.

"Ready as I'll ever be," says Walt, checking his tie is straight in the mirror. "Haircuts were a good idea—I feel younger—probably more handsome too. I think we should see the riverboats."

"I'm not going to argue with you, Walt. We need to make some money before we start spending it. Let's do what we came here to do, and we can have some fun later."

They set off from the Southern Hotel and visit three private gambling clubs that operate in St. Louis. At each club, Bill tells the man at the reception that they are considering becoming members, and in return, they are given a brief tour. Bill is convinced that this is the best strategy, and as they enter the Hyde Park Club, it appears that he is right. This private club is impossible to get into without an introduction from an existing member, but luckily, they make an exception for Bill and Walt when they explain they are only inter-ested in roulette.

They hear the subtle clink of glasses and gambling chips as they enter one of the larger rooms. Palm trees are in large urns, and ceiling fans give the place a feeling of freshness, with smoking only permitted in the cigar room. It is a world apart from the saloons and bars up the hill, with a business-like atmosphere and a hint of Riviera as colorful French landscape paintings adorn the walls.

Bill mentally notes the minimum and maximum permitted bets

on one of the four roulette tables and nods his approval to Walt. The club explains that temporary "visitor's membership" is available, and they agree to return within a few days. It's not Monte Carlo, thinks Bill, but it's a step in the right direction.

CHAPTER 25

*M*onday at Harry's proves to be busier than expected, which may be because it is the end of the month and many of the local workers have just been paid. Bill and Walt arrive early to set up and test their wheel. They use an Akron spirit level to verify the table is perfectly flat and spin the wheel 60 times to check for accuracy. It comes up black 28 times, red 26 times, and green zero or double zero six times.

"Perfect," says Bill, and they stack up the chips next to the wheel.

Two card games are in progress by five o'clock, and plenty of people are drinking at the bar, but no one has ventured to the roulette table aside from one person who had a quick look and thought better of it. Finally, at around half past six, one of Harry's customers approaches Bill and requests clarification on the table limits.

"Welcome," says Bill. "Here's the sign," pointing to his little plaque, which rests on a small stand at the side of the table. "One dollar minimum on outside bets and a half dollar on the numbers."

"So, I have to put two chips on this?" he asks, pointing to the middle thirteen to twenty-four dozen.

"Exactly," says Bill, "and the payout on the dozens is two to one, which means you keep your original stake and double it."

"Thank you," says the man and walks off back to the bar.

Eventually, it dawns on Bill that everyone is afraid of being the only player at the table, and some may be skeptical about the game's authenticity. The only way to get punters to commit is to have the table in use, and he remembers Hiram's trick of using dummy gamblers. He should recruit "fake gamblers" whose job would be to play as normal to demonstrate how easy it is to win. After all, he learned roulette by watching others. In the meantime, he suggests to Walt that he pretend to be a player, if only to get the wheel spinning.

"You can't actually keep your winnings," he whispers as Walt takes up a position at the middle of the table.

His plan works, as after Walt has been playing for around ten minutes, a few folks begin to gather around the table and eventually join in, albeit with only small amounts. Soon enough, Bill is in the rhythm once again, and he feels a surge of adrenaline as every two minutes or so, he calls out, "Place your bets." As it is early days for roulette at Harry's, Bill makes a point of calling out the winning number and corresponding winning chips, such as "double street six numbers," and then counting out the chips and announcing the amount loudly: "Twenty-two dollars to you, sir!"

At the end of the evening, they carefully drape the dust cover over the wheel. Hans is impressed with the setup and gladly accepts his cut.

"I took you two for a couple of losers when nobody took the bait," says Hans. "But the fake player was a good move, and I guess folks just need a couple of drinks inside them to get stupid with their money."

Walt is about to say something when he sees Bill's impassive look and decides to keep quiet. They are both thinking the same thing. It can't be this easy.

After reasoning that he has planned every last detail, Bill realizes one crucial element he has not thought through. What to do with their winnings and the $2,000 cash, which covers the value of all the chips? Does he trust Hans to look after their cut in the safe at Harry's, or do they risk leaving the place with cash? What is to prevent a couple of drunken opportunists waiting for them to leave and mugging them? Will they need extra security, or will that make them more of an obvious target in this part of town? He decides the best course of action.

"I'm not convinced," Bill says in a hushed tone, "that we should trust Hans with our winnings and take care of the table overnight, so let's keep our cut and take our chances. If we get held up, we'll say we don't have any cash on us as it's in the safe."

"Fine by me," says Walt, "but in my experience, I'm not sure telling robbers that we don't have any cash will do the trick. Let's leave at slightly different times each night to move the odds further in our favor."

"Agreed," says Bill. They exchange all the cash with Hans for as many high-denomination notes as he has and use every pocket and sock available to spread the money around. As they step out onto the street, Bill looks swiftly behind him at an imagined movement in the shadow of the ally. Nothing will be left if they lose this money, and Bill hasn't felt this anxious since his first pitch at the Bloomington Reds tryouts.

Despite the cold willing them to walk faster, they try not to attract attention and cautiously return to Walnut Street and the sanctuary of the Southern Hotel.

In the morning, Bill feels like a man who's run the gauntlet and lived to tell the tale as he goes downstairs for breakfast and picks up a copy of the *St. Louis Globe-Democrat*. He barely notices the headline stating that William McKinley has won the election and will succeed Grover Cleveland as the new President.

The following two nights at Harry's are a great success as word of the new roulette table spreads around the nearby steel company and the neighborhood. Most of the players are chancers with little idea of how to play the game, and the house winnings are steady. Inevitably, anyone who wins a large payout carries on playing and eventually gives it all back to the table.

The third night, however, finds them treading on thin ice. One player thinks that the way to break the roulette code is to bet solely on the middle dozen numbers. He stacks a considerable amount of chips on 13-24, and unbelievably, black 17 comes up twice in a row followed by red 23. He had three, $5 chips on both numbers, which means his payout is $525 each time.

The sheer audacity and unlikely fortunes of these consecutive wins sends ripples of excitement around the saloon, and soon enough, most of the patrons at Harry's have gathered around the table. Many know each other as they work together at the steel works and are all willing on the player as everyone wants to see the house beaten, and they may all get a free drink out of his winnings. Only Bill knows that another win would clean them out of their cash reserve, and they would be in serious trouble. Curiously, no one else places any bets, and everyone concentrates on the solitary player.

Bill tries his best to hide his anxiety and is impressed with Walt's ability to stay calm under pressure. Walt is unaware that this is literally the last of their money, although he does realize that this would wipe out their reserve, close their game for good, and probably destroy their reputation in St. Louis. The player has repeated his bets once more on the middle dozen, and all eyes are on the ball as it completes its laps around the track, then bounces off a canoe and jumps two frets before coming to rest in black 26, just the other side of the line of the player's chips.

As Walt starts to collect the chips on the table, Bill mutters a whispered prayer. Six new players hurriedly produce notes to be changed into chips, and Bill and Walt finish up with more winnings in the next hour than the entire proceeding three days. They are in the clear for now, but the events of this evening have proved that their adventure could so easily be brought to an abrupt conclusion. However, as Bill's roulette bible had predicted, the scales of fortune will nearly always tip in favor of the house in the end.

Bill and Walt sit in the hotel lounge on Sunday, looking like two long-distance runners at the end of a week of marathons.

"I have an idea," says Bill, "but it's risky."

"What exactly could be riskier than what we are doing?" asks Walt.

"Bear with me," says Bill, "It's just an idea. What if we hired two more guys to run the table at Harry's during the week, and we go and do what we came here to do, namely make a mint at the private clubs? I know this means diluting our takings at Harry's, but it would mean a steady income stream."

"Interesting idea, Bill," says Walt, "but I'm not sure I want to take a chance that we may get ripped off, and there are too many uncertainties."

After considering his argument, Bill agrees.

"You're right," he says, "let's stick to the plan. How do you feel about running the game one more week at Harry's? After all, Hans expects us to show up as usual tomorrow, and he would be pretty upset if we just turned up early and packed up the table. Considering the volume of bets we could put down, it would give us a better shot at Hyde Park."

"Sounds good," says Walt, "one more week, and then we'll be good and ready."

Wearing the plain suits they arrived in, Bill and Walt run their table at Harry's with pure professionalism without any showmanship that could result in mistakes. If there are no players at their table, Walt steps in as a dummy gambler and makes a big show of his winnings, which proves to be an effective system to encourage others to join in. Bill smiles each time this happens and can't help thinking that not only Hiram but perhaps Soapy Smith did teach him something after all.

Each evening, they deliver the cut of the takings to Hans, who takes great pride in telling everyone the roulette table was his idea and continues to take full credit for this new addition to his bar. On Friday, however, Hans's mood changes dramatically when they break the news that they will be moving on.

As they prepare for a quick exit, Hans blocks the door with his arms crossed.

"You should have given me more notice,' says Hans.

"No disrespect meant to you, Hans," says Bill, "but we have to move on."

"You must let me buy the wheel then," he says.

"Now listen here," says Bill, not wanting to waste any more time with polite conversation. "We had a deal and kept up our end of the bargain. We made you a tidy profit, but now it's time to move on, and our wheel is coming with us. The man you want to see is Sullivan on Locust Street, and he'll get you a wheel and everything else you need."

Walt positions himself next to Bill, standing at his full height, looking ready for action, which has the desired effect, and Hans backs down.

As they take the wheel back to the hotel, handling it with the same care they would afford a small child, Bill is once again considering his strategy. In his mind, he imagines gathering a formidable war chest to conquer Monte Carlo—the ultimate goal that drives his ambition. However, he knows that achieving this lofty aspiration will require traversing a long, challenging road. Walt's perspective echoes in his thoughts, reminding him they should also relish the journey. The perilous day last week, when they nearly lost everything, has put Bill in a new frame of mind. They should cherish the present and embrace the excitement and unpredictable twists that define their adventure.

"Walt," says Bill as they reach the entrance to the hotel. "We did well. You did well. We deserve a reward. Not the riverboat, I'm afraid, but definitely the Turkish baths."

"Good plan," says Walt.

"And shopping."

"Shopping?"

"Yes, Sir," says Bill. "We're going to become gentlemen in the morning."

Walt acquires new shoes and a walking cane, and they buy two new shirts each from Bracks on Washington and 8th Street. The last stop of the morning is to see Walter and Alexander Averill at Mills and Averill Tailoring, where they both have new suits measured and fitted within the hour. Bill notices a profound transformation in Walt from resembling a down-on-his-luck card player to a gentleman of means and affluence. He now walks with an air of confidence and is ready for the high rollers' tables.

The visitor's membership cards have proved to be a worthwhile practice for the Hyde Park club, resulting in more winnings for the house from the gambling tables. On their first night, Bill gets straight down to business, and Walt watches on in shock as he appears to stake their entire fortune on the third dozen in a series of coups that sees him winning considerable amounts in a matter of hours.

The sheer volume of chips on the table is enough to draw a sizable crowd, and there are so many chips on the bottom third of the grid that it is impossible to see the numbers in the squares. People gather to see this stranger who, to the untrained eye, would appear to be playing with reckless abandon.

Bill's system is simple and effective. He places a couple of "hedge bets" on red and odd, but he mainly stakes the high numbers, usually 28 to 36, in addition to split and corner bets that allow the maximum limits. He waits until the last possible moment before the croupier calls, "no more bets" before adding more chips, and therefore, there is no time to check the stacks to determine the total value of the stakes.

Even when Bill loses, the dealer has to count out the difference to ascertain the actual loss and the maximum permitted bet on any given number. This results in a considerable delay of play as the croupier counts out Bill's wins and losses. Eventually, the other players become frustrated, and Bill has the table primarily to himself for the remainder of the evening. Unlike the majority of other patrons at Hyde Park, he is not here for entertainment, and having the table to himself means no one is in his way, and he can reach around the grid easily to place his bets.

The onlookers at the table are talking in hushed tones between cries of excitement and astonishment at the sight of this man who never reveals a single emotion. Bill stands at the table, never sits, and only drinks water, small sips at a time to minimize bathroom visits. The most incredible spectacle of the evening is when he declares "change," which means he is cashing in his chips for high denominations to be changed at the cashier.

"But you're on a roll!" exclaims a bystander. Bill looks down at Walt, sitting in a chair near the wheel.

"Exactly," he says with a wink.

CHAPTER 26

*B*ill and Walt are in the lounge downstairs at the Southern Hotel when a stranger approaches them in an expensive-looking gray suit.

"Good morning, gentleman. I thought I recognized you from the club. You should get yourselves to New Orleans," says the man as he sips his coffee.

"Is that a fact?" says Walt. "So, who sent you? The fine gentlemen of the Hyde Park Club?" Bill remains impassive and looks at his pocket watch.

"Nobody sent me," says the man. "As I said, I saw you at the club and thought you may find New Orleans quite profitable. They don't call it the wickedest city in the union for nothing. There are gambling joints all over town, especially up by the Carrollton protection levee, where they run everything from craps, punch cards, Cajun bourré, cock fights, pinball payoffs, and even sports betting."

Bill and Walt exchange looks, perplexed by the stranger's unexpected eagerness to share his knowledge with them. A sense of suspicion lingers in the air, and Bill can't help but agree with Walt's assessment—the Hyde Park club might have sent the man to usher them out of town. The notion is not entirely unwelcome. After all, they have enjoyed a prosperous streak and built up a sizable cash reserve, so leaving while the going is good seems prudent.

Passing through Memphis, Tennessee, overnight, they arrive at Union Station in New Orleans. The famous architect Frank Lloyd Wright had been the draughtsman on this impressive station on South Rampart Street, and Bill is instantly filled with optimism by this first impression of the city's opulence. As the cab turns onto St. Charles Street, the sun is setting, and they are greeted by a colorful string of lights draped along the mezzanine balcony of the St. Charles Hotel. Entering the lobby, they see broad canopied trees in the center under four glass-domed ceilings, giving a welcome feeling of open space after the long train journey.

Bill has read that the city is quite overcrowded during Mardi Gras, but it is not too busy when they arrive to check in. The assistant manager on duty eyes the suspiciously large packing case accompanying them, but Bill uses a trick that he picked up from Gerent Duvalier— a neatly folded dollar bill is a sufficient incentive to prevent any questions.

Bill now has an actionable plan. There is no need to set up their roulette wheel this time as they have enough funds in reserve to head straight to a high-stakes table, which is exactly what they do the next afternoon at Dukes on Royal Street.

Murphy J. Foster, the Louisiana Governor, has recently outlawed the state lottery, which only encourages other forms of gambling. The casinos have agreed to pay a $5,000 tax, making scrutinization less complicated for the authorities. Bill and Walt tour eight casinos in the city until finally settling back on Royal Street.

Bill soon has a favorite roulette table at Duke's and plays steadily each evening for two weeks. He even starts sitting in the same position in the middle of the table. His bets are never extravagant as he tries various strategies including the "zig-zag split" from Bloomington and betting entirely on a single quadrant of the wheel. Slowly but surely, his winnings begin to accumulate, and each night, he sits in his room at the St. Charles, meticulously counting out the dollar bills and transcribing his notes detailing his bets.

Bill and Walt are walking through the hotel lobby one evening when they notice the bellhops have started to whisper behind their hands.

"Looks like they're starting to recognize us," Walt says, and Bill guesses that's right. He's done his best to stay calm no matter what happens while he plays, not to draw attention to himself in any way. But he knows onlookers have started to murmur that he must have a system, and yesterday, a reporter from the *Times-Picayune* had approached him in the casino lobby for an interview. Bill, of course, had quickly shaken his head, because as far as he is concerned, notoriety should be avoided at all costs. The excitement of seeing his name in the newspapers as a boy baseball player seems like a lifetime ago. This boy has evolved into a fully-fledged professional gambler who needs to keep his guard up.

"Then I guess it's time to get out of this town," he tells Walt.

Bill is beginning to feel that the prospect of perpetually journeying from one city to another is like ascending the rungs of a ladder. They sit in Bill's room that night with a large map of the United States stretched over the table, and Bill takes Walt entirely by surprise by pointing his pencil off the table, south of the border.

"Are you serious?" asks Walt. "What do you think your wife would have to say about this idea?"

"Haven't you always thought it would be exciting to go to Mexico?" says Bill, ignoring the question.

"Hadn't crossed my mind, to be honest," replies Walt. "Don't they speak Spanish down there?"

"Their gold is just as shiny, and they have eagles on their coins just like ours," says Bill.

"Far be it for me to question your judgment," says Walt, "but don't you think we should have an actual plan?"

"This is the plan, my friend," replies Bill. "Mexico is booming right now with an economy built on steel and beer. The railroad goes straight to Mexico City, and we'll get to see Texas on the way. After Mexico, we can head to California and then Alaska and the Klondike, depending on our situation. What d'ya say, Walt? Ready for an adventure?"

The journey is considerably longer than it appeared on the map. Bill, Walt and their roulette wheel pass through Baton Rouge, Lafayette, and Houston in Texas until finally crossing the border into Mexico at Matamoros. It is a surprise to both of them when they discover that the Mexican trains seem much more well-appointed than their American counterparts, with ornate upholstery and a full-service dining car.

The timing of their arrival into Mexico City does not seem ideal as an American armored cruiser, the USS Maine, unexplainably explodes in the harbor of Havana, Cuba, killing hundreds of American crewmembers.

President McKinley blames Spain and, ultimately, declares a state of war. Fortunately, the well-prepared US Navy manages to sink the Spanish ships at anchor in the Philippines, and within a month, the "Rough Riders" led by Colonel Theodore Roosevelt force the surrender of Santiago, Cuba. Bill and Walt keep a low profile as they remain wary of the repercussions for Americans in Mexico. They have no idea how people will react once they discover who they are.

Bill follows the unfolding of events two days later than they happen, as the *New York Times* takes some time to be delivered to Mexico City. They are staying at the Gillow Hotel on Isabel La Catolica Street in the center of the city, and on the day of the Spanish surrender, to their relief, there is much celebration in the streets as it turns out that the Mexicans have no sympathy for their old colonial masters.

They take the short walk from the hotel to the vast open space of the Plaza de la Constitución and can smell the sulfur from the fireworks as multi-colored rockets explode in the evening sky. Strangers embrace each other, and the mood is as if Mexico has won its own war against Spain, with people running around waving green, white, and red national flags. Bill has the impression that the Mexicans are fiercely proud of their independence, and the atmosphere is euphoric as word of the American victory quickly spreads around the city.

Spain cedes the territories of Guam and Puerto Rico to the

United States, which also annexes the Philippines. It is a defining moment in the history of the United States as there has not been a common enemy since the Civil War, and Bill and Walt breathe a sigh of relief as they have enough uncertainty of their own to deal with in the casinos.

As they near the Sierra Madre Oriental mountains on the train to northern Mexico, they come across a small casino in Monterrey and stay for two nights. There is a single roulette wheel, and Walt starts to look nervous as Bill continues to win. They get on well enough with the locals, but they are far from the familiarity of home, and the rules are different here—if there are any rules. One other player resembles a farmer sowing seeds as he scatters his chips around the layout compared to Bill's precision bets. Eventually, Bill wins on red 32, and it becomes apparent this little saloon does not keep the required reserve to pay out Bill's winnings.

A standoff ensues with the owner and some others shouting at Bill and Walt in Spanish, with them shouting back in English. People often tend to lose their civility when there is money at stake. One of the others acts as a translator and whispers urgently to the owner.

"Dos caballos," says the translator.

"Pardon me?" says Bill.

"Señor Vásquez asks if you would take two handsome horses as payment for the debt."

Walt and Bill exchange looks briefly. This is uncharted territory for them, but it is unnecessary for them to exchange any words— they simply nod in agreement.

"No caballos," says Bill.

The translator and Vásquez have another whispered exchange before Vásquez turns and heads out the rear door into another room. The translator smiles at Bill and Walt and raises his hand to indicate, "wait." Bill fears the worst as he has visions of Señor Vásquez returning with two burly sons and a loaded shotgun, and there is an awkward silence as they have no option but to stand and await the outcome of this standoff.

Within two minutes, which felt like an eternity for Bill, the door opens again, and Vásquez reenters the room. He holds a flat leather case in both hands, which he places carefully on the table between them. As he opens it, they see a red velvet interior containing a perfect set of a dozen silver knives, forks, and spoons. Even though the case is quite heavy and not entirely practical, Walt convinces Bill that this cache will serve as a nice memento of their time in Mexico, and so the utensils travel with them wherever they go from that day onwards.

"If times ever get hard," says Walt, "we can always sell the family silver."

Their journey takes them through Tucson and Phoenix in Arizona and on to Los Angeles, where they check into the Hotel Westminster with its distinctive red and white window canopies at the intersection of 4th and Main Street. At each stop, they have to carry both their bags, the roulette wheel, and the case of flatware, which is becoming tiresome, but Bill wants to hang onto the silver despite Walt urging him to look for a buyer.

"No time to unpack, Walt," says Bill, "I want to see the Pacific Ocean."

They take the electric tram west to Santa Monica and, without even speaking to one another, run across the sand, simultaneously remove their shoes and socks, roll up their trousers, and get the shock of their lives when a swell of seawater washes over their legs. They have quickly discovered that the ocean is not as warm as it looks.

Taking several steps back, Bill looks up at the majestic coastline. "I don't think we need to play roulette in this town," he whispers. "Let's leave it as we found it."

Two hours later, Bill and Walt are reading newspapers in the downstairs lounge at the hotel when Bill turns white.

"He's dead!"

"Who's dead?" says Walt.

"Soapy Smith! Killed in Skagway, Alaska, last week. July 8. Shot by a man named John Reid on the wharf. Wish I could buy that man a drink!"

"I've heard of him, of course," says Walt, "but why are you so happy he's dead?"

"Damn right, I'm happy! I learned how to play roulette at his place in Denver, but he smashed my old boss over the head with a cane. He was a dirty coward." Bill goes back to reading more of the article and Walt looks at him with quiet amusement. It seems his partner is not entirely without emotion after all.

In the morning, they travel north to San Francisco. On the train, as is often the case, a fellow passenger takes it upon himself to impart his wisdom when Bill and Walt tell him this will be their first visit to the city.

"San Francisco has been ruined by drink and gambling," he says, sounding like a preacher on the verge of launching into a Sunday sermon.

Encouraged by this information, they head straight to the place the preacher said to avoid in the northeast of the city—The Barbary Coast, which has become known as the "Paris of America." It is indeed a dangerous and sinful place where there are almost wall-to-wall drinking and opium dens, but more importantly, a bewildering selection of gambling haunts.

This time, they bring out their trusty roulette wheel and ply their trade for six days at a saloon on Pacific Street. They encounter sailors on shore leave, mining speculators, and dozens of people who work in the flourishing entertainment businesses in the area. All their customers are thrill-seekers of one type or another, and all have hard cash, which they seem to feel a desperate compulsion to gamble away as soon as the moon rises over the bay. On the fourth week, Bill and Walt spend two days straight on the punter's side of the wheel at the Moby Dick saloon on Trenton Street and walk away with a staggering $16,000.

The Barnaby Dance Hall is nicknamed the Forty-Nine Dance Hall after the 49ers, who were the original gold prospectors who arrived in 1849. Fifty years later, on November 1, 1899, it is Bill's thirtieth birthday, and he experiences the delights of can-can dancing for the first time. The waitresses are paid to dance with the customers and then direct them to the bar, where they receive an additional commission on drinks, which is an arrangement that often leads to misadventures for those less traveled than Bill and Walt. At one point, Walt makes the mistake of showing a thick bankroll as he pays for a bottle of French Champagne, and the girls swarm like bees to nectar. Bill sits back and surveys the scene. He should feel a sense of accomplishment, and even though he wants to live by Walt's ideals and live in the moment, he cannot quench his ambition to keep climbing the ladder to Monte Carlo.

"I've seen that look a thousand times," says Walt, raising his voice over the music. "You're up to something, aren't you? You have that faraway look like you're scheming or plotting some deviously cunning plan."

"You're not wrong," smiles Bill. "I think we should forget about the Klondike madness and go straight to New York City."

"Not a bad idea," says Walt, "but I think we should go and see some of the mining towns in Nevada on the way. Let's have another look at the map in the morning."

***

"BILL! BILL! WAKE UP!" Walt is knocking hard on Bill's hotel room door.

"What's going on?" says Bill as he opens the door and puts a hand through his hair.

"I've found a way for us to get to the Klondike." Walt seems out of breath, perhaps from running up the stairs. "We can take a steamship from here to Portland, Oregon, and then another to Alaska. Everyone's doing it—I found out from a kid who works at the docks."

"How far is it?" says Bill, sitting at the table by the window.

"Well, according to the kid, once we get to Norton Sound, we will have to get a paddle steamer up the Yukon River to Dawson City, and that bit is quite far. Only about a month. Maybe less if the weather holds."

"Walt," says Bill with a sigh. "You do realize it's November. I respect you, my friend, but this is possibly the worst idea you've had so far. The only people who survive up there are from places like Finland because they're used to the harshest winters in the world. We would probably freeze to death or be gunned down in the street, and nobody would ever find out where we were buried. We can visit some of the mining towns in Nevada, but let's not tempt fate."

"Understood," says Walt, a familiar hint of dejection in his voice.

They are staying on the ninth floor of the Palace Hotel on Market Street, which has a skylight over a garden court in its center filled with palm trees. The elevators are rosewood paneled, and their room has an intercom system should they wish to summon a staff member. As tempted as they are to stay put, the journey must continue, and so Walt puts the intercom system to good use by calling for a bellhop to carry the roulette wheel. The case with the silverware, however, never leaves his sight.

On the train to Nevada, they talk to a couple of travelers in the dining car and hear the news that the famous lawman Wyatt Earp is running a saloon in Nome. He obviously has a good sense of humor as he advertises his place as the "the only second-class saloon in Alaska." Many of the other famous gamblers, like Tex Rickard, William "Swiftwater Bill" Gates, and Louis "Goldie" Golden, play poker, but their decision to bypass Alaska seems justified as, from what they hear, it is a bleak and inhospitable place.

They stop in Reno, where Walt purchases a Model 95 Remington double Derringer with a shoulder holster.

"You realize that toy may only inflict a slight flesh wound on a rabbit?" jokes Bill.

"Maybe, but at least I can keep this toy in my pocket. Your old Colt never sees the light of day, packed away in a case somewhere. Anyway, it's just a deterrent, you know, for show."

The stories have enticed them to head south to explore the new silver mining towns, and from the train window, they catch glimpses of dilapidated mine entrances, their wooden structures fallen into disrepair. Bill ponders the arduous nature of such labor, where countless years are spent toiling away at rocks without even the solace of a comfortable bed at night.

Wearing their original old suits to deter attention, Bill and Walt try to keep a low profile as they head up north to Eureka, a place that has barely changed since the 1860s. A small stagecoach does regular runs the short distance from the train station to the center of town, and they haul the roulette wheel and their other bags up to a room in a small hotel next to the post office. Every second building appears to be a saloon, and they hear the tale of Ricky Grannon, who had broken the faro bank in one of the saloons there and bet $52,000 on one turn of the card. He lost and died of pneumonia shortly after.

The roulette table at Jackson House on Main Street seems like a good diversion, and the place is packed with rowdy gamblers and drinkers. It feels to Bill like a far cry from the relative civilization of San Francisco. A burly barman with a thick beard and calloused hands watches over his patrons from behind the bar, and Bill is sure he keeps a loaded shotgun under the shelf as this place looks like it has seen its fair share of disputes.

"Is this your own wheel, or does it belong to Jackson House?" Bill asks the croupier behind the roulette table. The man looks over at his partner, who is busy counting chips.

"It's ours," he says.

Bill exchanges a look with Walt. These guys are running exactly the same game as them, and a cursory glance at their fine shoes tells Bill they must be doing quite well.

"Change this, please," says Bill, handing over two five-dollar notes.

One of the first rules of Bill's roulette bible is "never chase your bets." If you are on a losing streak, the best thing to do is walk away. Despite everything he has seen in the years running the casino in Bloomington and on the road with Walt, Bill breaks the cardinal rule.

He has it in his mind that the low numbers will come up and continues to place bets on the first dozen, almost completely ignoring the higher numbers. He wants to replicate his very first win and so places chips on and around red five. Again and again, the ball comes to rest on a high number, and it is not long before Bill is in serious trouble. Walt is busy making new friends at the bar and doesn't notice what's happening, confident that his friend has everything under control as usual.

Bill comes up to the bar and takes Walt aside.

"How much do you think the silver is worth?"

"What are you talking about?" asks Walt in a whisper.

"The silver. How much could we get for it? I'm in a hole, and I need to win my money back."

"Bill. That's not the way, and you know it. Anyway, remember where we are. This is Eureka, and it only exists because they mine their own silver here."

"Fair point," says Bill, looking around for inspiration.

"We could have sold the silver in Los Angeles, like I said." Walt looks at an exhausted Bill. "Why not just quit for tonight? Everyone has bad runs occasionally. What is it you like to say? Live to fight another day?"

Will Darnbrough, the young gambler who has just gone through the west, at the heavy expense of roulette wheels along the route. About two months ago, Darnbrough was in Phoenix and made several good-sized winnings during his stay here. Then he went to Los Angeles and operated at various resorts on the coast, before trying the games in the northern mining towns. Before coming to Phoenix, Darnbrough visited the city of Mexico and there, as well as other places in the republic, he cleaned up large sums of money. At Tucson and Nogales, he won a few hundred dollars and then came to this city. Here he cleaned up several good-sized winnings, and in a little visit to Tempe, one afternoon, won about $500, breaking a game at that place.

Two or three of the gamekeepers at that place were aware of Darnbrough's dexterity at roulette and he was barred from some of the games. With Darnbrough was W H Adams a well-known gambler. The two work together and their system is probably the only one that has ever been successful in beating the roulette wheel. Pat Sheedy and hundreds of other experts have spent years in efforts to perfect plans to win from the wheel but Darnbrough is probably the only man in the world who could break the notable bank in Monte Carlo, if he were allowed to play there. It has been stated by writers who are not familiar with roulette that Darnbrough and Adams won by manipulation of the wheel,

but such is not the case. The alleged scheme was for Darnbrough to play and Adams to sit nearby. According to the story Adams's place was on a stool at the side of the wheel. He toyed with a light cane and nonchalantly watched the game as Darnbrough played and played heavily. Swinging the cane loosely, Adams would reach one end of it beneath the table and press against the bottom of the wheel, slowing it sufficiently to allow the ball to drop in some section covered by his partner. A pretty theory, but impossible since there is no opening by which the bottom of the wheel could be touched by the cane.
—*Arizona Republican, March 16, 1901*

Over breakfast, Bill and Walt agree it is time to return to civilization and head east.

They are traveling towards Walt's sister in Pittsburgh, Pennsylvania, in late January 1901 when they hear the news that Queen Victoria has died in England after a reign of sixty-four years. The funeral will take place at Windsor, and her successor is Edward VII. Bill wonders what life must be like in Windsor.

CHAPTER 27

$\mathcal{F}$ollowing a heartfelt conversation with his sister Kate, Walt makes a momentous decision—settling down and embarking on a more stable path is in order. It is clear to Bill that their nomadic and sometimes perilous lifestyle has come to an end. They will part as friends with many tales for the campfire, but Bill now needs to think about his own future. They agree that the roulette wheel should stay in Pittsburgh at Kate's house, and they give her the silverware set as a gesture of thanks for her hospitality.

Despite a fling on the roulette table at Pittsburgh's Duquesne Hotel, Bill is eager to continue his journey and sets off toward upper New York state. He wants to visit the place he has heard so much about—the Gold Dollar casino at 353 Main Street in Buffalo, NY.

The Iroquois Hotel intersects Main, Eagle, and Washington streets in Buffalo. It boasts that it symbolizes modern opulence and luxury that rivals anything else on the east coast. After checking in and a long soak in the bathtub, Bill heads back down to the street.

At the Gold Dollar, they play no-nonsense roulette, and there is no hesitation between spins as Bill loses $500 in minutes. He buys another $500 worth of chips and wins $1000 on twenty-six and thirty-two. After twenty more minutes, he has lost the $1000 but then wins $2300 as the ball jumps from the double zero and lands on black twenty-nine. The croupier calls over the two managers of the casino as he does not have the necessary funds to pay Bill in full. John Dunlap and James W Walsh are the managers of the casino, and they tell Bill that they will pay him $1400 with the remaining balance of $900 to be settled the following afternoon if he accepts an IOU. Bill has broken the bank, but without Walt to back him up, he sees little point hanging around, so he makes his way back to the hotel.

The following afternoon, Bill returns to the Gold Dollar to collect the outstanding debt.

Dunlap greets Bill with his arms folded and his chest puffed out —his attitude changed since yesterday. "You were here four years ago and skinned the game," he says.

Bill smiles. So, they're going to try to get out of paying him. "If you can prove by anyone that I was ever in Buffalo previous to yesterday, I'll give you a thousand dollars, cash."

"My associates in New York City know you. You're a cheat," Dunlap spits as his cronies move closer, surrounding Bill. He can smell the liquor oozing from their pores, the recently smoked cigars, and somehow, he hears his stepfather's long-ago voice: "You know the best way to win a fight?"

With a gesture of surrender, Bill raises his hands in a conciliary manner, diffusing any escalating tension. "All right, boys. No need to get persnickety," he says, acknowledging the setback with grace. To him, it's no different than striking out at the plate when you'd expected to hit a home run. He knows there must be a more sensible way to recoup his losses, so he turns and walks away.

Later that evening, a Buffalo policeman named David Cohen arrives at the hotel's reception with John Dunlap and requests an interview with Bill by sending his card up to his room. Bill comes down and meets Cohen, who wastes no time with pleasantries and confronts him, asking to verify his identity.

"This is my first time in Buffalo," says Bill. "If you want references as to who I am, ask anyone in Bloomington, from the policeman on the beat to the highest officer in the city. I should also add that this is the first time I have been shaken down for my winnings."

After a few minutes, Cohen concedes that this is a case of mistaken identity and tells Dunlap he wants nothing more to do with the matter. He states in his report that he found Darnbrough to be the "perfect gentleman" and concluded that the police department did not wish to pursue him. However, a reporter from the *Buffalo Review* witnessed the exchange in the hotel lobby and took it upon himself to investigate the story further.

Clearly, the Gold Dollar has gone to extreme lengths to avoid paying legitimate winnings by branding Bill as a cheat, although it is unclear why they should involve the police. Bill had six witnesses at the table, so there is no evidence of any wrongdoing on his part. The *Review* is not the only paper to run the story, and headlines begin to emerge, such as "Who Protects Gamblers?" and "Gambling Scandals Affecting Honor of Police Department."

Before long, the "Darnbrough Case" is developing into a scandal as the locals endeavor to create a web of mystery around the story. Bill definitely doesn't want anything to do with the publicity and decides to leave town. He takes the train along the south bank of Lake Erie to Cleveland and then on to Pittsburgh. Walt and Kate Adams are quite surprised to receive a note from Bill that he is back in town, staying in the Duquesne Hotel on Sixth Avenue. Walt calls the hotel, and they set a time to meet for a drink.

"I wish you'd been with me, Walt," says Bill. "I realize now that I may have taken your company for granted, and I am truly sorry for that."

"Well, Bill," responds Walt. "From what I understand, you like to believe you're a loner, but the truth is, you liked being part of the baseball teams, and Bloomington will always be home, if you know what I mean."

"Maybe so. I think the real issue here is, what's the point of experiences if you have no one to share them with? Years ago, somebody told me I would need a fireman's ladder to climb where I wanted to go. The question is, what will I see when I get to the top, and what happens next?"

GENERAL WILLIAM S. BULL, the Superintendent of Police, is placed in charge of the investigation and vows to "crush out all gambling and cause the arrest and punishment of the keepers of gambling houses."

A warrant is issued for Dunlap, who by now has become a fugitive. It turns out that Walsh and Dunlap are not the ultimate owners of the Gold Dollar as Frank Bapst, former chairman of the Democratic County Committee, and William H Kinch of German Rock Asphalt and Cement Company are implicated as the principles.

A request for a statement from Bill is issued, and they eventually track him down at the Duquesne Hotel.

On November 28, 1901, the *Buffalo Review* publishes a statement that Bill has given to the Pittsburg police and not long after, John Dunlap is arrested and sentenced to six months in the penitentiary. The police raid the gambling rooms of the notorious gambling boss, Pat Sheedy, confiscating his roulette and faro tables. As the scandal unfolds, the entire police department is investigated, although a "lack of evidence to secure convictions" is the often-quoted result. At one point, Senator Thomas C. Platt of New York is drafted in to aid the investigation. Ultimately, the "Darnbrough case" results in the closing down of all gambling establishments in Buffalo.

Bill is having dinner with Walt and his sister's family when he makes his announcement.

"Thank you for your hospitality, Kate. And Walt, thank you for being a partner in our incredible adventure, but the time has come."

"Time for what?" asks Walt.

Bill steadies his gaze and, with unwavering determination, reveals his decision.

"I am heading to New York City, and I'm going to go on my own." His words ring with a conviction that leaves no room for doubt or hesitation.

CHAPTER 28

"*I*s this seat taken?"

Bill is instantly on his guard—everyone in New York has an angle.

The man who stands in front of him is well-dressed, with a cravat in place of a tie, and he speaks with a surprisingly soft voice, considering his large frame. Bill sits alone at a table at Number 8, Barclay Street in Manhattan. This is one of the many illegal casinos in New York that does not have a name, just an address. The air is thick with smoke, and the ashtrays overflow with cigarette butts and cigar ends. This is a serious place for serious gamblers with no form of entertainment to be found—aside from gambling. Faro, poker, and roulette reside here, and the patrons conduct their business with no interest in distractions.

Bill raises his glass of beer in acknowledgment and looks up at the man, then around the room. There are only a few vacant chairs at the tables away from the roulette and card games, so it seems legitimate that the stranger would ask for a seat.

"Be my guest," says Bill, gesturing to the spare chair.

There is a silence between them for some time until the man speaks again.

"Have you been to West Twenty-Sixth?" he asks in barely a whisper.

"I have not had the pleasure," Bill replies, glancing at the man briefly. He is still relatively new to New York and finds it an intimidating city full of strange customs, so he must be vigilant.

"You look like what I would call a gentlemen gambler," the man continues. "Forgive me, but I was watching you. Watching you, watching the wheel, so to speak. You're not like the others in here who drink and gamble to the point of no return. I would say that your play is measured and calm."

"I see," says Bill, with a self-conscious glance down at his shoes as if something must have given him away as an out-of-towner. All his experiences since the pickpocket in Denver flow through his mind as he tries to figure out this guy's hustle.

The man has sensed his caution and gives a reassuring smile. Bill thinks that even snakes can look like they're sometimes smiling. The man extends his hand.

"My name's Altschul, Joel Altschul."

Bill looks at him and retains eye contact as he shakes his hand. "Bill Darnbrough."

"Pleasure to know you, sir," says Altschul. "I'm what you may call a scout, and I'm looking for gentlemen gamblers to invite to an exclusive private club. You see, I work for a man named Richard Canfield."

There is a loud crash as a glass explodes on the ground not far away from them, and at the same time, a man shouts, "Give me my damn money back!" The glass splinters across the wooden floor, and a large shard lands beside Bill's shoe. Bill and Altschul hardly flinch as the man is manhandled out of the front door by two muscle-bound suits. The entire episode lasts less than thirty seconds.

"You see what I mean," says Altschul. "This kind of joint is not for you. Why don't you drop by tomorrow? Number 23, West 26th Street. You'll be in good company—Reggie Vanderbilt and Bill "Bet-a-Million" Gates play up there. Tell them I sent you and go up to the second floor."

Bill's room at the Martinique Hotel has its own bath and a view of the open courtyard. Three dollars a day would get him a view of Broadway, but why pay 50 cents extra just for more noise? He is not an early riser, but it seems the rest of New York's 3.4 million people like to get things going as quickly as possible. The new motor cars sound their claxon-like horns constantly, and the only remaining quiet street is 5th Avenue, which does not permit cars, only horse-drawn carriages with uniformed drivers and footmen.

Bill lies in bed, trying to work out his strategy. Altschul is prob-ably right—to amass the necessary resources to get to Europe, he needs to be at the tables with Gates and Vanderbilt. If the Atlantic Ocean is the challenge, then New York is his springboard, and he needs to be in the thick of it instead of feeling like a spectator on the sidelines. He has started to overthink everything instead of keeping it simple—he needs to get out of the hotel and get some air.

Without a doubt, he would jump at the chance to drive around in one of those shiny new automobiles, but for now, Bill is a pedes-trian. A short walk from Bloomingdales on 59th and Lexington, he comes across a street market.

"Fresh apples, come and get your fresh apples," calls the boy as he juggles four bright green Medinas next to his cart. Mulberry Street is closed to all traffic, and as Bill moves slowly through the market, he sees women with blankets over their heads and shoulders —one carries a baby in one arm while counting out pennies with her other hand as she stands by the fish stall. It is September 1901, and the immigration station at Ellis Island sees an average of 1,900 new arrivals daily. The eclectic mixture of languages reminds Bill of Globeville in Denver. Small groups of people huddle together, speaking Yiddish, Russian, and German, and he also hears a lot of Irish accents as he takes in all the sounds. It doesn't feel like a single city here, but almost as if a group of countries have huddled together and erased their borders.

His little black notebook is crammed full of casino addresses, but many are crossed out as they have closed down or moved locations. Tonight, he visits Number 12, Ann Street, opposite St. Paul's Chapel at the south end of Broadway. The house's interior is dark compared to the well-lit street, and Bill thinks this must be what seances are like as everyone plays with noticeable anxiety. It seems to Bill that aside from the prospect of losing their money, people are also afraid of being arrested for gambling in an illegal establishment. Bill plays it safe on the roulette table with high numbers and hedge bets on the first dozen. Even though all the local police have been paid off, at any moment, he expects someone to yell, "Cops!" He can't help but think that these precarious days should be behind him, and he needs to find somewhere less foreboding.

BROOKLYN BRIDGE HAS THICK WROUGHT iron struts like lattice frames which means Bill can only catch glimpses of the East River as he takes the train from Lower Manhattan. The last stop on the line is Coney Island, where he has heard the lowest form of gambling takes place. "Every ride is a nickel" is a recent slogan, and Sea Lion Park is billed as a destination for working families. The most fascinating ride Bill sees that day is the "Human Roulette Wheel." About twenty people sit in the middle of a vast domed wheel that spins horizontally, picking up speed so that they drop off to the sides, unlike a roulette ball that drops into the middle. They look like they are having a lot more fun than if they were playing the actual game, as all they have lost is five cents.

As the light begins to fade, the shouting and laughter become frantic whispers and an eerie quiet descends in the park as if the wind had died during a yacht race. One by one, the rides and the music stop, and Bill hears a boy in a flat cap shouting, "The President's been shot!"

President William McKinley dies eight days later after being shot at the Pan-American Exposition in Buffalo by Leon Czolgosz, an anarchist who had concealed a .32 revolver under a handkerchief. Like most Americans, Bill is deeply troubled by the assassination, which reminds him how fleeting life can be. As Theodore Roosevelt takes office, Bill sees this as one more reason to hasten his departure to Monte Carlo—and certainly to never set foot in Buffalo again.

"WHAT DID you say his name was?"

Richard Canfield stands next to his trusted scout, Joel Altschul, at Number 23, West 26th Street, and they are watching Bill as he acquires another mountain of chips at the roulette table.

"Bill Deebra," answers Altschul.

"You mean Bill Darnbrough," says Canfield gruffly.

"You know him?"

"Sure do. He's the man who cleaned out Buffalo. Watch him. And find out where he's staying."

Monte Carlo to have a rival. With the cheerful assistance of the legislature of the state of New York, the village of Saratoga is set to become the Monte Carlo of America.
—Wilkes-Barre, Pennsylvania, February 26, 1902

Bill is oblivious to Canfield's interest until he receives an open invitation to the Saratoga Clubhouse. Altschul must have discovered where he was staying, although Bill guesses there is little that that man could not find out in New York.

Weighing up his options, Bill decides that bouncing between illegal casinos in New York is not getting him close to his goal. He needs to build a war chest for Monte Carlo. Arriving there without a substantial amount of currency is not an option, as he needs to be able to stay in the game for the duration. Unlike the regular visitors to the casino in Monte Carlo, Bill cannot simply go home or get a job to replenish his funds. He tells no one of his plans and, once more, boards a train with only a single bag.

Bill's timing turns out to be ideal as Canfield's New York club-house at 5 East 44th Street in Manhattan is raided, and even though he was not arrested, Canfield flees to England for four months.

Saratoga Springs is the perfect location for Bill's mission. He is two hundred miles north of New York City with few distractions, and hardly anyone knows who he is here. The casino's facade is a bland-looking three-story brick building, although the interior is the height of opulence. The entrance opens onto a central hall with a magnificent staircase, and the main gambling room is framed with statuettes and mirrors. The dining room is brand new with paintings of horses and stained-glass windows, although after some time, Bill hardly notices his surroundings, and people barely notice him sitting alone scribbling in his notebook.

He becomes a regular fixture at the roulette tables but never attempts risky bets, content to patiently watch the ball running circuits and collect modest profits. Baseball, Bloomington, and Libby are only shadows in the back of his mind as he slowly but surely saves his winnings. He opens an account with the Adirondack Trust Company, which can quickly transfer funds to "any bank in the world" whenever he desires.

At Canfield's casino, the entertainment is nothing short of spectacular, boasting captivating performances from luminaires like Lillian Russell and Florenz Ziegfeld. As the wins continue to come his way, Bill diligently deposits his earnings like clockwork every Monday and Friday, building a sizable reservoir of wealth. The steady flow of riches could easily afford him lavish luxuries—a new motorcar, gold pocket watches, and tailored suits—but he resists the temptations of immediate gratification. Instead, he possesses unwavering patience, biding his time within the confines of Saratoga, remaining focused on the ultimate prize: Monte Carlo. Every time he gazes up at the chandeliers, he wonders if the hotels in Monaco boast such exquisite fixtures—perhaps even more spectacular.

"I CANNOT DECIDE if I want you to continue playing and give me a chance at regaining some of my money or to encourage you to quit while you're ahead." The man offers his hand for Bill to shake. "Richard Canfield. It's a pleasure to make your acquaintance, Mr. Darnbrough."

"Likewise," says Bill, standing up from the table where he has been reading today's copy of the *Daily Saratogan* newspaper. He remains guarded, not easily swayed by appearances or flattery. As he continues to interact with Cranfield, he remains vigilant, using past experiences to discern friend from foe. The man exudes an air of arrogance. With his stocky frame and loud demeanor, Bill instantly distrusts him as it is clear he is only interested in winning his money back.

As Canfield walks away, Bill mutters, "I wouldn't even trust you to walk my dogs."

A NEWSPAPER ARTICLE catches Bill's attention in the summer of 1903. Horatio Nelson Jackson, Sewall K. Crocker, and their bulldog named Bud, arrive in New York in a two-cylinder Winton automobile, having driven from San Francisco in sixty-three days. They are the first people to drive across America. For Bill, the road to discovery leads far beyond the confines of his own nation, and this is the final inspiration he needs. He has enough capital in reserve and pictures himself driving an open-top car along the sunny shores of the French Riviera.

"So THAT's all you require, Sir?"

"Yes, that is all I require," replies Bill.

He is seated across from a studious-looking young man at the New York offices of Thomas Cook. He now has a one-way trans-Atlantic ticket to France on the White Star line with a room booked at the Hotel de Paris, Monaco.

"Oh," says Bill, "there is one more thing. I will need $4000 worth of Cook's Circular Notes."

"Very good, Sir," the agent responds. "These days, we call them traveler's checks."

PART III
THE EUROPEAN GAMBLER

1904-1909

CHAPTER 29

*A*ccording to ancient myth, Hercules passed through Monaco, and the Temple—Hercules Monikos, meaning Single House—was built in his honor, overlooking the Mediterranean Sea. He was followed by the Romans, Goths, Vandals, Danes, Saracens, and the Moors, who all recognized the strategic importance of the highway through the south of France between Spain and Italy. The Grimaldi family, originally from Genoa, has presided over the principality of Monaco, with a few minor interruptions, since 1227. Since that time, visitors have taken it upon themselves to bring their wealth to Monaco, and, in over 2000 years, there has never been a time where the Monegasque have had their goods taken from them.

Bill has traveled onboard the new steamship, RMS Majestic, owned by the British White Star Line, which sails from New York to Southampton and can accommodate 1,490 passengers. He is not a good sailor and frequently feels unwell throughout the voyage, spending most of his time impatiently walking up and down the promenade. Fortunately, he has one of the first-class cabins in the middle of the ship that is less affected by turbulence in the swells, and there is reduced noise from the engines down in steerage. When the ship's horn sounds as they pass a vessel traveling in the opposite direction, it is the loudest sound Bill has ever heard aside from the time he sat next to the church organ in Denver.

A well-stocked reading room provides Bill access to some interesting travel books, and he finds a copy of *Bradshaw's Illustrated Traveler's Hand-book in France*. This publication is incredibly useful for Bill as it details practical information, including maps, train routes, and essential French words and phrases. Most importantly, it gives a breakdown of the French currency, and Bill learns that 100 centimes make one franc, and 20 francs are called a louis. Bill finds it ironic that even though they beheaded their king during the revolution, they still name their silver coins in his name. He jots down notes in his pocketbook and intends to buy his own copy of *Bradshaw's Guide* as soon as possible. He will also need to open a bank account to deposit his traveler's checks and transfer money from Saratoga, but in the meantime, he can change dollars to francs at the main train stations at an "agent de change" office.

When he is on deck, the wind fills Bill's lungs, and seeing the swell of the ship's wake renews his sense of purpose. The feeling of perpetually moving forward over water to a destination is a new experience, and the anticipation is exhilarating.

The ship's final destination is Southampton, and after five days at sea, it berths en route at the port of Cherbourg in northern France. Bill buys his train ticket south, which will take him through Paris, Lyon, and Marseille to Monaco.

The western train station in Paris is the Gare Saint-Lazare, and Bill quickly finds a horse-drawn fiacre to take him to the connecting train at the Gare du Lyon in the south of the city. He has to fight the urge to spend a few days in what the guidebook calls "the most romantic city in the world." The thought of strolling along the banks of the Seine, gazing up at the Eiffel Tower, and savoring the finest French cuisine is painfully enticing. As the fiacre rolls along, the outdoor cafés and the magnificent facades are fascinating, but Bill reminds himself of the grand adventure ahead, and he knows the city will still be here when he returns.

After changing trains in Nice and heading east along the south coast, the view from his window gives a good impression, and Bill can see that Monaco is essentially two bluffs that encircle a small bay. The Mediterranean Sea is a magnificent greenish-blue and appears to change color as the train passes by an amphitheater of brilliantly white terraces, houses, and palaces.

This final leg of the railroad from Nice brings in well over one hundred thousand visitors a year, the majority of whom are English. Many of these pilgrims chose to remain and acquire semi-residency by building their villas in carefully selected spots. One of the undeniable attractions is that direct taxation in Monaco was abolished in 1869, the same year Bill was born.

Monte Carlo itself is one of the three districts within Monaco. It is undoubtedly the main attraction as it is home to the Hotel de Paris, the casino, and the Café de Paris, all facing each other in the Place du Casino. The amount of wealth on display is astounding to Bill, and he can't help but wonder how much money must pour into the casino.

Bill needs his credibility established at the casino from the outset, although it will take some time to acquire the respect of the gaming rooms known as Les Salle de Jeux. Even though they have his reservation and have been expecting his arrival, Bill assumes the confidence of a seasoned European traveler as he checks into the Hotel de Paris. The receptionist hands him a printed card with the hotel name on the front and his name and room number inscribed on the reverse.

His single room does not face the harbor, but the interior design is beautifully ornate, with abundant chintz and velvet. There is ample closet space for the various changes of attire required for gentlemen guests, in addition to a generous selection of balms and grooming products in his bathroom that would be befitting of a visiting French dignitary. Exhausted after the long journey, Bill decides that a short rest would be a sensible idea, although no sooner has he taken off his shoes and collapsed onto his bed than a surge of excitement rushes through him, and he jumps up again. The casino he has dreamt of visiting is only minutes away, and he cannot wait another minute to at least have a look, even if he doesn't place a single bet.

The Salle de Jeux is even more stunning than Bill had ever imagined, with hanging chandeliers that dazzle with thousands of sparkling electric lights. Beyond the atrium, the first room on the left is the gigantic and luxurious Salle Garnier, on whose walls hang magnificent tapestries and paintings. The room is encircled by twelve onyx columns accented with bronze bands, and above him, an enormous glass-domed ceiling features intricate engravings, including the significant date of 1889, marking the completion of this room.

The towering windows provide additional natural light as it is still only late afternoon. As he looks out to the south side, Bill can see the harbor and the yachts that have delivered their owners to this palatial paradise. A gold-plated sign beside the far doors reads *Salons Privés*, which does not escape Bill, as he needs to access the private rooms where the maximum stakes are played. Currently, he has a *commissariat special* card, which he was given when checking into the casino, but this will allow access only to the Salons Ordinaires. There is no doubt in his mind that there are more winners among the privileged members of the private rooms than there have ever been in the public spaces. He decides to buy a winter season Club Privé admission card for 400 FF in the morning. As the current exchange rate in 1904 is five French francs to a US dollar, Bill works this out as $80.

He cannot help feeling intimidated. Everyone is impeccably dressed, and there is a reverence to this place, with hardly any raised voices and not a trace of cigar or cigarette smoke. The environment stands in stark contrast to any of the gambling clubs, saloons, or casinos that Bill has seen. Here, Russian Grand Dukes and Duchesses effortlessly mingle with British Lords and German industrialists, creating an atmosphere of exclusive sophistication.

Two double-sided roulette tables sit majestically in the middle of the Salle Garnier, surrounded by a handful of players, onlookers, and what looks like a small army of officials vigilantly watching players, bets, spectators, and the croupiers. The Chef du Partie sits atop a high chair in the center of the hive, presiding over the proceedings like a tennis umpire. Bill stops beside an imposing marble pillar and stands perfectly still to capture the scene.

There is an order of play regarding Bill's education of his surroundings and plan of attack. He understands the odds, the house edge, and single-zero distinction with European roulette. However, he needs to gauge the atmosphere and note the habits of the croupiers, players, and spectators. He plans to be an observer for as long as he can hold out. There has never been a gambler in history who has managed to stick to his plan, as inevitably, with a game of chance, techniques must be adapted and altered. Nevertheless, preparation is paramount to give himself the greatest opportunity.

"Puis-je vous apporter un rafraichissement, Monsieur?" Bill's thoughts are interrupted by a smartly dressed waiter whose accent differs significantly from the little French he heard in New Orleans.

"Pardon me?" says Bill. "Do you speak English?"

"May I offer you a drink, Monsieur?" Bill is instantly relieved that the waiter speaks English, but he has to think about his answer for a moment.

"Thank you, I'll have a glass of red wine." The waiter bows slightly and scuttles off, as Bill thinks it is better to order a drink standing away from the action to understand the procedure for paying and tipping without embarrassing himself. The waiter may have detected his American accent and decided he was not well educated in French wines, as he would have requested a grape variety rather than simply the color. Bill thinks he needs to get all these details out of the way long before he takes his seat at the table for the first time. Also, perhaps he should learn some French.

From his vantage point, he has a good overview of the comings and goings of the Salle de Jeux. There is a vast amount of space for guests to drink and engage with each other away from the central tables, and this ensures that the players are not overtly distracted and keeps everyone entertained so that they will stay in the casino longer.

As if responding to an unseen signal, a continuous flow of guests pours in from the evening train from Nice. By the time they reach the roulette room, the gentlemen have already removed their hats and coats. Ladies accompany some of the men, and to Bill's pleasant surprise, he notices that many of the women are also enthusiastic gamblers. It feels like a theater stage, with the curtain rising to reveal the scenery and assorted actors. The women appear to be competing to see who can wear the most spectacular jewelry. Bill is amazed at the assortment of necklaces, bracelets, rings, and even tiaras on display.

"Are you a guest at the hotel, Monsieur?" asks the waiter as he returns with his drink.

"Yes, I am."

"Very good, sir. May I see your card?" The waiter produces a chit for him to sign, which answers the question of how one pays for aperitifs at the Salle de Jeux. Bill tips the boy, hoping he will remember him as an upstanding customer. There will come a time when he will be playing for hours without a break, and the servers will need to become his allies. In fact, everyone from the bartenders to the security guards will need to become his trusted adjutants as his battle is with the game itself, not the casino staff. The plan is to become a respected guest to whom the management would never hesitate to grant an unusual request should the need arise.

With this in mind, Bill decides to call on someone he thought could wait until tomorrow, but why not inquire now? He places his wine glass on a side table and makes his way to the cashier's office.

"Good evening," Bill announces through the glass partition. "I am a guest at the hotel, and forgive me, but I have yet to learn French. Do you speak English?"

"Certainly, Monsieur," the cashier replies, "Also Italian, German, and a little Russian. How may I be of assistance?"

"Excellent, thank you," says Bill. He needs to exude an air of confidence, but not to the point of arrogance. He knows courtesy will always trump an attitude of superiority. "May I please speak to the floor manager regarding opening an account?"

"Certainly, Monsieur. May I have your name, and I will fetch Monsieur Laget."

Less than two minutes pass before Bill is greeted by an exceptionally well-groomed and intelligent-looking man who could not be anything but French with his sharp suit and pencil mustache. Coming out of the office, he offers his hand, speaking perfect English with a heavy accent.

"Monsieur Darnbrough, welcome. My name is Pierre Laget, and I am the casino manager. Normally, I do not greet our guests in person upon their first visit to our establishment, but I understand you have traveled all the way from America. Please forgive me for being so blunt, but I feel obliged to point out that we do not usually agree on lines of credit for visitors to Monaco unless you have collateral in the form of fixed assets."

"I see," says Bill, employing a winning smile, "such as one of those fine villas I saw on the way here?"

"Welcome to the Salle de Jeux, Monsieur Darnbrough," says Laget, completely ignoring Bills' remark. "I am pleased we have had this opportunity to become acquainted, and if you would follow me, we can attend to the business of opening your account."

"Thank you, Monsieur Laget," says Bill. "It was a pleasure meeting with you, too, although I should point out that I have no intention of requesting a line of credit. I just wanted to know who was in charge around here."

CHAPTER 30

All the world's troubles seem very distant to Bill as he begins reconnaissance of Monaco. Following a breakfast of fruit and croissants, he ventures on to the Place du Casino to get a better look at the layout of the hotel and casino, which are conveniently situated next to each other. The hotel reception has given him a small leaflet containing a brief history of the buildings and a helpful map. He has definitely picked the best place to stay as it will be comparatively easy to navigate. There are no specific details of the interior of the private gaming rooms which Bill is seeking, although he is confident that he will find his way around after a few days.

According to his pamphlet, the famous Parisian architect, Gobineau de la Bretonnerie, designed both the Hotel de Paris and the casino, which were completed in 1863. This is quite surprising to Bill as he had thought the casino was older. Further reading reveals that the Opera House and theater were only completed eight years ago, and the Trent-et-Quarante gaming room is also a new addition. The details of the Beaux-Art style of design are followed by a description of the interior of the Salle de Garnier and its eight chandeliers, each weighing 330 pounds and made of Bohemian Crystal. This is a clever ploy, thinks Bill, to encourage readers back to the casino to see them just in case they have a temporary lapse of purpose.

Bill checks his pocket watch. It is noon, and his stomach is rumbling. After a short walk, he discovers the Petite Riviera restaurant and is directed to a small table outside. The waiter hovers briefly as Bill looks over at the other tables to see what everyone else is eating and drinking.

"Red wine, please."

When the waiter returns, Bill points with raised eyebrows at the "poulet roti au cresson salad" on the menu.

"Roast chicken et salad," says the waiter gruffly. Bill nods his approval and is already getting the impression that the Monegasque who cater to tourists probably all speak passable English but are not happy about it.

The wine is unlike anything Bill has tasted before—a deep velvet with an unexpected sweetness. As he takes in the scene, he savors this moment, realizing that Monte Carlo was well worth all the hard work to get here.

After lunch, he heads back to his room to freshen up and then to the casino office, where he purchases his Club Privé pass, which will gain him access to the private rooms.

He walks through the Salle Garnier and the Salle Schmit and, passing through the gallery with its magnificent paintings, turns right at the Salle Touzet. He stands still for a moment, craning his neck to admire the glass roof, the stained-glass windows, and the enormous canvases, each spanning over thirty feet, depicting the beauty of different seasons.

The familiar clicks of a roulette player shuffling his stack of chips echo through the room, but apart from that, the silence accentuates the grandeur of his surroundings. There is a reverence to this place that Bill imagines can only be found in Royal palaces.

Any moment now, he anticipates someone saying, "I'm sorry, sir, you don't belong here," but he straightens his shoulders and resolves that he will make it work somehow, no matter what obstacles arise. His confidence is reinforced by the realization that he possesses a significant advantage over most other patrons—he has experienced both sides of the table as both a player and a casino owner.

The main roulette table is the largest Bill has ever seen, with number grids on each side of the wheel, and all of its croupiers and the Chef de Partie are in attendance. Only one player is seated at the table at this time of day; therefore, twenty-three chairs are available. Bill removes one chair that is six places away from the wheel so that he has plenty of room to stand and place his bets. Numerous denominations of stakes are available in the game of roulette in Monte Carlo, ranging from casino plaques, French louis, and francs in coins and notes to gold. Fortunately, this table has adopted colored chips, unique to these particular roulette tables, that can only be used in the Casino de Monte Carlo. This is a 10 FF minimum bet table, and Bill decides to change 5,000 FF into 20 FF chips for his initial reserve and arranges little piles in front of him.

The croupier looks up and nods at Bill as he breaks the near silence.

"Faites vos jeux s'il vous plait, place your bets please," he announces.

The most significant attribute any roulette player can hope for is patience. Bill takes in the atmosphere and the layout of his surroundings and analyzes the style of the spinner. One of the features of the game of roulette is that some distinctions can alter the game's character. He knows full well that any variation in the veracity of the spin causes the ball to revolve for longer, and therefore there are fewer spins per hour. Walt was in the habit of spinning the ball quite forcefully, and even though there is no scientific or mathematical proof that this will determine the outcome, Bill must take note of this and any other eccentricities in the Salle de Jeux.

It does not take him long to see that his playing companion is not a newcomer to the game, although not an expert. He is a large middle-aged man with a thick, graying beard who appears to prefer growling to actual speech. He has a moderately healthy reserve and employs a risky Martingale progression strategy. The French have been using this method since the eighteenth century, and it involves doubling the bet after every loss so that the first win would recover all previous losses plus win a profit equal to the original stake. The man is betting exclusively on black, and the probability of hitting either red or black is 48.6%, as you have to consider the house edge. As Gerent Duvalier had initially pointed out, this is a single zero French table where the house edge is 2.7% compared to 5.26% in America.

One of the first lessons Bill learned from his roulette bible is that this system means that the longer you play, the higher your odds of losing become. The more you aim to win, the more likely you will lose. Over a short period, Bill sees that this player does not have nearly enough in reserve to succeed unless he is very fortunate.

"Good afternoon, Sir." Bill's concentration in watching the other player has meant that he has lost his peripheral vision and, in fact, all perception of anything else happening in the room. He has no idea where the waiter has come from or even how long he has been standing beside him with his tray. This is a far cry from his days as the wheel owner when the reverse was true. "May I offer you some refreshment, perhaps a drink from the bar?"

"Thank you, yes. I'll have a coffee, black." Bill wonders how the waiter knew to speak to him in English, and self-consciously looks down at his shoes again, as if they have given him away as a foreigner.

"Very good, sir," the waiter responds and disappears as quietly as he had appeared. This is Bill's moment to make an impact in the casino, and he needs a clear head, so the wine can wait for now.

He remains standing as he moves all his chips next to the numbers grid and waits for the croupier to set the ball rolling. Then, with incredible speed and agility, using both hands simultaneously, he places chips amounting to approximately 3000 FF on the numbers 28 to 36 with small hedge bets on 5, 11, red, and even. If a low number turns up, he could lose his entire stake, and the croupier will have to spend time counting out the difference as he has exceeded the table limit on a single number. This means his excesses will be returned to him, and the same will happen if he wins.

Bill stands, leaning slightly forward in anticipation with each spin. He is thinking of Dave Rowe in Denver, who always told him to *remember to breathe*. He tries hard to stay calm and does not even slightly flinch whether he wins or loses. His heart thumps each time the ball clatters around the frets, but he maintains a wholly detached manner even as a crowd begins to gather. It is only mid-afternoon, and Bill cannot understand from where these people emerged. Perhaps word has circulated there is a madman at the roulette table who doesn't seem to care if he wins or loses and appears to have money to burn. Just for good measure, he occasionally places outside bets with some stakes on the first and second dozens so that, unless the zero comes up, he will always win something back. Inevitably, sometimes he loses 5,000 FF, intermittently wins 10,000 FF, and, on balance, is up around 6,000 FF. On one occasion, on number 32, he wins 21,000 FF. The only noise he makes is scratching his pencil in his little notebook.

Bill occasionally notices Pierre Laget speaking to the Chef de Partie at his table and glancing his way. It looks like Laget is getting hushed updates on Bill's progress and orders some champagne to be sent to him.

As Bill himself used to do at the casino in Bloomington, it is not unusual for European casinos to ply the more enthusiastic patrons with drinks, especially if they are winning, as the casino would like the opportunity to win its money back. Bill declines the expensive wine and instead opts for plain water. At precisely six o'clock, he takes a break for a roast beef sandwich, which is brought to a side table. The beef is rare and bloody, and Bill feels the heat on his tongue from the horseradish sauce. No one dares approach him as he has a look of determination that may as well be a sign around his neck saying, "Stay away until I'm done." That is undoubtedly how he feels, and socializing can wait.

His right arm has begun to ache after so many years of throwing fastballs, but Bill keeps telling himself "this is just a matter of endurance." He looks up at the chandeliers, sparkling with hundreds of golden lights, and knows that if he is to stay in this incredible place, he has to earn that right. His throat feels raw, and the ice clinks as he sips his water. He must persist, and with each spin of the wheel, he places his chips using both hands.

After eight hours, he has hardly changed his betting sequence and always waits until the last possible moment to place his bets. The croupier has to spend so much time counting out the differences between his winnings or losses and the table maximum that there are only around twelve spins per hour, meaning that Bill often has the table to himself as no one else has the patience. This allows him to move his hands freely around the table, placing his chips without interference.

Finally, at eleven o'clock in the evening, the Chef du Partie calls time on the table, and Bill sits down to rest his legs and back. He pushes a 20 FF plaque to the croupier with a "merci"—his first word in French— and exchanges his chips for high-denomination plaques. He then walks to the cashier's office and asks them to keep his winnings overnight. They give him a receipt, and he writes the total in his notebook: 84,500 FF, which translates to $16,900. Bill glances back at the grandeur of the Salle Touzet and reflects, "If I were back at the *Rocky Mountain News*, I'd be on $420 a year."

On the balcony, outside the smoking room to the right of the Salon Rose, Bill stands overlooking the harbor and lights a cigar. It seems to Bill that everyone in France smokes, and he has taken to the occasional cigar as it makes him feel successful and confident. The rich tobacco aroma fills his nostrils, and he can relax for the first time today.

He wishes Dave Rowe, Clark Griffith, and Art could see him now. He knows his mother would disapprove, but she would approve of the winnings.

In the semi-darkness, another match strikes and briefly illuminates the face of a man who has appeared next to him. Bill is instantly on his guard, having won so much money, but does not show any sign of alarm.

A minute passes before the stranger breaks the silence.

"Do you know the fable of Sisyphus?" he says.

"Can't say I do," replies Bill, still looking straight ahead.

"In Greek mythology, Sisyphus infuriated the gods by cheating death, and he was punished by having to push a rock up a hill for all eternity. The problem was, the rock would always come down, so he was destined to perpetual frustration. The point is that his own ego was his worst enemy, and that's what most people who come here are up against."

"What does this have to do with me?" says Bill.

"Everything," replies the stranger, "because you have shown everyone fortunate to witness your trials tonight that you will not let your ego get in the way. You never doubled your bets or waivered from your numbers when you made big coups. That is not something we see here often, and I wanted to show my appreciation." He turns and offers his hand, saying, "pleased to make your acquaintance. My name is Charles Selby." Bill shakes his hand.

"William Darnbrough."

"Interesting. Darnbrough. That's an English name, but you have a distinctly American accent."

"My great grandfather George went over to New York from Yorkshire in the 1830s," says Bill. "Apparently, there is a Darnborough Street in York, but I don't know if that's true. I hope to visit someday to find out."

"Well then, we're practically related," says Selby. "My family hails from Yorkshire, too."

"Well, Mr. Selby," says Bill, "it is a pleasure to meet you, but if you will excuse me, it is time I turned in for the night. It's been a long day, but I'm sure our paths will cross again."

"I'm sure they will. Good night."

As Bill walks through the balcony doors, he turns to glance back. He questions whether this was purely a chance encounter or whether Selby has an agenda.

CHAPTER 31

*A*t the Hotel de Paris, personal mail is held behind the reception desk for collection, although a letter from the management will be placed under your door. As Bill heads toward his bathroom, he notices an envelope on the floor with the hotel's blue and gold coat of arms on the seal. Having led a nomadic existence for the past few years, a letter is something of a novelty, and Bill is intrigued to find that it contains a colorful pamphlet promoting the Opera de Monte Carlo at the Salle Garnier.

In two weeks, the famous Italian tenor, Enrico Caruso, will be performing the role of the Duke of Mantua in Verdi's *Rigoletto*. Bill's instinctive reaction is to wonder if the opera may be hosting a visit from Emma Juch. Would she remember him? What would she think of him now, considering his transformation from lowly mid-western baseball player to a gentleman of Monaco.

He sets the pamphlet aside and gets down on the floor to do his push-ups. The fine rug is soft under his hands, and he huffs an exhale each time he rises, knowing that what he is doing here in Monte Carlo requires even more endurance than pitching a double-header in one-hundred-degree heat in Kansas. He has replaced limbering up for a long stint in the baseball box for a demanding shift next to the roulette wheel. He will never be one of those players who sits at the table, talking and drinking with other players and onlookers. His game will be solitary and purposeful, with complete focus, and his double-handed, last-minute betting will require a fair share of athleticism.

A quick tour of the hotel's immediate vicinity is next on Bill's agenda, including a visit to Quinto's on Avenue des Spelugeus for a mushroom omelette. Quinto's has graduated from its early existence as a small café to a brasserie, and the food is cooked in the Italian style. Omelette may be spelled differently on a French menu, but it was an obvious choice compared to Vol-au-Vent, which would require further investigation. Bill makes a mental note to return so he can compare Signore Quinto's ravioli to Signore Mangini's in Denver.

Strolling back to the casino through the enchanting gardens, Bill notices the exotic plants and palm trees. He can't help but admit that Monaco is undeniably an alluring place to live as long as he can maintain a healthy bank balance.

In addition to his newly created casino account, Bill requires an actual bank account to transfer money between his account at Adirondack Trust in Saratoga and Monaco. This is easily achieved with a visit to the Banca Monte dei Paschi di Siena on the Avenue des Citronniers. He has read that this bank has existed since 1472, therefore, he has no doubt they can be trusted. The process for opening an account is surprisingly simple as he meets with the assistant manager, Mr. Niccolò di Buonaccorso. It becomes evident that being a guest at the Hotel de Paris carries significant influence in this town, like a valuable currency of its own. Mr. Buonaccorso is delighted to set up an account for Bill once he learns of his extended stay plans.

Bill retraces his steps to the casino and goes to a roulette table positioned on the far left side of the Salle Touzet. He deliberately chooses this table as it is away from the dappled afternoon sunlight that streams through the stained-glass windows. Once again, he stands opposite the third dozen toward the far end of the table. This time, he exchanges 10,000 FF and starts betting heavily around 29 from the start. He does not play neighbors of numbers on the wheel as many others do—instead, this time, he covers the adjacent numbers on the actual grid and transversal, which is a six-line bet. Mostly, he loses, and the croupier rakes in what looks like enough money to finance an invasion of a small country.

Bill reminds himself that the odds never change. This is hardly different than pitching in the bottom of the seventh with the bases loaded in a tie game—he might be about to lose, but he also might be about to win, and, plus, if he gets into trouble, he has more time.

He repeats the exact stakes each time. The wheel spins. The ball drops. He loses, and wins, then loses again. And then, on one spin, the ball leaps up to travel around the ledge above the numbered partitions. The cylinder revolves for an eternity, and two other players are making so much noise that other people come over to see what the fuss is about. Bill has rarely seen this happen, as he sees the cylinder revolving faster than the ball itself, which begins to wobble. Bill swallows hard and blinks. If the ball fails to dislodge and bounces anywhere but into the wheel, the croupier will call "rien va," and the ball will be respun.

The ball appears to slow. Then it speeds up again and dances on.

The crowd whoops and leans in, everyone's eyes fixated on the ball. Bill hears murmurs in French he doesn't understand, and someone is laughing.

Finally, as if it had been waiting for a considerable crowd to gather around the table, the ball drops with a final clink into number 29.

Word spreads quickly around Monte Carlo that a mysterious American has an infallible system. Many people assume that he must be cheating, as it is rare that a player can win at roulette with such consistency. One theory to resurface is that he is a wheel watcher and can somehow predict the outcome, which is why he waits until the last possible moment to place his bets. What they do not take into account is that he often has identical stakes on the table for four straight hours without a break. In addition, a wheel watcher looks for imperfections or biased wheels that require attention. This does not form part of Bill's strategy as it would take days of continuously watching every spin in the casino to determine any inconsistencies and he would need several accomplices.

The Chef du Parties check each of the seventeen tables in the Salle de Jeux each morning for any abnormalities. Also, since the days of the biased wheel player Joseph Jagger, a spirit level similar to the one Bill owned is used to determine that the wheel is perfectly aligned. The table is supported by eight legs, four of which bear the wheel's weight. If any slight defect is detected, a device can be used to ensure the cylinder level is true. Where the legs are fastened to the floor, there are brass caps that look like ornaments but contain screws that can be turned with a small key to raise or lower the legs accordingly. Only when the Chef is completely satisfied, 80,000 FF is allocated to each table before the casino opens at lunchtime.

Nevertheless, as Bill plays on, Laget and his entourage of security men watch him closely.

IN HIS FOURTH week at the Hotel de Paris, Bill receives a note requesting a meeting with Monsieur Titus Brico, the head of the *departement relations clientele* at the casino.

"You have made quite a name for yourself, Monsieur Darnbrough," says Brico. "Usually, the newspapers concern themselves with the comings and goings of the Grand Duke Nicholas Mikhailovich, the Comte and Comtesse de Sant Elia, Prince Frederick Charles of Hohenlohe, Count Ada Sierstorpff, or Baron Henri de Rothschild."

"It is not my intention to seek publicity," responds Bill, "but that does sound like I'm in good company."

"Yes, I understand," says Brico. "Nevertheless, we feel you should be rewarded for your endeavors and would like to offer you a room overlooking the harbor."

"I see," says Bill, "and how much will that cost?"

"Oh, Monsieur, this suite will be with the compliments of the casino for the duration of your stay."

"Well, in that case, thank you very much, Monsieur Brico."

"Certainly. Please follow me to the hotel reception, and we will make the necessary arrangements."

As they descend the front steps and head toward the hotel, Bill's mind is flooded with images of countless run-down rooms he has stayed in over the years. He can't help but feel grateful and blessed to have come this far and now be in such a remarkable place.

As he becomes a regular attraction at the casino, more people arrive to crowd around Bill's table and see if they can work out his system. They are often disappointed, as it is not unusual for him to lose considerable sums, although everyone wants to see the bank getting a good shake-up, so when he does win, his supporters give loud cheers. One evening, a crowd four deep surrounds his table, yet Bill remains completely calm, even when he wins 21,000 FF in one coup.

He prefers it when no bystanders are at the table, as he sometimes feels as if he is there purely for their entertainment. But what really bothers him are the *markers*. On a busy evening, a professional player will often jostle to take a seat at his table, but a *marker* does not actually play. Their tactic is to be prepared at any time to give up their place to someone else, and the usual fee is 20 FF.

One evening, a charming young woman is playing roulette at Bill's table. Her dark hair cascades in ringlets, and her eyes dart about, conveying a sense of anticipation for a significant triumph or a fear of impending loss. As Bill stands to take a break, she also rises and walks towards him.

"I have been watching your luck," she says. "You have great patience, unlike me."

Bill is taken with her soft voice and French accent. She exudes grace and beauty but it's a natural, understated allure, rather than an overdone, glamorous one.

"I find the more I practice, the luckier I get," replies Bill with a smile.

"Would you like to buy me a glass of champagne?" she says, in barely a whisper.

"Why not? I was taking a break anyway. My name's Bill, by the way, Bill Darnbrough."

"Monsieur Darnbrough," she says, "I think from your accent, you are American, no? You are certainly a long way from home. It is a pleasure to meet you. I am Eloise d'Alençon."

As their champagne is delivered to a small table at the side of the Salle Garnier, Bill is intrigued by Eloise. Is she a courtesan? Women in the casino do not generally flirt with men unless they have ulterior motives, but Bill's curiosity gets the better of him.

"Your English is excellent," he says. "I wish I could speak French as well as you speak English."

"How long are you staying in Monaco?"

"Well, I'm not sure. Quite a long time, I suspect. Are you from around here?"

"Nearby. I am from Nice. People from Monaco are not permitted inside the casino unless they work here."

"And you don't work here?" says Bill, fishing.

"Not exactly," replies Eloise in her most seductive voice. She is unashamedly flirting with him now, and Bill finds her irresistibly attractive.

They talk together for so long that eventually, all the tables have closed, and everyone else in the Salle Garnier has left for the night except the barman and one waiter.

"I have an idea," Bill says, taking another sip of champagne. "I would very much like to learn French, and you speak such excellent English. How about I pay you to teach me?"

Etienne is working late at the Hotel de Paris reception and is the only one who notices Bill and his new acquaintance climbing the stairs together at midnight.

ONE MONTH after he has checked in to the Hotel de Paris, Bill's wins at the casino are substantial, and more newspapers want the story. Great mystery surrounds the background of Mr. Darnbrough, and he remains somewhat of an enigma on account of his steadfast determination at the tables. Many decide that he is a millionaire banker from New York, although no confirmations are forthcoming as he does not attend the lavish dinner parties where people like to gossip.

Once the *Daily Mail* in England has got hold of the story of Bill's incredibly high stakes playing, the press works its magic, and even Camille Blanc and the casino administration begin to take a serious interest. Naturally, they would like to be on the winning side, which they often are, but on the other hand, Bill's good fortune is excellent publicity for the casino.

Bill has no interest in the speculation surrounding his good fortune and declines to be interviewed variously by the *Monte Carlo News*, *Vanity Fair*, and the *American Register*. However, they publish their stories anyway. Curiously, the *Milwaukee Sentinel* is the first to publish a special cable dispatch referring to him as the "American plunger." The plunger refers to his habit of pushing mountains of chips onto the grid with both hands instead of carefully placing little bets around the table, and it is a phrase picked up by many other newspapers.

BILL HAS SETTLED into a good routine after the first six months, and before commencing a long shift at the tables, he often finds a decent brunch at one of the fine restaurants or bistros within walking distance. One morning, on his way out to a late breakfast, he is greeted at the hotel's front door by a commissionaire who seems preoccupied with a gathering crowd outside the main entrance, and Bill soon sees why. There is a cream-colored, two-seater Renault Voiturette automobile parked just to the left of the main steps, and this has caused much excitement as it has an unusual retractable roof. Onlookers from around the square flock like pigeons to see the beautiful car. Bill had read of Marcel Renault's death during the Paris-Madrid race earlier in the year, and his brother Louis had taken over the business. He is looking at the Type D, Serie B, with an upgraded De Dion engine, and this car would cost about one year's pay for a middle-class French worker, or 3000 FF. Bill feels a stirring in his soul at the sight of it.

"Bonjour," he calls out as he touches his hat in acknowledgment to the driver and his companion as he walks past. They simply nod in acknowledgement and Bill wishes he knew more French to ask them questions about their magnificent motorcar. "More French lessons," he muses.

As if discovering a magnificent new automobile wasn't enough for one morning, Bill also gets to experience his first Vol-au-Vent. A large, round, light pastry dish containing fresh fish caught that very morning in the Mediterranean Sea arrives, and Bill congratulates himself for being brave enough to order it without having the slightest clue what it was. To speculate with vast amounts of money on the roulette table is one thing, but ordering local cuisine is often a gamble in itself.

As has become his custom, Bill is reading the *Monte Carlo Gazette* newspaper at the table, and the headlines are all about Anglo-French relations and the signing of the Entente Cordiale. This historic agreement means that France and Great Britain would finally be allies should the need to defend each other ever arise. There is also a piece regarding the construction of the Panama Canal and an obituary of Henry Stanley, who discovered the source of the Nile.

In his room that evening, Bill writes a letter to Raoul Gunsbourg, the director of the Opera de Monte Carlo, enquiring—or perhaps suggesting—that he contact the agent of Emma Juch to enquire about her availability to include Monaco on her next European tour. Bill feels more connected to Monaco now and knows the Hotel de Paris letterhead will have the desired impact.

At the bar in the Salle Schmit that evening, Bill sits alone at a table, preparing for his next roulette session, when an Englishman named John Haverstock introduces himself. Bill initially thinks he is just another casino dweller who needs someone to talk to, and Bill listens patiently to his stories.

"Have you heard of Baron Arthur de Rothschild?" says Haverstock, who continues without waiting for an answer. "He used to arrive on his yacht and was one of the first residents to have a private, purpose-built garage for his automobile at his villa. You know he had the curious habit of only betting on number 17 and occasionally zero. For a senior member of one of Europe's most powerful families that controls a vast financial empire and himself worth millions, playing roulette at all is quite astonishing if you ask me, but the manner in which he played, like so many other aspects of Monte Carlo, was quite bizarre."

"Are you familiar with London?" Bill asks.

"Why, yes, of course. I am from London. Why do you ask?"

"My family is originally from England, and I have always wanted to visit. I picked up a copy of *Bradshaw's Guide to France* a while ago, and I've been looking for his London version."

"Well, my dear chap," says Haverstock, "you've met the right man. You don't need Bradshaw—I can tell you everything you need to know."

Bill does have questions but decides they should wait. Perhaps, like Selby, Haverstock could prove useful. Maybe he should surround himself with people who can help bring him closer to his English ancestors. Perhaps Haverstock knows the real Reform Club where the fictional Phileas Fogg made his famous bet before departing on his journey around the world? He has come this far but needs to set a visit to London as a goal. What could be the harm if it's just a vacation? *There's always going to be one more rung on the ladder,* he thinks.

In the meantime, he needs to be disciplined and single-minded with no distractions until the possibilities present themselves—no distractions aside from the opera and French lessons, of course.

Many gentlemen who regularly attend the opera wear the latest fashionable white tie with tails or dinner jackets, and Bill needs to feel the part. He walks down rue Grimaldi and steps into Giovanni's Haberdashery to have a dinner jacket fitted. Fondly known as "De fil en aiguille," Giovanni's is the only haberdashery in Monaco. The whirring of a treadle sewing machine instantly brings back memories of his childhood in Bloomington. Monsieur Di Salvia, a master tailor, milliner, and fabric expert, impressively wields his tape measure with the precision of a skilled surgeon. Within a mere three days, a flawlessly fitting dinner jacket is delivered to the Hotel de Paris, and Bill is ready to make his mark.

There are only 524 seats in the Salle Garnier compared to its 2000 seat sister venue, the Palais Garnier in Paris. This gives a more intimate experience for both the performers and the audience. Bill has read that *La bohème* tells the story of Mimi, a poor French seamstress in Paris, and the tale seems interesting to him as he longs to visit Paris properly. He can almost touch the singers and tries his hardest to concentrate on the production, but the plot is difficult to follow aside from the fact that all her friends are so poor that they cannot help Mimi when she falls ill. *I could have taken care of her,* thinks Bill.

As the curtain descends and the company takes its final bow, the audience gives a standing ovation. Sadly, Bill is left wondering if perhaps it would be more prudent to bring a translator to explain everything next time. Or he could learn Italian.

The next day, Bill sets his London visit plans in motion, starting with a visit to Mr. Niccolò di Buonaccorso at the bank to acquire a banker's draft for use in England. He can transact at any major bank with the draft, although he doesn't expect to spend too much, apart from travel expenses, the hotel, and maybe a fresh new suit for the summer.

CHAPTER 32

$\mathcal{B}$ill traverses Paris's 11th arrondissement in an open-top fiacre from the Gare de Lyon to the Gare du Nord. It is not exactly the experience he had hoped for, as once again, he wanted to see the Eiffel Tower and the Arc de Triomphe, but the train-changing schedule means that his tourism activities will have to wait until his next visit. The architecture of the Boulevard Voltaire, with its café patios provides a glimpse into the life of Parisians, who seem far more fashionable and sophisticated than their southern cousins. His driver navigates the tram crossings and weaves his way at great speed, no doubt harboring a desire to emulate the great rally drivers that France is producing. The train from Paris to the Quai Chanzy in Boulogne-sur-Mer takes Bill through Abbeville and the enchantingly picturesque seaside town of Le Touquet. Even the train whistle seems to have a charm to it as they announce their arrival and departure at each station.

The French countryside seems a million miles away from the prairies of Nevada as stately homes and chateaux pass by his window in the first-class carriage. The deep green forest of Hardelot gives way to a view of the harbor and the magnificent twin-turbine steamships, one of which will take Bill to Folkstone on England's south coast.

The total travel time from Paris to London is seven and a half hours, which goes quickly compared to the trips Bill is used to in Kansas and Colorado. He feels great anticipation at the prospect of walking London's ancient, cobbled roads, but nothing has prepared him for the magnificence of London's St Pancras Station.

As the train pulls in, the spectacular iron and glass roof, held up by giant blue iron trusses, is unlike anything he has ever seen. Sixty million bright red bricks were used to construct the station in 1868, with eighty thousand cubic feet of cream-colored stone. As the porter collects Bill's cases, he has a chance to look more closely at the curious hand-carved stonework depicting dragons and gargoyles. Outside, there is a light mist, so he is grateful for the comfort of the closed carriage that will take him to his hotel. Nevertheless, his excitement gets the better of him, and he can't resist sticking his head out of the window to take in the sights as they pass through Bloomsbury.

The Hotel de Paris has arranged his lodgings at Brown's Hotel on Dover Street, which was started by James and Sarah Brown, the valet and maid to Lord and Lady Byron. The receptionist recognizes Bill's demeanor as a somewhat weary traveler and, wasting no time with idle chit-chat, has him escorted straight to his room in the adjoining St George's building overlooking Albemarle Street. That night, despite the aches from the long journey, Bill slips into a deep sleep on down feather pillows that smell of lavender.

The morning sun through the windows brings fresh excitement and anticipation as another adventure awaits. The plan, at least the original plan, is not to gamble in London at all. Monte Carlo is Bill's office, and England will be his vacation home. He feels the urge to become more sociable here and wants to meet English people. In order to fit in, he must find suitable attire.

Bill knows from his experience in Nevada that the best way to get to know a new town is to read the local newspapers. A courtesy copy of the *London Times* has been delivered to his room and he puts it under his arm as he closes the door. Albemarle Street is London's first one-way street because of the crowds attending the lectures on the advancement of science at the Royal Institution. It can be over-whelming to cross—even for someone familiar with navigating the haphazard traffic in New York. Horse-drawn carriages and automobiles are edging their way up to Piccadilly with bicycles and pedestrians all seemingly in a race to the death. After standing frozen on the hotel steps for a minute, trying to decide how best to traverse the street, Bill checks his pocket watch, turns around, and heads straight back to the safe refuge of the breakfast room inside Brown's.

A waiter materializes to refill Bill's coffee as he turns the newspaper pages and reads of the Japanese fleet defeating the Russians. He thinks many high-ranking Russian officials in Monte Carlo will have to return home, considering all the unrest in their country.

The sports pages would normally be more interesting to Bill, but they are dominated by the upcoming tennis at Wimbledon and the Open golf tournament. There is no mention of baseball in America, so Bill makes a mental note to find out how to have a copy of the *New York Times* delivered to his room.

The waiter returns and Bill politely places his hand over his cup.

"I was wondering," he begins. "Do you have any other brands of coffee? This one seems quite bitter."

"Ah, yes, Sir," the waiter replies, lowering his voice and leaning a little closer. "You see, we are a nation of tea drinkers and Brown's prides itself on our extensive collection of blends. However, we would be happy to order a special batch of coffee for you if you are planning on joining us again for breakfast."

"I have to order my own coffee beans?"

"Yes, Sir." The waiter looks cautious around to make sure their conversation is not overheard. "If I may so bold, sir, and if you are seeking an experience off the beaten track so to speak, a visit to Twinings on the Strand might be a nice adventure?"

"I see," says Bill, quite bewildered. "What happens there?"

"Well, Sir, it is the center of the world as far as tea is concerned and it has been there for quite a while. I highly recommend it to all our visitors."

The concierge gives Bill a pocket map of central London with an abundance of helpful information detailing the West End theatres, museums, and some larger shops such as Fortnum and Masons. He is standing outside the hotel, feeling more confident with the little map unfolded that shows him how to walk to Jermyn Street.

Bill soon discovers that aside from Albemarle Street, London is without a doubt, one of the finest cities in the world for walking. There are vast open parks, one of which, Hyde Park, is large enough to fit in the whole of Monaco. As he notices the passing ladies, he can't help but observe that they all have something in common—unfeasibly large hats that seem to defy gravity and somehow stay in perfect place despite the wind.

Lock & Co. is the oldest hatmakers in London and have maintained a shop on St. James's Street since 1676. Bill has decided that the Homberg is the most suitable design for him as it separates him slightly from the top hats and coke hats that are the fashion in London. Somehow, it makes him feel American, and this is not so much of a statement as an indulgence that just feels right.

Exploring St. James and Jermyn Streets could effortlessly fill up Bill's entire day if he wished, but for now, clothes shopping can take a back seat as there is another important matter he needs to attend to.

He steps off the pavement and hails a hackney carriage to take him east along the river Thames. After tasting less than appealing coffee this morning, Bill wants to understand why the English are so obsessed with tea. After the waiter told him about Twinings, his curiosity, and the cab, takes him to the small shop at No.216 Strand.

The double door entrance incorporates Queen Victoria's Royal warrant, a golden lion, and two Chinese figures to acknowledge that tea originated in China some 2000 years ago. A brown box labeled *T.I.P.S.* rests on a table by the entrance, which means *To Insure Prompt Service*. However, Bill doesn't have any spare change, so he proceeds through the narrow shop and selects a seat at the bar.

He spends the next hour becoming a tea expert. A young tea sommelier gives an enthusiastic lesson covering tea's history, growing, harvesting techniques, blending, infusing, and medicinal benefits. For the first time in years, the roulette table is out of his mind as his tea journey experience drifts between sweet lemon, vanilla, and creamy caramel. Just at the point of concluding that Earl Grey is his favorite, a voice behind him surprises him.

"Bonjour, Mr. Darnbrough!" Bill turns to see a magnificent hat adorned with flowers perched on top of an equally fragrant looking middle-aged lady smiling at him, but he cannot place her. His bewilderment is evident as the woman says, "You probably don't remember me. That is to say, we did not actually meet exactly." Finally, she gets to the point with, "I saw you in Monte Carlo, and you were quite marvelous." She puts out her hand, and Bill, who is standing now, accepts it as she continues, "I'm Mrs. Carruthers. My husband is Major Jock Carruthers."

"Great to see you," says Bill, somewhat embarrassed at being recognized, and that Mrs. Carruthers is so loud that now the other patrons of Twinings are all invested in the conversation. Bill initially thinks the best course of action is a hasty escape and is about to make a theatrical gesture of looking at his pocket watch when he remembers that he needs to make more of an effort to meet people.

"I have been so engrossed in this tea business," he says, feeling awkward and slightly hesitant at being confronted by an English lady for the first time. "It is nice to see you, and you must take your tea very seriously to be here?"

"Never mind about that," says Mrs. Carruthers, "where are you staying, and how long are you in London?"

"I'm not sure," says Bill. "I'm at Brown's for the moment, but we'll see."

She looks like she has sensed Bill's unease and says, "Well then, I will speak with my husband, and I am sure we will come up with something interesting for us to do together."

He feels relieved as he picks up his new Homberg hat and turns for the door. "Nice seeing you. Hope to see you again."

As he is on the pavement, searching for a Hackney carriage to take him westwards, Bill realizes that it has been a considerable amount of time since he has spoken to a woman. He hasn't held any meaningful conversations with anyone for months, as his single-mindedness in Monte Carlo has been all-consuming. There is no reason for him to have hurried out of Twinings now that he is in London, and perhaps he should have stayed longer for no other reason than to be polite.

A cab pulls up, and Bill tells the driver, "Brown's Hotel, please." Only after he is seated does he realize this is his first time in an electric cab. He had seen one in New York, but never actually taken one before. This is a Hummingbird, so named for the distinctive humming sound it makes, and it's unique black and gold livery. Bill is experiencing many firsts on this trip, and as he takes in the view of the Embankment, noiselessly riding alongside the Thames, he realizes that London is growing on him.

The following day, Bill gets to do something he has been looking forward to for as long as he can remember. He has scheduled an appointment at the Chelsea Town Hall on King's Road as assimilation into English society requires several modifications beyond suitable attire and a working knowledge of tea. In front of a Commissioner of Oaths, he officially declares his decision to change his name back to the family's original spelling, adding an "o" to become Darnborough once again.

CHAPTER 33

*L*ondon has four telephone exchanges named City, Mayfair, Kensington, and Westminster with eighteen thousand subscribers, one of which is the home of Major and Mrs. Jock Carruthers. In a matter of hours, Mrs. Carruthers has spread the word that she is acquainted with a mysterious American who has had extraordinary fortune at the tables in Monte Carlo. Many people would frown upon such knavish activities, but not Mrs. Carruthers's acquaintances, who are eager to entice him into their circle.

Alexander Graham Bell probably had no idea that a popular function of his invention would become a source for gossip and rumor. Nevertheless, this is how the telephone has evolved, and one of Mrs. Carruther's friends comes up with a cunning plan.

Bill does not receive many letters at Brown's as he does not advertise his address, so he is intrigued when an invitation to a garden party arrives one morning. Major and Mrs. Carruthers request the pleasure of his company at an afternoon garden party in Eaton Square the following Thursday. A discreet inquiry with Samuel Chambers, the assistant manager at Brown's, has determined that this will require a visit to Poole & Co of Savile Row to obtain suitable attire for a London summer garden party.

Bill feels quite accustomed to life as a London gentleman when he sees himself in the full-length mirror at Poole's. He does not know that Poole's has been dressing Maharajahs, Kings, Dukes, Tsars, and Emperors since 1806, as they treat each customer with the same respect even if they are simply looking for garden party attire. After his measurements are taken and he places his order, Bill decides the new style of straw boater hat does not suit him and instead opts for a cream version of his Homberg, which he purchases at Lock & Co. on his way back to the hotel.

THE NEW CLOTHES arrive just in time for the garden party, and he is anxious not to risk spoiling them with proximity to horses, so he hails an electric cab to Belgravia. It is surprisingly hot for May, and he is grateful not to have to wear a formal suit as he enters the gardens at Eaton Square, where he is greeted and welcomed after a brief inspection of his invitation.

The gardens are bursting with flowers, including red camellias, yellow tulips, multi-colored roses, and azaleas. A wind-up gramophone plays classical music, and a colorful mixture of ladies' hats dominates the scene as Bill spots Mrs. Carruthers near some tables with various hors d'oeuvres. A waiter with glasses of champagne on a silver tray intercepts him, and he helps himself to a drink, but before he can take a sip, a hand touches his shoulder.

"You must be the American from Monte Carlo!"

Bill turns sharply at the surprise but regains his composure quickly. "Yes, I suppose I must be."

"I'm a friend of Jock Carruthers. Name's Forsyth. Dominic Forsyth, formally of His Majesty's Scots Guards. Jock told me to look out for you," he says, looking up at Bill's cream-colored Homberg hat.

"Ah, the hat gave me away?"

"The ladies will love it," says Forsyth, "you look the part."

"The part?"

Forsyth leans in and lowers his voice with a half-smile. "As my mother always said, you can tell a lot about a man by the state of his shoes and his hat. You, sir, clearly have the credentials to match."

"Hello, Mr. Darnborough," says Mrs. Carruthers from underneath another unfeasibly large hat. "I see you've met Captain Forsyth."

"Excuse us, Dominic," she says, taking Bill by the arm and steering him toward a group of hats in heels. Mrs. Carruthers is on a mission to introduce Bill to all her friends. In fact, one in particular.

All the single young ladies want to talk to Bill as he is undoubtedly the most interesting of the guests. "What did you do before Monte Carlo? Are you enjoying the season? Are you going to Ascot this year? How long are you staying in London? Are you staying at a hotel? Which hotel?" Bill works out fairly quickly that if he takes long enough to answer a question, they fire off another one, and he can then decide which one to respond to. He does not brag about his baseball career, as he would have to spend hours explaining the difference between baseball and cricket. He also does not elaborate about his winnings, simply acknowledging that he has been fortunate. As for London, he tells the truth: "I will be returning to Monte Carlo in due course but have yet to set a date."

Mrs. Carruthers manages to steer Bill toward one particularly attractive young lady whom she introduces as Miss Katherine Tate whose dark eyelashes soften in the sunlight as she looks up at Bill from under a wide-brimmed hat. Mrs. Carruthers vanishes with a smile as if to signify that her job is done.

"So, tell me, Mr. Darnborough," Miss Tate asks, "why would an American come to dreary old England? America is so exciting."

Bill is struck by her confidence as she speaks freely but with a degree of refinement that he has not encountered previously.

"America is large and complicated," says Bill, trying his best to sound intelligent—at least on a philosophical level.

"Yes, I understand," says Miss Tate, "but don't you find it thrilling that you live in a place that is constantly evolving? I mean, you have people from all over the world wanting to go there because everyone is full of aspirations. Nobody goes to America to simply sit around all day talking about the weather, which is what we do here."

"The thing is," says Bill, "You all see the highlights and hear Buffalo Bill's tales of the exciting times in the Wild West. The truth is that it's more of a struggle. That's what I love about the south of France. It feels like you've achieved something in your life, and being there is a reward. Sure, people still have to go to work and feed their families, but there is a contentment that I have rarely seen anywhere else."

Bill notices how intently Miss Tate looks at him as if she's hanging on every word. He thinks she is probably an heiress or the daughter of a distinguished General. How incredible that he is here at a London summer garden party, speaking with such a lovely lady on equal terms. He thinks she is intrigued by him, perhaps even fascinated, and all Bill can think about is how far from the farm this boy has come.

Miss Katherine Tate has given Bill a shot in the arm, and he can now return to Monte Carlo with renewed vigor. He knows he needs to make a lot more money if he is to achieve anything close to his aspirations.

Before bidding farewells at Eaton Square, Captain Forsyth and Major Carruthers corner Bill by the gate and invite him for dinner the following evening. They tell him that they are members of a private club on Piccadilly called the Naval and Military Club, affectionately known as the In and Out, on account of the signs in the driveway to direct carriages. Bill hesitates for a moment and says he has a prior engagement and could they postpone to the following Monday. Amongst other things, he is anxious about having enough time to research what people wear to a dinner at the In and Out Club.

Once again, he calls on the expertise and experience of Samuel Chambers at Brown's, who informs him of the history of the place.

"It is a great privilege to be invited there, Mr. Darnborough," he relates. "The In and Out is an exclusive club for British Army and Navy officers. I assume your friends are members?"

"Yes," says Bill, "Scots Guards. I believe they served together in South Africa recently."

"I see. I have never been in there, but I can tell you that they will undoubtedly adhere to the strictest of dress codes with military uniforms or formal black ties and dinner jackets in the evening. I advise paying another visit to Poole & Co to get what you need. If I may be so bold, Mr. Darnborough, as I feel we have become firm acquaintances by now, may I give you one further piece of advice?"

"Yes, of course, Samuel, I have come to rely on your wisdom in these matters," says Bill.

"Even if you find yourself surrounded by Colonels and Navy Commanders, hold your own and do not show subservience as they would despise you for it. Stand tall, firm handshakes, that sort of thing."

"Good advice, Samuel, thank you. I imagine a place like that could be quite intimidating."

"I'm sure you will take it in your stride, sir."

Take it in my stride? Aside from the fact that Bill neglected to pack his dinner suit as he didn't imagine he would need it, he is wondering if Samuel Chambers has any concept of where Bloomington, Illinois, is in the world. A private military club in the heart of London surrounded by British Army officers relating tales of supreme courage under fire in hostile lands is so utterly alien to him. Then again, how hard could it be?

CHAPTER 34

Two letters arrive this morning. The first is from Libby.

He will never know how she managed to track him down to Brown's Hotel, but if there were any doubts before, now he knows for sure that their marriage is over. There are no threats or demands, and Bill can see that she has resigned herself to the fact that he will not be returning to Bloomington. Libby's last words are clinical as she informs Bill that a court will grant her a divorce on the grounds of desertion.

Guilt gnaws at him for his self-centeredness during his time with Libby and abandoning her after running the casino into the ground. Emotions don't come easily for Bill—joy or sorrow, but he has to keep moving without regrets. He knows Libby will probably resent him for the rest of her days but hopes she has a chance at finding happiness with someone more grounded than he.

What's almost more agonizing is that he betrayed Hiram and the trust he put in him. He stands up from the desk and looks out of the window. The street shimmers in the sun after a light rain, and his thoughts return to Hiram and his gratitude to the man who taught him so much about the game that propelled him into this new existence.

The second envelope has a Monaco post stamp and the printed emblem of the Hotel de Paris on the back. The letter requests he notify them of his expected return date under the pretext that they wish to ensure his room is prepared. No doubt they are under instructions from the casino to encourage his return, and it works, as his thoughts are of heading back to the roulette tables. Bill keeps methodical notes in his pocketbook regarding finances and has spent a small fortune in London, including his latest acquisition, a tailored dinner suit, wing-collared white dress shirt, and black bow tie. In addition, he has purchased a new pair of black brogue shoes from Crockett and Jones on Jermyn Street and a handsome polished maple umbrella from James Smith & Sons. As it turns out, a London gentleman is judged not only by his shoes and hat but also by his umbrella, which, even in this hot weather, is an essential accessory as it is liable to rain without warning.

The In and Out Club entrance is impressive compared to many of the neighboring addresses on Piccadilly, with its crescent driveway extenuating its reverence. Bill is greeted at the door by a uniformed non-commissioned officer who shows him to the reception, and they take his name. He is not allowed to enter the club until the member who invited him comes to fetch him. Major Jock Carruthers has metal Blakeys on his shoes which tap loudly on the polished floor as he strides purposefully toward Bill. He is wearing the red jacket of the Scots Guards and seems to be in his element here, totally in control of his environment.

"Glad you could make it, Bill," says Jock, "welcome to our little club." Bill is led through the entrance hall, which has enormous paintings of the battles of Wellington and Trafalgar on the walls and a vast portrait of King Edward VII splendidly displaying his British and foreign medals and honors. The flagstone floor gives way to a red carpet as they enter a hallway.

"I thought I'd give you a quick tour," says Jock, "we have quite a history here." There are cabinets displaying medals and regimental insignia, and next to the entrance to the smoking room are glass cases containing war-torn regimental color flags from distant battlefields. Mounted on the walls are large wooden roll of honor boards commemorating the club members who have died in battle. Jock has to turn and return to fetch Bill as he has stopped to look at the names that give their rank and the time and place they fell.

"Only the dead have seen the end of war," says Jock solemnly. "The club was only formed in 1862. If we had boards from the Crimea War up here, unfortunately, we would need a longer corridor."

The member's bar is crowded with an assortment of gentlemen, some in uniforms, some in suits. Unlike many of the saloons Bill has frequented, not everyone stops talking and looks his way when he enters. Jock introduces him to a navy Captain named John Jellicoe, who is probably ten years older than Bill, and another army officer called William Nesbitt. During a break in the conversation, Bill takes a closer look at a vast oil painting depicting soldiers in the midst of a harrowing battle. An inscription on the gilded frame reads: "Saving the Colours, the Guards at Inkerman, 8 Nov 1854." It is hauntingly magnificent and signed by the artist Robert Gibb.

Dominic Forsyth, who Bill recognizes from the garden party, appears with an extra glass for Bill.

"Greetings, Bill," says Dominic, "I hope Jock gave you the one penny tour?"

"I must admit, gentlemen," says Bill, addressing each of them at once, "this is not what I expected. In fact, I wasn't sure what to expect, but this is an honor."

"Well, the honor is ours, Mr. Darnborough," says Captain Jellicoe, "this is our no man's land. Here, we do not salute each other, irrespective of rank, and our members can kick off their boots, so to speak." Looking around at the exceptionally high standard of dress in the member's bar, Bill finds it hard to believe that there is much loosening of ties, let alone boot kicking off.

Compared to some of the meals he has been fortunate enough to have in Monte Carlo and London, their dinner is basic fare of chicken with boiled potatoes and vegetables. The camaraderie is evident as his new friends tell jokes and laugh loudly, and the wine flows freely until the port arrives and Bill witnesses for the first time the tradition of passing the port to the man on your left.

"It's a navy thing, Bill," says John, "port to port."

"Nonsense," says Dominic, "the army came up with this so we could always keep our sword hand free."

"You're both wrong," says Jock, taking the bottle over, "It's designed to keep the drink moving so we can all get some!"

Another roar of laughter and Bill raises his glass with the others, toasting their companionship, and, for a moment, forgets he's not one of them. Not yet.

A mist has blurred the streetlamps along Piccadilly as Bill walks the short distance back to Brown's Hotel. As he passes the gates of Green Park, he has a chance to reflect on his observations. He was expecting war stories, but none of the men spoke about their times in conflict, perhaps on account of his presence. They did not discuss their personal or family lives and, thankfully, said nothing about cricket. Most interesting to Bill is that they asked very little about his background. They seemed genuinely happy to have a guest in their midst, especially an American. Captain Jellicoe had asked his opinion about Roosevelt, but otherwise, there was only a mild inter-rogation, and even though these men came from entirely different backgrounds, they had made him feel like an old friend.

In his room at the hotel, Bill catches himself in the full-length mirror and decides the silk bow tie and dinner jacket were a good investment, although perhaps he will be more careful next time to remember to pack everything—just in case. All his new clothes will accompany him back to Monaco, along with the various other accessories he has picked up along the way.

Samuel Chambers is on the hotel steps to see the departure of the American and supervises Bill's large travel trunk containing his various suits, shoes, and hats.

"Would you like a copy of the New York Times delivered to your room next time you come to stay, Mr. Darnborough?" he says with a smile.

Bill laughs. "Good call, Mr. Chambers. I like your style. You didn't even ask if I was going to come back, let alone stay at Brown's. You're hired."

With all his Jermyn Street attire, at least he'll look the part of a

European gentleman, but a little piece of him is anxious that these are the only assets he has managed to accrue. He has spent nearly all the money he made in Monte Carlo last year, so he is starting off almost no better than he was a year ago. He was lucky at the tables last time, but will his luck hold?

———————

THE FRENCH COUNTRYSIDE turns purple with lavender as Bill travels farther south. The fields are in full bloom, and as he looks out of the train window, he thinks back to the endless wheat fields of Kansas and how each has a beauty of its own. He reflects that there is no better way to see the land than by train as he puts away his roulette bible and prepares to disembark.

As the carriage approaches the Hotel de Paris, Bill's concentration sharpens. Also his apprehension. It's clear to him he cannot do what he did last season and spend most of his cash in an effort to look the part. No, he must generate tangible assets. Everyone he has encountered in London has financial stability through family investments, careers, property, or military pensions.

Well before his trip to London, he had caught wind of the whispers and observed that some of the frequent lady gamblers seemed to show up with progressively fewer ornaments. The idea occurs to Bill: Is it possible for him to make an arrangement with the casino to obtain diamonds linked to outstanding debts? After much anticipation, he has come to the realization that what he really needs is some concrete security.

CHAPTER 35

he steps of the Hotel de Paris bustle with more activity than usual as crowds gather to admire the display of new cars. Camille Blanc, the son of François Blanc and current operator of the casino, enthusiastically has these splendid vehicles presented at the front of the building, fostering the illusion that anyone could win enough to afford one if luck favors them. This morning's showcased cars are two Renaults, a vibrant red Darracq, a Fiat 5-passenger Tourer, and a De Dietrich Spider with a chain drive.

Bill is captivated by their allure—their elegant contours and vibrant hues make them far more striking than their counterparts in New York. Reluctantly, Bill tears himself away, mindful that he has pressing matters to attend to.

Etienne Artolli at the hotel reception recognizes Bill immediately, and a porter is summoned, who hoists his travel trunk onto a trolly and escorts him to his room. A silver urn of fresh chrysanthemums and lilies is on the table by the window overlooking the harbor.

After a quick splash of fresh cold water on his face, Bill wastes no time and heads for the Banca dei Paschi to check on the health of his finances. While at the bank, he asks Niccolò for a recommendation for a diamond appraiser and a key for a private safety deposit box at the bank. He briefly stops at Le Café du Printemps for coffee and a baguette sandwich, then returns to the Salle de Jeux.

Bill takes his place at a roulette table and hands over some notes to the croupier.

"Monsieur?" The dealer has counted out his chips and pushed the piles toward him, but Bill shows no acknowledgment and seems to be staring into the middle distance. Something is troubling him, and he struggles to remain focused.

Tiers du cylindre is a strategy that covers one third of the wheel with only six chips. In order to cover twelve consecutive numbers, Bill places double bets on the splits: 5/8, 10/11, 13/16, 23/24, 27/30, and 33/36. He begins to lose heavily, and his hands become sweaty.

It's not working. He'll try *voisins du zero* on the other side of the wheel. That means nine chips on the neighbors of zero. He covers 4/7, 12/15, 18/21, 19/22, and 32/35 plus two chips on zero,2,3 and another two on a square bet covering 25, 26, 28, and 29.

He wins—then loses. Loses. Loses. Another spin, another sweeping away of his chips, and his pile diminishes. Seven times in a row, he loses. By around half past three, he has lost over 30,000 FF. "Time for a break," he thinks. His legs ache with tension like he's just run up a mountainside with an army chasing him. He cannot lose everything, not just out of the gate like this.

One of the Russians offers a greeting as he passes them in the atrium, but he ignores them and goes down the underground connecting corridor to the hotel and up to his room. There is a whiskey decanter on the table, and he pours himself two fingers worth.

As he sits at the desk, looking out over the harbor with boats straining to break free of their ropes, he tries to understand the cause of his irritability. He wonders what his father would say if he could see him now, sitting at this fine desk drinking expensive whiskey, looking out at the sparkling harbor full of gleaming yachts.

So why did Bill want so much more?

He takes off his jacket, does forty push-ups on the bedroom

floor, and goes to the bathroom to splash cold water on his face. He stares at his reflection momentarily before combing his hair—Lord, are there *more* gray ones?—and takes a few deep breaths. Now he is ready for action.

He chooses a different table in the Salle Garnier and takes a place on the opposite side of the croupier at the high number end.

After exchanging another hefty sum of cash, he waits until the ball is spinning and starts placing his chips on 26, 27, 29, 30, 32, 33, 35, and 36. He has a handful of hedge bets, including zero, 5, 11, and a split on 14/17 to ensure a regular return, but the big payoffs are always on the high numbers. *Remember to breathe.*

Playing with renewed vigor, in a style that is astounding to the gathering onlookers, he starts to exceed the maximum table bet limit on every spin. After only a few spins, the crowds are three or four deep at his table, and he finds himself jostled for position as players attempt to copy his bets. He keeps his spot by sitting in one of the chairs, but still, the outstretched arms come over his shoulders as others scramble to place their bets. Frustrated, he waits until the last possible moment to place his bets, and once again, the croupier has to spend time ascertaining the difference at the end of every coup. Impatient players start to leave, and Bill has his command of the table restored. *I'm back in the game*, he thinks.

Arthur Bourchier has never seen roulette played with such conviction. He is a famous English actor who loves to be the center of attention and sees this as an opportunity to get his name in the newspapers. He sits in one of the vacant chairs and exchanges some francs.

"Good evening," he says to Bill, who does not look up from the table.

"You're the American, aren't you?" he persists, now smiling and looking around at the spectators. Bill has seen Bourchier but has no time for his small talk. He has a tactic for this type of encounter, which he now employs. Out of his right jacket pocket, he extracts his small notebook and a pencil and proceeds to scribble illegible numbers. Once the ball is spinning again, he places his piles of chips on the exact same numbers using both hands. There are no square bets or streets, and he has no interest in outside bets. Eventually, Bourchier crosses his arms like a frustrated child, stops placing bets, and simply sits back to watch a master at work.

After nearly five hours of continuous play, Bill steps onto the balcony outside the Salon Rose and is alone. Most of the casino guests have caught the last train back to Nice, and Bill lights a cigar, finally allowing himself a smile. He turns to look in at the casino, and the sparkling chandeliers look like thousands of glittering diamonds. Diamonds.

Pierre Laget is not immediately amenable to the prospect of exchanging jewelry acquired from other players.

"My point is," says Bill, "the casino's greatest asset is this wonderful building," he looks up and gestures with his right hand, "and cash. If you want the burden of acting as a diamond clearing house, that's fine with me. All I am suggesting is that I make your work easier by taking some of the diamonds off your hands."

"It is not the policy of the casino—" Laget begins, but Bill cuts him off.

"I understand, but we all have to adapt. I am not proposing we break any rules, simply that we modify the policy as it would be a mutually beneficial arrangement."

Finally, Laget capitulates, and they agree that Bill will have his appraiser authenticate and value the pieces with the option to purchase them outright.

"Do you ever see him talking with anyone?" Laget is having a hushed conversation with one of the Chefs du Partie from a vantage point at the side of the Salle Schmit.

"No sir," the casino man answers as his experienced eyes survey the room. "He is possibly the most dedicated player I have seen in all my years of service, and he only takes breaks to use the facilities, and occasionally he eats some food."

"I hear he declines party invitations?" says Laget.

"I have heard that too, sir."

M. Darnborough is back again. This is without doubt the event of the week. People who don't often go into the rooms now make a point of visiting them to watch the stupendous play of this bold gambler. The only trouble is that it is almost impossible to get near the table where he is playing so dense is the throng.
　　—Monte Carlo Echo, December 12ᵗʰ, 1905

Each morning, Bill reads the newspaper to stay in touch with current affairs just in case he meets someone who should ask what he thinks of the latest war or political upheaval. Otherwise, even though he is surrounded by people every day, he resides in his own private world for months.

His concentration and single-mindedness mean that he only speaks with waiters, croupiers, and hotel staff. As the Christmas season approaches, the annual visitors from around Europe and beyond descend on Monaco. The train from Nice is packed with optimistic pilgrims, many of whom honestly believe they have a realistic chance of returning home as newly minted millionaires. Tourists come and go, as do one-off gamblers who imagine they have the magic touch, although most leave quickly and never return. Regular guests at the principality come for the social scene, and there are endless lunch and dinner parties to attend. Bill declines invitations to parties as he knows that most of the other guests will be hounding him for the secrets of his system for success.

The Monégasque are not permitted to enter the casino unless they work there, so it is the lively ex-pat fraternity that thrives on excess. The local gendarmes do not tolerate any unruly behavior, but the locals tend to look the other way as these are the people who are responsible for ninety-five percent of Monaco's income.

The first serious incident of driving an automobile while under the influence of alcohol happens that December. As he sips his coffee in the breakfast room, Bill reads the official report in the *Monte Carlo Echo* which states that a young man and his female companion, both from Germany, had perished while driving their Mercedes Simplex around the eastern end of the Avenue des Beau Arts. The newspaper reports that the male driver had consumed enough champagne to kill a horse before attempting to show off his driving skills around the town's roads.

Bill thinks about the magnificent motorcars he sees almost daily now outside the casino. He desperately wants to have one but now realizes that if he is going to drive around the treacherous roads of Monaco, he will need to become an expert driver.

He decides that the best person to inquire about this matter is Niccolò at the bank, as he is one of the few locals he can trust with a request of this nature. Pierre Laget at the casino would undoubtedly be as unhelpful as possible for fear that one of his most loyal and regular customers may spend his money on such frivolities as an automobile when he could be losing it at the tables instead. Bill doesn't need to qualify for the next Paris to Madrid rally, but he does need to learn how to drive proficiently, swiftly, and without mishaps.

CHAPTER 36

"*B*efore we can discuss your motoring intentions, Mr. Darnborough," says Niccolò as they make themselves comfortable in his office at the bank. "A matter of grave importance has been brought to my attention, which I wish to share with you."

Bill frowns. "Go on."

"As you can understand, Monsieur Laget at the casino and I are well acquainted with each other, and he has requested that I share some information with my, shall we say, regular customers. Our little town appears to have become quite an attractive place for criminals, especially of the pickpocket persuasion. Understandably, Laget does not want the casino to be associated with any undesirable reputation of this sort, and, equally, he wishes to protect his patrons from any wrongdoing."

"Of course, I understand," says Bill.

"As you know, all of the players in the Salle de Jeux carry cash and gold, as the tables will not accept checks or IOUs. Consequently, they are prime targets for pickpockets as large amounts of cash are carried around, which is usually easily accessible. I cannot think of any other place in the world where there is so much cash just walking around, and it must be the very pinnacle of the career of a pickpocket to arrive here."

Niccolò adjusts his silk tie. "We have a new Prefét du Police. You know, we call it the Surete Publique, which means public safety, which is exactly what it is for, but sometimes they can be, how would you say, a little too polite? I have the greatest respect for Monsieur Joseph Simard, and he has a groenendael dog, which is more like a wolf, but I just wanted to warn you to be on your guard."

"Well, thank you so much, Niccolò," says Bill, anxious to move the conversation along to the subject of driving. "I should tell you that I take every precaution to ensure the safety of my cash. Should I encounter a thief with a weapon, my wallet only has a few notes in it. I use different pockets, inside and out, within the lining of my hat, coat, and scarf. Socks are good, too." Bill smiles and sits back in his chair, although Niccolò does not seem as impressed as he would have hoped.

"That's good, Mr. Darnborough, very good," says Niccolò. "Have you ever had someone break into your hotel room without your knowledge?"

"I'm not sure," answers Bill. "I guess if I didn't know, I wouldn't know."

Niccolò is not amused. "This is a new method that you should know about." He picks up a printed card to ensure he has the details correct. "This is according to Theotime Farine, who I am told is a detective of the highest caliber. Apparently, he has protected the Russian Imperial family on many occasions and has received some of their highest orders and decorations. Anyway, there have been reports of thieves entering hotel rooms as the guests are sleeping. They use elaborate pincer keys to silently pick the lock, enter the room, and purposefully leave behind any obvious valuables like your wonderful pocket watch," he points at Bill's gold watch, "and proceed to remove all the loose notes from your pocketbook. The thief then leaves the room and locks the door behind him, giving the impression that it has been locked from the inside."

"In the morning," Niccolò continues, "you would not notice that anything of value was missing, and the room seems completely as you left it. For example, your pocket watch and cufflinks are where they should be. Only later, when you open your pocketbook, would you realize all your money is missing. At this point, you would assume that you had fallen victim to a pickpocket the night before, perhaps when you left the casino or walked through a crowded restaurant."

"Crafty little rats," says Bill, absentmindedly touching his wallet in his jacket pocket and looking at his watch. "As I said, I'm grateful for your advice, Niccolò, and I'm well aware that you wouldn't spend as much time as this with all your clients. But I still need to ask if you know anyone who can teach me how to drive?"

"Ah yes, let me make some inquiries."

Bill realizes that Niccolò is strictly in the asset protection business, and he should not have expected the banker to leap into action at his behest. He tries another tact.

"Perhaps I can return the favor and treat you to lunch?"

"That would be meraviglioso, as we say in Italian, Mr. Darnborough, although, regrettably, I have another engagement. Perhaps tomorrow?"

"Certainement," says Bill, realizing he has picked up the standard French response.

"Shall we say noon at Quinto's?"

"I should have guessed that you would choose the Italian place," says Bill with a smile and tips his hat as he leaves.

After making a sizable withdrawal from the cashier, Bill strolls back toward the Place du Casino, although this time, around the back through the magnificent gardens. He occasionally pauses to take in the fragrances, especially the roses. The leader of the army of horticultural geniuses, Monsieur Jules van den Daele, has recently been awarded the Knight of the Order of Saint Charles and made an Officer of the Order of Horticultural Merit. Horticultural magic is at work as the flowers of one type or another are always in bloom—the secret is that they are rotated with the seasons. Aside from his immediate ambition to own an automobile,

Bill hopes one day to have a garden of his own and not to grow food, like his father had to, but to grow fanciful flowers.

As he enters the Salle de Jeux, Bill is surprised that there appear to be many more people than usual walking haphazardly, many seemingly without a clear idea where to go. Perhaps they have recently announced something in the newspapers that has created an upsurge in visitors. He walks through the Salle Touzet and turns left into the newer of the two Salle Schmits, which only contains one roulette table.

No sooner has he taken his seat than a crowd starts to gather, and he realizes that the press must have been particularly attentive to his recent roulette activities. He had hoped that the excitement had died down by now, considering that he plays so regularly. Typically, the reporters would jump on stories of players who have significant wins in one sitting rather than follow the progress of a daily player.

> *Among the throng of players at the casino today was the Grand Duchess Vladimir of Russia. The American 'plunger' whose remarkable play at the tables has aroused so much attention – his name by the way is Darnborough, succeeded in netting £5,000 on Thursday, and on Friday his winnings amounted to £7,200. Yesterday he continued playing on the same system as hitherto, but Dame Fortune proved capricious, and he lost £4,000.*
> *—The Daily Mail, December 18, 1905*

"I met an Italian saloon owner in Denver years ago," says Bill, looking up at Niccolò as they study the menus. "Mangini was his name. He was an audacious character who had made his way to the American Midwest in difficult circumstances. Anyway, he ran a saloon serving Italian food and made me try his homemade ravioli. It was delicious. So, I thought I'd try that here, just for a comparison, you understand."

"I understand, Mr. Darnborough," says Niccolò. "Not that I am an expert, but you know we Italians take our food very seriously indeed. Here in Monaco, there are one hundred and twenty forms for exactly the same pasta, varying from the famous spaghetti, tagliarini, and cannelloni to the lesser known bombolotti, capellini, cornets, or little baskets." Niccolò is making gestures with his fingers to enhance his description. "Everyone thinks the shape is important, but it is not. The substance is the important part. Macaroni, for example, is made not with ordinary flour but with semolina, derived from the transparent, hard, for the most part, Russian wheat. They have a macaroni factory here in Monaco, you know?"

"Niccolò, you obviously know your pasta," Bill says, realizing that as he had to learn about tea in London, here he must become an expert in pasta. As the waiter arrives, Bill gestures to Niccolò that he can order the wine. When the bottle comes, Niccolò takes great pride in explaining that Sangiovese translates as "the blood of Jupiter." Bill only drinks one glass throughout the lunch, although Niccolò evidently has no essential meetings to attend this afternoon as the conversation becomes less formal with each glass. Though Bill is late for his usual appointed time at the tables, the magnificence of the ravioli with goat's cheese has him already planning on driving to Italy.

"Did you have any thoughts on my driving lesson?" he asks as they look over dessert options.

"Yes, a young German who lives here at the moment is an accomplished driver, and he would like to meet you."

"Excellent news! In that case, as promised, lunch is on me."

Bill keeps up the roulette momentum for five straight days, concentrating on numbers 29 and 32 and their surrounding numbers. Gradually, the stakes rise, and one night, he wins 300,200 FF, and on another night, he loses 90,000 FF. It is not unusual for the gallery to stand three or four deep around his table.

The newspaper reports vary wildly, and some speculate again that he is an American millionaire who has come very near to breaking the bank. Another report states that he has two ladies who always accompany him and sit on either side. One correspondent even says he has placed a little golden pig on the table and changed his tactics by playing the first dozen instead of the last.

The *New York Herald* carries reports of Bill's progress and is preoccupied with publishing exhaustive lists of guests at the casino.

One day, they announce the arrival of the Contessa di Santaflora, the Lady-in-Waiting to Queen Margherita, and Prince Michel Radziwill from the Russian Embassy in London. In addition, Conte Reglio di Castelletto, Baron Koyff, and Marchese Bourbon del Monte have all arrived and checked in to the Hotel de Paris. Bill has not heard of any of these people, but they have all heard of him.

CHAPTER 37

*J*ulius Beutler comes from a wealthy German family and aspires to become a famous rally driver. He was a navigator in the Paris to Madrid race in 1903, in which eight people died, including the renowned car maker Marcel Renault. The race was called off after inexperienced drivers crashed on the rough roads, hit trees, overturned, and often, the cars caught fire. Despite reports of over sixty participants wounded during that one rally, Beutler continues to follow his passion and supplements his lifestyle in Monaco by offering his services as a driving instructor.

Bill stands outside the Hotel de Paris momentarily, seeing Julius positioned proudly next to his Panhard et Levassor Type Q. He is exactly as Bill imagines a race car driver should look, with slicked back hair, polished boots, and long black leather gloves. A small crowd has gathered, and Julius is clearly enjoying the moment.

The car is magnificent, with a dark blue Victorian hood and a mahogany framed windshield for rear passengers. No expense has been spared on the design, and it looks powerful and restless, like a caged animal desperate to be let loose. There is no way that this belongs to Julius, Bill muses—he must have it on loan from a wealthy sponsor.

On his first lesson, Bill learns how to light the Ducellier head-lamps, which require him to unscrew the casings and ignite the acetylene flames. Thick concave mirrors combine with magnifying lenses to project the flame light, and Beutler insists that this is one of the essential things to master should Bill be driving at night or in the event of a breakdown.

"What's next?" asks Bill.

"Next, we start the vehicle, ya," says Julius, gesturing for Bill to get into the driver's seat. "This is the steering wheel, and the accelerator pedal is in the middle there," he points to Bill's feet. "The brake is this handle here," he says, pointing to the handle mounted on the outside, "and these are the mirrors."

"Excellent," says Bill, eager to get going.

"This is the choke," Julius continues, pointing to the cigar-shaped knob to the right of the steering wheel. "This is to adjust the mixture of fuel and air, and you need to burn more fuel at the start." He motions for Bill to get out of the car and follows him around to the front. The hinges must have been recently oiled, as the only sound is the slight squeak of the leather door strap as Bill gets out.

"Dies is de crank to start the engine. Always turn to the left, ya. Never turn, how you say, clockwise. Always to the left. Please repeat."

"Always to the left," repeats Bill.

"Good." Julius shoos him back into the driver's seat. "Check brake, please."

"Done." Bill feels exhilarated and anxious as his hands control the steering wheel for the first time. Julius cranks the engine, and nothing happens. He tries again, and still no sound. Bill tries to make sense of the dashboard. Is there something he should be looking out for? Is there enough oil and water? Perhaps it has over-heated? Finally, the engine sputters and shakes into life on the third time, and Julius rushes around and reaches over Bill to adjust the choke slightly.

"Third time lucky, eh, Julius?" shouts Bill over the noise, almost unable to contain his excitement.

Julius jumps into the passenger seat and points ahead.

"We go now, ya?"

"Sure, but why don't you take us around the corner first, and then I'll take over. I want to see an expert at work." Bill is understandably concerned that he does not make a fool of himself in the middle of the Place du Casino of all places.

Julius dutifully drives them down to Boulevard des Mouline, and once they are safely away from potential critics, they swap seats again. When the car is in motion, and after several lurches, Bill tries to act out something resembling confidence. Fear and excitement remind him of his first time playing roulette as he tentatively jolts down the road. He is more concerned about damaging the car than anything else and anxiously presses the brake more than necessary as his hands grip the steering wheel with the strength of a wrestler.

On Boulevard d'Italie, Bill has gained his confidence and performs his first three-point turn as Julius guides him through the newly invented reverse gear mechanism. Just for fun, Bill honks the horn several times and laughs.

"Just checking it works, Julius!"

While Bill is becoming accustomed to his latest adventure, the *Daily Mail* in London and then the *American Register* publish articles that include the fact that the *"American plunger of Monte Carlo, William Darnborough, stays at the Hotel de Paris in Monte Carlo."* Within one week, the letters start to arrive.

One of the more memorable of these first letters is from a mother in Brighton, England, who encloses a photograph of her daughter asking if Bill could buy her a piano. Otherwise, there are letters from actresses and all manner of people, some enclosing small amounts of money, with photographs, asking if Bill would play and return the winnings. His initial instinct is to try and answer as many letters as possible, although Hiram Lewin's warning words remind him to be wary of swindlers. How does he know if any of these pleas are genuine? He can't simply write checks to people he has never heard of and blindly send them money.

Strangers who are not regular visitors to the casino and do not appreciate the etiquette and unwritten protocols approach Bill more regularly now, seeking his advice. Does he have a strategy or a system that he can share? Perhaps he wouldn't mind staking 40,000 FF in return for a 50/50 split of the winnings?

This attention prompts Bill to hasten the purchase of his first car. Unlike Julius, he doesn't see this as a means to turn the heads of all the ladies in the Place du Casino but more as a form of escape. He has done his research well. Fernand Charron, Leonce Giradot, and Emile Voigt had formed *Automobiles Charron-Girardot-Voigt* and produced French-made cars under the CGV brand name. All three had been successful racing drivers for Panhard, and Charron won the Marseilles-Nice and Paris-Amsterdam-Paris races in 1898. King Manuel II of Portugal purchased a CGV in 1904, and Bill supposes that if it is good enough for a European King, then it is good enough for him. In addition, an automobile made in France would mean that spare parts would be easier to obtain.

The four-cylinder, 25 h.p, side-entrance tonneau has a top speed of 45 mph. There are four headlamps, two large ones on the front and two smaller ones on either side of the windscreen. There is a leather brace on the side to carry two spare tires. It seats four, and after a whole week becoming accustomed to driving it, Bill invites Julius and Niccolò for a motorized tour of Monaco.

Niccolò is supremely impressed with the new purchase as, aside from anything else, Bill finally has one tangible asset to his name. Julius, however, is less than thrilled as he tells them about a Darracq that has broken the land speed record of 104 mph in Ostend, Belgium. It seems evident that he despises being a passenger, although he most likely has agreed to come along as his instructor business relies on referrals.

They head east, and as they near the reservoir on Boulevard de France, Bill surprises his passengers by turning onto the Grand Corniche, a steep, winding highway. His scarf whips in the warm wind, and Bill grits his teeth against the dust and feels the pressure of the rising altitude in his ears as he leans over the wheel. His polished brogue on the pedal pushes the car faster, relishing the challenge of steering around the sharp, endless curves, even knowing there is no room for a second car to be coming down into

Monaco at the same time. He speeds past Mont des Mules as if he is racing at the Nice Rally. The road snakes higher and higher, and each time they turn a corner, they glimpse the harbor with its yachts and the azure Mediterranean Sea beyond.

La Turbie is a modest village with many outstanding features. Chief among these is the magnificent view as it overlooks the entire principality of Monaco from about two thousand feet. This is the first time Bill has seen Monaco from such an elevation, and as he looks down, he can see the Hotel de Paris and the casino in the distance, looking relatively small and almost fragile.

"What do you think of that, fellas?" says Bill as they all stare down into the distance. "It's a tough fight, you know, but I am sure I can beat them."

"What do you mean, beat them?" asks Niccolò.

"Down there is the greatest of all gambling resorts with organizational skills to match the Bank of England. Down there is a combination of the toughest specialists in the form of gambling on earth, and I am tackling them single handed. I am sure I can beat them." Niccolò and Jules simultaneously look at Bill, then down at Monaco, then back at Bill, who is smiling. He is looking down upon his enemy, and from this height and distance, the smallness of the casino only strengthens his determination to do battle with them at their own game.

The journey back to town takes much longer, and they have a much better view of Monte Carlo, but Bill is lost in thought. It never enters his mind that he could quit while he is ahead of the game. His whole life has been building up to this, the greatest of all opportunities to have the life he has dreamed of. Even if it takes eight hours a day standing at the tables, then that is what he must do. This is his life now. He could stop at any time and take a break, although he is a professional roulette player, possibly the best in the world, so he must stay the course and keep in the fight.

CHAPTER 38

*A*t the hotel reception, Etienne passes Bill a note that reads: *Heard you have purchased an automobile and hope that we could meet to discuss motoring in the Cote d'Azur and other topics.* It is signed by Jimmy Rothschild, Monaco. Bill receives many curious letters, notes, and messages regularly, although this one has caught him by surprise.

"Etienne, do you know a Mr. Jimmy Rothschild?"

"Well, actually, no, I do not," replies Etienne, and after a brief pause, "I know who he is, of course."

Bill raises his eyebrows as Etienne looks from side to side to ensure he is out of earshot of other guests and leans closer.

"James de Rothschild is a French relative of the late Baron Arthur de Rothschild, and I am reliably informed that he is presently staying at the family villa."

"How does he even know that I bought a car?"

"I cannot say."

Bill purses his lips. Etienne sighs and lowers his voice to a whisper.

"I honestly do not know why Monsieur Rothschild has contacted you, but I can say that he is a member of one of the most

256

influential families in the world, and it is no surprise that he is well informed."

Bill speculates as to the nature of Rothschild's hidden agenda. Does he have an angle? Is there a casino syndication that he does not know about? Although he died three years ago, Arthur de Rothschild used to play roulette. Could there be a connection? Eventually, Bill realizes there is no harm in simply replying to the note. After two exchanges of brief messages, Bill receives an invitation to meet with James Armand Edmond de Rothschild at his villa.

"I HEAR you are a decidedly private person, Mr. Darnborough," is Rothschild's opening line as they shake hands in his drawing room overlooking the harbor.

"That all depends on who you ask, Mr. Rothschild."

"Please call me Jimmy."

"Very well—please call me Bill."

Jimmy's butler arrives with a decanter of chilled white wine and pours glasses for both of them. Bill assumes it is probably one of the finest labels available. He looks around the room, appreciating the antique cabinets and tables, no doubt passed down from French and Italian noble families. They step out onto the balcony, and Jimmy has the air of someone surveying his kingdom.

"You heard about my new car?" says Bill.

Jimmy smiles. "Bill, we have something in common. Nearly everyone who meets us wants something from us. I imagine you have a fair share of people wanting you to place high stakes for them, expecting even higher returns?"

"Sometimes," replies Bill, impressed at Jimmy's perfect command of English, which has hardly any trace of a French accent.

"Well then," says Jimmy, "we are practically in the same business, but more than that, I suspect that your reputation for privacy stems from your desire to steer clear of people wanting to discover the secrets of your success." Bill says nothing and feels like he's watching the roulette ball spinning, waiting for it to drop. "My point, Bill, is that I don't want anything from you. Similarly, you don't need anything from me. From what I hear, you certainly don't require a line of credit." At this, Bill returns Jimmy's smile and feels a flush of relief. At least Jimmy has a sense of humor.

"There is one fundamental difference between us," Bill says. "Forgive me for being direct, but you have an extended family and have all manner of considerations that influence your every move. I can come and go without worrying too much about my reputation, and I am quite content to be the master of my own destiny."

"Too true, too true," says Jimmy. "I am bound by certain expectations although, trust me, like any family, ours is a colorful mix of heroes and scoundrels."

"I'm from the American Midwest," says Bill, turning toward Jimmy again and looking him squarely in the eyes. "We have a reputation for simplicity, but it's not that. It's honesty. We like to skip the bull and get to the point. So, forgive me, Jimmy, but why am I here?"

"I knew I would like you, Bill. You get straight to it—an excellent quality in a man. Especially around here." Jimmy waves his hand across the Monaco vista. "So many shallow people who pretend to be something they are not. Anyway, the real reason I asked to meet with you is that I want to start a car enthusiasts club and I wanted your opinion. Perhaps you would like to join me as a founding member? I thought we may call it the Automobile Club of Monte Carlo?" Bill laughs and is relieved that after such a buildup, this meeting turns out to be about joining a club.

"Jimmy," says Bill, "that sounds like a grand plan. I drove up to La Turbie two days ago, and what a ride!"

Bill feels like a barrier that existed between them has been lowered as if the formalities are concluded. Instead of an interrogation, warning, or who knows what, he has been presented with something to which he would voluntarily like to contribute.

"Good to hear," says Jimmy, "you see, at the moment, all they have here is the Sport Vélocipédique Monégasque, which is for cyclists, so I thought we should incorporate something similar to down the road in Nice, where they have a club run by Jacques Gondoin."

"By the way," says Jimmy smiling, "you know bull is actually a French word. It's bole, and it means deceit. I have been known to use it on occasion."

"Interesting," says Bill, smiling as he takes a sip of his wine, "I would have thought it was Spanish." He places his glass on the table and puts out his hands to imitate a Spanish bullfighter waving a cape. He is glad to see Jimmy just slightly startled by this and also glad to see him smile. He doesn't want to intimidate him but must ensure Jimmy realizes he cannot be pushed around.

Jimmy offers to take Bill to see the garage that Arthur de Rothschild had constructed in a customized recess underneath one side of the villa. "These are my lions," says Jimmy. "This one is from New York—it's called a Pierce-Arrow. They replaced the De Dion engine with a Pierce last year and I had it shipped over."

The beauty of the pearly body takes words away from Bill, and he is more than a little envious as he admires the magnificent vehicle.

"This other one is local," Jimmy continues, patting the fender of the next shining car in the row. "Well, local in that it won the Nice to La Turbie hill climb, although, as you can see, it's a Mercedes, so German by birth. It's called a Simplex. One of these also won in your part of the world. Have you heard of Grosse Point in Detroit?"

"I've read about it." Bill swallows as he thinks of the poor German couple who met their fate driving a similar car on the Avenue des Beau Arts.

"See how the engine is mounted over the front axle?" Jimmy says, pointing, "We have Wilhelm Maybach to thank for that design, and the frame is made of pressed steel. See how the engine is directly welded onto it—that keeps it low and aerodynamic. I'm expecting delivery of some cast-steel wheels in November to replace these fixed spokes. Pneumatic tires, of course."

Bill nods, his pulse racing. "Of course."

"It gives forty-four horsepower at a steady thirteen-hundred revolutions per minute, and you see this," says Jimmy, enthusiastically pointing. "That, sir, is a four-speed gearbox—four speeds and reverse. The top speed reached at the Ablis to Chartres race was nearly one-hundred and twelve kilometers per hour, that's seventy miles per hour in American English. Guess who did that? None other than William K. Vanderbilt, Jr. Bravo, America!"

Eventually, they bid their farewells, and Jimmy promises to send the details of the club proposal to Bill's hotel. As he climbs into his CGV, Bill is formulating a plan. He fantasizes about having a villa so that he can have a garage and fill it with a car collection to rival Jimmy's.

He snakes his way down the hill, loving the feel of shifting, the wind in his face, and the satisfying rumble of the motor surrounding him. No, he'll never have the family connections that Jimmy does. And, yes, over here, people set a lot of store by titles and lineage and such things, but Bill thinks, "I'm an American. I can be anyone I want to be if I have enough money."

CHAPTER 39

$\mathcal{P}$ierre Laget is on his tiptoes and clenching his fists as he stands at the edge of the room, watching the American play. The Salle Garnier feels like it has been transformed into an amphitheater, with a sizable crowd applauding Bill's savage stakes on the table. As he has become famous for, he is betting aggressively on the high numbers with maximum stakes.

Also at Bill's table is the Grand Duchess Maria Pavlovna of Russia, who is one of the few players in Monte Carlo who can play at this level. Bill occasionally glances up between spins at the Duchess's diamond-encrusted necklace, but he remains invariably calm under pressure. Even when the ball does not drop in his favor, he does not flinch. Laget bites his lip, watching the American and the Duchess have a run of good luck. Soon, a raised finger from the Chef du Partie signals Laget that a replenishment of funds is needed for their table.

Twenty more tension-laden minutes pass until the pivotal moment. Bill is rhythmically tapping his fingers on the table as the croupier calls, "Les jeux sant faits. The bets have been placed." The ball ominously descends, finding its haphazard way into the 32 pocket. The croupier's swift hand places the dolly marker on 32, prompting an intense exchange of glances with the Chef de Partie, who signals Laget once more. Laget's controlled façade falters perceivably as he breathes deeply through his nose, straightens, points his chin, and clasps his hands behind his back.

A crescendo of shouts and screams erupts from the gathered throng, a cacophony of excitement and chaos that permeates the air. A rush of onlookers converge towards Bill's table, all eager to witness the unfolding spectacle.

Bill quietly sits at the table, doing calculations in his notepad. His total winnings are 82,000 FF. Laget retains his resolute demeanor. Everyone knows that the publicity surrounding the American's good fortune will spread around the world, and this should only encourage more players to come and try their luck. Bill looks to his side and sees Laget looking earnestly in his direction.

The 82,000 FF Bill has just won translates to $16,400—enough money to buy a mansion in Manhattan if he wanted one, he figures, noting the calculations and totals. He pockets the notebook and stands up as many other guests and players congratulate him and offer him celebratory drinks. Rather than stick around to deal with an onslaught of questions, he stays for only one glass of champagne, then heads to his room and out onto the balcony, where he lights a cigar.

"London," says Bill out loud as he exhales and surveys the harbor. Perhaps this time, he can finally put an end to living out of a travel trunk, and he begins to seriously consider buying a place somewhere in England.

Bill hastily arranges a meeting with Niccolò di Buonaccorso at Banca Monte dei Paschi.

"You will return to Monte Carlo, Signore Darnborough?" asks Niccolò after Bill explains his travel arrangements.

"I can quite understand that if I didn't continue to bank with you," Bill replies, "this might result in the bank closing its doors ending five hundred years of service, but you have nothing to fear, I'll be back. There is one thing."

"Yes?"

"I will need a bank account in London so that I may transfer funds. I don't like surprises, especially unwarranted banking fees. So, who would you recommend?"

"Of course," says Niccolò, with a faint smile. "We have worked with a London partner for many years, and I will arrange an introduction to a senior advisor."

"Excellent," says Bill. "Who are they?"

"The bank is called Barclays, but they are quite young compared to us, as they have only been in business since the 1690s." This time, the smile widens, and Bill and Niccolò laugh together. Niccolò is one of only a handful of people Bill can speak frankly with and is completely relaxed in his company as he never asks about roulette.

Arrangements are made and telegrams are sent to various parties including Brown's Hotel. Bill does not want his CGV to remain at the hotel as they charge ridiculous rates, so he arranges for it to be safely parked and covered behind Hinault's garage just off the Boulevard d'Italie.

With a fair amount of ready cash evenly distributed around his person, Bill makes his way north again. Just as the connecting train is leaving Nice, a man knocks on the glass door of Bill's compartment. For a moment, Bill cannot place the short, slightly overweight man he sees, but in a second or two, he recognizes Charles Selby, smiles, and gestures for him to enter.

"It's been a while, Mr. Selby. Good to see you. Do you have any more Greek mythology inspiration for me?"

"Good to see you too, Mr. Darnborough, and I am impressed. I didn't know if you would remember me from our brief encounter on the balcony at the casino."

"Certainly! I may suffer from selective memory loss, but I am good with names and numbers." Bill looks at Selby's suit, probably Saville Row, and his shoes are highly polished, giving the impression that this is a man for whom appearance is essential. He may not be in the best shape, but he is clearly a man of means.

Charles grins. "If the papers are anything to go by, you are definitely good with numbers."

Bill has no desire to talk about his activities in the Salles des

Jeux. "Tell me, Charles," he says, "do you live permanently in Monaco now, or do you just visit occasionally?"

Charles shrugs and says, "I have been fortunate in business, and I'm not married, so I like to travel around. Monaco fascinates me, although I am unsure if I could call it home. Yorkshire is home and always will be. I come from a large family, and I want to be close to my people when I settle down. Until that day comes, I am simply trying to educate myself as best I can in the ways of the world. And you? Where in America do you hail from?"

"A small town in the midwest. I think I mentioned last time we met that my family left Yorkshire in the early 1800s. Back then, we were farmers, but that life wasn't for me. Like pushing the rock up the hill, if you know what I mean."

"Sisyphean, indeed," Charles agrees.

Bill laughs. "You know, Charles. You're the first person in a very long time who has asked me anything beyond gambling advice. I find it quite refreshing not to be asked about my *system*."

Charles laughs, too. "Bill, if I were to spend more than a few minutes at the tables, I could be taking this trip without a shirt on my back!"

"Well, I'm glad you have your shirt," smiles Bill, "or the ladies on the train might have something to say." The idea sparks a thought of Miss Tate at the garden party and his ambitions the last time he was in London. He wonders if Selby might have some interesting acquaintances. Anyway, it's been a long time since he's enjoyed anybody's company or felt like he had a friend. "Are you going to London?" he asks.

"Only for a few days, then I'll carry on up north."

"Well then," says Bill, "what do you say we go down to the dining car, have some lunch, maybe some fine wine, and do some chateau spotting as we whizz through the French countryside?"

"Sounds like a capital plan. Lead the way, sir!"

As Bill enters the dining carriage, he thinks how different this picture looks from the scene on the Kansas train returning to Denver with the Grizzlies. He misses all the boys and the talk of women and barfights, but that is a chapter in his life that has closed, and he is quite content to exchange beans for lightly salted quail's eggs today.

As the two men are eying the dessert menu, Charles gives a tiny half smile as if he's about to tell a joke and says, "Tell me, Bill, what's the difference between baseball and cricket?"

Bill laughs and supposes he has only himself to blame, as he had found himself telling Charles about his days with the Grizzlies. He raises his eyes as he considers the question. "It's probably easiest if I show you," he says. He looks down at their table, then stands and addresses the two gentlemen at the adjacent table. "Excuse me, sirs, may I borrow your salt and pepper?"

"Certainement," comes the reply from one of the Frenchmen with a wave of his hand.

Bill takes them, plus the salt and pepper from his own table, and places all four in a square, then goes over to where an elderly man and a lady at least half his age are drinking tea. "Please forgive me. May I borrow your sugar bowl?" The man simply nods his consent, and Bill returns to place the sugar bowl in the middle of the square on their table and sits down. "Now, this is how baseball works. Don't ask me about cricket because I have absolutely no idea. I'll do my best, and afterward, we can compare notes."

Bill points to the salt and pepper pots in turn. "This is the home plate, where the batter stands, this is first base, second base, and third base. The batter has to hit the ball, then run around these bases, but he can stop at any of them." He then points to the sugar bowl in the middle, "This is me in the pitcher's box. My job is to throw the ball in such a way that the batter misses. If he misses three times, he's out. Are you following this so far?"

"Yes, yes, carry on," says Charles.

"An inning," Bill continues, "consists of batters from each team taking their turn at bat until three batters are out. A game lasts nine innings but is extended into extra innings if the score is tied." Bill picks up a spoon and points around his miniature ballpark. "The fielding side consists of a pitcher, catcher, four infielders, and three outfielders. I guess that's about it. Whichever team gets the most runs wins."

"We do have a game similar to that in England," says Charles, "It's called rounders, although, from what I've read, baseball is more dangerous as doesn't the man who catches the ball wear protective equipment?"

"Definitely more dangerous," says Bill. "It's difficult to know for sure, but I think I can throw a ball at around ninety miles per hour. They're still trying to work out the best way to measure the speed, but it weighs about five ounces, so if it hits you in the head, you know about it. So, what's the difference with cricket?"

Charles allows himself a little laugh. "Well, it isn't that different, really. The team with the most amount of runs wins. We have eleven players on each side instead of nine. The batsmen don't run around anything, they run up and down what we call the wicket, which is marked at either end with stumps. I suppose the main difference is that our games can last five days."

"Five days!"

"Well, yes, those are called five-day test matches. The fielders have some interesting names, like silly mid-on and deep gully. Best not to go into too much detail."

"Silly mid-on?"

"Ah, yes. It's called silly because being that close is insanely dangerous!"

"Oh, right," says Bill. "We have one of those, too, and he's a third baseman. We call that the hot corner."

"Ah, well, good," Charles says with a smile. "We've settled all that."

Bill laughs again, feeling charmed by the man. He realizes he has almost forgotten what it was like to have a real conversation. Has he been *too* focused on his roulette play? He shakes off the thought. He has made out well, and no point second guessing himself.

"Tell me, Bill," says Charles, leaning in across the table, "what's it really like in the American West? I've always so wanted to see it."

"Oh, it feels like a long time since I was there," replies Bill, unexpectedly nostalgic, feeling the ache of how young he was back then. He sighs and brings himself back to the present. "But I think the frontiersman spirit will be alive for a long time. There is still oil and gold and silver to be found, but what's exciting is everything else that comes with that. Action. Building. Bustle. We Americans are always on about the next best thing, and we think every idea we ever had is brand new and started first with us. Pretty soon there will be roads for motor cars everywhere, which will bring more people, so they will build more towns and so on and so on. Who knows, maybe one day, someone will build their own Monte Carlo somewhere in America, and of course, we'll take the credit for inventing it!"

Charles laughs. "Will you go back?"

"Perhaps, but I want to see Italy and Spain. And I can go anywhere I want in my car. I'm drawn to the older parts of the world, somehow. You see, America is my mother," Bill smiles, "but Europe is my mistress."

"Ah, yes, the Italian ladies," says Charles, winking at Bill. "Well, I haven't been too far south, and I can tell you that they don't have any roads suitable for motor cars there either, but the north is fine. And the food is exquisite, of course."

Bill and Charles continue their journey together, and this time, the steamer departs from Calais to Dover, a shorter crossing than the last time to Folkstone. It also means Bill sees the gleaming white cliffs for the first time.

"Now you can see what Caesar and his Romans saw around two thousand years ago. All the locals were gathered up on the cliffs, chariots and spears glistening in the sunlight, and he turned right around."

"He turned around?"

"Yes," says Charles, "and came back again with eighty warships, and that's why we use Latin words in law and medicine now." The two men both laugh. "You know, we have a saying here," Charles continues. *What did the Romans ever do for us?* Of course, it's a joke, as they did quite a lot. For a start, they built all the great roads for their chariots that you can now use for your new motor car. Also, they gave us sanitation, irrigation, public order, and most importantly, they introduced us to wine!"

"Well, I had no idea," Bill says cheerfully and finds he's looking forward to continuing the association with his new friend in London. Also, in the back of his mind, he still thinks Charles is intriguing. Therefore, he must know some fascinating people. "By the way, Charles, have you ever met Jock Carruthers and his wife in Monaco?"

"Can't say I have."

"Perhaps I could arrange for us all to meet for a drink at Brown's or somewhere while you're in London. They have their own telephone, but how do I reach you?"

"I'll be staying at the Great Northern by King's Cross," says Charles. "Always stay there as it's so convenient to get up to Yorkshire as well. If you ask at Brown's, they can get a message to me easily."

"Very good," says Bill, and is instantly amused to notice he's beginning to use typically English phrases.

CHAPTER 40

*T*he attention to detail at Brown's Hotel is unequaled, and Bill is supremely impressed when he sees a copy of the *London Times* and the *New York Times* waiting on the drinks table in his room. Gratified that his status at the hotel has been elevated, he settles in a high-backed armchair to catch up on the baseball scores and trans-Atlantic news.

Both papers carry headlines about a recent sailor's revolt aboard a Russian battleship, the *Potemkin*. There are fears that this action, coupled with nationwide strikes, may lead to an uprising or, even worse, a revolution. Bill has played roulette with many Russian nobles and imagines that their visits may have to be cut short while they deal with issues at home. *Perhaps the Duchess should consider leaving some of her magnificent jewels in the casino safe,* he thinks.

In the baseball section, Bill catches up on the news about his old teammate from Bloomington, Clark Griffith, now the player-manager for the New York Highlanders in Upper Manhattan. His team came second in the American League last year, but it looks like they're struggling this season, having just lost again to the Boston Americans. Bill feels the loss of baseball from his life like a gaping hole in his chest as he reads how the New York Giants are dominating the National League. Joe McGinnity and Christy Mathewson are pitching their way to victories at home and on the road. That could have been him pitching at the New York Polo Grounds Stadium in front of over thirty-thousand people.

He folds up the newspaper and sits for a moment, looking out the window at the busy London street. He does not often feel homesick, but now he's had the wind knocked out of him, and he goes to his travel trunk to retrieve the one thing that has traveled with him this entire time. Clark's signed baseball has become a perpetual good luck talisman, and as he throws it up and down, the memories return.

Determined to look forward and not dwell on the past, he rallies and walks to the desk to use the telephone. His meeting at Barclay's Bank is scheduled for two o'clock tomorrow, so he still has plenty of time to make calls. He dials the operator and asks for Mayfair 2096, Jock Carruthers's number, to arrange drinks. He then redials the operator and passes a message to Charles at the Great Northern Hotel. He feels the slight frisson of his success as he replaces the receiver back in its cradle. He is planning his first London party.

Returning to personal duties, Bill is hanging suits and shirts and folding socks, contemplating his battle plan for infiltration into London society. True to form, he shuns the offer of a valet from Brown's as he prefers to take care of unpacking duties himself. He has emptied his trunk and neatly arranged his wash kit in the bathroom when he realizes the little leather box containing his cufflinks is missing. The shirt he is wearing has standard buttons on the cuffs, which he always wears when traveling for fear that he may have to surrender cufflinks to a thief. He will now need to visit Jermyn Street straightaway, as all his good shirts require cufflinks.

As he crosses over Piccadilly to St James's Street, he finds himself at the window of the tobacconist, Robert Lewis, and the rich aroma wafting out into the street lures him in. He is led downstairs to a walk-in humidor, where the tang of fresh cigars is even more pungent, and he notices there is a new extractor fan to remove stale smoke. Some boxes have little Cuban flags imprinted on their labels, reminding Bill of the flag he saw at Soapy Smith's saloon in Denver. How the same cigars could be purchased and smoked in such vastly different circumstances is quite astounding. So is how far he's come. Emma Juch probably wouldn't even believe it if she saw him now, sitting in a sumptuous leather armchair, crossing his legs to admire his perfectly shined Loake & Co. black brogues.

There are dozens of classes of cigars to choose from, including Virginian, oriental, and Cuban, so Bill decides on a sampler packet of four, five-inch *robusts*, and he is reasonably sure he will return another day and go for the Montecristos.

Returning to street level, he is about to cross the road on the corner of Jermyn Street when a loud horn makes him almost lose his footing. He stands back and admires the motorcar. It is a Panhard for sure, similar to Julius's, although a racing version. Possibly as large as a 13.5-liter, 50 HP, which he estimates would cost around two thousand American dollars. Bill has that much with him right now. As the wheeled beast heads up to Piccadilly, honking all the way, Bill wistfully considers when he'll have a chance to upgrade his CGV.

The glass cufflink cabinets at Deakin & Francis contain an overwhelming selection of gold, silver, base metal, enamel, and personalized dress sets. Erring on the side of caution and aware that a man's character may be judged by his choice, he decides on one pair of gold oval links, a set of sterling silver knots, and one pair of mother-of-pearl studs.

The letter of introduction is addressed to the assistant manager, Mr. Anthony Farquhar, and the bank in Monaco has given Bill a copy, which he now presents at Barclay's Bank as instructed. He is shown to a small waiting area outside Farquhar's office, and while he waits, the clerk offers him tea, which he declines.

"Mr. Darnborough?" says Farquhar as he opens his door after a few minutes. "Welcome to London. Tea?"

"Good afternoon, and no, thank you." Bill wants to get straight down to business and is anxious that securing a bank account in England is not as straightforward as in Monaco.

In his favor, he has no requirement for an overdraft, mortgage, or any other financial instrument the bank offers, simply an account that permits him to access funds transferred from Monaco.

"I have your note of introduction from Banca Monte dei Paschi," says Farquhar, looking at the letter on his desk. "May I enquire as to your residential status in the United Kingdom? Do you intend to live here permanently?"

Thinking fast, Bill answers, "Yes, I am currently a permanent resident at Browns Hotel." He considers adding that his grandfather was English but keeps this information in reserve.

"I see," says Farquhar as he removes his glasses. Bill fears the worst, as a bank account is essential if he intends to make London his home one day. Monaco is a beautiful resort town, but it has become a means to an end for Bill. He wants to lean forward in his chair and speak in plain language to Farquhar but has the impression that this man is a stickler for bank protocol and needs to play by his rules.

"It would appear from this note," says Farquhar, now holding up the letter, "that our friends in Monte Carlo hold you in quite a high regard, and therefore, I see no reason why we should not open an account for you here." Bill keeps his roulette face on and tries hard not to break into a smile.

"However," continues Farquhar, "I must stipulate that you provide us with an initial deposit of two hundred British pounds."

"That will not be a problem," says Bill.

As he walks back up to Piccadilly, Bill turns right toward Leicester Square and sees a stand advertising discount theatre tickets and decides it would be a great idea to see a west end play on this trip. The attendant gives him a pamphlet with times and prices, which he takes with him to the café outside the Alhambra, although there are no spare tables, so he goes instead to the bistro opposite the Café de Paris.

He looks down the list of plays and sees endless musicals, including a production of *The Blue Moon* at the Lyric, *The Little Michus* at Daly's, *Mr. Popple of Ippkleton* at the Apollo, and *The White Chrysanthemum* at the Criterion. None of these seem appealing. A special notice is given to the new Waldorf Theater, which opened at the end of May and features the Italian opera *Il Maestro di Cappella*. However, Bill thinks this may be a bad idea just in case he falls in love with the lead soprano again.

At the end of the page is a listing for Weston's Music Hall on High Holborn, where the entertainer Charles Coborn has returned after an extensive European tour to perform, among other songs, "The Man Who Broke the Bank At Monte Carlo." Bill looks around at the other people having lunch and whispers out loud.

"Why not?"

That evening, Bill is seated toward the back of Weston's Music Hall. He imagines this crowd is very different from those at the world-famous Covent Garden Opera, but wearing a dark suit, he blends in with the showgoers sitting on the hall's sides, overlooking the tables in the middle where other patrons eat dinner. There are long balconies on either side of the great room, and the stage has a large semi-circular arch with long purple drapes on both wings.

In contrast to the serenity of the Denver opera, everyone is talking loudly, and the clink of glasses and cutlery on plates is only slightly dulled by the thick blanket of cigarette smoke bellowing up to the ceiling.

Coborn, dressed in top hat and tails, takes to the stage, and his first song, "Two Lovely Black Eyes," goes almost unnoticed, although when the piano plays the first chord of the next song, the entire auditorium erupts in cheers. Everyone in the audience knows the words to the song by heart, except Bill.

As I walk along the Bois Boulogne
With an independent air
You can hear the girls declare
He must be a millionaire
You can hear them sigh and wish to die
You can see them wink the other eye
At the man who broke the bank at Monte Carlo.

Bill cheers and claps along with everyone else and, simultaneously, thinks how fascinating it is that in Monte Carlo, he is surrounded by crowds who think he is there purely for their enter-tainment, and here he is in London, witnessing something not entirely dissimilar. Even though Coborn has been performing this song in reference to the crooked Charles Wells, Bill feels a certain sense of pride, knowing that he is somehow connected to the lyrics. Not wishing to dwell on the psychology of the matter and enjoying the anonymity, Bill decides not to stay for a drink at the bar and heads outside. He asks the cabby to take the route down the Embankment, and seeing the River Thames glistening in the misty moonlight, Bill thinks again about how this is starting to feel like home.

"You wouldn't believe it, would you?" says the cabbie, as if they had been in the middle of a conversation.

"What's that?" asks Bill.

"Well, guv'nor," continues the cabbie. "Out there," he points, "beyond all this fog, there's a great big empire."

Bill looks out over the river again, not sure how to respond. This was the moment he learned that London cab drivers can be surprisingly philosophical.

"Amazing," says Bill, thinking how he wants to be right in the middle of it.

CHAPTER 41

"*I*sn't it extraordinary?" says Emily Carruthers. "You can live in your own town all your life and not visit the finest hotels. I mean, thank you, Bill. We would probably never have come here if it weren't for you. What a lovely place." She looks around, admiring the sumptuous decor. She is wearing an embroidered dress that hangs gracefully, and the pink ribbon woven through her collar brings out the blush of her cheeks.

As he is not usually in the habit of entertaining, Bill has made a special effort to reserve a sizeable round corner table in the Brown's hotel bar. Charles Selby, Jock, and Bill drink whisky, and Emily Carruthers has an elderflower. He had considered ordering champagne, then second guessed himself and was glad because all the men wanted Scotch whisky anyhow.

"The folks here have been incredibly helpful," says Bill. "When I first arrived, I had no idea where to go or what to do. I must admit that the farthest I've been is down by the Embankment, as everything I need is right around here, although I want to explore more."

"I think one of London's greatest attributes is the parks," says Jock. "Have you been to Kensington Gardens or Hyde Park or even down the road to Green Park or St. James's?"

"A little," says Bill, "I like the parks, but I have more exploring to do. I read something about Kew Gardens by Monsieur van den Daele from the Monte Carlo garden."

"Good idea," says Charles, "The botanical gardens there are stunning. Make sure you see the Temperate House and the Palm House. In fact, that one might remind you of the palms behind the Hotel de Paris. And, I can say with authority that a number of pretty ladies like to stroll there, and there's always the chance that one may drop a glove for a gentleman to retrieve."

"So, Mr. Selby," says Emily, wishing to change the subject, "How did you meet Mr. Darnborough?"

"Actually, we met in Monte Carlo," replies Charles, "on one of the balconies at the casino."

Emily's eyes brighten, and she sips her drink. "Are you a gambler?"

"No, not really, just a happy coincidence. We traveled together on the train as I am on my way to Yorkshire."

"Yorkshire is lovely this time of year. Where are you off to?"

"Just south of York. A town called Selby."

"Oh! You're Charles Selby." An awkward silence follows, and Bill feels a flush of shock as he realizes the town is possibly named after his friend's family.

"Ascot!" says Jock, turning to his wife, "we were going to tell you about Ascot, Bill."

"Oh, yes," says Emily. "Bill, will you come to Ascot with us this year? You know, the horse races—it's the biggest event of the summer, and the King will be there. And we have badges for the Royal enclosure this year and wanted to invite you. We saved you a badge."

Bill grins. "I have only two questions. When is it, and what do I have to wear?"

"It's next week, and you will need a top hat, sir!" says Jock.

More drinks arrive, and Bill's little party is very relaxed as they talk about things to do in London in the summer. Bill, meanwhile, is trying to imagine Ascot and has a thought.

"Speaking of Ascot, how were you planning on getting there?"

"The train," says Jock, "everyone takes the train from Waterloo, and it's only about an hour and a half."

Bill raises an eyebrow coolly. "I saw a fine motorcar this morning, nearly ran me over, in fact, and I was thinking, perhaps I could persuade someone to loan me one for the day?"

"Capital idea," says Jock, "but none of us own motorcars. Hardly anyone in London does. We just don't need them." The others return to the conversation, but Bill is determined to make a better-than-excellent impression on his new friends. He can't change his background, get a degree from Oxford, or become a British Army officer, but he does have an idea that should have a lasting impact.

"My friends have just invited me to Ascot," Bill tells Samuel Chambers at Brown's after the others have departed, "I want to show them a little favor in return."

"Yes, sir?"

"How might I go about borrowing a motorcar for the day? That is to say, do you know where I can hire a motorcar?"

"I see," says Samuel, looking down at his desk. "This here," he continues, pointing down, "is what I call my big book of just about everything in London. Will you require a vehicle for four persons or just two?" Bill's smile widens as he pulls out a shiny gold sovereign coin and it passes from his hand to Samuel's in one swift movement.

"Four. For next week, Thursday. We'll have it back to the owner by Friday afternoon." On an afterthought, Bill turns and leans in closer, saying, "By the way, if anyone asks, you don't know my background, just that I am prepared to pay a cash deposit."

Samuel gives a curt nod. "Understood, sir."

"I'M GOING to make one thing, no, two things very clear," says Bill. He is seated opposite a thin, mustached man who had the audacity to interrupt him while he was reading the *New York Times* at breakfast in the hotel. He had requested a private conference.

Once Bill saw that the man wouldn't take no for an answer, he led him to the corridor behind the bar, but he was not happy about it. "First, whoever you are, your timing stinks. I take my time for breakfast and reading my newspaper very seriously and do not appreciate being disturbed. Second, I drank too many whiskies last night, and I'm in a foul mood, so out with it."

The man smiles as if Bill has told a joke. "Sir, I represent certain parties who wish to retain your services should you deem such services to be available."

Bill sighs and rubs his aching temples. "Just speak to me in plain English, will you?"

Again, the strange smile. "My client would like to invest in you. Rather, he would like to invest in your skill and considerable rate of return at the roulette table."

Bill frowns. "As you can see, I am not presently near a roulette table, nor do I plan to return to one for some months."

The man tents his fingers. "I have been sent here merely to ascertain your openness to the idea, and I am authorized to inform you that the investment will be considerable, and the split would be fifty/fifty. My client has expressed absolute trust in you and respects your time, so the timing is up to you."

"I get it," says Bill. "Understand this. I play nice with the good ladies and gentlemen of this fair city. However, when it comes to my business, I will not be fooled, intimidated, coerced, manipulated, or anything else for that matter. Do I make myself clear?"

"Crystal clear, sir."

"By the way," says Bill, "how did you find me?"

Now, the smile is thin. "You're good at what you do, and I'm good at what I do."

The prospect of high returns gambling other people's money is not instantly appealing to Bill, as sore losers do not sit quietly in his experience. But he thinks perhaps he should be open to the proposal in case he ever finds himself low on his own resources.

"This is not something I will engage in without meeting with your client," he says. "And another thing. I'm not taking cases of cash on the train to Monaco for some bandit outfit on the other side of a civil war."

"I understand," says the man, "and I appreciate your time. I will leave you now, and my apologies again for interrupting your breakfast. By the way, my name is Mr. Jones, and we will be in touch." As Bill watches him leave, he rubs his temples again. Just when he thought all he had to do today was buy a suit.

Bill returns via the dining room to sign for his breakfast and leaves the hotel by the Dover Street exit to head to Barclays Bank. He does not need to meet with Anthony Farquhar today, but to simply to check the transfer came through from Banca Monte dei Paschi and that his statement is in order.

The next stop is Poole & Co., where Bill needs to be fitted with a classic morning suit, including a tailcoat, a double-breasted waistcoat, striped trousers, and a wingtip white collar shirt. The assistant at Poole & Co. does not like to be hurried.

"You see, sir," the assistant says, "We pride ourselves on exacting standards here."

"What if I paid you double the asking price?"

"That, sir, would not help your cause. I understand you are in a rush, but even Mr. Churchill must wait his turn."

"I see," says Bill, looking around at the mannequins with chalk outlines and embedded pins.

"Unless," says the assistant.

"Yes?"

"Well, this is most unusual, sir. If this is a considerably urgent request, as you say, we may have one option available to us."

"Yes?"

"A gentleman almost precisely fitting your measurements recently ordered a morning three-piece, and unfortunately, he is no longer in a position to make use of his wonderful new suit."

"Right," says Bill, trying hard to conceal his impatience. "May I see it?"

"Of course, sir. One moment, please."

As Bill looks at himself in the mirror, admiring the tailor's craftsmanship, he turns to face the assistant.

"By the way. What happened to the gentleman who ordered this suit?"

"Deceased, I'm afraid. Nasty business down in South Africa, I am informed. Poor chap never got to wear his suit."

He arranges for his Ascot attire to be delivered to Brown's, and after a brisk walk across Piccadilly, he is back at Lock & Co. However, for his top hat, Mr. Vaghela, the master hatter, insists on a perfect measurement.

He uses a tape measure for the initial dimension, and then fits Bill with a device called a conformitor. Next, he inserts a piece of paper, and the conformitor punches little holes in the paper that outline the exact size of Bill's head. Mr. Vaghela then has the outline to calibrate the other sizing tool, the formillion, whose wooden keys are used to match the cutout, and the conformitor is put inside the hat. The master hatter, who clearly takes his profession very seriously, softens the fabric using steam and a brush, makes some slight adjustments, and presents Bill with his new top hat. Only when the process is complete does Mr. Vaghela allow himself a slight smile.

His outfit is completed with a rose gold cravat, and everything is put on account.

As it has started to rain, Bill hurries back to the hotel and is greeted in the courtyard by Samuel Chambers, who looks like he has just returned from battle.

"I think you will like this, Sir," says Samuel. "I have found you a motorcar for next week."

"That was quick," says Bill, "did you have to twist some arms?"

"Not exactly. Most of the car owners I spoke with were less than happy with the idea of someone paying to drive their motorcars. However, one of our regular guests told me he liked the idea of you paying him when he's not using his motorcar."

"Excellent, so what do we have?"

"It's something called a—" Samuel looks down at his big book of everything, "Wolseley. I don't know much about the technical specifications although I can say that it has enough room for a driver and three passengers. The owner is well known to us here at Brown's and just suggested a daily rate of—" he passes Bill a slip of paper with a number written down along with a separate line for the deposit.

"I see," says Bill, grateful that he checked with the bank that his funds had arrived. "How do we make arrangements? Can they have it delivered to me here?"

"Ah, well," replies Samuel, "that's the one little snag. You would need to collect it from Richmond."

"Richmond! Not the one in Virginia, I hope?" Samuel looks blankly at Bill as he has clearly never heard of Richmond, Virginia, so Bill follows up with, "Never mind, is it far?"

"Not really," Samuel replies, "you can get a train from Victoria Station easily."

"Excellent news, well done," says Bill as he passes Samuel one of his folded £1 notes. "Can I have his details as I think it best if I take over from here?" Bill is already thinking how all the ladies at Ascot will be mightily impressed with his Wolseley.

CHAPTER 42

*T*his is the first time Bill has taken the "tube," and he has to put his faith in British engineering as the idea of traveling in a train underneath all the streets and buildings is pretty daunting. Since it is mid-morning and he's traveling against the general flow of people still headed into central London, he's fortunate to find a seat with ample space.

He takes an electric train on the Piccadilly Line from Green Park to Earl's Court, then has to change and get on a steam train to complete the journey on the District Line to Richmond. This section of the trip is overground, so he gets a good view of Hammersmith and Chiswick on the way. Bill finds he can breathe a little easier when he can see his surroundings, and it is a picture-perfect summer's day as he arrives at Richmond station. He finds a Hummingbird cab outside the station, and the ride to Oliver Bain's residence on Marlborough Road only takes a few minutes.

"As I mentioned on the telephone, Mr. Darnborough," says Bain, "I only use my motorcar for weekend rides in the countryside, as I take the train most days into the city. Would you like to see her?"

"Thank you, yes," Bill remarks, flicking away a bit of soot from the train tunnel he just spotted on his shoulder.

Bain leads Bill past a privet hedge and toward a garage. "This is a work of art, in my opinion. Herbert Austin is one of our finest designers." Once inside, Bain pulls off a smart dust cover sheet to reveal a British racing green, 24 h.p., 5.2-litre, Wolseley Landaulette that looks like it has never been used.

"Have you driven one of these?" he asks.

Bill is admiring the car's lines. "I've not had the pleasure. I have a French CGV, which I keep in the south of France, although the roads are more rugged down there, of course." Bain eyes Bill up and down but says nothing.

"I will take excellent care of her, of course, Mr. Bain," continues Bill. "I'm taking some friends down to Ascot, and I thought this would be more fun than the train."

"Perfect for the occasion," says Bain, "she'll fit right in, considering she's practically Ascot green! You know, Queen Alexandria has one just like this. Four-speed gearbox and a chain drive."

"Please forgive me for asking, Mr. Bain, but what business are you in? The only reason I ask is that I'm thinking we should go into the car-hire business together if we could buy a nice line of Wolseleys." They both laugh at the idea, and Bill feels that he has succeeded in making Bain more at ease at the prospect of loaning out his pride and joy to a complete stranger.

"Right, jump in," says Bain, "I'll take us for a little ride around Richmond Park and explain how everything works on the way."

They set off together at a gentle pace, and Bill is relieved to be the passenger as people are crossing the road seemingly without checking to see if there is any approaching traffic. They turn right at Queen's Road and then through the gates to the park at Sawyer's Hill as Bain turns to Bill and raises his voice over the engine noise.

"By the way, as you are American and live in France, you may have noticed that we drive on the left side of the road over here. That's quite important. Also, if you look in the glove compartment in front of you, there's an up-to-date road map from the Royal Automobile Club."

"Perfect, thank you," says Bill.

"Shipping," says Bain.

"I'm sorry?"

"Shipping," repeats Bain. "You asked what line of business I am in. We run a shipping company. But I like your idea of a motorcar hire company. Perhaps we should talk about that some more if you can bring back this girl in one piece? Fancy a spot of lunch? I know a place."

Bill looks at his pocket watch, even though he has no particular agenda for the afternoon.

"Certainly," he says. As they continue through the park, Bill sees nannies walking with small children and some pushing babies in prams. There are elegant ladies with umbrellas to shade them from the sun, and he notices a gentleman sitting on a bench, feeding bread to pigeons. He spots a group of young boys laughing as they roll a hoop with a stick, much as he used to do with his friends growing up in Bloomington. He wonders what may become of these boys, growing up in the new century in middle-class Richmond instead of Illinois. They pass by woods and lakes, and at one point, there is a glimpse of the city in the distance as they reach the top of the hill. Bain has seen Bill's gaze and stops the car.

"Come and have a look at this," says Bain. There is a clearing with a telescope mounted on a stand. "This is called King Henry's Mound. If you look through this," he motions to Bill to come forward, "you can see towards the Tower of London. They say this is where Henry VIII stood on the day of Anne Boleyn's execution in 1536. They let off a firework when she lost her head, which cleared the way for Henry to marry Jane Seymour."

"Fascinating," says Bill, turning the telescope a little to the east and recognizing St. Paul's cathedral. "Quite a view," he says, thinking that if he is going to buy a house in London, it would be somewhere near Richmond Park.

Bain turns around and points to the right, and he is clearly now enjoying his new role as a tour guide.

"Over there is Hampton Court Palace, and there," he points to the left, "that's Wimbledon."

284

"Which way is Kew Gardens?"

"Oh, yes, you must go and see the Palm House. It's back where we came from, down there."

They get back into the Wolseley, and Bain steers them down to the river, where they stop at the White Cross pub, which has seats and tables right on the banks of the Thames overlooking the edge of Eel Pie Island. Bill observes the noticeably cleaner water than at the city's Embankment. White swans gracefully mingle with ducks on the serene surface. "The Cross," as it is called, has been around since 1780 and serves Young's Ale on tap. It is not exactly what Bill would call refreshing on a hot summer's day, but he drinks the warm beer as a courtesy to his host.

"Tell me, Bill," says Bain, "where are you living in the South of France?"

"I'm in Monaco at the moment. Monte Carlo."

"How wonderful! What do you do there?"

Bill wonders if a man about to lend him his brand-new Wolseley will be distrustful if he discovers he is a professional gambler. He decides honesty is the best policy and flashes Bain a smile. "I play roulette."

"I knew it! You're the American plunger! I've read all about you in *The Times,* and I thought your name was familiar. Is it all true? They say you've broken the bank, just like that Wells fellow."

Bill laughs. He hears his mother. The things people will say when they get an idea in their heads that's just plain wrong. "You know, Mr. Bain, I've been fortunate. But I should add that I am not at all like Wells. He was just lucky, and now he's in prison. I actually live in Monte Carlo, and I play consistently. I don't win every day, and I haven't technically broken the bank." He grins. "Yet."

"What a life," says Bain, with a wistful smile and shake of his head. "Forgive me for appearing crass, but how on earth do you keep the ladies away? Or maybe you don't. I'm sorry, sometimes I forget to put my brain in gear before engaging the mouth." Bill laughs along with him, wondering which stories Bain has read. He decides not to ask.

"You know, Bill," says Bain, "I like your style. You're welcome to

285

have my girl for the week, although I have to ask, where will she stay in London before you go down to Ascot?"

"I've reserved a space at the London Motor Garage on Wardour Street. They'll clean and deliver her to my hotel and guarantee top-notch security."

"Good to hear," says Bain, taking another sip of his ale.

Bill can't hold back his enthusiasm. "Apparently, they can hold up to two hundred cars, so I'm looking forward to seeing all the different makes and models. The garage behind Piccadilly Circus on Denman Street has an electric elevator to move cars between floors, but I wasn't convinced that was the safest option, as I didn't want to risk any dings on your lady."

Bain smiles at this reference to his Wolseley as a "lady." "She sure is a beauty, isn't she? Did you see how they all stop and stare?"

A waiter brings out their lunch, a plowman's—cheddar cheese, well-baked bloomer bread with butter, apple, pickled onion, and ham.

"I thought you could tell all your friends back home in America about the traditional English pub lunch," Bain says, and Bill toasts to that with his ale.

When they return to Bain's house on Marlborough Road, they bid farewells, and Bill hands over an envelope with the payment plus the agreed deposit. In return, Bain lends Bill his driving goggles for protection against high-velocity insects.

Following Bain's advice, Bill takes the route back to London south of the river, turning left at Vauxhall, although he misses the turn and ends up taking the Lambeth Bridge across the Thames. This brings him to Westminster and Parliament, where carriages fight with motorcars for the right of way, and there is considerable confusion even amongst the locals. People cross the roads, seemingly without regard for traffic, and often stop in front of him to stare at the magnificent vehicle. Each time he stops, Bill mutters "left, left, left" under his breath to remind himself which side of the road he is supposed to be on.

Just as he fears he may never get used to driving in London, he finds himself at Buckingham Palace and weaves slowly around toward St. James's.

He parks directly outside the entrance to Brown's, wholly exhausted and quite traumatized. He leaves instructions for the London Motor Garage to come and pick up his vehicle and heads straight to the bar.

As the barman pours him a Scotch whisky, he starts to feel proud of himself as he has overcome one of the most significant challenges a man could face. Driving across London without hitting any horse-drawn carriages, bicyclists, or pedestrians.

"To safe passages," he says to the barman, then downs the shot, imagining the looks on his friends' faces when they see the flawless Wolseley.

CHAPTER 43

The following day, Bill is drawn to the beautiful reading room at Brown's and quickly realizes that he should continue his education while in London. Curiously, the log fire is burning even though it is mid-summer, which lends tranquility to the setting. The library is available for hotel guests, and a leather-bound register details the book title, your name, and the date on which you borrowed the book. The shelves are impressively well-stocked with current literature, including Joseph Conrad, H.G. Wells, George Bernhard Shaw, Henry James, Jack London, Mark Twain, and W. Somerset Maugham. There is even a children's book by J.M. Barrie called *Peter Pan in Kensington Gardens*. Bill reflects that the only book he has read with any degree of enthusiasm since leaving college in Bloomington is his roulette bible, and he thinks it is high time he follows Hiram Lewin's example and expand his knowledge of the world through literature.

He selects *The Napoleon of Notting Hill* by a little-known author called G.K. Chesterton, and as Bill settles down in a comfortable Chesterfield wingback chair, he is fascinated from the outset. It talks about cheating the prophecies of the twentieth century and how the motor car is faster than the coach, although it will eventually be replaced by something even faster. He can see a part of himself in each of the characters, especially Auberon Quinn, who has the ability to see the humor in life.

Just as Adam Wayne's army is mounting its first defense of Notting Hill, a waiter appears in the room and asks if Mr. Darnborough would like some lunch. How could it be lunchtime already, thinks Bill and realizes that he has not moved from his armchair for hours. He cannot remember a time when he has sat still for so long and marvels at G.K. Chesterton's talent for intrigue and suspense. Reluctantly, he places a specially designed Brown's Hotel bookmark on his page, closes the book, and carries it with him to the dining room.

After lunch, Bill has planned a trip in the Wolseley to Kew Gardens, and if there was ever an argument as to who has the right of way on the roads of London, the answer is the cabs. Bill gives them a wide berth as even the omnibuses fear the seemingly reckless abandon with which the drivers hurl their passengers around corners at breakneck speed. He thinks that his trip to Kew Gardens serves two purposes. He is fascinated by the prospect of seeing the Palm House and the wonderous botanical kaleidoscope of the Temperate House. Secondly, he is learning very quickly how to navigate pedestrians, bicycles, buses, and especially cabs. He is almost certain that by the time he does the long distance to Ascot, he will have complete confidence, especially driving on the left side of the road.

Bill realizes he may be trying to distract himself from Mr. Jones's request for a meeting, but there is much to learn at Kew. The one piece of interesting trivia he intends to share with anyone who will listen is how the Palm House is heated. A chimney stack is disguised as an Italian campanile bell tower that serves as an exhaust for the underground boilers. A subterranean tunnel brings coal to heat the boilers, and the only way visitors can notice where the tunnel is located is during winter when the snow does not settle along its path. The Palm House itself is a vast Victorian greenhouse that looks, feels, and smells like a rainforest. At least, that is how it is advertised, and Bill sees no reason to argue the point, considering he has never been to an actual rainforest. The air is humid with an earthy but fresh scent, and Bill notices the leaves glisten with moisture from the artificial showers. Ascending a wrought-iron spiral staircase, its white hue sharply contrasting against the sea of greenery, Bill emerges onto a walkway nestled within the dome's apex.

Enormous bamboo shoots and towering palm fronds extend overhead, enveloping him. From this elevated vantage, he gazes through the expansive windows to his left, where his view stretches down to a serene lake. Bill feels like he has taken a trip to a distant land, transported by the experience within the Palm House's lush confines.

The term "rush hour" is an Americanism that Londoners have quickly adopted. Bill is driving into the city against the general flow of late afternoon traffic, although his trip takes considerably longer than the journey out. After studying his RAC map, he decides to take the Hammersmith Bridge route, a mistake he will only make once. The concentration required to ensure that not a single scratch should appear on Bain's "girl" is considerable, and after a very close shave with a London omnibus, he is immensely relieved to reach the safety of Dover Street and the hotel entrance. Once again, he passes a sovereign coin to the doorman and leaves instructions for the London Motor Garage to fetch the Wolseley.

This time, the RAC map accompanies Bill upstairs as he prepares his route to Ascot. According to the book, he should go via Windsor. Or maybe Twickenham. Having second thoughts, he requests the hotel operator connect him with Jock Carruthers and speaks with him briefly to confirm pick-up times and their accommodation, as they are due to stay one night in Ascot. Jock can act as navigator, Bill decides, though he highlights his chosen route with a thick line of blue ink, just to be sure.

The following morning at ten o'clock, Mr. Jones and his client arrive for their meeting, which is held in a discrete board room on the first floor of the hotel.

"Good morning, Mr. Darnborough," Jones begins, "Please allow me to introduce my client, Mr. Johnathan Fairfax."

Fairfax is short, stocky, and blond, dressed in a black suit that has been brushed so much it shines.

"Good to meet you, Mr. Fairfax," says Bill as they shake hands. "Let's get straight to it if you don't mind. How can I be of assistance?"

Fairfax smiles as they take their seats. "That suits me just fine, Mr. Darnborough. What I am about to propose is an amalgamation, a partnership, or a coalition if you like. It is quite straightforward. I would like to bankroll your roulette in exchange for a fifty/fifty split of the winnings."

"You mean a syndication?" says Bill as his eyes narrow.

"Not exactly, as that would imply a combination of investors. What I am proposing is a partnership, and I would be the sole investor."

"You do understand that roulette is a game of chance, sir? Contrary to what you may have read about me in the papers, I do not have an infallible system, and there is no nefarious, covert mechanism by which I can guarantee to win. I do not bribe any of the casino officials, and there are no biased wheels left in Monte Carlo, as they check them meticulously every morning. I would like you to think about how you may react if you were to lose your investment. This is something I have to deal with every single day." Fairfax is about to respond, but Bill raises his hand and says, "Before you answer my first point, I want you to listen carefully to the second.

"If the administration suspects that gamblers are attempting to win back their losses with money that does not belong to them, they will act against such players. I've seen it happen. Very little escapes their watchful eyes, and high-stakes players like me are watched even more carefully than most. One player, who was part of syndication, was deemed by the casino director to be, as he put it, an agent. We all have admission cards, and, at the drop of a hat, they can inscribe on the card, *representant de commerce*, that is to say, commercial traveler. That alone would be reason enough not to renew an admission card."

"Sir," says Fairfax, and he seems annoyed. "I am prepared to invest £20,000."

"That is a great deal of money, sir," Bill says, after a moment of silence. "Are you prepared to lose it? You understand there are no guarantees in my business."

"I understand that, sir."

Bill nods curtly and says, "Why don't you give me your card, and we can both think on it."

Fairfax tries to argue, but Bill's mind is made up, and when he walks out of the room with Fairfax's card in his jacket pocket, he decides not to take him up on his offer. Not unless he finds himself in a very, very desperate situation.

CHAPTER 44

*A*t the hotel reception, there is a message from Jock Carruthers. It simply reads: "We should take the train to Ascot." Bill immediately goes to the telephone booth and calls the Carruthers' home.

"I am so sorry, Bill," says Jock, "but we've talked it over with quite a few people, and it just doesn't make sense to try and get there by motorcar. I should have given you more notice, and I must offer sincere apologies."

"Not to worry," says Bill, unable to conceal his dejection, "at least allow me to drive us to Waterloo station, and we can leave the car for the day."

"Is there a safe place to leave it there?" asks Jock.

"Good point," says Bill. "No problem. I am sure the train will be more practical. I'll come to your house at nine," he continues, with less conviction in his voice, "and we can take a cab together to the station."

"Right oh," says Jock, "see you then."

With a knot in his stomach, Bill disconnects the call. He had spent a small fortune hiring the Wolseley and was looking forward to driving through the English countryside. Thinking about his eagerness to dazzle everyone, perhaps he might be overdoing it. Why should he have to infiltrate English society anyway? Who is he trying to impress? Maybe people will just accept him for who he is —with or without fancy cars and suits? But, still, he has a desire to become one of them. These people are genuine and interesting compared to the façade of Monaco.

On Thursday morning, Bill meets Jock and Mrs. Carruthers at their home in Kensington. Bill feels the tightness of his collar, although is pleased to see that Jock has on a suit almost identical to his. He should have known that Poole & Co. would do exactly right by him—or at least the poor soul who originally ordered it. It is a perfect summer's day in London, and the intricate lace, puffed sleeves, and sweeping skirt of Mrs. Carruther's dress rustle gently in the breeze. Bill wonders how many pins she has used to secure her giant hat so that it does not move atop her head as the cab takes them past Trafalgar Square, up the Strand, and over Waterloo Bridge.

The station is teeming with gentlemen in top hats and ladies resplendent in their summer dresses. The train is packed with race-goers, and it is standing room only, especially for the men, as there is an understanding of etiquette that seats are reserved for the ladies. Even though there is great excitement in the air, hardly anyone speaks to each other on the train. Bill thinks back to his days traveling with the Grizzlies and notes the contrast.

"Why is everyone so quiet?" he whispers to Jock.

Jock holds a finger to his smiling lips, but it still takes Bill a few moments to understand. The English prefer to travel in silence. He grips the hanging strap to keep his footing and, as the train rattles along, contents himself with looking out the window at the rolling green countryside and finds that he enjoys traveling in silence, too.

The atmosphere at Ascot is unlike anything Bill has experienced before. He feels like he has been invited to an immense party, where everyone greets each other as if they are old friends. As they approach the racecourse's gilded entrance gates, men in green uniforms wearing military medals are inspecting entry credentials. Mrs. Carruthers fastens Bill's Royal Enclosure badge to his left lapel, patting it in place with a sincere smile as she trills, "By invitation only." Having assumed anyone could simply buy a badge, Bill is still trying to make sense of this as they gain entry.

"These gentlemen are mostly retired soldiers," Jock explains. "the Greencoats were started by Queen Anne in the 1700s. Originally, they used to herd wayward spectators off the racetrack, but these days, they are just here to help out." Just like Oliver Bain in Richmond, Jock clearly enjoys playing the role of the guide. "If you get lost, find one of these gentlemen, and he will be able to steer you back to where you belong."

Bill is amazed at the sight of so many top hats and ladies with umbrellas to protect them from the blazing sun. Not a single cloud graces the deep blue sky, and even though the grandstands offer shade from the midday sun, most visitors are out and about. Bill notices that, unlike in the park, the gentlemen do not raise their hats to every lady they pass, as that would be impractical considering there must be thousands of people here today. He has a feeling he'll know the right one when he sees her, somehow.

"Thursday is known as 'Ladies' Day' at Ascot," says Mrs. Carruthers, "but I really do not understand why." She waves her arms gracefully to showcase her dress and splendid hat. "We look as wonderful as this on any given day." Bill smiles in agreement and remains captivated by the ceaseless procession of English high society passing before him.

"The ladies used to get free entry on Thursdays," says Jock, "equal rights and all that." Mrs. Carruthers slightly frowns at this comment but says nothing in response.

"This is what it's all about," says Jock, waving his hands around. "Half of these people come for the occasion and to see the Royal Family—they have little interest in the racing itself. They may place a bet on the Gold Cup, but they don't really study the form."

"How do you study the form?" asks Bill.

"That's the horse's performance record," says Jock, "essentially, you look to see if it has a good chance of winning its race by previous results."

"Thank you. I see," says Bill, "we use the same term in the

States. What I mean is, how do you *know* it?"

"Didn't I give you one of these?" Jock pulls out a race card from his inside breast pocket. "See here, on the right are the most recent races, and the numbers one to nine show the position they finished in the race. If there were outside the first nine, then there's just a zero. It's a little like your baseball statistics, I imagine. All these letters mean something, like this one, *B.F.* means it was the favorite to win in its last race but was beaten. This one," he points, "*B.E.* means big ears. That's how Emily determines the favorite."

"It does not!" says Mrs. Carruthers, laughing, "and nor do I pick a favorite by the size of its ears. I like a good girth, though, as it shows more room for a big heart and lungs. That's what you need over these long distances."

"There may be something to that," considers Jock. "When they come into the parade ring, you'll see punters looking carefully at the riders and horses for things like confidence and temperament. Anyway, let's go and get a glass of bubbly, shall we?"

As they move toward the grandstand, they pass a stall selling programs, and Jock buys one for Bill, which contains a loosely inserted race card. Bill quickly scans the card, although he doubts he'll be placing any bets today. He thinks it's probably wise to stick to what he knows, as the idea of losing his hard-won French francs on the horses in England is not at all appealing.

Armed with glasses of champagne, they stand at a raised table in their private box, and Bill can see the whole course from this lofty position. On the other side of the racetrack, he sees men in flat caps and straw boater hats, in stark distinction to the silk top hats on their side. Not too long ago, he thinks, he would have been on that side of the fence.

"This is called the straight mile," says Jock, pointing to the left; "that's where the Royal family will come in their carriages after lunch."

"It's quite a spectacle," says Bill.

"Part of history!" says Jock. "The Royals have been doing this every year since the 1820s. As I said, the Royal procession is many people's highlight of the day. On each of the five race days, the carriage takes a slightly different track down the course to protect the ground. Some people say that the going of the course can be determined by listening to how the carriage runs on the track."

"I wish I could do that with a roulette ball," says Bill, momentarily letting his guard down as the champagne begins to take effect.

"No matter how often you come to this," says Mrs. Carruthers, "it really is a special event. There can't be anything else like this in the world."

In between races, Harry and Emma Crichton join them for a light lunch. Colonel Crichton is a friend of Jock's from the In and Out Club, and Lady Emma is a landscape artist of some renown. Mrs. Carruthers spends most of the time trying to entice Lady Emma to come to the south of France to do some landscapes while the gentlemen try to convince Bill of the merits of cricket over baseball.

At two o'clock precisely, the open-top Royal Landau carriages arrive, each drawn by four magnificent Windsor Greys. King Edward VII and Queen Alexandra wave to the cheering crowds on either side of the track. Many racegoers wear ties, although Bill is pleased to see that the King has a cravat like his.

"Who's that with the King?" asks Bill.

"Aside from Queen, you mean?" says Jock. "Let's see," he says, opening up his program. "King Alfonso of Spain."

"He's staying at Buckingham Palace," says Mrs. Carruthers, "looking for a bride, I think." Bill feels a visceral start, then wants to laugh—perhaps he has the same mission as the king of Spain!

"The other gentleman with them is Richard Marsh," says Jock, "he's the King's trainer. Trains his horses, I mean." He laughs.

There are large boards on the other side of the track with the horses' names and riders for the races, along with the betting odds. Smaller stands at the rails divide the enclosures where the bookmakers' chalkboards display the latest odds. They wear cloth flat caps and use dirty rags to rub out the chalk numbers and rewrite updated odds according to the volume of wagers placed.

"Are you going to have a flutter?" asks Jock, turning to Bill.

Bill grins. "I'm not much of a gambler."

"Very well," says Jock, giving Bill a sideways glance with a smile. Turning to Mrs. Carruthers, he says, "Darling, how about you?"

"I'm going to wait until the Gold Cup," she replies.

The first race is at half past two, and the crowd erupts in a cacophony of shouting as they all scream for their own favorite to make it to first past the post. Gentlemen and ladies, who are usually reserved, yell at the top of their lungs. Bill is reminded of how people's characters and personalities change so profoundly when they are around a roulette table or a baseball diamond. At the end of the race, he sees several people still cheering, although most are tearing up their betting slips in disgust. Nevertheless, like acts in a play, the show continues as many more events remain.

Two more races are completed, new champagne bottles appear, and old ones disappear as everyone takes their turn to give Bill random updates on the proceedings.

"Let's go down to the parade ring to look at the contenders for the Gold Cup," Mrs. Carruthers suggests.

As they approach the paddock, Bill can see owners and grooms attending to their horses.

"See how all the jockeys wear different colors?" says Jock as he turns to Bill. "That's to indicate which stable they belong to. I mean, who the owner is."

"Hello, Jock," says a man who simultaneously lifts his hat to Mrs. Carruthers.

"Amherst, how the devil are you, sir?" says Jock as they shake hands. "Lord Amherst, please allow me to introduce my wife, Mrs. Emily Carruthers."

"It is indeed a pleasure," says Amherst. "And this," says Jock, "is our good friend from America, Mr. William Darnborough."

"Welcome to Ascot, sir," says Amherst.

Bill nods in return as Jock says to Amherst, "John, I haven't seen you at the club for a while. Are you in London at all these days?"

"Not as much as I would like," says Amherst. "I've been in Australia, as a matter of fact. We bought a cattle ranch in New South Wales."

"How brave of you," says Mrs. Carruthers.

"Not really," says Amherst, "they're not all heathens and criminals down there, you know. It's just a devil of a journey, but I am glad I came back for the summer in England, and what a day!" he says, looking around, as the loudspeaker announces the next race, the much-anticipated Gold Cup.

"Get ready for two and a half miles of thunder," says Jock as he places a £5 bet with the nearest bookmaker, and Mrs. Carruthers puts the same amount on a horse named Zinfandel, owned by their friend, Thomas Ellis.

"And they're off!" cries Jock as the loudspeaker echoes his words. Over 90,000 spectators cheer as the field moves around the track at break-neck speed. The commentator sounds as if he is on the verge of a heart attack as he relays the change of positions as the race nears its climax. At the finish line, it is difficult to tell which of the two leaders came in first, and there is a moment of quiet as the crowd awaits the verdict. Finally, the loudspeaker announces the winner.

"Zinfandel, ridden by Morny Cannon!"

Mrs. Carruthers is bouncing on her heels, and in typical English fashion, Jock tries to calm her down.

"Congratulations!" says Bill, "how much did you win?"

"Twenty-five pounds!" shouts Mrs. Carruthers. It must have been 4/1, thinks Bill. Not a bad payout with a £20 profit on a £5 stake.

"This sure is a lot more fun than sitting at the tables," says Bill.

"Still not your bag, eh Bill?" asks Jock, raising his voice over the noise of the still cheering crowd.

"Not for me, sir," says Bill, "although this has been a mighty fine day out!"

"Let's go down to the paddock and congratulate Mr. Ellis," says Mrs. Carruthers, who has the glow of a winner that Bill has seen so many times before.

The stewards strain to hold back the crowds who gather around Morny Cannon as he dismounts Zinfandel. The Royals remain in their box, although the King has been clapping for the winners, signaling his respect, especially to Thomas Ellis. Bill cannot help but think how extraordinary his life has become in a comparatively short time. Even though he has yet to buy a house or meet the right woman, here he is, dressed in the attire of the British aristocracy, having lunch with ladies who are actually titled and gentlemen who have medals on their chests given to them by a King. That same King is now sitting only sixty feet from him as the band of the Grenadier Guards strike up the National Anthem, and 89,999 people know all the words. Bill can't help but join in the chorus when it comes around for the second time, "God save our gracious King, long live our noble King." Jock looks over as the song ends and gives Bill a hearty slap on the back.

"Welcome to England, dear chap!" Jock says, and Bill grins and thinks maybe, just maybe, he has arrived.

That night, he dreams of his mother, sitting at the kitchen table back in Bloomington, sipping from a cup of coffee and telling him, "You've always thought you were special, Bill, but you know all you'll ever be is your father's son."

He wakes up in a sweat. It had felt so real, like a visit from beyond the grave. Although, as far as he knows, his mother is still alive.

"Don't try to bring me down," he says aloud to the room as if she's sitting right there in the wingback chair over by the wall. "I'm not going to let you do it." But he's wide awake now and finds himself fretting about all the things he's done and not done, all the places he's trying to fit in where he doesn't—not quite. He feels like a man hanging from a ladder with his hands all slippery with sweat.

He can't help but dwell on the fact that England is so incredibly different. The class system is so inflexible that even possessing vast wealth seems inconsequential. People seem unfazed by modern automobiles, elegant attire, or extravagant gold cufflinks. An authentic English gentleman boasts a lineage from a venerable school, bears a military officer's commission, is affiliated with an exclusive members-only club, and wields clout in financial and diplomatic circles. Doubt resurfaces as Bill thinks the prospect of fully integrating into London's high society might, after all, be an unrealistic aspiration.

CHAPTER 45

*T*he passengers on the train look increasingly uncomfortable as the temperature rises. Despite his strong temptation to take a few days to stop in Paris on his journey south, Bill ultimately decides against it due to the scorching heatwave currently sweeping through France. Considering how everyone raves about Paris in the spring, Bill chooses to wait until then to fully enjoy the experience.

The hotel staff greet him as if he has returned home, and the familiarity of his rooms at the Hotel de Paris is welcoming. It certainly feels like home to Bill, and he is more comfortable in these surroundings, knowing he has a purpose and an agenda. Instead of just spending money, he intends to make some.

There are dozens of letters and messages, and Bill realizes that he needs to create a system to sort correspondence into separate files. Most petitions concern noble causes and charities, and Bill does not dismiss these as he will never forget the good fortune that has come his way and decides that, eventually, he will share in his good luck. Many of the letters are investment opportunities, which can be divided into two categories. Those expressing a proposition in a new commercial venture and those wanting him to become part of a gambling syndicate. Many of the other casinos have requested that he come and play on their tables as, no doubt, they could use the publicity. There are offers of free accommodation and travel expenses, but the only one that is of interest to Bill is the casino at Nice.

Finally, there is a variety of bizarre correspondences that genuinely baffles Bill. Requests for marriage are becoming quite regular, although perhaps most unexpected and sad are submissions from parents proposing that Bill adopt their children. *You are in a position to give our daughter the education we cannot give her.* All the solicitations are remarkable in their own way, and many are very compelling. As much as he would like to respond to each of them, aside from the inability to check their credibility, he must continue building his fortune before considering benevolence. Perhaps, in the future, he may create a foundation, although such an enterprise is a long way off for now.

In the first two weeks back in Monaco, Bill does not even look in on his beloved CGV motorcar. He politely declines invitations from Rothschild and others as there are London accounts to be paid, and he must remain focused.

Bill chooses to go to work in either the Salle Garnier or the Salle Touzet, depending on the availability of space around the roulette wheel. He stands at the tables from noon until at least nine in the evening every day, often up on the balls of his feet like a boxer. He does his push-ups in the morning and takes a brisk walk up the hillside after coffee and the newspapers.

Occasionally, he may break from his work for a light supper, although mostly, he prefers to have sandwiches brought to the table. His concentration is hardly interrupted, as the winter crowds have not yet arrived. He knows Pierre Laget watches him carefully from the edges of the rooms, but his concentration rarely wavers. He focuses on numbers twenty-five through thirty-six and alternates only slightly with street and square bets. For two months, aside from zero, five, and a fourteen/seventeen split, he hardly places a bet anywhere on the first or second dozen numbers, and his winnings are steady.

As he always stakes over the maximums at each spin, the croupier's call of "Rien ne va plus" is only heard around twelve times per hour. Many spins go by without a single coup, and whether he wins or loses, Bill simply scribbles numbers in his notebook and carries on as if nothing has happened. He doesn't feel afraid of anything—not right now.

The exploits of the American "plunger," Mr. Darnborough, continue to create considerable attention at the casino, and there is always an interesting throng at his table. Mr. Darnborough adheres to the same system of play which I have already described in these columns, and fortune still favors him. At the close of yesterday's sitting, he rose the winner of no less than £6,000.

Mr. Darnborough resumed play again today and continued to pursue his usual tactics with great success, his winnings at the time of telegraphing having amounted to £5,000.

It is computed by competent observers that up to the present, his visits to the tables have resulted in a net gain of £27,000.
—Daily Mail, Nov 12, 1906

Bill receives a letter from Jimmy Rothschild explaining that the creation of the Monte Carlo Automobile Club is gathering pace, and he is requested to attend a meeting. They assemble in the private Salon Ravel in the Hotel de Paris at the appointed time, and Jimmy introduces everyone, stressing that this is an informal gathering. Present are Jacques Laffite, Jean-Pierre Tambay, Jules Hublot, Jimmy, and Bill.

"Firstly," begins Jimmy, "we need to establish feasibility. Jacques Gondoin is doing an excellent job over in Nice with his new Automobile Club, but we felt it necessary to have our own version right here. If you look at the agendas, you will see that I have outlined several propositions, and that is precisely what they are at present. Propositions.

"The idea is to create an organization where car enthusiasts can gather to discuss any manner of topics relating to the pastime of motor car pursuits. Our mission is to attract members from all over the world, and in addition, we would function as a local lobbying group. There are certain aspects that we could influence. Such things as re-tarmacking the roads in Monaco to ensure smoother driving, road safety, and access to service providers such as drivers and mechanics. Essentially, we will enhance the motor enthusiasts' experience, both on and off the roads. So you see, we have our work cut out for us, and I need each of you to commit to your roles for an initial period of one year."

Bill is thrilled to be included in the group but is still a little confused as to his role so he raises his hand. "I'm honored to be considered as a founding member," he says, "especially considering that I am a foreigner, but I don't know how much use I can be to you."

"Bill," says Jimmy, "I appreciate your modesty, although you are one of our greatest assets. Monaco itself owes you a debt of gratitude for creating so much publicity. Now that you are a motoring enthusiast, visitors will try their best to replicate your achievements. We are all aware that you do not crave attention, but it has to be said that you are a representative of the spirit of Monaco. We will employ a club secretary for the enrollment paperwork, etcetera, and an accountant, of course. Otherwise, I think we will find that the club will naturally evolve in the same way that the popularity of the motor car is evolving."

Bill is impressed. It's clear that Jimmy specializes in allaying any fears and that, to him, this is just another gentleman's club, which suits Bill fine.

Jimmy explains that he will use his private secretary to draw up the registration details and a mission statement to file with the relevant authorities, and they agree on the next meeting time. It occurs to Bill that their members would probably pay handsomely just to have the Monte Carlo badge displayed on the front of their cars, let alone have access to all the other benefits that membership may bring. Bill takes Jimmy aside when the others have left.

"Excellent speech, Jimmy. Just one thing. You didn't mention the idea of creating a new race in addition to the Nice to La Turbie climb. I realize there will be some issues with dangerous corners and such, but don't you think it's time we looked at running a car race in Monaco?"

"Let's go for a drive, Bill," says Jimmy. "I think you mentioned you'd been to La Turbie before? I know a great place for a spot of lunch."

Bill is immediately in awe of Jimmy's confidence behind the wheel of his Pierce-Arrow. He navigates the tight corners easily, and, at this time of day, the road is quite clear, so the hill climb is swift. Aside from the occasional horse and cart, the only serious obstacle they encounter is a stray chicken.

"Imagine our obituaries," shouts Jimmy over the wind, "James Rothschild and William Darnborough killed on the Monte Carlo to La Turbie road by a chicken!"

They arrive at the summit and take a moment to survey the scene below. On this perfectly clear day, the Mediterranean Sea blends with the blue sky on the horizon, and from this height, Monaco looks serene.

"You see that," says Jimmy, pointing to the ruins of a tower, "this is the Alpine Trophy that was built over two thousand years ago to celebrate the great victory of Octavian Augustus. He has the dubious distinction of having expelled all the local tribes, and this tower is known as 'Turris Viae,' meaning a Tower along the way. That, my friend, is why it's called La Turbie."

"I could happily settle here," Bill says. "It feels like a place untroubled by the goings on below."

They secure a table on the terrace at the Le Petite Poucet, a place Jimmy seems to know well. A waiter wearing a red fez hat brings them a carafe of white wine and, a few minutes later, arrives with his pencil and notepad to take their order.

"We have Charolais beef from Burgundy or fish," he announces.

"With apologies to the Chef," says Bill, "may I have the beef well done?"

The waiter does not change his expression or look up from his notepad. "You will have ze fish."

Jimmy just smiles as the waiter walks away. "We're not in Monte

Carlo anymore, Bill. The provincial restaurants in France are like that. Quite particular about their cooking. You'll get used to it."

Bill is still slightly shocked, but Jimmy is ready for a new subject. "Tell me. Are you planning to be in England next spring?"

Bill gathers himself. "Certainly. What do you have in mind?"

"My great-aunt has a place near Aylesbury, and I have asked her if I can have a gathering there at the end of May. We're making the arrangements already, and I would be honored if you would join us."

"Well, thank you, Jimmy, that would be fine. Where's Aylesbury? Isn't that where the ducks come from?"

Jimmy laughs. "Exactly! It's not far from London, but you would be staying over the weekend, so bring a toothbrush."

As they drive back down to Monaco, the wind rustling their hair, Bill is thinking about all the decisions he has made that have brought him to this moment. An invitation to a party at the Rothschild estate. Even Clark Griffith wouldn't believe it. *This changes everything*, he thinks. Perhaps this will be his badge of entry into English society.

CHAPTER 46

At the casino today, Mr. Darnborough, the well-known American "plunger" played from twelve to half-past three with varying luck. He was watched with unusual attention by a crowd of interested spectators, and in the end, was the lucky winner of £2,000.

Amongst visitors to the inner rooms today were the Grand Duke Nicholas and Mr. Arthur Bourchier.

—Daily Mail, December 29, 1906

*I*t is a three-hour drive to Cagnes-sur-mer, just outside of Nice, so when he is there, Bill often spends the night at the Winter Palace Hotel on Boulevard de Cimiez or the Hotel des Anglaise. Fortunately, the new Palace de la Jetée has a fine casino and provides a perfect escape from the constant recognition at the casino at Monte Carlo. The Jetée-Promenade looks like a floating island as it is built on a pier upon which tourists can "walk over the sea." After sunset, it shimmers in the moonlight with turrets, minarets, and a thirty-five-meter dome topped with a gold-plated trident. The sounds of clinking champagne glasses, laughter, and songs from the concert hall float across the water, and visitors are irresistibly attracted, as if drawn by a magnetic force.

Bill rapidly acquires a routine in Nice, dividing his time between days out exploring and evenings at the roulette tables. On New Year's Eve, he plays nonstop for four hours and ends up 165,000 FF to the good. The volumes of his stakes are enormous by now, but the trick is knowing when to quit for the night. This would certainly be enough to buy a thirty-room mansion in Manhattan, and he arranges for his winnings to be transferred directly to the Banca Monte dei Paschi. Inspired by this new-found wealth and spurred by the allure of a different setting away from Monaco, Bill sheds his inclination for a low profile. He impulsively purchases two cases of Dom Pérignon Champagne and, as if by magic, finds himself surrounded by a multitude of new acquaintances at the Hotel des Anglaise.

Back in his suite, he sits down at the desk with his notebook and scribbles some calculations. He gets out his bank books and studies them. The account balances go wildly up and down, and they're up now, but definitely not enough, he thinks.

The following day, a photographer captures the moment that Karl Hermann is speaking with Bill on the steps of the casino. The picture is widely circulated in international newspapers, with a caption that reads: *Mr. Darnborough, on the left of the picture, is initiating Monsieur le Director Adjoint Hermann into the mysteries of bank-breaking. It would appear that M. Hermann is not losing a word.*

When he returns to Monte Carlo, Bill wastes no time and immediately heads to the Salon Privé. He has not forgotten his first win at roulette at Goodfellows in North Bottoms, Lincoln, Nebraska, where he won on number five. He often places a couple of chips on red five as a hedge stake when he is betting on the high numbers. His strategy this evening is to keep chips on 5, 11, 17, 23, and all numbers from 28 to 36. He has a double outside bet running on red and odd to ensure small wins are regular.

There are five other players at the table the moment the ball lands on red five. The croupier's swift hand sweeps away all but the winning chips, the marker on the victorious number proclaiming its supremacy. One of the other players to his right, an Italian, judging by the extravagant attire and the amount of exaggerated arm swinging, lets out a loud groan, signaling his frustration. Bill is passed his winnings, leaving his original two chips on red five. After the next spin, the croupier calls out, "Cinq rouge encore!" as incredibly, red five comes up again. The other chips strewn across the grid vanish into the abyss, but Bill still wins a sizable amount on his original stake.

When five comes up a third time, the murmurs around the table increase, and other people come over to see what's happening. Chairs grate on the floor as more people move from their positions to see what all the commotion is about. Word quickly spreads of the phenomenon occurring at Bill's table, and a crowd starts to gather. A thin, bespectacled man with a pencil mustache can be seen frantically doing sums in his notebook as he tries to calculate the odds of recurring numbers when the ball lands on five for a fourth time. Applause and shouting ensue, and more people arrive and place their chips on the five. By now, it is impossible to make out the number five, as when the croupier calls out, "rien ne va plus, no more bets," the square is covered in stacks of chips as each player has decided that this is history in the making, and he wants to say he was there.

Bill's usual impassive countenance has been replaced with an expression of stunned disbelief as he sees all the rest of the chips whisked away at each turn. The guests that were on the balcony have come in, and there is more shouting than he has ever witnessed in the casino. As if driven by a collective consciousness, the crowd is now willing the little ball along its merry dance as it bumps several times against the diamonds before finally coming to rest yet again in red five. This time, the shouts and cheers could probably be heard in the harbor as Russians, Germans, French, Italian, and English men and women all celebrate this extraordinary event.

This remarkable occasion goes down in history as one of the few times it has occurred. Naturally, Pierre Laget and the casino are overjoyed at the publicity it will generate.

American's strange system at Monte Carlo. Darnborough, who is known as "The American Plunger," has for some weeks past attracted a good deal of attention at Monte Carlo, where he has made and lost huge sums of money at the tables. It is said that he never begins to put money on till the ball is spinning, and then hurries on piles of gold, the croupiers having to count it after each coup to ascertain if he has exceeded the maximum, in which event the surplus is withdrawn before accounts are settled.

Here, roughly, are his figures for a few days: Monday, won $20,000; Tuesday, won $38,000; Wednesday, lost $30,000; Thursday, won $30,000. He takes losses and winnings alike with admirable equanimity, and while the onlooking throng emits involuntary gasps of excitement when the ball settles, Darnborough looks unconcerned.

This greatly adds to his reputation in the gambling-room, where sang froid is cultivated by most but attained by very few.

—The American Register, February 1907

Even though Bill strongly desires to spend more time in England, he is still proud to be an American, especially this morning as he reads the headlines. President Teddy Roosevelt has been commended for his successful peace negotiations between Japan and Russia. Bill peers around the newspaper to see the Grand Duke Nicholas Mikhailovich sitting across the room reading a book, seeming entirely unaffected. He is a bear of a man at 6'3" with an eccentric sense of humor that all the young ladies adore. Doubtless, they also have a penchant for his wealth. Last night, Bill had seen him gamble away about 100,000 FF.

"Sir? Mr. Darnborough? May I have just a moment of your time?" The voice belongs to a young man who looks as if he has barely started shaving.

"Yes?" says Bill, looking up from his paper.

"Please forgive me, but I was hoping you could give me some advice. You see, I am getting married soon and I wanted to make enough to put down on a house. Do you have a system that I could use?"

"Keep your money and go home to your bride," says Bill, and

returns to reading the newspaper. The young man stands in front of Bill in stunned silence until, eventually, Bill folds his newspaper.

"Listen," he says, taking pity on the boy. "The only serious gamblers in this place are here for the duration. You cannot simply arrive with a few francs and hope to double your money."

The Grand Duke glances up from his book.

"But—" the young man begins.

"No buts," says Bill. "I didn't come here to give lessons. Be on your way, and I wish you well."

The Duke looks at Bill and signals a nod of approval.

At the Hotel de Paris reception, Etienne has held back one letter from Bill's usual mailbag. He hands it personally to Bill as he passes through, and both men can see clearly that it has the blue and gold crest of the Rothschild Family as a seal.

"Good man," says Bill, realizing once again that he is picking up typically English phrases. He wonders if he will lose his American accent if he ever lives in England. He passes a customary folded French franc note to Etienne. The envelope contains his invitation to Jimmy's weekend gathering at Waddesdon Manor, so he organizes for a telegram to be sent accepting the invitation and makes plans to travel to England once again. The first thing he does is write to Oliver Bain in London requesting to rent the Wolseley for a long weekend.

CHAPTER 47

"*A*s I mentioned in the telegram," says Oliver Bain as Bill walks with him to the side of his Richmond house, "I have had an upgrade."

Bill can hardly believe his eyes as Bain carefully pulls off the dust cover to reveal a brand-new Rolls Royce. Specifically, it is a British racing green, twenty horsepower, Harrington side-entrance Tonneau. Bain lovingly strokes the curved mudguard as he comes around to the front with its Grecian-shaped radiator.

"This is a work of art, in my opinion," says Bain. "Frederick Royce and Charles Rolls are two of our finest designers." Bill is speechless as he walks around the magnificent vehicle, almost afraid to touch it. *It even smells expensive*, thinks Bill as he takes in the leather interior.

"Now, listen up, Bill. If we didn't know each other and I didn't trust you, there is no chance I would entrust this lady into your care. However, considering that you mentioned an invitation to join the Automobile Club of Monaco and, of course, our financial arrangement, please take good care of her."

They embark on another excursion to Richmond Park, taking turns behind the wheel to help Bill become accustomed to the Rolls.

Bill then drives with deliberate caution back to Brown's and is so excited about driving the magnificent car up north that he hardly sleeps.

AFTER HIS INVITATION is inspected and accepted at the gatehouse to Waddesdon Manor, Bill finds himself on a long driveway surrounded by fields of blue cornflowers and wild, white daisies in full bloom. The drive meanders around imposing fir and cedar trees, and footmen are strategically positioned to prevent guests from taking a wrong turn. The formidable house looms over him as he edges the car around the final corner. For a moment, he thinks he has been transported back to France as the main residence resembles a French Renaissance chateau.

Two footmen hurry to his aid as he brings the Rolls to a halt, and a butler appears at the front door and requests a further inspection of his invitation.

"Mr. Darnborough, sir," says the butler, "Mr. Rothschild has requested your company at three o'clock for a tour of the grounds. You will be staying in the bachelor's wing. Please follow the valet." A young man in a green uniform picks up his travel trunk, and they walk down a long corridor in silence, turn right, and then another long corridor before a flight of stairs. Bill thinks he will get lost in this place at least once over the weekend. He catches his reflection in a mirror and realizes that his face is caked in dirt from the drive, and there are large white circles around his eyes after removing his goggles.

He is grateful for an opportunity to clean up a little in his room, and he passes a coin to the valet after declining his help to unpack. In 1907, it is not uncommon for country house parties to last three or four days, so Bill came prepared with a half-sized travel trunk for his attire changes. Old habits die hard, and Bill is still in the practice of hanging his own clothes. Only after the valet has gone does he wonder if it is appropriate to tip in a private house. He is so used to living in hotels.

He retraces his steps to the middle of the house as best as he can remember and finds Jimmy waiting outside on the gravel driveway.

"Bill!" Jimmy exclaims, "Welcome to Waddesdon! How was the drive?"

"Windy! But sublime in the Rolls. Thank you so much for inviting me, Jimmy." Bill is surveying the scenery. "Quite a place."

Jimmy grins. "We're just waiting for two more people, and then I'll take you on a little tour. We have a nice, cozy gathering this evening, but more guests will follow tomorrow."

Just then, a couple enters from the side hallway, the man in a black suit fussing with his pocket watch, the woman sailing ahead like a ship expecting to be admired, holding out her hand to Jimmy. Jimmy introduces them as John and Emma Hardacre.

"You two jump in the back," says Jimmy to the Hardacres as he gestures towards the bright red, four-seater car parked in front of them, "and, Bill, you ride up front next to me." Mrs. Hardacre appears mortally offended at not being the center of attention, but they all take their seats as Jimmy says, "This, my friends, is a Humber Beeston, brand new. I've only driven it around the estate so far, so I haven't had a chance to really open her up, but she goes like the wind." Bill notices how Jimmy's French accent has almost entirely disappeared since he arrived in England, and he is clearly enjoying playing the role of the English country gentleman.

"The first thing you should know," says Jimmy, driving slowly to lessen the engine noise, "is that my great-uncle Ferdinand bought this land from the Duke of Marlborough, when it was just a hill. He used the same French architect who adapted Chateau de Mouchy." He points behind them as they drive up the center of the north lawn. "Same turrets at the chateau. They had to lay eleven miles of water pipes from Aylesbury and make a branch railway line for the gasworks. There was central heating in '81 and electricity in '89. Queen Victoria came for lunch the year after that, and she made them turn the lights on and off for ages."

Even Bill is aware of Queen Victoria's reputation for staying at home during her later years, and he realizes this must have been a big deal for the Rothschilds, who are undoubtedly a dominant element of society.

"After Uncle Ferdinand died," continues Jimmy, "his sister, my great-aunt Alice, took over, and everything you see from now on in the gardens is mainly thanks to her. She employs over one hundred gardeners here and, hold on." Jimmy has overshot the turning and reverses to turn left beside a fountain. As the car climbs over a small hill, they see a magnificent cast iron and glass aviary rising from the surrounding rose beds.

"Let's have a look and see what we can see?" says Jimmy, and he stops the car and opens the small back door for Mrs. Hardacre. They stroll around the bird sanctuary, marveling at flamingos, ibises, African cranes, and an extraordinary collection of exotic birds.

"This is the most marvelous thing I have ever seen," says Mrs. Hardacre, "how did they get all of these beautiful creatures here?"

"Good question," replies Jimmy. "Ferdinand commissioned the majority of the rare species to protect them from the evil bird stuffers at the British Museum and bred them to be released at a later date. A previous guest tried to debate the morality of breeding birds in captivity, so you will just have to take my word for it—we protect many endangered species here. Aunt Alice bought in the noisy ones like the Kookaburras from Australia, the laughing Jack-asses, and the parrots."

Bill and the Hardacres take their time moving from one area to the next, and Bill stops to read the inscribed mounted cards explaining the bird's native habitats. Each enclosure has been care-fully designed so that its occupants can fly, waddle, wade, or swim as appropriate.

"Let's get on, shall we," says Jimmy, as he looks at his pocket watch and gestures for his guests to resume their positions in the Humber.

"This is Wilderness Valley," says Jimmy as they are surrounded by a stunning kaleidoscope of colorful wildflowers stretching far into the distance. "We're going back up to the house now for tea, but I promise to show you the stables in the morning."

Bill catches glimpses of the south front through the trees, but nothing prepares him for the sight of the fountains and statues on the raised garden with the majestic façade of the manor and its turrets beyond. Jimmy pulls the handbrake, and as they walk up to an entrance to the right, Bill notices how the doorways are framed with palm trees strikingly similar to the palms at the Hotel de Paris in Monte Carlo.

Fortunately, Jimmy has the good sense not to introduce Bill as "the famous gambler from Monte Carlo" or the "American roulette player." Instead, he simply introduces him as "my good American friend." Bill is grateful as his profession often leads to awkward questions, and he would prefer merely to blend in.

Two other guests join them in the conservatory. David Montague looks like a rower with his light blue jacket and straw boater hat, and his wife, Jane, is in her twenties and wears a cotton summer dress. They easily slip into casual conversation with Bill, relating how he really should visit Oxford, and he feels grateful that things seem to be a lot less formal than expected.

After tea, they walk through the house to the main entrance on the north front, and there are now four people playing badminton on the lawn. The shuttlecock makes a noticeable swish as it sails through the air, and it looks like these guests are regular visitors as they have made themselves feel right at home. *Perhaps they are family members*, thinks Bill.

Jimmy has disappeared, so Bill takes this opportunity to explore the house a little more. He stumbles across a room containing suits of armor, swords, and shields, which are displayed in contrast to the French elegance of the rest of the house. A helmet has been placed on an Italian chest of drawers, and a small, mounted card explains that it is part of a suit of armor given to Emperor Charles V by the Duke of Mantua in 1536. At the end of the corridor are a billiard room and a smoking room, and, aside from the fact that only single men are accommodated in this part of the mansion, Bill begins to realize why this part of the house is called the Batchelor's Wing.

The famous Rothschild wine collection is on show tonight as Emma Hardacre holds court at her end of the dining table while Jane Montague scowls at her husband for laughing a little too hard at Mrs. Hardacre's jokes. Toward the end of dinner, Jimmy proposes a toast.

"To my wonderful great-aunt Alice," says Jimmy as he stands with a raised glass. "As many of you know, Aunt Alice has been gracious enough to lend us her house for this weekend. I should remind you that even though she is not here at this precise moment, she has eyes and ears everywhere, so you'd better behave yourselves."

After a sumptuous dessert of fresh strawberries and ice cream, which have been grown and made on the estate, the gentlemen retire to the billiard room. However, they move to the smoking room when it becomes clear that cigar smoking is more popular than billiards. Jimmy sees Bill from across the room and comes over.

"Hope you enjoyed the day, Bill? So good of you to come all this way. By the way, I finally heard back from the chaps about the Automobile Club. The general consensus is that we can join forces with the cycling crowd and just change the name to Sport Velecipedique Monegasque et Automobile Monegasque. Alexandre Noghès's son is going to take over the proceedings as president, and there is talk of organizing a rally from Paris. Let's wait until we get back, and then we can set about changing the name to the Automobile Club de Monaco."

"Sounds like a good plan, Jimmy," says Bill, already making a mental list of the people he could invite to join.

It turns out that John Hardacre and David Montague are both accomplished cricket players and, to Bill's relief, are more interested in learning about baseball than roulette. Signaling an attentive footman, Bill asks, "Do you happen to know if there are any sugar lumps in the kitchen?"

After adequately demonstrating the fundamentals of baseball using sugar lumps, Bill is one of the first to retire as the rigors of the journey up from London without a chauffeur catch up with him.

Following breakfast the next morning, Jimmy invites them all down to the stables, and Bill sees grooms and stable lads hard at work when they arrive. Jimmy takes his time to greet them all, and they return a respectful acknowledgment by touching a finger to their hats. Bill can see that this is a place where Jimmy is most at ease as, for a moment, he seems to have forgotten his guests and pays far more attention to the horses.

"Welcome to the future Waddesdon Stud," says Jimmy. "Mark my words, we'll have some thoroughbreds here one day, and a Gold Cup winner will come from these stables."

One of the other guests, Neville Hibbert, has walked to the end of the coach house to admire the parked motor cars. Bill joins him as he seems to be examining the Rolls.

"Are you a motorcar man?" asks Bill.

"Ah, good morning, Mr. Darnborough," says Neville. "Unsure at this point. I am fairly certain that I would like to own a Gold Cup winner, although I am positive that I would rather own this beauty." Neville looks up from the car at Bill and then down at the car again as if making an unseen connection.

"It's yours, isn't it?"

"I borrowed it from a friend in London."

"Good for you," says Neville, "do you need a navigator for the trip back?"

"Certainly!" says Bill. "That is an excellent idea. I would welcome the company."

After Jimmy explains the considerable details of his plan for a stud farm, he comes over to the cars.

"Greetings, Neville," says Jimmy cheerfully. "Has Bill told you about our little car club in Monaco?" Neville looks suspiciously at Bill.

"Not exactly, but I have volunteered to be his navigator on the trip down to London, so I am sure we will find time to discuss it." Bill smiles at Neville but fears there may be a fair amount of interrogation later in the day. So far, he has managed to keep his background a mystery from the other guests as they have not shown particular interest. They probably assume he is in banking, considering he is a friend of Jimmy de Rothschild.

As the stable tour concludes, the group heads back up to the house, and they can hear cheering and clapping as they come around the east wing. Bill blinks hard at the astonishing sight of a man in a carriage drawn by four zebras.

"Walter!" Jimmy exclaims and turns to the ladies gathered outside the front entrance and his tour party from the stables.

"This is my fantastic cousin, Walter!" shouts Jimmy. "A gentleman, a scholar, and a man who really can speak to the animals." Lord Walter de Rothschild, the second Baron and nephew of the late Ferdinand de Rothschild, is quite a sight to behold. He has a generous black beard with an imposing frame, and he holds a long horsewhip in his left hand as he raises his hat to the ladies with his free hand.

Bill has only seen photographs of zebras and is the first to approach them, although not too near for fear that the Baron may whip him for being impertinent. The others all stare or snigger, but Bill has questions.

"Can they be trained? Like horses?" he asks.

"Certainly," replies the Baron.

"Walter," interrupts Jimmy, "please allow me to introduce my good friend from America, Mr. William Darnborough."

"Pleasure to make your acquaintance, sir," says the Baron, raising his hat once more.

"And I, yours, sir," replies Bill. "I imagined these beasts in one of P. T. Barnum's circus tents but never expected to see them in the English countryside, let alone pulling a carriage. This is spectacular. Did you bring them over from Africa?"

"Walter," says Jimmy, "is an eminent zoologist and runs the Natural History Museum in Tring."

"In case you are curious, sir," says the Baron, "horses and zebras both come from the equidae family, but there are some noticeable differences. The main one being that a zebra is naturally skittish, so do not get too close. They have a built-in nervous disposition on account of a fear of natural predators, you understand."

"I see," says Bill, as he takes a step back, just in case.

"Furthermore," continues the Baron, "you may conclude this animal is simply a donkey, or mule, as you may refer to it, with stripes. It is not. They may be slower than horses, but they are surprisingly agile and can turn well at speed, which is how they avoid capture."

Bill is looking at one of the most bizarre sights he could have imagined, but in less than two minutes, he has been convinced that having a carriage drawn by four zebras is a perfectly logical scenario.

After a light lunch served on the south lawn, the other guests begin to arrive. Many have traveled long distances and are shown to their rooms to rest and freshen up. Bill and Neville move to a bench that faces the house and have a good vantage point to see the new arrivals as they come to take in the view. Bill concludes that arriving early has many advantages as he remembers the dirt on his face from the day before. He feels much more relaxed as he crosses his legs and takes a generous puff of his cigar.

"Jimmy tells me you live in Monaco?" says Neville. "Is it sunny all year round?"

This is how all conversations in England start, thinks Bill. *It's always about the weather.* "We get a howler of a wind in the spring, but most of the time, driving around the corniches is spectacular."

"What are corniches?"

"The roads that are cut into the mountains. Majestic and treach-erous at once. There are hairpin bends, and you never know what may be around the next corner, so if you're sight-seeing, the trick is to be the passenger."

"What kind of car do you drive down there?"

"A French Charron, but I have my eye on a Darracq." Bill laughs. "I'm certain it will be easier to stable and feed than Jimmy's stallions."

Just then, a striking couple appears on the south patio. The gentleman is tall and slim with a tailored light suit, and his female companion has a slender form, a magnificent wide-brimmed hat, and carries a parasol. Neville and Bill are sufficiently far away so as not to necessitate a formal greeting and simultaneously raise their hats instead.

"Who could that be?" Bill inquires, his gaze firmly locked on the captivating women before them.

"Oh, dear," says Neville dryly. Then, he slaps the bench between them and says, "All right, old chap, time to go change for drinks, and I suppose you'll have a chance to meet her then."

"But is that her husband?"

Neville gives a little smile. "Her uncle, I believe. The coast may well be clear, as you Americans like to say."

Bill and Neville make their way to their respective bedrooms in the bachelor's wing, and Bill takes advantage of a few minutes of solitude and lies down on his bed. Once more, he looks up at a ceiling with a crystal chandelier hanging like an enormous piece of sparkling jewelry, and he thinks back to the days of water-stained plaster in dead-end towns. Finding himself in a French manor house in the middle of the English countryside is starting to feel quite surreal, and he can't get the picture of that enchantress on the south patio out of his head. Neville has refused to tell Bill her name, though he obviously knows who she is, which Bill finds maddening. Well, at least he has the right clothes to make a good impression. As long as he can keep from embarrassing himself, maybe she won't realize he isn't truly one of them.

CHAPTER 48

*C*ocktails are served on the north front lawn overlooking the fountains and the fields beyond. Jimmy ensures everyone is introduced to each other and takes special care to make Bill feel as welcome as possible. While keeping one eye out for the radiant woman he had spotted earlier, Bill is trying to master a memory technique, which involves repeating the name of the person he is introduced to out loud. Mrs. Hardacre's husband plays cricket with Montague, who is married to Jane, and they live in Oxford. Eventually, Bill reminds himself that he doesn't need to remember everyone's names as it is more likely that they will remember him.

And then he looks to the doorway, and he sees her.

The sash of her white gown encircles the most petite waist Bill has ever seen on a woman. She seems to have an ethereal quality about her, and she moves elegantly with a soft smile. Bill wants to approach her immediately but fears that would be too American. He walks over to Neville instead and speaks in a low tone. "Sir, you must tell me who she is."

Neville smiles. "Oh, all right, then. That, sir, is Miss Frances Erskine-Shaw. And I respect your good taste."

"Miss Frances Erskine-Shaw," Bill repeats out loud as he thinks there is a certain music to the name. "And the gentleman?"

"Her Uncle Charles. Who, by the by, has been, shall we say, very protective since her father died some years ago."

Neville sips his drink. Bill glances across the lawn at Miss Erskine-Shaw, who has gracefully extended her gloved hand to David Montague. Bill hasn't seen a more captivating woman since Miss Emma Juch all those years ago in Denver. Deep in thought, he takes a sip of his drink, contemplating the best approach to engage her.

What words could he possibly use to attract her attention? In this moment, he grapples with a sense of unworthiness, realizing that to win someone like Miss Frances Erskine-Shaw, he'll need more than just his current finances. He knows someone like her would expect a pedigree, not a man who amassed his wealth at the roulette tables, unlike the illustrious Rothschild lineage.

Bill feels like he's nineteen years old again, plotting a way to take Emma Juch to dinner. Only now, it feels like the stakes are much higher, and the odds seem far more challenging to overcome. Neville laughs slightly as if he knows exactly what's running through Bill's mind. "Poor old chap. Would you like me to introduce you?"

"Good God," says Bill. "Yes!"

"GOOD EVENING, MR. ERSKINE-SHAW," says Neville as they approach. Uncle Charles does not offer his hand to shake as he is holding a champagne glass and instead nods and gives a suspicious glance in Bill's direction. Bill is staring at Miss Erskine-Shaw, and seeing this, Neville hurries ahead with the introductions.

"Good evening, Miss Erskine-Shaw. How nice to see you again."

"Good evening, Mr. Hibbert," says Frances.

Neville adds, "May I present Mr. William Darnborough from America." Bill steps forward.

"So, Neville," says Uncle Charles, completely ignoring Bill, "are you staying out of trouble?"

"Yes, Sir," answers Neville, "so far, so good."

Bill is at a loss for words only for the second time in many years. Miss Frances Erskine-Shaw has her light auburn hair swept up in a fashionable pompadour and carries a white lace parasol to shield her eyes from the evening sun. Her eyes. They are hazel, soft, and warm. Her nose is pert, her mouth a perfect bow to complement the flawless symmetry of her face, and when she smiles at Bill and holds his gaze, it feels as if they have already had a secret conversation. No superlative in existence would be enough to describe her loveliness, and yet a strange familiarity about her further complicates Bill's efforts to form whole sentences.

"My," he manages, "the weather is perfect for us this evening."

He immediately regrets his opening line.

"Yes," says Uncle Charles, "not too hot, not too cold. Eventually, they will develop a better system to predict meteorological parameters."

Now he's done it, thinks Bill. They are going to talk interminably about the weather, and then she will turn away in search of more interesting conversation, and he will have lost his chance forever. But Miss Erskine-Shaw catches his eye and breaks in. "We have relatives from Philadelphia, Mr. Darnborough." Her voice is smooth and elegant, and the sound of it causes a mild electric shock to Bill's heart. "Is that near where you are from?"

He cannot seem to think straight with those hazel eyes on him. He reminds himself he is no ballplayer anymore but a man who shops at Poole & Co., wins piles of money in Monte Carlo, and drives a smart French motorcar. He puts back his shoulders and smiles. "Very close. I've spent a great deal of time in New York," he says.

"Oh, my," she says, with a coy smile of her own. "You probably had a grand adventure there."

Charles Erskine-Shaw breaks in. "Our family has quite some connections in the United States," he says gruffly, and Bill senses that the man already does not like him, nor the way his niece is looking at him.

"Is that so?" Bill says warmly, hoping to ingratiate himself with the possessive uncle.

Frances answers before her uncle has a chance. "My great-grandfather was Baron David Erskine, who was the British Ambassador to the United States during the presidency of Thomas Jefferson. My great-grandmother was the daughter of General Cadwalader, who fought with Washington at Valley Forge. She was called Frances, too."

"That's truly extraordinary," Bill remarks, unconsciously leaning in a little closer. He yearns to have this conversation privately, away from the watchful eyes of Neville who probably finds it amusing and Uncle Charles, who appears rather annoyed.

Uncle Charles decides to throw his weight in again. "So, what do you do, Mr. Darnborough, and what brings you to these fine shores?"

Before Bill has a chance to jeopardize any possibility of ever speaking to the Erskine-Shaws again by coming clean about his profession, he is saved by the house butler, who announces dinner will be served.

Neville and Bill walk together toward the dining room, following the Erskine-Shaws at a discreet distance. Bill is hoping he will be seated next to Miss Erskine-Shaw as he catches glances of her ankles from under her layered skirt and rustling petticoat.

They enter the marble-clad dining room, which has large rococo framed mirrors on the walls from the Paris house of the Duc de Villars. Bill pauses to look closely at the designs with extraordinary inlays of cresting waves, palm fonds, bats, and dragon wings. The table is set with dozens of roses, malmaison carnations, and six large silver candle stands. The food at Waddesdon is legendary, and Bill can soon taste why.

Dinner starts as a relatively subdued affair, and the convention appears to be that the guests do not talk over the table but rather to the people to their immediate left and right. Bill sees Miss Erskine-Shaw at the other end of the table, and she appears to be in a deep conversation with a strikingly handsome middle-aged man. He is immediately filled with jealousy, and it is clear that he has already developed a longing to be near her, a longing the likes of which he hasn't experienced before.

Jimmy must have recognized that the dinner party needed a little cheering up, as once the main course arrives, he proposes a toast.

"My Lords, Ladies, and Gentlemen. Guests and friends from near and far. Welcome to Waddesdon and enjoy the pheasant. I can assure you that it was reared, shot, hung, plucked, and cooked right here on the estate."

At this point, Bill glances at his neighbors to check that he is using the correct silverware in the assigned order, as different dishes of roasts and salads are served. He is seated next to Emma Hardacre and Clara Butt, who is sure that Bill enjoys hearing all about the various singing engagements she has performed for important members of the aristocracy.

Following a dessert of delicacies and artfully arranged sugar fruit pyramids, the dinner draws to a close, and Jimmy announces that the gentlemen will adjourn to the smoking and billiard rooms. Bill ponders the fate of the ladies as he observes them heading toward the library. He finds this custom rather curious, but his primary preoccupation is finding a way to have another conversation with Miss Frances Erskine-Shaw.

Once the cigars are lit, and everyone is armed with a glass of cognac, Bill sits in an armchair beside Neville.

"It is none of my business, of course," says Neville, as they settle down, "and I would quite like to be able to wish you the very best of luck in your endeavors."

"But?" says Bill.

"No buts," says Neville, "only, I was brought up to understand the fact that life is full of disappointments, and the Erskines are a very old and respected family with Royal connections, so I pray that you are not setting yourself up for a Shakespearean tragedy."

Bill laughs at the reference and takes a sip of cognac. His nerves are on edge, and the drink burns nicely down and calms him. "All right, then, Neville, what would you do in my position?"

"Well, dear fellow," replies Neville, who also takes a sip of his cognac. "I would commence the quest with a request to correspond. The uncle will pull up the drawbridge if you are too forward with

Frances, so why not become better acquainted over a reasonable amount of time?"

"Good God," says Bill. "That sounds ridiculous. That could take months. Years!"

"May I remind you, Bill, you are no longer in America. It isn't about the hustle and grab and buy here, but finesse and charm and receive." Neville grins, toasts Bill slightly, and takes another sip of cognac.

Bill sighs, knowing Neville is right. If he's to have any hope of success in this matter, he must rein in his American impatience. He must cultivate an aristocratic nonchalance. "If I were paying you as my navigator, Neville, I would double your salary. You have become my guide in more ways than one, and I am grateful for your counsel."

The house butler arrives and whispers something in Jimmy's ear, who then stands to address his guests.

"Gentleman, I am informed that the ladies have gathered in the music room and request the pleasure of our company. As most of you know, we are to have the delight of some music and song provided by Signori Paolo Tosti and Miss Clara Butt."

Bill and Neville stand and make their way to the music room as Neville whispers, "Watch out for 'Abide with Me.' I hear she sings it in the bath."

Miss Butt is over six feet tall and has a surprisingly deep voice that commands the entire music room, although Bill can't focus to listen. He's stealing glances across the room at Miss Erskine-Shaw, who is seated with her uncle. On one occasion, she catches him and smiles, then raises an eyebrow to pretend to be offended and looks back at Miss Butt as if the singer has her full attention. Bill almost laughs out loud.

At the end of Miss Butt's fourth piece, which did not include "Abide with Me," two footmen serve handmade chocolates from Switzerland on silver trays. The guests begin to mingle, and Bill knows he must make a move before Miss Erskine-Shaw is whisked away by her uncle. He maneuvers his way through the crowd of people before coming face to face with Uncle Charles, who appears to be blocking his way like a knight guarding a princess.

But Bill's confidence is high from that glance they'd exchanged, and he is determined not to be put off. "Good evening, Mr. Erskine-Shaw. I was wondering if I may continue our fascinating conversation regarding your family connections in America?" Frances is now standing beside her uncle, giving Bill a little smile, which dares him to continue.

"My own family hails from Yorkshire," he offers. "In fact, I'm reliably informed that there is a Darnborough Street in York."

"Really?" says Charles, and Frances smiles.

"We do so enjoy meeting people who have at least one street named after their families," she teases, and his face burns—damn, what an American gaffe to make, in this place!—but he grins to show her he can take it.

"When did your family decide to make the courageous voyage to America?" she continues.

"My grandfather George went over in the early 1800s and purchased land in Pennsylvania. I do not believe he was any sort of an ambassador," he teases her back, and she smiles and lowers her lashes, giving a nod that says *touché*.

"It is very interesting that we should have an American here tonight." Uncle Charles says stiffly. "How do you know Mr. Rothschild?"

"Ah, well," replies Bill, "we met in Monaco, and we are forming an automobile club together." Charles and Frances exchange a glance at this news, both with raised eyebrows, and Frances takes this opportunity to interrupt.

"That is wonderful," she says. "We were in Monte Carlo last summer. I do so love the sunsets and the warm breezes." She looks at her uncle again and, with an infectious smile, says, "I do hope we may have an opportunity to revisit Monaco soon, Uncle Charles. Perhaps in the summer?"

Charles frowns, and just as Bill realizes that the conversation is coming dangerously close to the point where he may have to divulge his profession, another guest, the handsome gentleman who was so eager in conversation with Frances at dinner, arrives and greets Charles.

"My dear friend, Charles, I was hoping to have a chance to speak with you this weekend. Good evening again, Miss Erskine-Shaw."

"Frances," says Charles, "you remember Piers Pemberton? He came to the house in Kensington some months ago."

"Yes, of course," replies Frances, "we were seated next to each other at dinner." She gives the man a courteous nod. "Mr. Pemberton."

Bill briefly entertains the notion of escorting Pemberton outside and terminating this conversation forcibly. However, he swiftly dismisses the idea, recognizing that unleashing the youthful boxer inside him would unquestionably shatter any hopes he might have with Miss Erskine-Shaw for all time. He may break Pemberton's jaw, but it's not a worthwhile trade-off.

With another glance at her, he can't help wondering if he has a chance at all. Certainly, he's been thinking of trying to meet the right woman, a companion for life to share in his good fortune, but now that he has, he sees she is so much more than he could have imagined. Eventually, the fact that he is a professional gambler will come to light, probably sooner rather than later, and he cannot decide if it is better to come clean now or hope that he can charm her into liking him enough that, by the time she finds out, it won't matter as much. She may be out of his league, but he has nothing to lose by trying.

Pemberton is more interested in a conversation with Charles after all, and as he leads him off to one side for a private discussion, Bill takes the opportunity to speak to Frances.

"I enjoyed meeting with you this evening, Miss Erskine-Shaw."

She gives him a warm little smile as she looks up at him. "I do not think my uncle likes you at all," she pronounces.

Bill is shocked, at a loss, trying to think what to say.

She goes on. "I find that quite an intriguing circumstance."

Bill is so surprised he laughs. "Well, then!"

"Are you going to ask to write to me?"

Bill swallows and glances around. He feels like he's caught in a net and never liked any feeling better. "May I be so bold as to ask if I may write to you, Miss Erskine-Shaw?"

She cocks her head as if considering the request but says nothing. Bill blurts, "Also, I keep rooms at the Hotel de Paris, and I would be honored to invite you and your uncle to stay there whenever you decide to visit Monaco." He immediately regrets this last statement, and Frances is still not responding, and he fears he has taken a step too far.

Then, she smiles. "My word, Mr. Darnborough, you *are* quite bold." As he looks into her eyes for a moment, Bill senses once more that there is a private communication between them as Frances continues, almost in a whisper, "Mr. Rothschild has my address."

CHAPTER 49

ollowing Neville Hibbert's advice was never going to be easy, but Bill knows he has to use tactical finesse in his campaign to win the heart of Miss Erskine-Shaw. Back in Monaco, he decides to revisit the idea of having a separate place to live in the village of La Turbie. He drives up the Grand Corniche and arrives at the fountain on the road opposite the Hotel de France. Walking around the side of the hotel and seeing the spectacular view down to Monaco from this elevated position, Bill decides that this is the perfect spot. The hotel manager is Jean-Luc Baptiste, who recognizes the name William Darnborough from the newspapers and is quite surprised to see him here.

Monsieur Baptiste understands Bill's request for anonymity and is more than happy to accept two months' payment in advance for a room with a double balcony. Bill's only issue now is that he will need two of everything: two toothbrushes, two shaving kits, two sock drawers, and everything else, as he plans to divide his time between the Hotel de Paris and La Turbie. Once in his room, the first thing he does is sit down with a glass of white wine and write to Frances Erskine-Shaw.

The construction of his first letter is one of the most challenging undertakings in recent years as Bill scrunches up many inane drafts that find their way to the wastepaper basket. He guesses that Uncle Charles may have an opportunity to read his correspondence and, therefore, chooses the tone of his letter accordingly. It's not too familiar, yet not overly formal like a communication from the bank manager. His primary objective is to elicit a response, and he is in no hurry to overstate his desire to see her again, as this would only scare her away. Worse still, Uncle Charles may forbid her from corresponding with him entirely.

As he looks up from the desk, admiring the view of the principality below, the evening sun has turned the harbor a deep crimson color, and one by one, lights are turned on as if signaling to each other that all is well.

The scene inspires him to use what he has learned from the English writers he discovered in Brown's library room and he begins the letter with a flowery description of the view from his window. Then, he recalls how she had teased him for his boldness and also seemed to like it, so he decides to continue in the same vein— though not in a way her uncle could object to. Conflictingly, he also needs to keep in mind Neville's advice to take things slow. *Now, Miss Erskine-Shaw,* he writes, *I could continue to talk about the weather and the scenery, but I would rather truly get to know you, instead. I could ask you what your favorite color is or who is your favorite author, but, being American, I would like to ask you instead what your greatest ambition in life is and what you would like your life to look like in five years. Please reply as soon as possible because (again, being American) I simply cannot wait to hear your response.*

He thinks it's best to keep it short and not overwhelm her with the thousand questions he would *like* to ask. He signs the letter, *Yours truly, Bill Darnborough,* and seals it up with satisfaction, writing the Hotel de Paris on the envelope as a return address. "Who could resist replying to that question?" he thinks, and, glancing out at the skyline again, he can't help but hope that someday he will be sharing beautiful views like this one with Miss Frances Erskine-Shaw.

The following evening, Bill drives down to Monte Carlo but does not head straight to the Salon Privé, instead choosing to sit on the balcony of the Salon Rose with a cigar. As he watches the yachts bobbing up and down in the harbor, he overhears an interesting tale of J.P. Morgan, the famous American financier who has arrived in the harbor on his new yacht, the Corsair. Apparently, he had an argument with one of the Directors at the casino, saying he would refuse to play roulette until they raised the table limits to 20,000 FF. They declined, and Morgan left. Seems like a reasonable request, thinks Bill, content with his relationship with Laget and his standing at the casino after all this time. All it takes is a friendly word with Pierre on a quiet afternoon in a corner of the Salle Touzet, and the limits are negotiable.

Three nights later, Bill is beside himself at not having received a reply yet from Miss Erskine-Shaw, which he realizes is ridiculous. She probably hasn't even received his letter yet. He is seated at a table on his own in the smoking room after a particularly intense evening of double-handed betting, almost to the point of exhaustion as he has been standing at the table for hours. He feels like he has earned the whisky he is drinking.

"You haven't returned my messages, dear boy." Bill turns to see John Haverstock standing over him with a drink in his hand.

"Well, well, John, how good to see you! Please forgive me, I've been preoccupied."

"I heard some news of that—the newspapers adore you."

Bill laughs. "John, you're a sight for sore eyes. Since I returned, I've been so entirely committed to the tables that I haven't even been near the harbor or the gardens, let alone seen anyone. People come and go, and many want to talk to me, but I've been so focused on playing that I feel possessed."

"Well, this is what sets you apart from the usual crowd. People come in here, on this hallowed ground," John waves his hands around the ornate surroundings of the casino, "they expect to win big and go home without any effort. They see chaps like you and assume it's easy. You and I both know that is not the case. For most of us, this is a sport, just like the races. For you, it's a business. In fact, for you, it's an industry. Nobody here has the experience or the commitment that you have. Consequently, very few will ever attain your level of success either."

"Nevertheless," John continues, "I think it is high time you pay attention to your health. Forgive me for being so blunt, but if you would consider me a friend, I would like to suggest that you take a break occasionally."

"I've had lots of breaks, John," says Bill. "I couldn't be happier."

"I'm not referring to holidays, Bill. Don't you think it would be a good idea to take a breath once in a while in between sessions down here? Even bankers go out in the evening and have fun on weekends."

"You may have a point."

"Yes, any decent doctor will tell you that the mind needs to rest as well as the body. What you need is a distraction. How about golf?"

"Golf?"

"Yes, golf," says John, "you know, small defenseless white ball that you can hit as hard as you like whilst enjoying a brisk walk in the countryside."

"I'm not sure about that," says Bill. "For one thing, it would be very time-consuming. How long does it take to get around a golf park?"

"Course," says John, "It's called a golf course. Around four hours, depending on how the players in front are getting on. There are rules regarding time, of course. For example, when I'm knee-deep in the rough at Nice, I have about four minutes to look for my ball until I have to drop another one and carry on. That happens far too regularly, I'm afraid."

The roulette tables have all shut down for the night, and the barman clinks glasses as he tidies things up.

"I'll think on it," says Bill. "Where can I find a good book about golf?"

"That's the spirit, Bill," says John, "I've got just the one. I'll drop it off at the hotel reception for you. There is one other thing. I think you'll like the members at the Nice club as they won't pester you about roulette. It's an unwritten club rule, similar to a London gentleman's club if you like. We never discuss business."

"That's a good thing," says Bill. "Of course, there's no business to discuss in Monte Carlo besides the casino. I was thinking yesterday that if we took the casino away from Monaco, all they would have left would be the macaroni factory."

"Too true," says John, "In fact, they should give you full residency as a reward for all the publicity you bring the place."

After they bid each other good night, Bill considers John's comment. What could he get away with in terms of casino privileges? Perhaps Laget would increase the maximums even more? As for golf, perhaps being known as a golfer might elevate his social status in English society? Would Frances see him as more of a gentleman if his pastimes went beyond gambling and a love of motorcars? Anyway, he needs something to keep his mind off waiting for a letter from Frances.

He has become such a regular feature of the casino that visitors expect to see him at the tables every night, and people speculate about his whereabouts if he is absent. No letter arrives from Frances, and, in part to keep his mind off that fact, Bill slips back into the routine of long hours standing at the table. It begins to take its toll.

Early one afternoon, a waiter comes up to him. "Pardon me, Monsieur, can I fetch you a drink?" Bill takes a moment to register, looks at his pocket watch, and realizes he has been at the table for at least twenty minutes without placing a single bet. The wheel will not be spun unless a bet is placed, and he is entirely unaware if any other players have arrived and departed.

"No, thank you," he says to the waiter as he passes all his chips to the croupier to exchange for large denominations. "Cash me in, Monsieur. I'm off to play golf."

The Nice Golf Club at Cagnes-sur-Mer has a curious first hole as you have to cross the eighteenth fairway to get to the tee. It is a 350-yard par four, and Bill steps up to the tee box for the first time with Alfred Covington, the resident professional at the club who also acts as the local instructor. Alfred presents Bill with a set of clubs.

"This is what you'll need," he says, "a bulger driver, brassie, spoon, brassie niblick, cleek, lofting iron, mashie, iron-niblick, and a putter."

"Got it," says Bill, although if he hadn't been standing there, looking at Alfred's weapons of choice, he would not have believed this is what they were called. He looks nervously down the fairway of the first hole, concerned that Alfred will detect his obvious anxiety. Fortunately, it appears that Alfred has seen this look of apprehension many times before.

"Let's get out to the practice field," says Alfred, "and we'll have our first lesson."

Unlike baseball, the objective of golf is to keep the ball within the playing area, and it soon becomes clear that while Bill has the strength and hand-eye coordination to hammer the ball considerably further than most, accuracy will require some refinement. "Keep your head down, sir, and your eye on the ball," is a repeated phrase of Alfred's as Bill tries to hide his frustration. The mashie soon becomes his favorite club as it is a mid-range, loftier club than a driver and has less opportunity to head out toward the Mediterranean Sea.

Alfred concentrates on modifying all of Bill's baseball habits, especially adapting his grip and swing. "You do need a firm grip, but it looks like you're trying to strangle a snake," says Alfred. "Both hands work together in unison," he demonstrates, "that's how we will prevent the ball going too far to the left or right." Next comes the swing, which Bill initially finds difficult as he is used to swinging so fast. "It's all about timing," says Alfred, "everything about this will feel wrong, but with practice, you'll be hitting them straight down the fairway in no time."

Bill is one of Alfred's more promising students right from the start, as he has no problem spending hours by himself hitting balls in the practice field. This is how he trained in baseball, and he is determined to get as good as possible before venturing onto the course. The temperature drops to 48°F in the early winter evenings, and even as the light is fading, Bill can still be found hitting a bucket of balls or on the putting green.

John Haverstock introduces him to two of the founding members, John Langford-Browne and James Hay-Gordon, who secure his club membership, and Bill is well on his way to his first full round of golf.

As golf practice is very time-consuming, the usual suspects at the casino in Monte Carlo are beginning to wonder what has become of Bill. The newspapers do their merry dance with speculative reports that he has become obsessed with driving and has gone on a tour of southern Europe. The few people who need to know his whereabouts know where he is, which suits him just fine.

What doesn't suit him is that he still hasn't heard from Frances. He writes to her again, several drafts, then finally crumples up the final effort and sends nothing. Bold is one thing, but overeager is another. He just hopes this isn't another time in life when all his dreams will go up in smoke.

On the day before Bill's first round of golf at Nice, the force of nature that is the mistral has decided to make itself known. The mistral is a strong, dry wind that blows down from the Rhone Valley to the Mediterranean Sea, and even though it may be a bright, clear day, the wind brings a severe cold snap. Bill likes to think that he is one of those people who is prepared for all eventualities, although this turn of the weather is not something he even noticed the year before. Now, he has a drive along the coast to Nice in an open-top motor car and has a round of golf to complete.

Alfred has shown great patience and given Bill all his knowledge concerning the theory of golf. For this reason and out of respect, he cannot simply telephone the Nice Golf Club and cancel his game. As he makes his way to the Boutique Alpine shop on the aptly named Boulevard de Suisse, he thinks the newly formed Automobile Club of Monte Carlo should open a shop selling driving gloves, goggles, and coats.

One of the benefits of an unexpected mistral wind is that it ensures that most sane golfers occupy themselves with indoor pastimes instead of subjecting themselves to a day of almost perpetual frustration. Alfred and Bill have the course to themselves, which works out well for Bill as there is no shortage of "correction shots" meaning he is encouraged to try the same shot on more than one occasion. This is, after all, "merely a practice round," Alfred kindly reminds Bill as they trample in the long grass looking for lost balls.

"This is painful," Bill cries out over the howling wind at one point.

"How so?" asks Alfred.

"I can hit a baseball traveling at nearly a hundred miles per hour, and this little guy," he points down at the ball, "Is just sitting there, perfectly still, begging me to hit him as hard as I can."

"I have an idea," says Alfred, "try not to *hit* the ball. Concentrate on your follow-through and swing slowly. Don't concern yourself with where the ball may be going because you don't have to run after it when you've hit it."

In the golf clubhouse, they have a moment to relax with a drink and reflect on the day's antics. Alfred demonstrates a talent for optimist language, which is rarely heard at a baseball park.

"You show great promise, Bill, as you have all the natural abilities required to be a first-class golfer. All that is required now is more practice."

"At least," says Bill, "if I prove myself to be above average at golf, not a soul will ask me to share my *system*. As you say, it is simply a matter of try, try, again."

Alfred sits further back in his chair and turns to look out over the course and beyond to the sea. Eventually, he turns to Bill with a pensive look.

"You see, golf is like life," he says. "You can hit a perfect shot and end up in a terrible spot or hit a bad shot and have an easy next shot. I watch some of the old boys around here who can't hit it that far, but they post good scores as they don't go for glory with every shot. Straight up the fairway every time. I suppose it's because they have reached a point in life where they don't need to prove anything to anyone anymore." Bill turns to Alfred and smiles. He is wondering if that time will ever come for him.

He arrives back at the hotel and checks at the desk for his mail. He is no longer hopeful, and yet—there it is! Among the piles of letters from strangers wanting him to marry their daughters or gamble their life savings away, a letter addressed in a decidedly elegant hand, the right corner of the envelope sporting the postage stamp, *Kensington*. He tears the envelope open.

Dear Mr. Darnborough,

    I hope you'll forgive the delay in my response to your letter. You see, until I received it, I hadn't realized that I was expecting my life to continue for the next five years (at least) in the same old patterns of garden parties and luncheons and trying to choose the right hat for each occasion, so I've been in quite the spin at the suggestion that I might have some choice in the matter or even make a change in direction. I suppose American ladies are used to the idea of ambition. Do you find me awfully dull and terribly English, as that it is such a novel concept to me?

    Yours truly,

    Frances Erskine-Shaw

    P.S. My favorite author is the poet Elizabeth Barrett Browning. My favorite colour—oh, I am so frightfully pedestrian—is blue. But what shade of blue, you may wonder?

Dear Miss Erskine-Shaw,

    Contrary to finding you boring, I could not find you more charming. A poet for your favorite author. It seems to me, though, that you didn't answer my principal question. What did you conclude regarding your own ambitions? And, yes, I am certainly wondering what shade of blue.

    Yours truly,

    Bill Darnborough

    P.S. Please call me Bill.

Dear Bill, (gosh, that feels racy),

    It seems to me that a lady does not discuss her ambitions, at least not with a gentleman she met at a weekend house party. May I ask what yours are? I do not even know what you do. How can I know whether it is safe to confide in you at all?

You may continue to call me Miss Erskine-Shaw.

Yours truly,

F.E.-S.

P.S. You are likely to find this scandalous, but, as for the shade of blue, think of Van Gogh's "Starry Night." Surely you have seen it? It has a depth that startles one—it is vivid and yet serene.

DEAR MISS ERSKINE-SHAW,

Forgive my boldness, but though I have not had the good fortune to have seen the painting you mentioned, it seems to me that with your description of Van Gogh's blue, you have described yourself exactly . . .

Bill crumples up this effort and starts over, only to find himself writing nearly the same opening line again. But he feels it's time to go more into depth. He cannot help himself, in fact. He describes to Frances—he cannot think of her by any other name—a few things about his background. Certainly not everything. He leaves out his mother and Libby, for example. Nor does he mention his profession or how he has acquired his money. But he wants Frances to understand how far he's come and how far he intends to go. He writes of being signed as a young professional baseball player and exploring the mid-west until finally arriving in the fantastic metropolis that is New York. *I have been prosperous in business affairs and now have the great fortune to spend my days in Monaco.*

He tells her he imagines a country estate, not unlike the one where they met. He tells her he thinks he can make enough money to buy one. The letter is two pages long by the time he's finished, and he ends by asking when he might be fortunate enough to see her again.

NO REPLY COMES, and no reply comes. Day after day, nothing.

Has he shared too much? Shot himself in the foot? He curses himself for the mistake. He should have kept up the short, breezy notes. It felt like he had been getting somewhere. Now he has shared the truth—or some of it—about who he is and been too forward and blown his chances. He thinks that the life he has led is so utterly alien to her that she probably laughed at his letter, tossed it into the fire, and forgot about him entirely. Who did he think he was, anyway, writing to her like that? What a goddamned American gaffe. How uncouth to discuss his money, his *ambition*! Of course, of *course*, she is more suited to a British gentleman who has a title and a seat on the board of a venerable bank.

He has forgotten the way things work over here, forgotten Neville's caution about finesse. *Money can't buy you everything, after all,* he thinks, and it feels almost like his heart is broken, and he can't believe he's been such a fool, especially at thirty-nine years old. He is acting like a foolish young man. He decides he must focus on his work, which is the only place where his future lies now.

THE *NEW YORK TIMES* is available in Monaco in 1909, and Bill reads that Fred Clarke's Pittsburg Pirates have won the World Series, beating the Detroit Tigers 4-3. He remembers his boxing days at school in Bloomington when he always got back up, even if it meant a repeated punch in the face. He was the scrappy kid who practiced pitching until it was too dark to see the ball, and it is the same with gambling as no matter how many times that damned roulette ball landed on the wrong number, he knew eventually, it would bow to his will.

Somehow, he cannot muster this sort of optimism about Frances, not anymore, but he is determined he will keep it up at the tables. However, when he returns to the casino that afternoon, things do not go his way, and he struggles to focus on the game. One of the croupiers is completely taken aback when Bill raises his voice and swears as he hammers his fists on the table, which he has never done before.

Maybe I'm in a rut, he thinks. *Maybe I just need to get out of here. Maybe nothing means what I thought it did—maybe I have everything all wrong.*

As if perfectly on cue, that afternoon, an Englishman named Beresford arrives in the most beautiful car Bill has ever seen and parks at the steps of the casino just as Bill is leaving. They exchange the customary greetings and introductions, and Beresford proudly explains that his car is a seventy horsepower, four-cylinder, De Dietrich racing model.

"It's a dandy car," says Bill. "Seventy horsepower, you say? Do you want to sell it?" Beresford, who is, in fact, The Honorable Seton Robert de la Poer Horsley-Beresford, looks completely caught off guard.

"I've just bought it from Charles Jarrott and driven all the way through France," he says.

"I see," says Bill. "Who's Charles Jarrott?"

"He's the famous British racer who won the Circuit des Ardennes and came third in the Paris-Madrid race in a De Dietrich."

"I don't doubt its pedigree," says Bill, who is determined to have this prize without giving Beresford an opportunity to haggle. "How about I pay you one-third on top of what you paid for it? Cash."

"Well, that's very generous, sir," says Beresford, "but that would set you back more than ten-thousand French francs."

"I'll give you twelve-thousand cash. Wait there." Five minutes later, Bill returns with the money, and a stunned Beresford hands over the papers.

Bill drives the car straight up the Grande Corniche to La Turbie and explains to Monsieur Baptiste at the hotel that he is going on an automobile trip and may be some time. He gets back in his De Dietrich, whispers "Seventy horsepower" under his breath, and cranks the engine.

CHAPTER 50

"Quanto veloce va la tua macchina?"

Bill has acquired a firm grasp of the French language, yet when the Italian asks about the speed of his car, his response is nothing more than a smile. Sixty miles beyond the French border, he has finally stopped in Albenga, as he needs three things: benzina, acqua, and gabinetto—petrol, water, and a toilet. Fortunately, the French words, essence, eau, and toilette are enough for the garage manager to understand, and being so close to the border, most of the locals have a good understanding of French. Unfortunately, Bill cannot comprehend all the questions regarding the specifications of his De Dietrich, and it sounds to him as if the man is swearing at him. The exaggerated hand gestures help a little, although it is clear that this encounter will not result in a long-lasting relationship between them unless Bill takes the time to learn Italian.

The decision to drive east from La Turbie feels spontaneous to Bill and has given him a renewed sense of adventure. He had no idea what to expect on this side of the border and is impressed that the Italians have done a first-class job tarmacking the main coastal road to accommodate motorcars. Many of the country roads have deep ruts going back two thousand years to the Roman chariots, although Bill thinks he and the vehicle will be in good shape as long as he sticks to the coastal route.

Sixty miles farther, he arrives in the port city of Genoa, which has remarkably similar architecture to the buildings that have become so familiar to him in Monaco. He stops at the Piazza Acquaverde as he sees the huge sign of the Grand Hotel Savoia above the palm trees.

There are no English language newspapers at the hotel, which gives Bill a feeling of being cut off from the rest of the world. He seeks to avoid publicity, yet complete seclusion and isolation are not desirable either.

He takes out his recently acquired map of northern Italy and draws a pencil line north to Milan, then west to Turin, and finally south to the French border. Each segment spans approximately one hundred miles, suggesting the possibility of additional stops along the way. The last stretch from Turin to Monaco covers over two hundred miles and will necessitate at least two extra nights of stopover, with Savona being his choice for one of them.

On the bedroom wall is a mural depicting an armada of tall-masted sailing vessels in the Genoa harbor, with an inscription in Italian that Bill cannot quite interpret. However, he does recognize the name Cristoffa Corombo. As he stands on the balcony, he looks out over the recently constructed marina and then turns to make another attempt at deciphering the inscription.

It dawns on him that this must be the hometown of Christopher Columbus, but he distinctly recalls from his school days that Columbus set sail from Spain, not Italy.

These days, there are pleasure boats that take people up and down the coast and even a ferry that takes vacationers all the way to the island of Corsica. How different everything looks now, thinks Bill, with electric lights casting shadows on the sidewalks, and how fortunate he is to be able to drive up and down the coast and even across borders in a motorcar. His mind wanders to the future of transport as since the success of the Wright brothers in America, the Frenchman Louis Bleriot has flown a plane across the English

Channel. Before long, aircraft will be able to fly passengers across oceans, perhaps even within a decade, he thinks. As he continues to muse about the future, he realizes that this trip is doing the job he'd intended—taking his mind off the silent Miss Frances Erskine-Shaw.

In Milan, Bill stands in the Piazza del Duomo and stares at the giant Milan Cathedral, which is the largest man-made structure he has ever laid eyes upon. In a pamphlet, he is reliably informed that it is the second largest church in the world after St Peter's Basilica in Rome and can hold over forty thousand people. Continuing his Italian journey of discovery, he arrives at the Royal Palace in Turin, which has an armory in which Bill sees one of Napoleon Bonaparte's swords and a breathtaking collection of weapons.

His suite of rooms at the Hotel Torino has a balcony overlooking the spectacular snow-capped peaks of the French Alps. The trip has been outstanding, and Bill's thoughts drift to Jules Verne's Philias Fogg, who passed through Turin with his trusted manservant, Passepartout, on their way to Egypt.

Bill takes his time on the final leg as the magnificent Alps are always to his right, and he frequently stops the car to take in the view and inhale the fresh alpine air. The distant, unseen force of the wind blows the cloud's shadows over the mountains, which change color and shape, resembling moving glaciers. Every so often, the sun will catch a piece of distant rock, and a flash of light is reflected as if someone is signaling to him down below.

He made the right decision to come by himself as passengers or even a chauffeur would undoubtedly have become irritated with his constant unplanned diversions. He spends two nights in the tiny town of Mondovi and another night in Millesimo, where nobody knows who he is, just that he has a nice motorcar. His final pitstop is the coastal town of Porto Maurizio at the mouth of the river Impero, surrounded by fields of vibrant yellow and orange flowers and perfectly manicured olive groves. Bill cannot recall ever seeing so many vivid colors all at once, and for a moment, he wishes that he were an artist so he could capture the scene and have it framed on a wall somewhere—perhaps in England.

He tries not to think of Miss Erskine-Shaw and her particular shade of blue. That was just a distraction, in the end, and it's unlikely that she will write again, so it's time to keep moving forward.

***

"BUONASERA, ETIENNE," Bill says as he enters the reception of the Hotel de Paris, confidently using one of the four phrases he has picked up recently. The lobby is a welcome sight, with its familiar equestrian statue of Louis XIV dominating the scene. "Any letters?"

"Buonasera, Signori Darnborough!" replies Etienne, fully aware that Bill has been in Italy. "Why, yes, as a matter of fact." He smiles knowingly and holds up a stack. "Have you enjoyed your journey in Italy, Mousier?"

"Perfectly enchanting," replies Bill, "that car is the best investment I have ever made." Bill makes a mental note to find out if Jimmy Rothschild is in town as he has a sudden urge to show off his latest acquisition now that it has been on a proper test run. He also wants to book a lunch with Niccolò from the bank to share his experiences of discovering Italy. "Now, my letters?"

Bill is sure he can detect a smirk as Etienne hands over the bundle. His eyebrows shoot up as he sees the letter at the top of the pile. The unmistakable elegant handwriting and the Kensington return address on the reverse side of the envelope. Does Etienne know? No time to ask—hotel staff know everything. He grabs his key and takes the stairs two at a time up to his room.

Dear Mr. Darnborough, the letter opens. *You have given me a great deal to think about once again.*

At first, Bill is so excited to see that she has written five full pages and, yes, her handwriting is widely spaced, but still, five pages! He can barely concentrate on reading, and he just skims, picking up lines that seem promising.

Your background is quite intriguing . . .
I appreciate the thoughts you make me think . . .

I have the sense you may be different than most gentlemen I've encountered in my life, which is refreshing . . .

He skips to the end. *I think someday you and I will see each other again, Bill, though I cannot say when.*

It's enough to make him want to jump up and click his heels. He feels his heart and all his recent dreams restored.

He sits down immediately to write back to her. He doesn't want to appear too eager but doesn't see the need to cloak his enthusiasm. He tells her about his recent Italian adventure and concludes the letter, *and I heartily look forward to the day when I will see you again.*

Refreshed from his expedition and with renewed vigor and purpose due to hearing from Frances, Bill is back doing what he does best at the roulette table. He tries to keep a low profile, often playing in the newly built Salle Medecin, the casino's last private room. When gambling is in progress, this room is closed to everyone except members, and there is less hysteria when the croupier sweeps away towers of chips or when he places his marker on a loaded number.

One evening, Bill is up 14,400 FF and wins a further 22,800 FF on number 31. He loses nearly everything over the next hour but claws his way back with some clever hedging strategies. He looks relaxed and in control, but inside, he is tense with the anticipation of every spin. In all his years, he has never had such a good run in one sitting.

He has a street bet on zero, 1, 2, and 3, with further coverage on 5, 14/17, and 21/24. Play at the other tables stops, and the crowd around Bill's table begins to grow. The comments and ripples of whispers start to turn into gasps. Eventually, he wins again on the third dozen, this time on 28, and the gasps become cheers.

His winnings have depleted the available funds of the table.

Pierre Laget stands off to the side, hands clasped behind his back, watching Bill play. He has been observing Bill all these months he's been here at this or that wheel—months that add up to years— watching the American making his little notes and strewing chips like a farmer planting seeds. Never a change to the expression on his face, whether he's up or down by thousands.

Laget had been told that this man was a *nobody* from *nowhere*. And yet, right now, the croupier is speaking to the Chef de Partie, who signals to Laget, who gives a little nod to agree to replenish the table to the tune of a further 40,000 FF. Laget and the anxious spectators continue to be dazzled as the American begins to resemble a crazed New York architect as his mountains of chips on the table take on the form of model skyscrapers.

"He will lose," Laget mutters out loud. "The odds are he will lose it all."

And yet, the American is having an exceptionally long run of good luck, with the ball landing in multiple high numbers. The volume of his winnings far outweighs his losses. Laget's hands are beginning to sweat as a larger crowd gathers, gasping and cheering with each roll and rattle of the wheel.

Within another two hours, all the additional funds belong to Bill, and the croupier and the Chef de Partie simultaneously announce that the table will be closed. Bill anxiously looks around, unsure how to react as he has never seen play suspended in this manner.

More people from the adjoining rooms barge into the Salle Medicin to witness the scene as Pierre Laget takes charge of the proceedings. The entire room has fallen silent aside from inquisitive whispers, which are met with shrugs as no one seems to know what is happening.

A black cloth is ceremoniously brought out from the office of the Directeur and draped over the table as a sign that the bank has been broken. The original operator of the casino, François Blanc, created the tradition of the black cloth, and it serves a dual purpose. The most obvious is that it will give the table time to replenish the funds necessary to continue playing. However, the actual reasoning is that it will create publicity for the casino.

Bill has remained impassive throughout the proceedings, but when the balance of his winnings is paid, a huge crowd has gathered around the table, and Bill looks up at the chandeliers and punches the air with both arms.

No doubt, word of his accomplishment has spread around the entire building, and this time, there is cause for celebration. This is

Bill's World Series win, and he orders a case of champagne to be shared by all present.

"You can hear all the girls declare!" Someone in the crowd shouts, "He must be a millionaire!" Spontaneously, the Salle Medecin erupts with the chorus to the song: "He's the man who broke the bank at Monte Carlo!"

The celebrations continue until the casino closes, but only when Bill is back in his room does the magnitude of what has just happened begin to sink in. He beat them at their own game! This could change everything. Does it mean he has enough? Enough that Miss Frances Erskine-Shaw might consider him a suitable match?

He can't sleep out of excitement, and the elation isn't over the money, not exactly.

Bill is on a high the next few days, though he doesn't let his celebrity status go to his head. He goes to work at the tables as usual. He shows no emotion, not even when the bejeweled crowds gather around and gasp and cheer. Privately, though, he is thinking of writing to Frances Erskine-Shaw with an invitation—for her and her uncle both, of course—to come to Monaco. He envisions finding some engrossing distraction for Charles, then whisking Frances off on a romantic adventure up into the hills. Perhaps a drive in the De Dietrich to Grasse, the perfume center of the world, or a walk around the castle at Eze. Maybe even further to see the Alps or Cap d'Antibes at sunset?

He is winning large amounts of money nightly now and losing hardly at all. There's no doubt he's on a lucky streak. He thinks if she'll just give him a chance, he can prove to her that he's good enough. Good enough even for her.

DISASTER STRIKES.

Dear Mr. Darnborough, Sir,

Imagine my surprise when my uncle drew my attention to a little (or, well, not so little) article in the Times *about your escapades the other night in Monte*

Carlo. I thought you were a car collector, likely one of Jimmy's numerous bankers, a respectable gentleman. It may be that I am old-fashioned, but the truth is, I just cannot associate in any way with a man who is a notorious gambler. Consider this our final correspondence.

Sincerely,

Miss Frances Erskine-Shaw

The publicity surrounding his big win may have just cost Bill his future happiness, and he is sick to his stomach for days. He writes to her three times, asking her to reconsider. No reply.

"She cannot associate in any way with a man who is a notorious gambler." Bill considers Frances's words carefully. He has made this life for himself, and his existence depends on gambling. If his mother hadn't murdered his father and moved them to Bloomington, he would be running the family farm by now. Fate intervened, and he had no control over his future—but now he does.

He considers a new profession and comes up blank as to his possibilities. No job on earth would pay what he makes at the tables, and he thinks investing what he has is too big a risk. Aside from diamonds, he knows nothing about investing and doesn't even know where he would start. What if he could win enough to quit? Would she give him a chance, then?

And then he realizes: *There will never be enough to quit.*

PART IV
THE GAMBLER'S GAME

1910 – 1911

CHAPTER 51

MONTE CARLO BANK IN LOSING GAME

Will Darnborough follows up success from years ago and nightly wins thirty thousand dollars . . . ranked one of the most successful players at Monte Carlo . . . Darnborough has not returned to America for many years since his tour of the west . . . his system has been markedly successful, but it is believed that except in diamonds, of which he has a superb collection, he has failed to invest his winnings. During the last week, according to a cablegram from France, it has been observed that Darnborough plays 29 oftener than any other number, which has started a run on 29 at roulette.

—American Gazette, December 23rd, 1910

The only item in Bill's diary for today is a pre-arranged lunch with an acquaintance he'd met a year or so ago through Jock Carruthers, Sir Edward Hutton. This is a great relief because Bill feels exhausted after another long stint at the tables last night. The details of whether he won or lost elude him, requiring him to consult his notebook for the exact amounts. Is he losing his edge? Losing his stamina? He hates to think about it, so he puts the thought aside.

They meet at Quinto's, and Bill is grateful for the complete disinterest Hutton shows in gambling, as he seems more inquisitive about people rather than their money. There is a good connection between them from the outset, which is made easier because they have both dined in the hallowed sanctuary of the In and Out Club in London. If Jock hadn't informed him of Hutton's resume, he would have no idea from his down-to-earth manner that Lieutenant-General Sir Edward Hutton is the former General Officer Commanding the Australian Forces, General Officer Commanding Militia of Canada, and had served in the Anglo-Zulu war, both Boer wars, the Anglo-Egypt war, and the Nile Expedition. As if all that wasn't impressive enough, he was also Queen Victoria's Aide-de-Camp in 1892.

As far as Bill can see, irrespective of his background, Edward Hutton is simply a man who seems relieved to be away from it all and wants to know as much as possible about life on the Riviera. It transpires that he has just arrived from London, and he says the most exciting thing he's done in months was to attend the funeral of Edward VII, who had died at age sixty-eight last May.

"You know his horse won at Kempton Park that day," says Sir Edward.

"Really?" says Bill.

"Indubitably," Sir Edward continues. "Apparently, he was informed of this just before he died, and therefore, we can assume he passed away in quiet contentment."

At the end of lunch, Bill recognizes that Sir Edward is, in fact, entirely alone in Monaco and so invites him to come with him on a road trip to Nice next week, telling him to bring evening-wear as they will be visiting the casino.

Bill tries not to think with regret that there hasn't been a single woman he's found worthy of even thinking of taking on a drive in the last two years since Miss Frances Erskine-Shaw cut off their correspondence. There's no sense regretting it, and he scolds himself because it's better to stay focused on his work and keep up his stamina.

He sets off for Nice the following Wednesday with Sir Edward after stopping at the Alpine shop to acquire another pair of driving goggles.

The Promenade des Anglaise in Nice is busy with tourists enjoying a break from the brutal winter weather in Northern Europe. The midday temperature in December rarely dips below 60°F, and the locals are easy to spot as they are wrapped up with scarves and gloves as if setting out on a trek to the Antarctic. In contrast, the northern visitors appear dressed for springtime. The gentlemen raise their hats as they pass by the ladies, and many also raise their hats to Bill's De Dietrich as he finds a suitable place to park. Bill has arranged lunch with two additional friends at Le Duc restaurant in the Hotel Westminster overlooking the Bay of Angels. Sir Edward is clearly taken with the Florentine frescoes and murals that adorn the Grand Hall as his head is tilted at an angle for quite some time, and Bill has to turn around and respectfully steer him toward the restaurant. Once seated, Bill takes a moment to explain who will be joining them.

"Isidore de Lara," says Bill, "is an English composer I met at the Salle Garnier. He's been here for about the same amount of time as me, and I've also asked an old friend, John Haverstock, to come along. Since none of you have much in common, it should be an intriguing gathering."

Sir Edward laughs. "Clever boy, Bill. I presume there will be no talk of war or gambling, and that is exactly how we like it."

"Exactly," says Bill.

It turns out that John, Sir Edward, and Isidore do have something in common to talk about, which is the latest cricket battle known as the Ashes which is played biennially against the Australians. It is the middle of summer in Australia, and the English visiting team is struggling against a formidable side. Inevitably, the Englishmen have accused the Australians of some underhanded tactics. As the conversation continues, John has noticed Bill staring out the window at the seascape.

"Bill, I've always wondered what everyone finds so attractive about America?" asks John. "Why do so many people want to go there?"

Bill looks around at his guests and considers his answer carefully. "Land," he says. "At least initially, that's what it was. My grandfather farmed the land in Philadelphia before moving to Illinois, and I doubt he could have owned so much land in Yorkshire."

"It is interesting how so many Americans are buying property down here," says Isidore. "After Phelps Allis bought the prince's summer palace, plenty of Americans are buying up the great properties all over the Riviera now."

"Ah, yes," says Bill, "however, they are not necessarily a good reflection of the majority of people, as they are the ones who have done exceptionally well in oil, the railroads, mining, and so forth. Life can be tough in America. I've seen Russians, Poles, Slovaks, Czechs, and Hungarians working long hours in stockyards, tanneries, and factories just to put food on their plates. In fact, the difference, and what made the Atlantic crossing worth the risk, is that they live as free men. As long as they don't break the law, they cannot be persecuted for their beliefs, and there is a great sense of pride across the nation. I saw it in the crowd at the baseball games, and it feels like the whole country is a collaboration where people want to help each other rather than create obstacles. Look at the rate of progress in terms of technology. With cars, telephones, electricity, and radio broadcasting, things are moving so fast. Imagine this. I am certain that fairly soon, I will be able to get from here to New York in a flying machine in the same amount of time it takes me now to take the train to London."

"How fantastic," says John, "I would love to see some of those new buildings. I read that the Metropolitan Life building is fifty floors high! Imagine the view."

"Well, I hope they never allow buildings like that here," says Isidore, "we like the Riviera just the way it is."

"Fascinating," says Sir Edward, "you know, Bill, I think you are a good ambassador for the Americans. You've used nothing but your wits and determination to get to one of the most exclusive destinations in the world, and I take my hat off to you, sir." Bill considers this statement for a moment, and the others seem to be looking to him for a response. He smiles, thinking of the joy he's felt so many nights in Monte Carlo, popping champagne after a big win, and looks out the window again. Joy has felt elusive for a while now.

"Well, gentlemen, it's difficult to say if all of that will truly succeed in getting me where I really want to end up," he says because, at this moment, he isn't even sure where that is.

Except, just then, he glances across the restaurant and sees her. Frances Erskine-Shaw.

It *is* her, isn't it? He cranes his neck to see. Yes. He's certain of it. And he recognizes her uncle, Charles, as well. His thoughts race. What are they doing in Nice? Is there a chance they're headed for Monaco to visit Jimmy? And then he sees another man—young, quite handsome, definitely English, by his dress and bearing—seated with Frances and her uncle, and Bill's stomach clenches to think perhaps she has married in the years since he last saw her. A travesty, he thinks—and yet, he has to find out. He forgets all about finesse and the English way of doing things. He is seventeen years old again and winding up to throw a fastball across the center of the plate. "Excuse me, gentlemen," he says and doesn't notice his friends' reactions as he gets up, drops his napkin onto the table, and strides over to where Frances Erskine-Shaw is having lunch.

He is standing at her elbow when he says, "Miss Erskine-Shaw." She looks up, and her eyes widen in surprise and what seems like pleasure, then quickly narrow as a curtain almost visibly comes down over them. "It's Bill Darnborough," he reminds her.

She sets down her fork. "I remember you," she says coolly. It is the height of rudeness to have interrupted her luncheon, it is clear.

There is a frightful pause. Uncle Charles is glaring. Then, with an air of amusement, the young man comes to Bill's rescue, standing and putting out his hand for Bill to shake. "Mr. Darnborough! Aubrey Erskine-Shaw. I'm Miss Erskine-Shaw's cousin," he says, with a grin toward Frances, who is shooting him a dagger-filled look.

Bill is viscerally relieved. *Her cousin.*

The young man continues. "You're the American gambler, are you not? My cousin has spoken of you!" He almost winks at Frances. "We're planning to spend time in Monte Carlo just after

Christmas—I don't suppose you could give me a few pointers at the tables, old chap?"

Bill thinks this kid—the cousin—is a gift from God. Aubrey grins at Frances like this is all a big joke, while she appears on the verge of hurling a piece of silverware at him. Uncle Charles is frowning. "I hardly think— "

"Oh, come on, Father," says Aubrey; "it will be a great adventure!"

"I would be more than pleased," Bill tells Aubrey. "In fact, for old friends, I would love to host you entirely and show you all the best that Monaco has to offer." He is thinking on his feet now, trying to find a way to appease and distract Uncle Charles to secure time with Frances. He needs a chance to win her over, but a glance at her shows it may take a significant amount of time. He needs days on end, possibly a week. "Any interest in shooting, sir?" he blurts. "I know a fellow who can take you!"

And, miracle of miracles, Uncle Charles' face lights up.

CHAPTER 52

"*P*erfume," John Haverstock advises with a serious nod when Bill returns to the table and tells his friends what has transpired. Frances Erskine-Shaw is a woman he has been unable to put out of his mind for over two years. "You must drive up to Grasse and buy her some," continues John. "It's just north of here, and it is the epicenter of perfume creation. The locals have harvested lavender, jasmine, myrtle, mimosa, and orange blossom there since the 1740s. Several ladies have assured me that a bottle of perfume from Grasse means far more than one from anywhere else in the world."

Bill, who knowns of Grasse, but never been there, is willing to do whatever it takes, and Sir Edward laughs and agrees to the ride. They spend the night at Hotel des Anglais, where the manager is very excited to ingratiate himself with Sir Edward by informing him that the Englishman Henri Ruhl built the hotel. Bill is so preoccupied with thoughts of Frances that they refrain from gambling, and after an early start, they make it as far as Cagnes-sur-Mer for breakfast.

Another three-hour drive and Bill parks the De Dietrich outside the Guerlain's perfumery in Grasse. Sir Edward announces that he's going to take a walk and sets off, and Bill enters the shop beside the perfumery, which has a little bell on the door that announces his arrival. The powerful aromas and the sight of hundreds of bottles on the shelves are overwhelming, and Bill is relieved when a pleasant looking young assistant offers some guidance.

"Bonjour, Mademoiselle," beams Bill in a near perfect accent, which has the effect of a rapid verbal response that Bill cannot understand as the assistant has assumed he speaks fluent French. Bill explains that he is seeking something subtle for an English lady, perhaps with roses.

The assistant speaks incredibly fast, and Bill finds her difficult to follow. However, he does understand keywords such as violet and jasmine as she shows him various bottles and offers samples to smell by spraying different perfumes on little white cards.

Eventually, he settles on a bottle of Après l'Ondée by Jacques Guerlain. The translation is "after the rain shower." The assistant, who has introduced herself as Madeline, explains that it is a delicate combination of orange blossom, violet, and spicy anis. The notes are of a springtime garden after a downpour.

The bottle is made from Baccarat crystal and has a spherical stopper, which should keep the contents safe. Madeline wraps up his tiny treasure with the dexterity of a talented surgeon, and the little package is swaddled in fine paper and placed in a box for the journey back to the coast.

Sir Edward congratulates him, laughs again, and says the lady has little chance of resisting, but Bill, though hopeful, isn't so sure about that.

"TIR AU PIGEONS," says Beresford, who is explaining the French version of pigeon shooting. Bill has managed to track down the Englishman who sold him the De Dietrich, as he is reliably informed that he is the leading expert on the pastime of shooting just about anything. He has reserved a table positioned behind the glass partition at the rear of Café Riche, a strategic selection aimed at ensuring the utmost privacy for their conversation.

Inviting Beresford to an expensive lunch is the best way Bill knows to entrust him with the details of his predicament. What is true is that he had exaggerated his connections in the shooting world to Uncle Charles, and now he must try to get up to speed.

"There is no need to bring your own guns," Beresford continues, "the club will provide them, along with ammunition. Also, there is a fine restaurant at the shooting pavilion at Cap d'Ail."

"Maybe pigeon shooting wouldn't be the best diversion," says Bill, second-guessing himself. "Perhaps it would be easier just to take them to the races at Nice."

"Yes," says Beresford, "except you did promise the man, and going to the races would mean you would have to sit with them, which would defeat the purpose. How about trap shooting? If you will pardon the expression, there is no harm, no foul. It is far easier to arrange, and you would be free to take the lady for a drive in the countryside. By the way, are you certain the gentlemen in question will be acquiescent to your suggestion? I don't wish to sound judgmental, and I realize that this is the 20th century and all that, but if this uncle is as possessive as you describe, would he not insist on accompanying the young lady in question?"

"Good point, Beresford," says Bill, "I will only discover that when I ask, I suppose, but I'm going to give it my best shot, if you'll pardon the expression."

At the hotel, Bill has invited Sir Edward for a drink in his suite, and they share a full-bodied bottle of claret. During their conversations, Bill realizes that Sir Edward and he have much more in common than an observer may recognize. It transpires that the life of a senior military officer can be quite solitary as he cannot fraternize with the ranks as much as he would like, and he appears to have been "on duty" for decades without a break. Bill has always found it difficult to trust people and has distanced himself from commitment, and he has begun to understand why. Sir Edward is one of the first people he has encountered who, should he ever find himself needing assistance, would do whatever was within his power to come to his aide. Undoubtedly, he instilled a high level of trust among the men under his command, individuals who placed their lives in his hands every single day.

There is a knock at the door, and a hotel valet presents Bill's mailbag. They have been bringing his mail to his room for some time now as they simply lack the space to accommodate it all behind the reception desk. However, the delivery is notably later than usual today.

"Time I was off," says Sir Edward.

"So soon?" says Bill as he dumps the mail across the table. Since Sir Edward took part in the perfume-buying expedition, Bill feels they are good friends, and it's been some time since Bill has had a good friend.

"That's quite a lot of post, old chap," Sir Edward says, eying the pile. Then, something catches his eye, and he picks up an envelope, looking at the return address. "It can't be. Hiram Maxim? Is he a friend of yours?"

"Can't say I know who he is," says Bill. "A lot of strangers write to me."

"He's the man who invented the machine gun. If it's the same chap I know."

"Let's open it and see," Bill says, holding out his hand, and when Sir Edward hands it over, he opens it and reads the letter out loud.

> *My dear Darnborough.*
>
> *I wish you would write me of the results of your play at Monte Carlo. If I remember rightly, you played ten hours a day for twenty eight days consecutively and that your stakes were from six to thirteen thousand francs at each coup. If you staked 400 times a day this would be 89,600,000 francs which is £3,584,000 sterling. If the bank had captured its full percentage of this it would have amounted to £96,864, but instead of that you neutralized the zero and came out about £10,000 ahead. Is this so? On one occasion I believe you won £20,000 in two hours. Will you kindly write me giving me as much information as possible on the subject and oblige.*
>
> *Yours sincerely, Hiram S Maxim. M.G.*

Sir Edward laughs. "Either he wants to learn how to play like a professional, or he's writing a book."

Bill laughs, too. "It sounds like he's writing a book."

CHRISTMAS IN MONACO is a curious time of year as while the Monegasques have families to visit and presents to give, the casino crowd tends to carry on as usual. Bill is not especially religious, although he does attend the midnight mass service at the Saint Charles church to indulge in the majesty of the superb choir. Most of Monaco's affluent, semi-permanent residents attend the Christmas service as it gives them a sense of belonging to the community beyond the glitz and glamour of the parties. Bill is no exception, and it has the bonus of making him feel like an upstanding member of society rather than someone known purely as a gambler. He has received several invitations to Christmas lunches, although this year, he chooses to retreat to the peaceful surroundings of the Hotel de France in La Turbie. The only event he is due to attend is the masked ball at the Hotel de Paris but right now, he is preoccupied. He finds himself contemplating his upcoming rendezvous with Miss Erskine-Shaw like a pitcher preparing for the biggest game of his life.

> By far the most discussed person on the Riviera now is W.N. Darnborough, the American who recently won so heavily at the Monte Carlo roulette tables. He went to Nice for a spell of golf, but now he is back playing again. He is still winning and is now well over $400,000 to the good. He is regarded by the croupiers as the heaviest and luckiest player ever known at Monte Carlo.
> —The New York Times, page 3, December 25, 1910

BILL DRIVES BACK DOWN to Monaco on Boxing Day and drops in at the Le Hermitage Hotel. He discreetly gives the concierge a folded-up 5 FF note in exchange for the promise of a telephone call to inform him that the Erskine party has arrived safe and sound.

Beyond that, he must simply wait. He would hate to appear too enthusiastic, too *American*. He has Neville's long-ago advice ringing in his ears. Also, he has the picture of Frances wanting to throw a spoon at her cousin's head.

When a message arrives at the Hotel de Paris for Bill, it's not the message he's waiting for, but after a moment of disappointment, he's glad to be asked to call Jimmy Rothschild.

"The rally has turned out to be quite a sensation," explains Jimmy as they sit down over a coffee in the discrete area of the front lounge. "Anthony Noghès has done an excellent job of organizing, and we expect around twenty-five participants driving Peugeots, Wolseleys, De Dions, Panhards, Levassors, and many others. Most are leaving from Paris on the twenty-first of January, and others are coming from Rome, Saint Petersburg, Brussels, Lisbon, and Geneva in Switzerland."

"This is extraordinary," says Bill, slightly confused. "How will they time everybody if they are coming from all these different places?"

"Good question," replies Jimmy, "the judges are awarding points for all sorts of things." Jimmy pulls a small card from his pocket and reads: "One point per kilometers per hour with a maximum of twenty-five kmh, one point per one hundred kms covered, two points per passenger, including a mechanic, zero to ten points depending on the degree of comfort, zero to ten for elegance of the car, zero to ten for the state of the frame upon arrival and zero to ten for aesthetical appearance." Jimmy sits back and smiles as he puts the card back in his pocket.

"Fantastic, Jimmy. But the judges seem more concerned with the cars than the drivers' ability."

"Precisely, dear chap. What we have here is the start of something marvelous that will undoubtedly result in considerable investment in motorcar manufacturing and probably encourage people to invest in the automobile industry. Still, I agree the actual business of driving skill is taking a back seat, and it will be a huge feat of endurance to navigate your car all the way down here in the middle of winter. I imagine they have considered the terrible tragedies caused by reckless driving during past events and want to make sure that the public realizes that it is not simply about speed, but also safety and comfort."

"I see. Well, I'm grateful I'm not one of the judges."

"Would you prefer to be one of the drivers?" asks Jimmy with a wry smile.

Bill gives a similar smile in return. "You know I love driving, Jimmy. But I have to think of my future these days."

"What am I missing?"

"Well, you remember Frances Erskine-Shaw from your party at Waddesdon? I have my sights set on her quite firmly. She's coming to town any day now, and I have offered to host her and her cousin and uncle." He doesn't mention that Aubrey is a much more enthusiastic participant than Frances.

Jimmy laughs and shakes his head. "I wish you the very best of luck, Bill, and I hate to cast a shadow over your dreams and aspirations, but I rather prefer your chances as a late entry into the rally."

Bill laughs, too. "Well, what do I have to lose, Jimmy?" he says, but then he is stricken with the sudden feeling that he actually stands to lose everything this time around.

CHAPTER 53

*T*he telephone beside the bed rings like the trill of an orchestra of crickets, so loudly that Bill is wide awake in a split second. How strange to have a telephone in his room now. And yet, this is the modern world. Annoyingly convenient.

"This is William Darnborough," says Bill, as he places the listening piece to his ear and holds the base of the phone with his other hand.

"Good morning, Mousier Darnborough. This is Dominique at the hotel switchboard, and I have a Monsieur Erskine on the line for you.

"Merci, put him through," says Bill as he swings his legs over the bed and sits upright.

"Hullo, Mr. Darnborough! Bill!" It is undoubtedly Aubrey and not Charles, and Bill is relieved. "We made it down! How are you?"

They exchange some pleasantries and then discuss potential plans. "How about a drive tomorrow?" Bill suggests. "And then lunch?"

"That sounds marvelous, Bill!"

"The three of you, I mean."

366

"Ah, yes. Well, we'll see if my cousin can be convinced." Aubrey laughs, and Bill's heart falls to his ankles.

"You must convince her, sir."

Aubrey laughs again. "I will do my utmost, sir." Bill tries to retain his optimism. After a telephone call to La Réserve restaurant in Beaulieu and optimistically securing a table for four just inside the balcony, he realizes he must distract himself from his jitters. He spends the remainder of the morning going through his mail, which contains the usual assortment of requests for donations and syndications *to be created in the uttermost confidence.*

At lunchtime, he takes a walk down to Hinault's garage on the Boulevard d'Italie to ensure the De Dietrich is in perfect condition for the trip. He needs to ensure that there will be no mechanical mishaps, especially as he anticipates three passengers. It is a sunny afternoon, and he still needs a bit of a distraction, so Bill retrieves his driving goggles from the glove compartment and drives east to Roquebrune-Cap-Martin. No matter how many times he goes on these little expeditions, he always finds somewhere previously unexplored simply by parking the car and walking around.

As he looks further east at the snow-capped peak of Monte Saccarello in the Ligurian Alps and the Mediterranean Sea to his right, Bill again imagines the impossible know-how you would need to translate these colors onto canvas. He takes a deep breath of the clean, crisp air, and there is almost complete silence, as if everyone in the village is asleep. Few tourists venture this far past Monaco, and he pats the engine hood of the De Dietrich, giving thanks for allowing him the opportunity to explore. He only hopes Frances will like the car, although she is not a woman to be won over by a mere motorcar. If only it could be so easy.

The Hotel de Paris is busier than usual that evening as they host the winter masked masquerade ball in the opulent Salle Empire. A myriad of crystal lights dangle from the gilded ceilings in chandeliers, casting a radiant glow on the marble columns and intricately sculptured archways. Guests arrive early to ensure they are seen, which is a curious paradox as they hide behind masks anyway. Bill is wearing a classic Bauta mask, which is more practical than most as it only covers the top half of his face, making speaking and drinking easier. The costumes are variations of 18th-century French aristocracy with colorful gowns and oversized wigs, but Bill has opted for a straightforward dinner jacket.

He has no idea if the Erskine clan is due to attend but feels confident he would recognize Frances even behind a disguise. He is torn between wanting to see her and hoping she'll stay away because what if he says something wrong and she cancels tomorrow's drive? At least if he puts his foot in his mouth tomorrow, when they're miles away from town, she will be relying on him for a ride back, giving him time to rectify any mistake.

And all of this is assuming she'll come along on the drive.

As the party goes on, Bill starts to feel like a prisoner in his own castle and fueled by three glasses of champagne, he works up a private stew of resentment against Frances and her high standards. Why should he be ashamed of being a gambler? Why should that mere fact have caused her to give him the cold shoulder? So many people bet on the horses at Ascot and play the odds on the stock exchange, so why is his game any different? And he's a success! A wealthy man!

Undoubtedly, the Erskine family would approve of him if he were a banker or a lawyer, although why these professions are considered especially noble is beyond him. Often, those men are far less scrupulous than he is. He should be proud of his achievements, as he has made more money than most people will ever see in their lifetimes, and, considering his background, that is no mean feat.

His background. Of course, that is going to be another obstacle. He had been putting that fact out of his mind, but he has to face it. He doesn't come from the *right* family—not even close—and that is unalterable. And even if he could win Frances over to the point that she'd overlook his origins, her uncle Charles certainly is beyond persuasion.

Bill swipes another glass of champagne from a passing tray and surveys the crowd, looking for Frances. Forgetting her is a lost cause if he hasn't managed to do so in all this time they've spent apart. He must win her over, whether he has any prayer of the family's blessing or not.

Amidst the crowd of passing masks, Bill's heart quickens as his gaze falls upon her. There she is, the captivating Miss Frances Erskine-Shaw, a vision of pure radiance. She is wearing a magnificent Italian carnival-style mask that veils her delicate features with an air of mystique, but Bill is in no doubt—it is she for sure. Her eyes, concealed behind the mask, hold a hint of intrigue and allure, and, as far as Bill is concerned, the dimly lit ballroom seems to brighten in her presence. Her gown, a masterpiece of flowing blue silk, cascades gracefully around her, accentuating her every movement with an ethereal elegance.

At this moment, despite the impulse urging him to approach Frances, Bill makes one of the wisest decisions of his life. After too many glasses of champagne, he knows he would only make a fool of himself, especially as he had spotted Uncle Charles and Cousin Aubrey nearby. Instinctively guarding his dignity, he chooses to slip away before they catch sight of him. His countless hours at the roulette table have instilled in him the value of patience, and he also needs to maintain a clear head for tomorrow's trip.

The road into Beaulieu-Sur-Mer is lined with olive and palm trees, and Bill is careful not to cause any sudden jolts as he brings the De Dietrich to a halt outside the main entrance to the hotel. He pulls up the brake lever and parks next to a large grassy mound with the words *La Réserve* spelled out in flowers in its center. The engine noise and the wind have ensured that his passengers have remained entirely silent throughout the hour-long journey from the Hermitage Hotel. Only Frances appears unfazed as she had the foresight to wear a warm winter fur coat. Bill is grateful for the road noise as he has been all but speechless in her presence. His relief that she decided to come along for the drive has not diminished since the moment he saw her approaching with her uncle and cousin stationed on either side of her like bodyguards. Now, the fresh air has brought some pink to her cheeks, accentuating her high cheekbones, and her eyes are soft, even in the sunlight.

Bill observes that she's wearing a smaller-than-usual hat, and he admires her practicality, a trait he finds rather impressive for a woman accustomed to city life. He had ensured the roof cover was closed and the windows sealed, but without any heating, the wind during the journey reminded everyone that it was still December.

The pink and white façade of the building ensures it stands out, and once Bill has informed the man at the entrance of their reservation for lunch, he escorts them through the marble-clad lobby to the restaurant. Palm trees are in every corner, and a magnificent black Steinway & Sons grand piano stands near the far wall, suggesting that La Réserve has an abundance of entertainment in the evenings. As the maître d' shows them to their table, Bill turns to him with a question.

"Excuse moi, Monsieur, cela vous si nous jetions d'abord un coup d'œil rapide a la extérieur?"

Frances looks astounded, and Bill guesses she must be thinking, *the gambler rake speaks perfect French?* Charles frowns, but Aubrey grins. "Capital idea!" He grabs his cousin's elbow. "Come on, Fran, let's go and take in the view!"

As the four of them stand on the grass looking back at the classic Belle Epoque design building, Bill is careful not to ignore Charles and Aubrey and addresses all of them.

"Pierre Lottier came here from Nice in 1880 and set up a seafood restaurant. The rooms were only added a few years ago." He turns to Frances. "What do you think, Miss Erskine-Shaw? Do you like it?"

Frances sniffs slightly. "It's quite fine," she says, as the others nod and turn to look out to sea.

"I had hoped you might like it," Bill says to Frances. "I thought it might be close to your particular shade of blue."

Frances blushes and casts her eyes down in a way that Bill finds so endearing but he keeps talking to avoid embarrassing her.

"It's called La Réserve," he continues, "after Lottier's fish tank, which he dug out to store the catch of the day. That's why I like it because the seafood is completely fresh, and you can watch from the restaurant as the fishing boats come into the bay." He turns and extends an elbow to Frances, hoping she'll walk arm in arm with him back inside. She merely gazes at it like it is a fish that has passed its prime and walks on by, which makes him want to laugh, makes him more determined than ever to win her over.

As they read their menus, Charles looks up and fixes his stare at Bill across the table.

"Mr. Darnborough, for an American, you seem to have a decent command of the French language. How long have you been out here, exactly?"

"I arrived in Monaco in '04, so nearly seven years now," replies Bill. "I find it quite straightforward to speak the language, but understanding the replies can be tricky."

"Yes," says Charles, "the accent is very harsh down here compared to Paris."

"I think your accent is excellent, sir," says Aubrey. "What do you think, Fran?"

She sniffs again, gazing over her menu. "I think it's possible that it would not get him shot." Bill laughs out loud, and, to his thrill, she looks up at him and smiles.

Their lunch is an exquisite combination of amberjack, grilled redfish, and sweet potatoes, with French cheeses for dessert. Even Charles is forced to admit that La Réserve was an excellent choice for their excursion. Bill has been observing him carefully throughout the meal and quickly anticipates any potential interrogation. As it seems such an inquisition is imminent, he makes his first metaphorical chess move.

"Do you by any chance know of the Honorable Seth Beresford?"

"Can't say I do," replies Charles.

"He is a world-famous marksman and spends a lot of time here. I mentioned to him that you had expressed an interest and wondered if you gentlemen may enjoy some clay pigeon trap shooting this weekend? Beresford is very well connected and can arrange for you to shoot on the Tir au Pigeons at Cap d'Ail if you would like." Charles and Aubrey exchange glances, and it is clear that they are keen on the idea.

But it looks like Charles is pretending to be gruff about it. "Well, I'm not sure—" he begins before Aubrey cuts him off.

"Oh, Father, that would be spiffing! I've always wanted to have a go of it down here. Please, let us go?" Charles narrows his eyes at his son as Bill attempts to close the deal.

"The guns, ammunition, and someone to man the trap will be provided, and there is also a restaurant at the pavilion, and I will arrange lunch for you both. My treat." Charles and Aubrey exchange looks again. They entirely ignore Frances, as if she is invisible, though Bill figures this is to his advantage.

"Would Saturday afternoon work?" Aubrey ventures. Bill seizes on his opportunity.

"That's great," he says, "I know you'll have an excellent day." He turns to Frances, who is looking impassively across the palm-lined shoreline. The low winter sun has come around a little and threatens her shade, so he calls a waiter over and requests that he move the curtain slightly.

"Miss Erskine-Shaw," says Bill, "while the gentlemen are shooting their clays, would you like to join me on a drive up to the gardens at Eze?" This is a calculated move as he knows it would be far easier for Charles to forbid her from going anywhere alone with him should the suggestion have come at any other time. Frances meets his gaze coolly as Uncle Charles gives a slight harrumph.

"I suppose it's checkmate, then," she says. "Shall we say 11 o'clock on the steps of the Hermitage on Saturday?" She favors Bill with another smile, and Bill grins back, hardly able to contain his thrill. He is finally getting somewhere, he thinks, and he doesn't notice the glare that Charles is shooting him or Aubrey's grin.

As they drive back toward Monte Carlo, silence is maintained in the De Dietrich as they pretend to be interested in the scenery instead of having to raise their voices over the noise. Bill feels quietly content that everything seems to be falling into place as best as he could hope for.

That evening, Bill decides there is no chance that the Erskine party would gain entrance to the Salons Privé as they would have mentioned it at some point during their excursion. It is curious that they never once referred to the casino or that he has made a considerable fortune at the tables. Perhaps they are holding their cards for the right moment. He makes his way to the Salle Medicin, confident that he can afford some distraction, if only for one evening. As he places a sizable volume of chips on the high numbers and hears the familiar, "rien ne va plus," he looks up at ceiling panels that depict women and cupids.

"Fifty thousand francs for your thoughts," comes an English accent from behind him. Only John Haverstock would have the nerve to speak to Bill when he is in the middle of a game, but Bill is evidently relieved to see him as he extends his hand.

"John, how good to see you. I must stop playing anyway, as I cannot seem to focus. Losing concentration can be an expensive business." He gestures to the croupier to change his chips and scoops up his stake, passing a generous denomination chip back to the croupier before he leaves the table.

They procure two glasses of red wine from the bar before making their way to the smoking balcony in the recently extended casino area. This exclusive enclave is reserved solely for members of the Salle Privé, adding to Bill's intrigue upon discovering John's presence in this distinguished setting.

"You're not a regular visitor to these parts, John. Have you been seduced by the dark magic of the roulette wheel?"

"Well, Bill," John replies, "I have had some success back home and thought I would take the opportunity to turn it into a retirement fund of sorts. I have, of course, had the additional good fortune to watch the master at work, and it turns out I am quite good at this." Bill is immediately filled with a sense of foreboding as he knows it is more than likely that John will end up losing everything. He weighs his response thoughtfully.

"John, I hope I can consider you a good friend, and as such, will you permit me to speak my mind freely?"

"Of course, Bill, I would appreciate it."

"The reality of gambling is that 99 out of 100 people end up returning to the tables again and again until there is nothing left. In my experience, the people I have witnessed continue to play on out of sheer greed, even if they're on a winning streak. Those who have lost nearly everything borrow more money and sink further into the abyss. I don't mind telling you that I have quite an impressive collection of diamonds to prove it."

"I understand and appreciate your concerns, Bill," says John; "however, my ambitions are realistic—I am sure of it. I still have some property back in England, and I will never touch that, and I am trying to be careful with my winnings thus far." Bill realizes that there is little more he can say to dissuade John from his cause. It is much like trying to persuade an alcoholic to quit drinking when the reality is that they can only decide for themselves when the time is right.

"John, I wish you all the very best of luck, and I mean that sincerely. Nevertheless, as your friend, I want to make something perfectly clear. Only one person in the history of this place has made it back home with their winnings intact. Joseph Jagger, who I am sure you have heard of by now, returned to Yorkshire about thirty years ago. The rest, like the Russians, for example, either have so much money that it doesn't matter how much they lose, or they keep playing until there is nothing left."

Bill takes a moment to check that John is still listening before he continues.

"In my case, people around here see me at a table betting the maximum stakes permitted and assume that I am blessed with a lucky angel on my shoulder. The truth is far from that. Every single train journey I took across America, from the days when I played professional baseball, I studied strategies and systems, and I learned from the best before running my own casino and watching hundreds of players. Nobody in this town knows my background, but I traveled all over America with my own roulette wheel, setting up shop in some of the most disreputable places on earth. Only after that did I start playing properly for myself. Even then, I never played with my own money as I was winning it from people playing on my own wheel. When I arrived in Monte Carlo, I had already been at this game for many, many years, and I had a vast amount of capital in reserve, which enabled me to bet consistently with the highest possible stakes."

"I see," says John, taking a sip of his wine and a puff of his cigar.

"Do you?" asks Bill. "I would hate it if you were unsuccessful in your endeavors, John. I realize that you must be doing well, or you would not have made your way to this room. I can see what's happening around here, though, as I have heard they're expanding the private rooms. All this suggests that the casino is making money hand over fist. I'm certain that in a few years, this place will be packed all year round as travel becomes easier, and honestly, I feel nothing but sympathy for the poor souls who will leave without any fond memories whatsoever and are filled with regret. I simply want to make certain that you know what you are doing."

John is silent for a moment before looking back up at Bill.

"Do you think you will walk away with no regrets, Bill? Do you think your luck extends that far?"

Bill almost wants to laugh, but then he recalls the certain tilt of Frances Erskine-Shaw's head this afternoon when he'd helped her out of the car and confirmed their plans for Saturday. *Do you think you're going to walk away with no regrets?* The question haunts him through the entire sleepless night.

CHAPTER 54

"I thought it was straight ahead?" says Frances as Bill turns the De Dietrich a hard right on Avenue de Lattre de Tassigny.

"That's Eze-sur-Mer ahead of us," says Bill, "we're going up into the hills, to Eze Castle."

Beresford had done a fine job organizing the shooting party, and Charles and Aubrey had set off from the hotel well before Bill arrived to pick up Frances. She arrived at the hotel reception looking like a light breeze had carried her down the stairs. Not too ostentatious, yet elegant with a winter green dress under a long black coat. She has a gentle, refined manner that only comes with a privileged upbringing and the best English schooling. Her thick, auburn hair is piled under her hat. Bill feels like a schoolboy and is again in awe of her visual charm.

The road is steep and winding, and only once they have reached 1500 feet above sea level does the full view become evident. Bill parks the car, and they can see all the way along the coast in both directions. It is a perfectly clear day, with a pale blue sky, and the mistral winds are still a few months away, so there is almost complete silence as they take in the scene.

"I've never been up here before, Mr. Darnborough," says Frances, "as we don't have a car when we stay in Monaco. It really is marvelous."

Bill turns to her. "Please, call me Bill when we're not around the others."

"Very well, and you may still call me Miss Erskine-Shaw." Bill looks quizzically at her before she breaks into a wide, beautiful smile. "Now, Bill, can we see Genoa from here?"

"Genoa?" says Bill, trying to regain his composure. He thinks she is the most extraordinary woman he has ever met. "Not quite. That's around the coast over one hundred miles away," he points eastwards. "Funnily enough, I was there not long ago. Wonderful architecture."

She turns and begins to walk away, and he hurries to follow.

"My grandmother is buried there," she says, "and I've never been. She was also called Frances Erskine. Frances Cadwallader-Erskine in fact."

"The General's daughter?"

She laughs. "Good memory. Yes, the General's daughter."

"What about your parents?" asks Bill.

"Well, my father was called James, and he died when I was thirteen, and my mother had already died the year before, so that's why Uncle Charles became my guardian." She ends with that and purses her lips.

"That must have been very painful," Bill ventures. "To lose both your parents at such a young age."

"Hmm," she says, and it sounds like an affirmative.

"I lost my father when I was about that same age," he says.

She looks at him, her eyes widening in slight surprise. "Really? Oh, I think you may have mentioned that in one of your letters? That's why you moved."

"Yes." Of course, he is not going to tell Frances Erskine-Shaw that there is some chance that his mother was responsible for his father's death. He is just glad to see that she seems to be softening toward him, even if the softening is ever so slight. "Shall we go and have some lunch?" he says with a mischievous smile. "I've arranged a little surprise, and then I'll tell you everything you need to know."

She frowns slightly. "I do dislike surprises," she grumbles, and Bill feels a lurch in his stomach, but he's committed to following through on the plan.

"Bear with me," he says, offering her his elbow again. This time, she takes it, and her closeness quickens his pulse once again. They walk up the cobbled stone path to the castle's gates and are greeted by a footman who emerges from a sentry box.

"Bonjour, Monsieur," says Bill, "nous sommes les invites du prince—Mr. William Darnborough et Miss Frances Erskine-Shaw." Frances looks bewildered as the footman nods an acknowledgement, opens the gate, and directs them up the path. Once they are out of earshot, she stops and turns to Bill.

"Mr. William Darnborough, what is going on? What did you mean, we are guests of the prince? What prince? Why didn't you warn me? I should have worn something more appropriate!"

"Not to worry," says Bill, "His Highness will not be joining us for lunch. It's just the two of us."

"Oh, I see," says Frances, "well, that's just fine. Honestly, would you be so kind as to enlighten me? What is going on here?"

"I'm just calling in a favor," says Bill, "the young Prince Wilhelm of Sweden just bought this place, and I asked him if we could use one of the balconies for lunch. The view is magnificent."

Frances turns to look at Bill again, and her heel catches one of the cobblestones. Bill's reactions are fast, and he catches her in his arms, saving her from a frightening fall on the hard stones. "Oh, good Lord, how embarrassing," she says as she disengages from his embrace and looks at him with a soft expression he cannot read.

"Pardon me," he says as she turns away, though he cannot imagine what he is asking to be pardoned for when he has just saved her from a potentially terrible fall.

At the castle entrance, they are met by another footman, who leads them up a maze of paths that wind between an assortment of medieval-looking buildings and culminates at an expansive patio with black iron railings. The view is indeed spectacular from up here as they look down on the town of Beaulieu-sur-Mer from 1500 feet. There is no wind, but there is a chill in the air, and Bill is pleased to see that two Hartley & Sugden gas-lit heaters surround the table that has been set out for them. They do not enter the private rooms of the castle and are directed to take their seats at the table, upon which silverware and crystal glasses are laid out in perfect order. Their napkins are embroidered with the crest of the Swedish royal family with crowned golden lions astride azure shields, and an ornate wine cooler stands ready to perform its duty.

"Well, Bill," says Frances as they are left alone for a moment, "maybe I don't hate all surprises, after all." Bill smiles, fixing his gaze on her, not even tempted to look off at the incredible view. A house footman returns with a bottle of white wine and without speaking a single word, pours a tasting sample for Bill. It is clear that they will not have an opportunity to decide which wines they would prefer or even the food, considering that this is not a restaurant, and they are guests at a private home, albeit one without a host.

They are given a starter of asparagus soup, and when they are alone again, Frances puts down her napkin and takes a deep breath.

"So, tell me, Bill Darnborough, how long have you been a professional gambler?"

Caught off guard by her straightforwardness, Bill tries to remember the dozens of answers he had rehearsed.

"I believe," he says, "that a man should not be defined by the manner in which he makes his living."

"Perhaps," says Frances, without skipping a beat, "but a man will always be defined by the means by which he acquires notoriety. Do you think you will ever stop?"

Bill is on the back foot now and has no option but to go on the defensive. "I should point out that I am not a habitual gambler, Miss Erskine-Shaw, and I do not feel an uncontrollable urge to bet on boxing bouts or at the races. I have spent twenty years becoming a successful roulette player, and I sit at the most prestigious tables in the world. There is a difference."

Just at that moment, the house footman reappears and refills their glasses before taking their starter plates away.

"Did you enjoy the asparagus soup?" asks Bill.

"Yes, thank you," replies Frances, forcing a smile and re-folding the napkin on her lap. She fixes him with a hard stare, and Bill realizes that this could be a defining moment if their relationship is to have any future.

"In the springtime," he says, "the bougainvillea and mimosa blossoms are quite magnificent up here."

"I am certain they are," says Frances, taking another sip of her wine and looking away out to the Mediterranean. Bill is frantically thinking of a way back in, as this is obviously not the moment to discuss the appeal of the local flora and fauna.

"Frances," he says, and she arches an eyebrow. "Excuse me. Miss Erskine-Shaw. Everything I have done is a means to an end. When I play roulette, I play for hours at a time, nearly always on my feet. I am not a big socializer and have no interest in the gossip of the town. If I had chosen a different path, say an insurance agent or an accountant, then I would be working in a dreary office somewhere and not have the opportunity to be sitting at the top of a castle in the south of France with the most beautiful lady I have ever set eyes on."

"Oh, honestly." Frances shakes her head a little. "Do you really think I'm going to fall for that old line." She then gives him a dazzling smile.

Bill leans back in his chair. Has he averted disaster? What is her meaning? He has no idea, and before he can ask, she switches the topic.

"Bill, how did you organize for Charles and Aubrey to go on a shooting day? That was a very cunning ploy."

"What can I tell you?" he replies, "same way I organized for us to be here at the Prince of Sweden's castle for a private lunch. People like me."

She laughs out loud. "And you are modest, as well!" she jokes, pressing a finger to her chin. "But you're hiding something, I can tell."

He is hiding many things, of course, and he feels properly chastised. What can he say? Ought he defend himself, or deny it—or lay his soul bare before her and hope she approves of his honesty if nothing else?

"I am going to ferret it out," she says.

Fortunately, just then, their main course of lobster thermidor arrives, and Bill decides he'd better try to take an offensive strategy. If he keeps playing defense, he's going to be sunk.

"So, tell me, Miss Erskine-Shaw," he says after the waiter has gone. "If you could live anywhere in the world, where would it be?"

"Good question," she muses. "Well, I do like the idea of exploring the world, but I also need stability in my life. I love England and English people, on the whole. Somewhere on the south coast, so that France is never too far away, a place with views across the sea, nice and peaceful without all the noise of the city. Somewhere where I can see the stars at night. I like London, but I find it quite dirty and loud these days, especially with all you maniacs driving around, blowing your horns at all of us." She has a broader smile now, and Bill notices her perfect teeth, which is another sign that she has had a good upbringing, considering the state of most English people's teeth.

"That sounds lovely," says Bill. "I would like to see more of Italy. Perhaps I could take you to Genoa one day?"

"Bill. Let's not get ahead of ourselves. You really are very American, aren't you."

She says *American* as if it's a pejorative, and yet, if she had been wearing a suit of armor, Bill thinks perhaps he has found a chink. She is a picture of refinement in everything she does—the way she sits up straight with the posture of a ballerina, and she holds her knife and fork with delicate hands. But he is starting to detect a sense of humor that the English are so famous for. A hint of sarcasm and irony in her language gives him the impression that she would be the perfect companion. She has the qualities of a lady and doubtless a stern side when required, yet there is something playful about her character that he cannot resist. He takes another bite of the lobster and can taste the cognac and gruyére cheese in the sauce.

The butler arrives out of the shadows and takes away their

plates to an unseen kitchen.

Frances smiles. "So, Bill, do you find yourself having to fend off all the ladies, you know, considering your success and celebrity status in Monte Carlo? Ah! Maybe *this* is what you're hiding."

Bill sips his wine, thinking she is quite determined to torture him. And yet, if she didn't like him, she wouldn't be bothering to— would she? He doesn't want to tell her that, since they met at Waddesdon years ago, she's been the only woman on his mind at all.

"As a matter of fact, no. I keep rooms up in the little village of La Turbie precisely to avoid unwanted attention. I have some friends, including Jimmy Rothschild and John Haverstock, but I avoid most tedious dinners and drinking parties. This town has been my home for many years now, and I have no time for social climbers and people who come here for the season just to be seen. The newspapers have written all sorts of things about me, but you will never find a single thing referring to my scandalous personal life simply because there isn't one. I should tell you, though, that I was married once. In Bloomington, Illinois. A long time ago."

"Oh! Well, that's a bit of a scandal."

He still is not going to tell her about his mother. "Not really, and we were just too young, and we made the mistakes that young people make."

She appears to consider this, then asks, "Any children?"

"No children," says Bill, and she gives him a tiny, approving smile.

The butler reappears and replenishes their glasses before presenting their dessert of traditional Swedish semlor buns, soft with whipped cream, marzipan filling, and a trace of cardamom flavoring. Frances falls silent, usually a sign that the food is exceedingly good, although Bill is nervous and anxious to know what she is thinking.

After dessert, Frances requests Ceylon tea, and Bill has a small coffee.

"Have you ever been to Twining's on the Strand?" Bill asks as Frances sips her tea.

"Yes," says Frances, "isn't it wonderful? I adore tasting all the teas and imagining the faraway plantations they have come from in exotic places like Burma and Assam. Have you traveled to the Far East at all, Bill?"

"Not yet," he replies, "would you like to go and see some tea plantations?"

"Oh, Good Lord. You are so *American*," she says and laughs, an infectious laugh that Bill wishes he could hear every single day.

"Good heavens," she says then, "what is the time? I should be getting back, shouldn't I?" She smiles as if daring him to deny it, but Bill can only sputter that he supposes so, and he gestures for the footman to bring their coats and assists her in putting on hers.

Bill maneuvers the De Dietrich carefully down the windy roads to Monaco, and at the entrance to the Hermitage, Frances turns to him.

"Wasn't that quite odd how the servants did not utter one word to us? Perhaps they don't speak English? Anyway, please send the prince my regards," she says. "That really was quite wonderful, Bill. You are full of surprises. And, as it turns out, you may call me Frances."

He grins, feeling like she's given him the world. "When will I see you again?" he asks.

"Honestly," she answers with a slight brow furrow, "I cannot say. Charles and Aubrey do not entirely dictate my life, but while we are here in Monte Carlo, unless you can come up with another devious plan to divert their attention, I believe we shall be returning to London in a few days."

"That doesn't give us much time!"

"Us, Bill?" She laughs as if this is the funniest thing she's ever heard.

"Well, I don't mean to be presumptuous," he sputters. "It's just that I was rather hoping to see you again." She sighs and gazes at him with an impassive look.

"I don't see how I could find the time, honestly," she says, "but you may write to me again if you wish, and perhaps our paths may cross again when you are in England." She leaves him with a smile, and his heart feels caught in her fist, which, after all, is no surprise.

CHAPTER 55

$\mathcal{A}$t the Hotel de Paris, there is another message from Jimmy Rothschild detailing a pre-rally party to be held at his villa. Bill goes upstairs to his desk, starts to reply to Jimmy and other letters, and is reminded of the French phrase *laisser-aller*, alluding to the unrestrained freedom he has become accustomed to. The truth is, though—to his shock, he realizes now—he no longer wants it. After today, all he wants is a life with Frances Erskine-Shaw. Is it too soon to propose? How would his life change if she accepted him? Would she tolerate his roulette playing and living part-time in Monaco? She did ask him if he would ever stop gambling. The motorcar adventures would undoubtedly be different with a passenger.

Honestly, he doesn't care. Maybe, he thinks, it's time for a change. Although there is the problem of money, does he have enough? Well, the answer is no, certainly not. However, he comes to the realization that he can at least purchase a house. In England. A fine country house for Frances, as she deserves. And certainly, once she sees how reasonable a solution—to the problem of maintaining the lifestyle she is accustomed to—is for him to continue coming to

Monte Carlo once or twice a year to replenish their funds, she'll have no objection.

A knock at the door brings him back to the present. A valet apologizes for the delay in delivering his edition of the *New York Times*. The front page is dominated by news of the revolution in Mexico. It seems to Bill that American companies are siding with the rebels, including Pancho Villa, in a bid to overthrow the dictator, General Diaz. Russia's Tsar Nicholas and Emperor Wilhelm of Germany are meeting to agree on spheres of influence in the Middle East. Much more interesting to Bill is a small article about Arthur Knight, who has successfully acquired a patent for his newly invented steel golf clubs.

When he falls asleep, he dreams of Frances walking away from him in the far distance. He is swinging a steel golf club at a teed-up ball, thinking he'll get her attention by hitting it in her direction, but he misses, and misses again, and his teeth are clenched because the last thing he wants to do is hit her with the ball—he might *hurt* her! —and yet, if he could just get her to *turn*!

On his way to the breakfast room in the morning, Bill stops by the reception to check for messages—he is hoping that Frances has called, that perhaps she'll say she has time to see him today or tomorrow, after all—and Etienne gives him a letter that has been hand-delivered from the Hermitage Hotel. From Frances! Bill sits down with a coffee and opens it, his heart soaring.

In an instant, he crashes to earth.

Dear Bill,

I write to you just two hours after we have parted company, before I can lose my nerve, both to say thank you for the beautiful day and also to tell you news that I suspect you won't much like, and news I am beginning to realize I should have told you before. You see, Uncle Charles has decreed that I marry Piers Pemberton, and they are in the process of arranging it, as if I am a horse to be traded or a property to be bought and sold. I am not entirely pleased, as you can imagine, but I also don't see what choice I have when Uncle Charles has done so much for me over the years. This evening, my uncle informed me that negotiations have reached the stage that we are to spend the next two weeks at Mr. Pemberton's estate in Bordeaux so that he and I may get acquainted in time for a May wedding, as I have only met him twice briefly. We depart on the early train and will no doubt be gone before you read this. Bill, I hope you can forgive me for indulging for a brief while in the illusion that I am free to do as I please and have my own ambitions, as you so alluringly suggested to me years ago. I apologize, Bill. I really did have a lovely time with you. I will never forget the day I dined as a princess would.

  F.E.S.

Bill bangs his fist down hard on the breakfast table, and a spoon falls to the ground with a clatter. Other guests look around at him, and whispers ensue, although Bill is oblivious to their pettiness as he gathers his composure and leaves the room.

Counsel is required, decides Bill. Jimmy Rothschild is a good friend, although too young and not experienced enough in matters of serious relationships to be relied upon in this case. Bill calls down to the reception and is connected to the concierge's desk. "Find me Sir Edward Hutton," he says. All the years of passing little folded banknotes to the staff at the Hotel de Paris entitle him to make such demands, and they are happy to oblige.

Within the hour, news reaches Bill that Sir Edward is still in Monaco and staying at the Hotel Metropole. Bill sends a note over requesting a meeting as soon as is convenient, and fortunately, Sir Edward receives the message almost immediately as it is still early in the morning. He telephones Bill, and they arrange to meet for lunch.

"My advice to you," says Sir Edward after patiently listening to Bill's dilemma, "is to hold hard."

"Excellent, Sir Edward," says Bill. "What exactly does that mean?"

"When negotiating for peace, for example, even though every fiber of your being is telling you to act with great haste, quite often the best course of action is to be patient."

"Thank you, Sir Edward," says Bill, "although I am fairly certain that I am not at war with Frances and have no need to sue for peace. Yet."

"Oh, but you are, dear boy," replies Sir Edward, "and please stop calling me sir. Edward will do just fine. The thing is, you are in the middle of a battle, and you need all parties to lay down their arms and come to a parlé."

"A parlé?"

"Yes, a negotiation to bring about the cessation of hostilities. The family is the cause of her defection, and they are prejudiced as they fear the unknown. This is how wars start. They haven't had the chance to get to know the real William Darnborough. Perhaps even Miss Erskine hasn't—not enough to know she'd be lucky to have you, in any case. The William Darnborough that I know is an upstanding gentleman of the highest pedigree who is as concerned for the lowly cleaning staff as he is for members of the most affluent in the land. You are generous not simply because you possess wealth, but because generosity is part of your personality. The rub of it is that thousands of people think they know you because they have read about you in the newspapers, but they don't know you and probably never will."

"I see," says Bill, "but what does any of this matter when her uncle has promised her to someone else who—"

"I am reminded," interrupts Sir Edward, "of something I read years ago. "Know your enemy." Sun Tsu, *The Art of War*."

Bill has no desire to know Charles Erskine. He frowns and taps his fingers on the table. Sir Edward laughs at the scowl on Bill's face. "You know them better than they know you."

Bill remains silent and agitated.

"Look here, my boy," continues Sir Edward. "You need to show the kind of courage that you're so famous for in the casino. Have faith in your abilities. The good news, Bill, is that she wrote to you about her situation. Perhaps it was a plea to you to put your case forward and to rescue her, as it were. At least, it could be seen as an invitation to try."

Bill's eyebrows shoot up. "Then I'll have to go to London!"

Sir Edward sits back and smiles. "Right, my boy. You'll wait patiently for a month, and then you'll go to London."

Bill pens a note to Jimmy, gracefully declining the invitation to the pre-rally party. Despite receiving numerous subsequent invitations to New Year's Eve gatherings in Monaco and Nice, he decides to spend a few days up in La Turbie, feeling disheartened.

There are no social charades up here, and the locals are out on the main street in their hoards with plenty of fine wine and champagne as they welcome in 1911. Bill stirs and begins to hum along with "La Marseillaise," as he isn't familiar with the lyrics, given that the French national anthem is not commonly sung in Monaco.

Despite the chill in the air, there is dancing in the streets and alleys in La Turbie, and Bill is glad he decided to come here to try and forget his troubles. Nevertheless, when he retires to his room, he feels quite dejected, and the alcohol does not help his feeling of loneliness. How can it be, he wonders, that he has more money and success than he has ever dreamed of and yet can feel so entirely alone? He wants badly to travel straight to Bordeaux and unearth the exact location of this Pemberton's estate. He imagines blustering in, stating his case, and whisking Frances away. No. It's the wrong plan and one that would set them up for a lifetime of pain with her family—if she even agreed to go with him.

Sir Edward is right. Bill will have to wait until she's settled back in London. He'll have to hope the visit to Bordeaux is terrible and that he can find her in London and make her happy enough that Uncle Charles relents.

It's going to be the longest two weeks of his life.

Bill returns to work at the roulette tables, driven by the desperate urge to win enough money to outshine Pemberton and win over Frances. How much is enough? He has no idea, so he plays for far longer hours than usual, like a man possessed. He cannot bear to think of Pemberton, wooing her with country walks through the vineyards of Bordeaux. He is not, he tells himself, losing control despite drinking too much and smoking too many expensive cigars.

A welcome diversion occurs when the Monte Carlo rally comes to town, and Bill is with Jimmy Rothschild and Anthony Noghès to welcome the first driver to make it to the finish line. A strong contingent of journalists has arrived after news had reached Monte Carlo that Captain Von Esmach is due to cross the line first, having driven over one-thousand miles from Berlin. The drivers have left on consecutive days depending on their point of departure, with eighteen cars due in Monte Carlo on January 25.

They have driven over mainly rutted, unpaved gravel tracks in dire conditions, and the jury gathered at the finish is a testament to the importance of the race. Chaired by Baron van Zuylen, President of the French Automobile Club, the other members include the Presidents of auto clubs from Italy, Belgium, the United States, Germany, Russia, Switzerland, Portugal, Sweden, Denmark, Austria, Spain, and England. Their task is to determine points based on comfort, distance traveled, number of passengers, and vehicle condition once it has arrived.

The route is lined with onlookers who stand perilously close to the edge of the roads, waving flags of the competing countries. A huge crowd has gathered at the Place du Casino as they eagerly await the arrival of the intrepid daredevils. An almighty cheer goes up as Von Esmach's Durkopp rounds the final corner at the Avenue de la Madone and crosses the finish line.

Spectators jostle to get better positions as the sound of each engine alerts them to a new arrival, which kicks up the dust as it comes around the last bend.

The jury's deliberation goes well into the night and even the following day as Von Esmach and the other drivers are forced to wait patiently to hear their decision.

All the competitors and their cars that have survived the trip are on parade outside the casino the next afternoon, and finally, the winners are announced. Henri Rougier from Paris, in his Turcat-Méry, takes the glory and 10,000 FF in prize money, followed by José-Antonio Aspiazu in a Gobron, also from Paris. Third place is awarded to none other than Bill's driving instructor, Julius Beutler, in a thirty-five horsepower Martini which he had driven from Berlin.

When the dust has settled, Bill meets with Jimmy for a drink in the bar at the Café de Paris.

"I've decided," Bill says, "that this time I go to London, I'm going to drive my De Dietrich down Piccadilly. They can put my bags on the train because if my driving instructor can make it all the way from Berlin, then I can make it to London."

"Beutler probably didn't stop to stay in the finest French hotels on the way," says Jimmy.

"Well, that may be, but I am still in a race of sorts."

"Ah, yes, the lady Frances." Jimmy sighs. "I'm afraid it's hopeless, Bill. Even if she weren't engaged to someone her uncle's picked out for her, it would still be hopeless, I'm afraid."

"I'd put the odds about even, myself," Bill boasts, though, of course, that isn't true.

Jimmy laughs, rising with his hand outstretched. "Bill, I wish you good day, good luck, and will see you in England. Oh, and by the way, did you notice that all the rally drivers had a mechanic with them? You should consider taking Hinault's son, Claude with you. I hear he's quite useful and would probably enjoy the adventure."

CHAPTER 56

*T*here are many more cars on the roads in London in early 1911, although Bill's De Dietrich stands out as one of the more magnificent beasts as he comes to rest outside the entrance to Brown's once more. Samuel Chambers is instantly on the steps to greet Bill and is quick to inform him that his bags have arrived before him and his room is prepared with a recent copy of the *New York Times* on his desk.

"Thank you, Samuel," says Bill, turning to inspect his car. "It has been a long journey. They had to hoist her onto a cargo ship, and customs was painful but well worth it to have this beauty here with me." Bill keeps it to himself that his wonderful motorcar broke down several times during the trip through France. Without Claude Hinault and the recent emergence of French motor mechanics, he would probably still be stuck on the side of the road somewhere near Lyon. Hinault Junior was more than happy to accept Bill's generous envelope stuffed full of French francs and get on the south-bound train from Calais.

"Can you call the London Motor Garage on Wardour Street and ask them to send someone to pick her up? You may want to mention that it is a De Dietrich and should be treated with the utmost care."

"Certainly, Mr. Darnborough," says Samuel, "I'll see to it right away."

The following day, Bill's first port of call is Hancocks jewelers in the Burlington Arcade.

"Good morning," says Bill, "I am seeking something colorful for a lady. A ring that signifies friendship, rather than engagement."

"I see," says the attendant, "I hope we will be able to assist. My name is Mr. Raymond, and I would be remiss if I did not direct your attention to this." He opens one of the glass drawers, pauses to put on a pair of velvet gloves, then removes a black box.

"This is a Burmese ruby," he explains. "Many ancient crowns were decorated with rubies as they represent good fortune and courage."

"Really?" says Bill, who pretends not to know anything about jewelry this early on in proceedings.

"Yes, Sir. This yellow gold ring has fourteen round, brilliant-cut diamonds surrounding a 1.45 carat oval ruby. This one has facets which allow it to shimmer in the light as it moves around."

"Quite nice," says Bill. "Do you have any other suggestions?"

"Yes, sir, please bear with me one moment." Mr. Raymond moves around to another glass display case and is on the point of extracting another ring when Bill interrupts the proceedings.

"Why is that medal there on the wall?" He is looking at a framed military medal with a silver cross and a crimson material.

"That, sir, is the Victoria Cross, the highest medal for valor awarded for conspicuous gallantry in the face of the enemy. We, at Hancocks, are the only makers of the Victoria Cross."

"Really?" says Bill, "that is incredible. What an honor it must be."

"Yes, it is, sir. The medals are cast from bronze from cannons captured from the Russians after the siege of Sevastopol during the Crimean War in 1855. I have to say, sir, that it is a solemn task that we have, as many of the recipients have fallen in battle, so the awards are posthumous."

"I see," says Bill, standing up straight given the gravity of the conversation; "nevertheless, a great honor."

"Yes, Sir," says Raymond, placing a further offering on the glass table. "This, sir, is a rare opal with a kaleidoscope of colors. The Romans thought that the opal was the most powerful stone as it contains all the colors of the other gems and symbolizes hope, purity, and trust."

"That makes sense," says Bill, closely inspecting the ring. He has reservations. "Perhaps a ring may be a little premature. How about brooches?" he asks. Raymond returns to the first glass cabinet and retrieves two diamond brooches for Bill to inspect.

"That one," says Bill, indicating the one on the right.

"Excellent choice, sir," says Raymond, "As you can see, this is a dragonfly. Approximately two inches by two inches. Very popular at the moment. This one is set with gold and silver diamonds throughout with garnet cabochon eyes. If you look here," he continues, turning the piece around, "there is a single fastening pin. A combined total of 4.5 carats."

Bill glances at the price tag and barely raises an eyebrow. "I'll take it," he says. "I want you to hold the ruby for me. Can you use my own diamonds in the ring if I bring them to you next time?"

Standing outside the Burlington Arcade, Bill looks across Piccadilly at Fortnum & Mason and spots Hatchards, the bookstore next door, with a sign above the window, *Established 1797*. In that instant, it occurs to him that perhaps a gift as extravagant and ostentatious as a diamond brooch may not be the most thoughtful offering for Frances. He needs to show her that he has been listening and appreciates her unique sensibilities. A brooch is just too easy.

The cab ride from Brown's Hotel to 89 Kensington Garden Square takes Bill through Mayfair and over the north side of Hyde Park and Kensington Gardens. This is the first time he has seen the parks from the north side, and the winter months have stripped the trees of their color. Despite the cold, hundreds of people walk in the park, some governesses and nannies pushing prams, and others are out simply to exercise and get some fresh air.

The square itself has a private garden in the middle, and all the houses have little signs on their black railings, often with the words "Tradesmen's Entrance" denoting the stairs to be taken by delivery men. Bill climbs the four steps to the front door and makes sure his cravat is straight before pressing the doorbell.

A young woman in her early twenties opens the door. She is wearing a housemaid's obligatory black and white uniform, and she looks Bill up and down.

"Yes, how may I help you?"

"Good day," beams Bill, feeling as nervous as he did stepping into the pitcher's box in Denver for the first time all those years ago. "May I please see Miss Frances Erskine-Shaw? My name is William Darnborough."

"Do you have an appointment?" comes the reply. Bill is unprepared for this response and needs a moment to regain his confidence.

"I have come all the way from Monte Carlo to see Miss Erskine-Shaw, and I have a gift for her."

"I see," says the maid. "If you would be kind enough to leave the gift with me, I will make sure she receives it." This is proving to be more complicated than Bill had initially anticipated.

"I am much obliged, Miss," says Bill, "although I must insist that I hand deliver it personally to Miss Erskine-Shaw. Is she here today?"

"Oh, very well," she says, "wait here, and I will enquire if milady is receiving guests." Bill flashes one of his sincerest smiles at the woman, and she reluctantly invites him to wait in the hallway, which is a welcome relief from the bitter cold outside. As he takes in his surroundings, Bill notes that ferns and palm plants appear to be the fashion in London as well as Monaco, as it looks as if a section of Kew Gardens has been specially transported to Kensington. The house seems noticeably quiet and peaceful, save for the loud ticking of a grandfather clock that stands in a corner like a sentry on guard.

A few minutes later, Frances emerges on the landing, one flight of stairs up. At first, she frowns, and then her expression shifts to a slight look of anxiety as she descends the stairs.

"I mentioned before, I don't appreciate surprises," she says in a hushed tone. "Did it not occur to you to call ahead?"

"Nice to see you too," says Bill.

She reaches where he stands and looks up at him. "Are you here to complicate my life, Bill?"

"Frances," he begins, trying his hardest to sound confident. "Miss Erskine, I mean. When you tripped outside the castle, and I caught you, I know you felt something. I certainly did. In fact, from the moment I saw you at Waddesdon, I knew that fate had brought us together."

Frances smiles. "That sounds like a terrible line from a West End play."

"I know," says Bill, "But there is something I need to say to you."

Frances cocks her head. She does not look displeased. "Well, I suppose you have come all this way." She closes the door, and they sit opposite each other in armchairs in front of the fire, which crackles with smoldering coal and wood.

Bill is trying to read her mind. She probably thought he wouldn't come—she hadn't asked him to. They barely know each other aside from exchanging letters. But then there was that moment on the cobblestones at the castle. That little flicker of something he hadn't felt before. Just a moment. Not nearly enough to upend her entire life, her uncle's plans for her, and her duty to her family. And yet, the fact that he has come must have impressed her.

He leans toward her, his elbows on his knees, a small smile on his face. "Is it too much to hope that the visit to Bordeaux went badly?"

"Did you come all the way from Monte Carlo just to torture me, Bill?"

"Good God, no!" he answers earnestly. "I came because I couldn't stop thinking about you."

She sighs. "Don't you see there's no use, Bill? I'm not free."

"But that can't be, Frances," Bill says earnestly. "If you want to be free, you make yourself free. No matter what it takes."

She stands abruptly and steps toward the fireplace. "If you

really want to know what happened in Bordeaux, then I'll tell you."
Bill looks up at Frances from his chair and gives a serious-looking
nod.

"The fact is, it was horrible, but I put on a smile and did what I
was expected to. At meals, Uncle Charles and Pemberton droned on
endlessly about shooting. Honestly, I think he and Uncle Charles are
a match made in heaven. Pemberton, by the end, claimed to be in
love with me. He had not asked me a single question, let alone
listened to an answer. No part of him had come closer than a few
feet of me, and in his presence, I had the sensation that we were
both made of stone—not a recipe for a successful marriage."

Bill understands now. Uncle Charles must have feared Frances
was destined for a life of solitude, and when Pemberton took him
aside at the garden party, it must have been to ask permission to
marry his niece. It would have appeared to be a perfect solution.

"Do you want to be free, Frances?" he says quietly as he stands.
She does not turn or answer him.

"I brought you something," he says, and, at this, Frances sighs.
Bill guesses there must have been dozens of suitors over the years
who have tried to dazzle her with jewelry as if she could be bought
for the price of a trinket.

"I cannot accept a gift from you," she says.

"Yes, you can," he says gently, and when she turns, he is holding
out a paper-wrapped, beribboned package that appears to be a
book.

"All right, then." She sits down and unwraps the brown paper.

"The book is a first edition of the sonnets of Elizabeth Barrett
Browning."

Tears spring to Frances's eyes. "Oh!"

"I hope you don't already own that one," Bill says.

"How did you know?" Frances says, glancing up at him as she
pages tenderly through the volume. "She's my favorite."

"You told me. In a letter. Remember?"

"You were paying attention," she laughs. "To me."

"Yes, of course," he says, his confidence returning. Right then, she meets his eyes, and Bill can see the depth in them. She looks terrified.

"Bill," she says firmly, standing up with the book in her hand, letting the brown wrapping paper fall to the floor. "Thank you for this. But I must be sure that you understand my position. After my parents died, Uncle Charles took me in without hesitation and has provided for me all these years. And now he is asking me to marry a particular man so that the Erskine-Shaw family's future is secure, and I have agreed to do so."

Bill's mouth turns up into a tiny smile. "Well, if that's all it is."

"Oh, I am full of angst, am I not?" she says.

His smile broadens. "Lucky for you, all I will ask is for you to take a walk with me in the park. How about tomorrow? Kensington Gardens? I'll bring my umbrella, just in case."

She laughs again. "Yes! A walk! Yes."

CHAPTER 57

A new batch of recently published books has arrived in the reading room at Brown's Hotel. Bill is on the crest of a wave after his well-calculated gift to Frances but wants to expand his knowledge by gaining a deeper understanding of how English families operate. Of course he is looking forward to their walk tomorrow, but he needs more arrows in his quiver if he is to prevent her wedding to the *other guy* in May. He has read a review on *Howard's End* by E. M. Forster which suggested it would give him some insight into England's social makeup and conventions. Plus, he imagines Frances may have read it, and he would like to talk with her about it, or at least not be entirely ignorant if the topic of E. M. Forster comes up in conversation.

As far as Bill can tell from the story, the English class system seems relatively rigid compared to America, and his chances of assimilating are slim at best. Most of the characters in the book live in London, but they despise it and would prefer to live full-time in the countryside. The one underpinning aspect of the plot is that a family home is placed above nearly everything else, so E. M. Forster has convinced Bill that there is only one course of action if he hopes to woo Frances away from a life of misery with Pemberton. He has to look south of London to buy a house. Somewhere for Frances to call home that is neither too near nor too far from the city and also close enough to the coast for excursions to France.

"THAT SEEMS MOST IRREGULAR, BILL," Frances says to him as they stroll through the park the following day. Every now and then, the sun peeks through the clouds, but the air is so frigid that Frances's words produce a visible whisp of steam each time she speaks. "You want me to drive with you to Elmbridge to look at a property?"

"I need a lady's opinion," he says. "I'm apt to make an American gaffe."

She laughs. "Oh, well, when you put it that way. I see you're desperate. When are we going?"

"Day after tomorrow."

"My, you don't waste time, do you?"

BILL IS unaccustomed to waiting for anything other than a roulette ball and has an entire day to continue his education in the reading room at Brown's. The next book that captures his eye is by P. G. Wodehouse, who has just published a novel called *A Gentleman of Leisure*. Bill finds the plot quite convoluted but cannot help drawing conclusions based on his own current predicament. The central characters, Jimmy and Molly, find their happiness put in jeopardy as they fear upsetting her father. At one point, Jimmy spends a year traveling around the world to try and forget about Molly but comes back to her in the end despite everything that stands in their way.

Bill hopes the Erskine household is not familiar with the story as it is about a bachelor gemstone thief from New York who has a shady history and knows all the "wrong" people. His mission now is to try and distance himself from even a hint of a dubious past and

JAMES DARNBOROUGH

convince Frances that he is now a reformed "gentleman of leisure" with all the time in the world to concentrate exclusively on her happiness.

THEIR JOURNEY WILL TAKE them about twenty-five miles south of London to the county of Surrey, and Bill picks up Frances from Kensington Garden Square at ten o'clock. As they are driving together in the De Dietrich, both wrapped up in hats and scarves, Frances turns to Bill and has to raise her voice over the roar of the engine.

"I do like your motorcar." she says.

"Excellent," says Bill, "I thought you would approve."

"Approve of what exactly? Another surprise? You do realize that I know exactly what you are doing."

"Well," says Bill, also raising his voice to be heard, "I have lived in the Hotel de Paris in Monte Carlo and Brown's Hotel in London for the last seven years. Not exactly what you might refer to as stability, and yet, here I am today, taking you to see what I think may turn out to be the beginning of a state of permanence. Are you familiar with the French phrase faute de mieux?"

"Of course," she replies.

"Well, then, you know that it means to desire a better alternative. I have been thinking about that for a long time now, and I'm hoping you might be thinking of it, too."

She casts a sidelong glance at him, raising an eyebrow, yet he notices her cheeks redden as she looks away. They drive in silence for the next half hour and arrive at the little town of Chessington. Bill slows the car down on the high street, and there is an awkward exchange of glances between them as they pass a church and look at each other for a moment and then straight ahead again. The road opens up once more, and Bill turns to Frances.

"I told the property agent to meet us at the house at two o'clock," he says. "He's coming from Epsom. That gives us time for a pub lunch if that suits you?"

"As long as they have a fire," Frances replies as she claps her gloved hands together to warm up a little.

They stop on the Portsmouth Road for a hot meal at a hotel called Fairmile, which used to be a coachman's inn in the seventeenth century. Bill notices that Frances seems perfectly at home in a local restaurant, which is a far cry from private castles in the south of France. They both order the leek soup and roast chicken to warm up after the freezing car journey.

Bill only drinks water as he will never forget the young German couple who perished in Monaco and has vowed never to get into a car after drinking alcohol. He thinks Frances has noticed this and is sure she has given him a smile of approval.

"How are you enjoying the chicken?" asks Bill.

"Thank you, it is really quite good."

"You sound surprised."

"Well, to be honest, Bill, I don't often have the opportunity to dine in country inns, and I have to say I am surprised. Pleasantly surprised."

They get back on the road for the last leg of the trip, and as they turn into the driveway, Bill points toward the gate.

"See the sign? This is it, Little Orchard."

A tall man in a long overcoat holds a file and hovers at the entrance. He looks like he has been waiting out of the cold inside the house but has heard the car approach and now comes toward them with an outstretched hand, looking extremely happy to see them in the way that house agents always seem to be.

"Mr. Darnborough?" asks the man.

"Yes, good day to you, sir," says Bill, gesturing to Frances, "This is my trusted advisor on all property matters, Miss Frances Erskine-Shaw."

"My name is Hamilton-Smith. It is a pleasure to meet you both," he says. "Please allow me to show you the house and grounds, and I will answer any questions you may have along the way."

The house is surrounded by a large lawn with a glass conservatory attached to the east side containing exotic palms and ferns—

undoubtedly a trend, thinks Bill, thanks in part to new heating technology. There are six bedrooms and four reception rooms, but it feels quite dark inside on this gray, cloudy day, despite the large sash windows. Hamilton-Smith enthusiastically details how well the current owners have taken care of the place. There does not appear to be a single chip in the paintwork or a spot of rust anywhere in the kitchen or bathrooms. Once they are outside again, he explains the innumerable benefits of the area with Epsom nearby and the road to London, giving direct access to the city through Wimbledon. Frances remains silent throughout the tour, and Bill has the impression that she is not entirely convinced. When they have a moment to themselves, she takes the opportunity to share her thoughts.

"It is a lovely house, Bill, but don't you think you would prefer to be a little further south? All I'm saying is that the further south towards the coast you go, you could have some land with nice views. A view of the sea, even. Of course, this is entirely your decision, and I am simply offering an opinion."

Bill turns to look again, imagining himself in the shade of the conservatory on a summer's afternoon with P.G. Wodehouse. The house seems easy to maintain and would be close enough to London to go to plays and concerts. Bill walks back to the front door where Hamilton-Smith is pretending to be busy with his file of papers.

"Thank you for your time today," he says, "but I will need some time to consider whether to put in an offer. You will have my answer within two days."

As they drive back to London, Bill thinks that even if that house is not exactly right, he has achieved what he set out to do in that Frances will now be convinced that he is serious about settling down in England.

He parks the car at the curb in front of her uncle's townhome and walks her up the steps to the front door. His heart catches in his throat when she turns to him with a goodnight smile. "I think we'll have to visit several more homes in the coming days, don't you?" he blurts, without thinking. "So that we can be sure we've found the right one? It's vital to me that you're happy with the choice."

Her eyelashes flutter slightly. "It's funny," she says. "I think you're actually sincere."

"Of course I am."

A sorrowful look washes over her face. "But I'm afraid I can't, Bill. You don't know the grief I took from Uncle Charles just to go with you today. I'm supposed to be preparing for my wedding, you see?"

Can it be that she genuinely doesn't understand Bill's intentions? Can it be that she is not going to relent? After the initial shock of this realization, Bill feels the weight of disappointment settle on his chest. Should he just blurt out a proposal? No. She'll laugh or cry or run inside and slam the door in his face—he's sure of it. He remembers the advice of his friends. *Finesse. Patience.* "I wish I could convince you otherwise," he says quietly.

"I keep telling you it's hopeless, Bill," she says, and there seems to be a sadness in her voice. "Good night. Thank you for a lovely day." And she is gone, the door clicking shut behind her.

Bill wallows in misery for thirty-six hours straight—he just cannot see his life without her, not at all—and then he remembers Sir Edward's words of wisdom, and there is a flicker of optimism. He just needs to take a new tack. This is the biggest game of his life. At the very least, he needs to get her to the point where she'll agree to a parlé.

He doesn't think of Frances as his adversary, but, just now, there is only one way he can think of the situation: he needs to get her to capitulate and sweep her off her feet to the point that she is utterly powerless.

He needs, he decides, to present her with the perfect English country house. Pemberton may have the estate in Bordeaux, but Frances wants to live on the south coast of England. Bill knows because she told him so. Somewhere with a view of the sea.

Over the next two weeks, Bill takes several trips south on reconnaissance missions. People ask him about his car each time he stops at a local village pub for lunch or just a coffee. It was a good idea to bring the De Dietrich over to England as it gets him around the country lanes at quite a pace. He visits two golf courses, West Surrey and Walton Health. The former was founded in 1910 by a local landowner, John Eastwood, and the second boasts Winston Churchill as one of its members.

He soon realizes, though, that he is wasting precious time. Far away as it seems, he needs to go to the coast. He leaves early one morning and keeps driving on the London Road all the way to Portsmouth. He goes directly to the office of a local house agent to inquire about possible properties coming up for sale. He is looking for something elevated, with a good view across the sea and a sizable amount of land that would not require too much maintenance. The agent listens intently to Bill's description and tells him about Theodore Roosevelt's visit to the New Forest the year before. There is a small village on the other side of Southampton called Brockenhurst, with a lodge that has just come on the market. The agent makes a telephone call to his colleague who is handling the sale, and a time is set for the following morning for a visit to the property.

Bill takes the agent's recommendation to stay in a room at the Forest Park Hotel in Brockenhurst, where he finds the receptionist is also eager to share the details of Roosevelt's visit when he hears Bill's American accent.

The "lodge" turns out to be an imposing Tudor-beamed mansion with six bedrooms and enough space to raise a large family. The grounds are expansive and well-kept, with an abundance of perfectly manicured flower beds and meadows backing up to woodland. Birdsong fills the air, and it is clear that spring is coming as there is a freshness that Bill finds exhilarating compared to the gray dampness of London.

Frances is exactly right. This is the perfect location to live. Country life will suit him just fine, and he can always take a room at Brown's should business or leisure require him to visit London. The concierge at the hotel has told Bill about Bramshot Golf Club in between the towns of Fleet and Farnborough, so he goes to investigate. The clubhouse is more extensive than expected, with boarding rooms in addition to a restaurant and snooker room, and the club has recently hosted the Anglo-American Club, so this would be an ideal course for Bill to play.

However, that is a side consideration if Frances doesn't agree to marry him. If she ends up in Bordeaux with Pemberton, this will all have been for nothing.

CHAPTER 58

"*C*hange of plan, Mr. Raymond," announces Bill as he enters Hancocks and closes the door firmly behind him. No doubt, Mr. Raymond had eagerly anticipated re-setting the ruby ring with Bill's diamonds, but that will have to wait. Today, Bill is seeking an engagement ring with different specifications. Having visited his security box at Barclays Bank, Bill now presents a little pouch of diamonds to Raymond, and together, they create a custom ring.

"This will sit low on the finger," says Raymond, "which makes it a practical ring to wear." He starts sketching out the design on a pad with the skill of an artist. "We will end up with an 18-carat gold and platinum cluster with two further intertwined clusters of diamonds, and it will look like an elaborate figure of eight. They are well-matched, and these stones are nice and bright. A reeded design will be set into the shank on the band with more diamonds."

"It looks like a perfect design, Mr. Raymond," says Bill, "and I hope it has the desired effect."

"I had an idea about the box if you would like to see it," says Raymond as he steps over to another cabinet and opens a drawer.

"This is blue leather with a velvet pad and satin hood. Easy to open and yet perfectly secure brass hinge clip closure."

"Excellent," says Bill, "when will it be ready?"

"Give me nine days."

"I'll pay £10 extra if you can do it in five."

Bill has been ignoring most of his letters, and many have remained unanswered as he is so preoccupied with the new house and matters of the heart. However, he always ensures that there are no overdue balances on Jermyn Street or Saville Row. The telephone has changed everything, and along with the motorcar, Bill notices that life seems to have picked up its pace considerably. Everyone seems impatient, and the streets are louder, with horns replacing the sound of horse hooves. Or maybe it's just he who is so impatient.

"I THOUGHT I had told you a proper goodbye," Frances says, looking up at Bill just inside the front door. Bill is unsure, although it looks like she is happy to see him. It's been more than three weeks since their drive down to Elmbridge, and they haven't spoken in all that time. Maybe she had even thought he'd gone back to Monaco. Bill envisioned her undoubtably occupied with dress fittings, hat selections, choosing china patterns, and various other preparations, of course. He thinks that the estate at Bordeaux probably already has five sets of china, but even Bill knows it's incumbent upon an upper-class bride to start afresh with her own. Frances looks up at Bill, who is smiling down at her.

"I've been busy with a few things," he says, "but I was hoping today you might join me for a walk."

"I see," says Frances. "You do realize it's late March already, and I've been preparing for my wedding in May." She looks back inside the house. "There's no one else here at the moment. Let me get my coat and the house key."

The air is much milder in the park than the last time they

walked together. Spring has nearly arrived—yellow daffodils and tiny shoots of green are poking through the soil.

"The thing I can't abide," Frances says, "Is how all these salesladies tell me all day long that my life is just beginning. For one thing, I'm twenty-seven years old. For another, getting shipped off to France to marry a stranger? It feels like I'm being sent into exile. Like my life is over, rather than just beginning." Bill wishes she would change the subject, but it's obvious there isn't an alternative topic of conversation available at the moment.

"If you really don't want to go to France," he says quietly, "you don't have to."

"I keep trying to explain it, Bill. I do have to. I held onto my so-called independence as long as possible, and now this is the consequence. This is my duty."

"Don't you understand, Frances?" he says, his voice now having a strange, quiet intensity. "This is not just something you're going to do two months from now to fulfill an obligation to your uncle. This is not your duty. It is the rest of your life. Living in a strange country with a man you don't love. Having children with a man you don't love and living day in and day out with him. Growing old with him. Taking care of him if he gets sick. I know something about being married to someone I didn't love, remember, and I wouldn't wish it on my worst enemy."

"How do you know I don't love him?"

Bill laughs slightly.

His toes feel pinched in his shoes as they walk along the straight path under a tunnel of tall trees. Bill stops walking and looks at her —she looks troubled, more distressed than he has ever seen her.

"Well, maybe love isn't the most important thing, then," she says.

Bill holds up his hands, half a shrug, half a gesture of peace. "I'm not trying to argue with you. Listen, though, I have some news I wanted to tell you. I bought a house. Down near Portsmouth. Quite a nice place. High on a hill overlooking the sea. Tudor style with six bedrooms. Would you have time to drive down with me and see it?"

"You're not serious, Bill?"

"Completely. Come with me to see it, will you? Please.

BILL PICKS Frances up around the corner from Uncle Charles's house three days later. She has lied to Charles and said she was in for an exceedingly long day of shopping with a friend. "Last minute needs for the trousseau, you know!" she had said. "We're so close to running out of time!" Charles had harrumphed with barely a glance at her and returned to his newspaper.

Riding in the De Dietrich, heading for the coast, Bill loves the feeling of the wind on his face. He hopes Frances will think he is the perfect driver: fast, but not too fast. He has never had the sense that he's being reckless, nor does it feel he is not in perfect control—until right now.

"Bill!" she shouts, "there's smoke coming out of the front of the car!"

"Ah yes," says Bill, as he pulls the De Dietrich over to the side of the road. "It's not on fire—it's steam from the radiator. Not to worry, we just have to let it cool down." He disappears around the back of the car and returns with a large water can, which he sets down in front of the vehicle.

"You're so calm," says Frances. "Does this happen often?"

"Oh, yes. I like that she shows her personality occasionally."

"She? Are you implying that the fact that your motorcar is temperamental that it should be feminine?"

"No, not at all," says Bill, looking directly at Frances as he unscrews the cap on the watering can. "You're joking with me, aren't you?"

"Maybe a little," she smiles.

As Bill had predicted, Frances loves the Tudor house and the estate overlooking the sea. "It's perfect, Bill," she exclaims once inside, taking off her hat and twirling to look up at the soaring ceiling of the front foyer. "Divine. You're going to be so happy here. Who *wouldn't* be happy here?"

As she finishes the circle she is turning, without warning, Bill is down on one knee, holding open a tiny box containing a sparkling diamond ring. "Could you be happy here, Frances? That's all that matters to me," he says.

Tears begin to well up in Frances's eyes. "How dare you try and ruin my life," she whispers. "Everything is already planned."

"But, I'm giving you the chance to be happy. I will do anything, Don't you see? Is it the money? I'm sure I have more than that guy you don't love. I can always get more."

"And you could lose it all, too," she snaps. "I hate that you're a gambler! I didn't want to mention it before, but I can't tell you how much I hate it. It is so uncouth. So hideous, really. Hideous!"

LATE THAT NIGHT, Bill pulls the De Dietrich to the curb in front of Uncle Charles' house. It has been an exceedingly long day of driving, and he's seething with frustration. He and Frances have spent the last hour in utter silence. He believes she's being unreasonable and coming up with excuses. Throughout the entire drive back, he contemplated selling the house because the whole dream of it feels ruined. *The English are such snobs,* he thinks to himself as the De Dietrich idles at the curb.

"Aren't you going to walk me to the door, Bill?" Frances says, and she sounds as riled as he feels. Without a word, he opens his door and climbs out, strides around, opens her door, and reaches for her hand. As she places her palm in his and stands up, she trips slightly on the curb and stumbles toward him. He holds her up and reaches for her waist. In some far recess of his mind, he wonders or even hopes: Has she planned this?

"Bill," she says, looking up at him so closely that he can feel the warmth of her breath and skin. "I'm afraid I might be an awful fool."

The little box with the ring still inside feels cold and heavy in his jacket pocket. He can't stop himself. He kisses her. He can feel her shock, but in a moment, she kisses him back, then, just as quickly, pulls away.

"You really shouldn't," she says, very close to his mouth. "But maybe just once more."

FOUR DAYS LATER, Frances summons him by telegram and meets him at the door with her coat and hat on, pulling the door shut quietly behind her with a murmur about how Uncle Charles can't know that Bill is there. Bill's palms are sweaty despite the spring chill in the air. The other night, after their kiss, he'd asked her what it would take for her to reconsider, and she'd said she'd think about it, and now, after four days of pacing and fuming and being unable to eat or sleep, he's about to get his answer.

"I've been thinking," she begins, as they start off down the street, and he interrupts.

"Pardon me, but can you just cut to the chase, Frances?"

"Oh!" She looks at him. "Pardon me. Mr. American. Yes. I've concluded that I like you, Bill."

It's like she's stabbed him. "But you don't love me, so why turn your life upside down?"

"You haven't let me finish," she says coolly.

He is suitably chastised. He stays quiet as they walk on. A light mist is coating his face. He wishes he could be sure she is warm enough, but it seems foolish to ask right now.

"What's been on my mind, Bill," she begins, "is throughout my life, there have been very few men I genuinely liked. My father let me down when I was young, and his passing was the worst disappointment. I've come to the conclusion that I'm afraid of love because, from my experience, it brings pain. Above all, I dread losing things. If I don't allow myself to deeply care for anyone or anything, it means I don't risk losing something that holds importance to me. Do you understand? It's because my heart was shattered when I was young."

Bill swallows. This is more than he bargained for, yet he's

hanging on her every word, hanging so much that he's almost swinging on each one, and with every swing comes a little prayer that this will all break his way. He has felt it deeply, these last few days, how miserable he would be without her. "I think so," he says.

"You bought that lovely house, Bill, and there's a way in which I can see the whole thing, far more than I can see a life in Bordeaux. I can see marriage, as you've proposed. Filling that lovely house with children." She blushes slightly.

"Yes?" At that moment, he's never wanted anything more.

"But where I get hung up, Bill, is when I see, five years down the road, and I'm the mother of three or four children, and you come home from Monte Carlo and tell me you've lost the house. We're destitute, and we have nowhere even to live."

"But that would never—"

She interrupts. "You see, what I haven't told you about my father. He drank. He drank everything away. He lost everything. And then he died. And I was thrown to the mercy of my uncle. And I can tell you, Bill, if I marry you, I'll have no uncle to return to. I am going to be disowned. Do you see how serious this is for me, Bill? Do you see what a risk it would be, in all ways, for me to marry you?"

He swallows again. His heart is pounding again. This is not what he wanted to hear, not at all. He is resigning himself to returning to Monte Carlo, making himself richer and richer and more and more miserable, all to no avail.

"And yet." She stops, and they turn to face each other. "In your presence, Bill, I have felt excitement. Joy. Even passion." A slight, endearing blush again. "You have made me feel seen and listened to. You have made me feel what it could be like to be free. To be loved. Truly loved." She is blinking back tears.

"I do love you, Frances!" he exclaims, and she smiles a little.

"I don't know if I believe you, but I want to," she says. "And, if I can see my way through that, then I can see it all. I can even see that I could choose my happiness over the wishes of a man who would trade me like a horse."

His heart is soaring. "You mean—?"

She nods slightly and can't hold back a little smile. "All I need is for you to promise me that you'll stay with me in England and you won't return to Monte Carlo. I need you to promise me security. I need you to promise me that you won't gamble again, Bill."

His soaring heart drops to his shoes. "But how would I make enough money to support us? Gambling is my only business."

"You'll think of something, Bill. Won't you?"

Bill is looking at Frances and knows he can't possibly let her go. He realizes he has never before feared losing anything, and now the thought of losing her makes him feel he's teetering on a tightrope with no net below.

He's reinvented himself many times before and can certainly do so again. He knows the millimeter difference between striking out and hitting a home run, and he knows the right thing to do is adjust his swing. Was it Hiram Lewin who said, "Once you find true love, hang on to it with all your might"—he can't remember, but the words are ringing true. Bill finally understands that since his dream of getting to the majors was taken away from him, he hasn't had a true purpose in life. He is just like the roulette ball, going around and around, slowly losing speed.

It is clear that this is the moment when he has to make the choice between the life of a gambler and the love he has for Frances. He gazes into her eyes, seeing the sincerity and knows that he is about to make the most important gamble of his life. There can be no turning back.

"Then I'll give it all up, Frances," he whispers, trying to fathom what all this might mean. "All that matters to me now is you." And he means this so much that it startles him, thrills him, and makes him feel as if he's never even been alive before. "I mean that. I truly do," he adds as if that could be enough to make her understand the depth of his feelings.

Frances smiles. "In that case, my answer is yes." As he is standing there, shocked and thrilled, she laughs. "And thank good-ness you have a car because you realize we're going to have to sneak my trousseau away in the dead of night."

"Frances—"

"Wait," she says, putting a finger to his lips. "I need to tell you something. One of the reasons I love Elizabeth Barrett Browning."

"Yes?" says Bill.

"I was about thirteen when I found out that she made a daring elopement with Robert Browning, and they married in secret to evade her father's disapproval."

BILL AND FRANCES are married with only two witnesses in a quiet ceremony at the register's office in Lymington, Hampshire, five miles from their new home in Brockenhurst.

As they stand on the steps outside the registry office, Frances tilts her parasol to shield her eyes from the sun and hide them from public view as she kisses Bill. There is no Uncle Charles to frown disapprovingly now, just the two of them.

"Shall we go home, Mr. Darnborough?" she says.

Bill smiles. He knows it's a cliché, but he finally feels like the richest man in the world.

"Yes, Mrs. Darnborough. Let's go home."

ACKNOWLEDGMENTS

Bill Timmins and Peter Venison for sharing their unrivaled experience in the hotel and casino business; Tim Brunold, Jay Sanford, and Bob Sampson for vintage baseball expertise; Henri Ferero, Tetiana Brico, Yasmine Jedda, Morgane Grandclement and Rudy Tarditi at the Monte Carlo Casino; Ellen Baker, Bob Wallace and Kate Love for editing mastery; and Denise, Lisa and Mindy from the Easybreezy book club. Kudos to the countless newspaper archivists around the world who tirelessly upload millions of pages to the internet. Finally, it was originally suggested that this project be written as a screenplay although my wife, Priya, convinced me to spend nearly three years creating this book instead, and I am forever in her debt.

CHARACTER LIST

ADAMS, WALT H — GAMBLER
AGRID, JOSEPH - GUEST, MONTE CARLO
ALFONSO OF SPAIN, KING — MONARCH
ARKINS, JOHN — NEWSPAPER EDITOR
ARKINS, MARGARET — JOHN ARKIN'S WIFE
ARTOLLI, ETIENNE — CONCIERGE, HOTEL DE PARIS
AMHERST, LORD HUGH — GUEST, ASCOT
ASPIAZU, JOSÉ-ANTONIO — RALLY DRIVER
BACKMAN, JOHN — BASEBALL PLAYER
BAIN, OLIVER — SHIPBROKER
BAPTISTE, JEAN-LUC — HOTEL MANAGER
BERESFORD, HON. SETON — SPORTSMAN
BERGER, TUN — BASEBALL MANAGER
BEUTLER, JULIUS — RALLY DRIVER
BLANC, CAMILLE — CASINO OPERATOR, MONTE CARLO
BLANC, FRANÇOIS — CASINO OPERATOR, MONTE CARLO
BRICO, TITUS — CLIENT RELATIONS, MONTE CARLO CASINO
BROWN, JAMES AND SARAH — FOUNDERS, BROWN'S HOTEL
BURKETT, JESSE — BASEBALL PLAYER
BUTT, CLARA — OPERA SINGER

417

CADWALADER, GENERAL JOHN — REVOLUTIONARY WAR
COMMANDER
CADWALADER-ERSKINE, FRANCES — DAVID ERSKINE'S WIFE
CAMPBELL, JOCK — NEWSPAPER EDITOR
CANNON, MORNY — JOCKEY
CARRUTHERS, EMILY — SOCIALITE
CARRUTHERS, MAJOR JOCK — ARMY OFFICER, BRITISH
CARSEY, KID — BASEBALL PLAYER
CARUSO, ENRICO — OPERA SINGER
CHAMBERS, SAMUEL — ASSISTANT HOTEL MANAGER
CLARKE, FRED — BASEBALL MANAGER
CLARKE, WILLIAM — EXPLORER
CLINE, MONK — BASEBALL PLAYER
CODY, BUFFALO BILL — SHOWMAN
CONLON, JOHN — POLITICIAN
CONNER, JACK — BASEBALL PLAYER
CONNERS, WILL — BASEBALL MANAGER
COORS, ADOLF — BUSINESSMAN
COVINGTON, ALFRED — GOLF PROFESSIONAL
CRICHTON, COLONEL HARRY AND MRS. EMMA — GUESTS, ASCOT
CURTIS, BEN — TRAIN ROBBER
CURTIS, JIM — BASEBALL PLAYER
D'ALENÇON, ELOISE — COURTESAN
DARNBOROUGH, WILLIAM "BILL" — BASEBALL PLAYER, GAMBLER
DE LARA, ISADORE — MUSIC COMPOSER
DE ROTHSCHILD, BARON ARTHUR — ARISTOCRAT
DE ROTHSCHILD, BARON FERDINAND — BANKER, POLITICIAN
DE ROTHSCHILD, HENRI — PLAYWRIGHT
DE ROTHSCHILD, JAMES "JIMMY" — ARISTOCRAT
DE ROTHSCHILD, LORD WALTER — BANKER, ZOOLOGIST
DE SALVIA, GIOVANNI — MASTER TAILOR, MONACO
DE VILLE WELLS, CHARLES — GAMBLER, FRAUDSTER
DEVON, JACK — BASEBALL PLAYER
DI BUONACCORSO, NICCOLÒ — ASSISTANT BANK MANAGER
DOLAN, TOM — BASEBALL PLAYER
DUNN, SERGEANT — POLICEMAN

DUVALIER, GERENT — GAMBLER
EDISON, THOMAS — INVENTOR
EDWARD VII, KING — MONARCH
ELLIS, THOMAS — HORSE OWNER
ERSKINE, BARON DAVID — AMBASSADOR TO THE US, BRITISH
ERSKINE-SHAW, AUBREY — GENTLEMAN, ENGLISH
ERSKINE-SHAW, CHARLES — GENTLEMAN, ENGLISH
ERSKINE-SHAW, FRANCES — LADY, ENGLISH
FAGAN, BILL — BASEBALL PLAYER
FIELD, EUGENE — NEWSPAPER EDITOR
FITZGERALD, DAN — BARMAN
FLAHERTY, MICHAEL — BARMAN
FLANAGAN, DANNY — BASEBALL PLAYER
FORSYTH, CAPTAIN DOMINIC — ARMY OFFICER, BRITISH
FOURNIER, HENRI — BASEBALL PLAYER
GAFFNEY, "HONEST" JOHN — BASEBALL UMPIRE
GALLAN, WILLIAM — POLITICIAN
GLEASON, BILL — BASEBALL PLAYER
GONDOIN, JACQUES — FOUNDING MEMBER, NICE GOLF CLUB
GRAHAM-BELL, ALEXANDER — INVENTOR
GRIFFITH, CLARKE — BASEBALL PLAYER
GUNSBOURG, RAOUL — DIRECTOR, MONTE CARLO OPERA
HACKETT, CHARLIE — BASEBALL MANAGER
HALL, JOHN — JUDGE
HAMILTON-SMITH, EDWARD — REAL ESTATE AGENT
HARDACRE, JOHN AND EMMA — GUESTS, WADDESDON MANOR
HARDCOURT, JOHN — NEWSPAPER EDITOR
HAVERSTOCK, JOHN — HOTEL GUEST
HAY-GORDON, JAMES — FOUNDING MEMBER, NICE GOLF CLUB
HEALEY, JOHN — BASEBALL PLAYER
HERMANN, KARL — CASINO DIRECTOR
HIBBERT, NEVILLE — GUEST, WADDESDON MANOR
HINAULT, CLAUDE — CAR MECHANIC
HIRSCH, IKE — SALOON OWNER
HOFFMAN, FRANK — BASEBALL PLAYER
HOHENLOHGE, PRINCE FREDERICK — GUEST, MONTE CARLO

HORAN, ANDREW — POLITICIAN
HUTTON, GENERAL SIR EDWARD — ARMY OFFICER, BRITISH
JAGGER, JOSEPH — GAMBLER
JARROTT, CHARLES — RACING DRIVER
JELLICOE, CAPTAIN JOHN — NAVAL OFFICER, BRITISH
JOHNSON, SPUD — BASEBALL PLAYER
JONES, JASON — ASSISTANT TO MR. FAIRFAX
JUCH, EMMA — OPERA SINGER
KEEFE, TIM — BASEBALL PLAYER
KEENAN, JACK — BASEBALL PLAYER
KELLY, KING — BASEBALL PLAYER
KENNEDY, BRICKYARD — BASEBALL PLAYER
KILMOREY, VISCOUNT - GUEST, MONTE CARLO
KNIGHT, ARTHUR — INVENTOR OF THE STEEL GOLF CLUB
LAGET, PIERRE — DIRECTOR, MONTE CARLO CASINO
LANE, HARRY — CASINO OWNER
LANGFORD-BROWNE, JOHN — FOUNDING MEMBER, NICE GOLF CLUB
LEWIN, HIRAM T — SALOON/CASINO OWNER
LEWIN, LIBBY — HIRAM LEWIN'S DAUGHTER
LEWIN, RUTH — HIRAM LEWIN'S WIFE
LEWIS, FRANK — LAWYER
LOTTIER, PIERRE — RESTAURATEUR
MACULLAR, JIMMY — BASEBALL PLAYER/MANAGER
MADDEN, EUGENE — SALOON OWNER
MAGOON, CHARLES — LAWYER
MANGINI, SIRO — SALOON OWNER
MANNING, JIM — BASEBALL PLAYER
MARSH, RICHARD — HORSE TRAINER
MATHEWSON, CHRISTY — BASEBALL PLAYER
MAXIM, SIR HIRAM — INVENTOR
MAYBACH, WILHELM — CAR DESIGNER
MCCLENNAN, BILL — BASEBALL PLAYER
MCGARR, CHIPPY — BASEBALL PLAYER
MCGINNITY, JOE — BASEBALL PLAYER
MCHUGH, MIKE — SALOON CUSTOMER/BRAWLER
MCNABB, ED — BASEBALL PLAYER

MIDDLETON, THOMAS — POLICE OFFICER

MIKHAILOVICH, GRAND DUKE NICHOLAS — ARISTOCRAT

MILLHEIM, JOHN — BUSINESSMAN

MITTLER, JOHN — CHEF

MONTAGUE, DAVID — GUEST, WADDESDON MANOR

MORGAN, J.P — FINANCIER

MORSS, SAM — NEWSPAPER OWNER

NELSON, WILLIAM ROCKHILL — NEWSPAPER OWNER

NOGHÈS, ALEXANDRE — FOUNDER, MONACO AUTOMOBILE CLUB

NOGHÈS, ANTHONY — FOUNDER, MONACO GRAND PRIX

O'BRIAN, BILLY — BASEBALL PLAYER

O'DAY, HANK — BASEBALL PLAYER

O'LEARY, TOM — BASEBALL PLAYER

OAKLEY, ANNIE — SHARPSHOOTER

PADEREWSKI, IGNACY — PIANIST

PARKE, ALICE — BILL'S MOTHER

PARKE, CHARLES — BILL'S STEPFATHER

PARKER, BANJO — SOAPY SMITH'S HENCHMAN

PATTON, OWEN — BASEBALL PLAYER

PAVLOVNA, GRAND DUCHESS MARIA — GUEST, MONTE CARLO

PEARS, FRANK — BASEBALL PLAYER

PEIKER, MARY — LANDLADY

PEMBERTON, PIERS — BUSINESSMAN

POWELL, JIM — BASEBALL PLAYER

RAYMOND, MATTHEW — JEWELER

RENAULT, LOUIS — CAR MANUFACTURER, RALLY DRIVER

RENAULT, MARCEL — CAR MANUFACTURER, RALLY DRIVER

RICHARDSON, HORACE — CIGAR MANUFACTURER

ROAT, FRED — BASEBALL PLAYER

RONCAGLIA, AUGUSTINE — SALOON OWNER

ROOSEVELT, THEODORE — US PRESIDENT

ROWE, DAVE — BASEBALL PLAYER/MANAGER

ROWE, JACK — BASEBALL PLAYER/MANAGER

SCHMIDT, GEORGE — BARMAN

SCHMIDT, HANS — SALOON OWNER

SELBY, CHARLES — LANDOWNER

SHAFFER, NED — SPORTS COLUMNIST

SIERSTORPFF, COUNT ADA — GUEST, MONTE CARLO

SILKS, MATTIE — BROTHER OWNER

SMITH, JEFFERSON "SOAPY" — CONMAN

SMITH, JOSEPH — FOUNDER, THE MORMONS

SPALDING, A.J — BUSINESSMAN

STANLEY, HENRY — EXPLORER

STEELY, HANK — BASEBALL PLAYER

SULLIVAN, JOHN — CASINO EQUIPMENT STORE OWNER

SULLIVAN, SLEEPER — BASEBALL PLAYER

SWEDEN, PRINCE WILHELM OF — ROYAL FAMILY, SWEDISH

TATE, KATHERINE — GARDEN PARTY GUEST

TOMNEY, PHIL — BASEBALL PLAYER

TOSTI, SIR FRANCESCO PAOLO — COMPOSER

TWINEHAM, ART — BASEBALL PLAYER

VAGHELA, JAYESH — MASTER HATTER, LOCK & CO.

VAN DEN DAELE, JULES — HORTICULTURALIST

VANDERBILT, CORNELIUS — BUSINESSMAN

VANDERBILT JR., WILLIAM. K — MOTOR RACING ENTHUSIAST

VÁSQUEZ, SEÑOR — SALOON/CASINO OWNER, MEXICO

VILLA, GENERAL PANCHO — REVOLUTIONARY, MEXICO

VON ESMACH, CAPTAIN — RALLY DRIVER

VON ROTHSCHILD, ALICE CHARLOTTE — ARISTOCRAT

WAINWRIGHT, GEORGE — SPORTS COLUMNIST

WATKINS, BILL — BASEBALL PLAYER

WATSON, PEG-LEG — TRAIN ROBBER

WEBSTER, J.R — LAWYER

WERRICK, JOE — BASEBALL PLAYER

WHITE, BILL — BASEBALL PLAYER

WHITEHEAD, MILT — BASEBALL PLAYER

WILSON, TUG — BASEBALL PLAYER

YOUNG, CY — BASEBALL PLAYER

ZANG, PHILIP — BUSINESSMAN